when I am laid

Mon coeur s'ouvre ta
voix –
    Samson et Delilah
        Saint - Saëns

            from
Gavotte – Mignon
    Thomas

Sonnet – Agnew Bakrison
Lullaby – Menotti

            Iher
            21-25 –

THE VIKING PORTABLE LIBRARY

HEMINGWAY

The Viking Portable Library

HEMINGWAY

◇◇

Edited by Malcolm Cowley

NEW YORK · THE VIKING PRESS

1944

COPYRIGHT 1944 BY THE VIKING PRESS, INC.
PUBLISHED BY THE VIKING PRESS IN SEPTEMBER 1944

SECOND PRINTING SEPTEMBER 1944
THIRD PRINTING NOVEMBER 1944

PRINTED AND BOUND IN U. S. A. BY THE COLONIAL PRESS INC.

CONTENTS

35797

INTRODUCTION

GOING back to Hemingway's work after several years is like going back to a brook where you had often fished and finding the woods as deep and cool as they used to be. The trees are bigger, perhaps, but they are the same trees; the water comes down over the black stones as clear as always, with the same dull, steady roar where it plunges into the pool; and when the first trout takes hold of your line you can feel your heart beating against your fishing jacket. But something has changed, for this time there are shadows in the pool that you hadn't noticed before, and you have a sense that the woods are haunted. When Hemingway's stories first appeared, they seemed to be a transcription of the real world, new because they were accurate and because the world in those days was also new. With his insistence on "presenting things truly," he seemed to be a writer in the naturalistic tradition (for all his technical innovations); and the professors of American literature, when they got around to mentioning his books in their surveys, treated him as if he were a Dreiser of the lost generation, or perhaps the fruit of a misalliance between Dreiser and Jack London. Going back to his work in 1944, you perceive his kinship with a wholly different group of novelists, let us say with Poe and Hawthorne and Melville: the haunted and nocturnal writers, the men who dealt in images that were symbols of an inner world.

On the face of it, his method is not in the least like theirs. He doesn't lead us into castles ready to collapse with age, or into very old New England houses, or embark with us on the search for a whale that is also the white spirit of evil; instead he tells the stories he has lived or heard, against the background of countries he has seen. But, you reflect on reading his books again, these are curious stories that he has chosen from his wider experience, and these countries are presented in a strangely mortuary light. In no other writer of our time can you find such a profusion of corpses: dead women in the rain; dead soldiers bloated in their uniforms and surrounded by torn papers; sunken liners full of bodies that float past the closed portholes. In no other writer can you find so many suffering animals: mules with their forelegs broken drowning in shallow water off the quay at Smyrna; gored horses in the bull ring; wounded hyenas first snapping at their own entrails and then eating them with relish. And morally wounded people who also devour themselves: punch-drunk boxers, soldiers with battle fatigue, veterans crazy with "the old rale," lesbians, nymphomaniacs, bull-fighters who have lost their nerve, men who lie awake all night while their brains get to racing "like a flywheel with the weight gone"—here are visions as terrifying as those of "The Pit and the Pendulum," even though most of them are copied from life; here are nightmares at noon-day, accurately described, pictured without blur, but having the nature of obsessions or hypnagogic visions between sleep and waking.

And, going back to them, you find a waking-dreamlike quality even in the stories that deal with pleasant or commonplace aspects of the world. Take, for example, "Big Two-Hearted River," where the plot—or foreground of the plot—is simply a fishing trip in the northern peninsula of Michigan. Nick Adams, who is Hemingway's earliest and most personal hero, gets off the train at an abandoned sawmill town; he crosses burned-over land, makes camp, eats his supper, and goes to sleep; in the morning he looks for bait, finds grasshoppers under a log, hooks a big trout and loses it, catches two other trout, then sits in the shadow and eats his lunch very slowly while watching the stream; he decides to do no more fishing that day. There is nothing else in the story, apparently; nothing but a collection of sharp sensory details, so that you smell or hear or touch or see everything that exists near Big Two-Hearted River; and you even taste Nick Adams' supper of beans and spaghetti. "All good books are alike," Hemingway later said, "in that they are truer than if they had really happened and after you are finished reading one you will feel that all that happened to you and afterwards it all belongs to you: the good and the bad, the ecstasy, the remorse and sorrow, the people and the places and how the weather was." This story belongs to the reader, but apparently it is lacking in ecstasy, remorse, and sorrow; there are no people in it except Nick Adams; apparently there is nothing but "the places and how the weather was."

But Hemingway's stories are most of them continued, in the sense that he has a habit of returning to the same themes, each time making them a little clearer—to himself, I think, as well as to others. His work has an emotional consistency, as if all of it moved with the same current. A few years after "Big Two-Hearted River," he wrote another story that casts a retrospective light on his fishing trip (much as *A Farewell to Arms* helps to explain the background of Jake Barnes and Lady Brett, in *The Sun Also Rises*). The second story, "Now I Lay Me," deals with an American volunteer in the Italian army who isn't named but who might easily be Nick Adams. He is afraid to sleep at night because, so he says, "I had been living for a long time with the knowledge that if I ever shut my eyes in the dark and let myself go, my soul would go out of my body. I had been that way for a long time, ever since I had been blown up at night and felt it go out of me and go off and then come back." And the soldier continues:

I had different ways of occupying myself while I lay awake. I would think of a trout stream I had fished along when I was a boy and fish its whole length very carefully in my mind; fishing very carefully under all the logs, all the turns of the bank, the deep holes and the clear shallow stretches, sometimes catching trout and sometimes losing them. I would stop fishing at noon to eat my lunch; sometimes on a log over the stream; sometimes on a high bank under a tree, and I always ate my lunch very slowly and watched the stream below me while I ate. . . . Some nights too I made up streams, and some of them were very exciting, and it was like being awake and dreaming. Some of those streams I still remember and think that I have fished in them, and they are confused with streams I really know.

After reading this passage, we have a somewhat different attitude toward the earlier story. The river described in it remains completely real for us; but also—like those other streams the soldier invented during the night —it has the quality of a waking dream. Although the events in the foreground are described with superb accuracy and for their own sake, we now perceive what we probably missed at a first reading: that there are shadows in the background and that part of the story takes place in an inner world. We notice that Nick Adams regards his fishing trip as an escape, either from nightmare or from realities that have become a nightmare. Sometimes his mind starts to work, even here in the wilderness; but "he knew he could choke it because he was tired enough," and he can safely fall asleep. "Nick felt happy," the author says more than once. "He felt he had left everything behind, the need for thinking, the need to write, other needs. It was all back of him." He lives as if in an enchanted country. There is a faint suggestion

of old legends: all the stories of boys with cruel step-
mothers who wandered off into the forest where the big
trees sheltered them and the birds brought them food.
There is even a condition laid on Nick's happiness, just
as in many fairy tales where the hero must not wind a
certain horn or open a certain door. Nick must not follow
the river down into the swamp. "In the swamp the banks
were bare, the big cedars came together overhead, the
sun did not come through, except in patches; in the fast
deep water, in the half light, the fishing would be tragic.
In the swamp fishing was a tragic adventure. Nick did
not want it. He did not want to go down the stream any
further today."

But fishing is not the only activity of his heroes that
Hemingway endows with a curious and almost super-
natural value. They drink early and late; they consume
enough beer, wine, anis, grappa and Fundador to put
them all into alcoholic wards, if they were ordinary
mortals; but drinking seems to have the effect on them of
a magic potion. Robert Jordan, in *For Whom the Bell
Tolls*, is the soberest of Hemingway's heroes, the child,
as it were, of middle age. Nevertheless he finds that a cup
of absinthe "took the place of the evening papers, of all
the old evenings in cafés, of all the chestnut trees that
would be in bloom now in this month . . . of all the
things he had enjoyed and forgotten and that came back
to him when he tasted that opaque, bitter, tongue-
numbing, brain-warming, stomach-warming, idea-chang-
ing liquid alchemy." There is much that he wants to remember, but also the fear of death that he wants to
forget, and he personifies liquor as "the giant killer." On
one occasion he reflects that writing about his fears might
help him even more than drowning them in absinthe. He
says to himself, after worrying about all the lives that
have been lost as a result of his activities behind the

Fascist lines: "But my guess is you will get rid of all that by writing about it. . . . Once you write it down it is all gone." Hemingway himself sometimes seems to regard writing as an exhausting ceremony of exorcism. And, as a young man after the First World War, he had painful memories of which he wanted to rid himself by setting them all down.

II.

He was born on July 21, 1898, in Oak Park, Illinois, where his father was a physician. He went to school there, too, but what he regarded as his real home was a house in Michigan near the tip of the southern peninsula. The house was full of children all summer, for there were two boys and four girls in the family. In those days, the first-growth hemlock woods came down almost to the shore of the lake; and back in the woods was a settlement of Ojibways who lived by cutting the hemlocks for tanbark. Then one year all the woods were gone, "and there were only stumps, dried tree-tops, branches and fireweed where the woods had been." Ernest ran away from home when he was fifteen years old; that may have been the time he met the Battler beside the railway track near Mancelona. In 1917 he was graduated from Oak Park High School, where he had played football and had been chosen to write the class prophecy. He didn't go on to college, but instead got a job on the *Kansas City Star;* a few months later he went to Europe as a volunteer ambulance driver. He was badly wounded on the Italian front; he was given a silver medal (besides the Croce di Guerra); and after being patched together in a Milan hospital he served for a time in the Italian shock troops, the Arditi. One of the sights he could not forget was of the Austrian dead lying on their faces with their pockets turned out and each body surrounded by postcards and letters from home, a surprising quantity of paper. Another memory that became a nightmare was the evacuation of Smyrna by the Greeks, who left their baggage animals to drown. But that was something he saw four years later, when he was sent to the Middle East as a correspondent for the *Toronto Star*.

In Paris, which would be his home for many years after the war, he set about learning to become a writer. He had met Sherwood Anderson, who sent him to Gertrude Stein with a letter of introduction. He also became a good friend of Ezra Pound's, and he sometimes helped Ford Madox Ford to edit the *Transatlantic Review*, although his name did not appear on the masthead. These four—but especially Pound and Miss Stein—seem to have been his principal teachers; and what they gave him (or rather, what they confirmed in him) was an ideal of complete objectivity. When he sent his early manuscripts to Pound, they came back to him blue-penciled, with most of the adjectives gone. Miss Stein was content to make general comments, but they were usually followed. He afterwards said to John Peale Bishop, "Ezra was right half the time, and when he was wrong, he was so wrong you were never in any doubt about it. Gertrude was always right." As soon as he had saved a little money, Hemingway quit his job as a correspondent and devoted all his time to his stories. Once at a dinner in Paris with Dos Passos and the Lincoln Steffenses, he insisted that anybody could write. "You can," he said to Mrs. Steffens, making the gesture of giving her a left hook to the jaw; in those days he always gestured like a boxer. "It's hell. It takes it all out of you; it nearly kills you; but you can do it. Anybody can. Even you can, Stef. . . . I haven't done it yet, but I will." And Steffens adds, in his autobiography, "I think he thought that writing was a matter of honesty and labor."

"I was trying to write then," Hemingway tells us at the beginning of *Death in the Afternoon*, "and I found the greatest difficulty, aside from knowing truly what you really felt, rather than what you were supposed to feel, and had been taught to feel, was to put down what really happened in action; what the actual things were which produced the emotion that you experienced. In writing for a newspaper you told what happened and, with one trick and another, you communicated the emotion aided by the element of timeliness which gives a certain emotion to any account of something that has happened on that day; but the real thing, the sequence of motion and fact which made the emotion and which would be as valid in a year or in ten years or, with luck and if you stated it purely enough, always, was beyond me and I was working very hard to try to get it." In those days he seems to have regarded stories as, essentially, machines for arousing emotion. You didn't put the emotion itself into the story, any more than you would make a reaping machine out of wheat or a sewing machine out of cloth and thread; but you picked out the sharp details from life that had aroused your own emotion and, if you described them accurately, in their proper sequence and without closing your eyes to violence and horror, you had something that would continue to arouse the emotion of your readers. That was the method Hemingway followed in his early sketches and, within its self-imposed limitations, it was extremely successful. It was even successful beyond those limitations, for his pictures proved to have a vast power of suggestion. Take, for example, two of the "chapters," or interchapters, from *In Our Time*. Chapter III reads in full:

We were in a garden in Mons. Young Buckley came in with his patrol from across the river. The first German I saw climbed up over the garden wall. We waited till he got one

leg over and then potted him. He had so much equipment on
and looked awfully surprised and fell down into the garden.
Then three more came over further down the wall. We shot
them. They all came just like that.

There is nothing more. There are no editorial reflec-
tions on the horrors of modern warfare. There is, in the
story itself, no emotion whatever except the "awfully surprised" look of the first German who was shot. But the
story has the power of arousing emotion in the reader,
who tends to put himself either in the position of the English riflemen or, more likely, in that of the Germans climbing the wall to their deaths. And the wall itself is so vivid
that, for the reader, it tends to become a sort of metaphor
for all the impassable obstacles we see in nightmares: the
swamps in which our feet are mired, the endless steps, the
river that must, and cannot be crossed. Moreover, Hemingway returns to the same type of image in the following
interchapter:

It was a frightfully hot day. We'd jammed an absolutely
perfect barricade across the bridge. It was simply priceless.
A big old wrought-iron grating from the front of a house.
Too heavy to lift and you could shoot through it and they
would have to climb over it. It was absolutely topping. They
tried to get over it, and we potted them from forty yards.
They rushed it, and officers came out alone and worked on it. It was
an absolutely perfect obstacle. Their officers were very fine.
We were frightfully put out when we heard the flank had
gone, and we had to fall back.

Here the sense of nightmare becomes more definite.
The reader begins to feel that the "absolutely perfect
obstacle" is a symbol for other obstacles recurring in
Hemingway's novels: for the wound that divides Jake
and Brett (in *The Sun Also Rises*); for the death in child-
birth that separates Frederic from Catherine (in *A Farewell to Arms*); and even for the bridge that must be de-

stroyed (in *For Whom the Bell Tolls*) at the cost of the hero's life. Moreover, the picture of a wall reappears in the two interchapters that follow. Chapter V begins: "They shot the six cabinet ministers at half-past six in the morning against the wall of a hospital." Chapter VI begins: "Nick sat against the wall of the church where they had dragged him to be clear of machine-gun fire in the street." In Hemingway's unconscious mind, all these walls may have been the images of death, though I doubt that he regarded them consciously as symbols. He was trying in those early days to state everything behavioristically, and it was not until later that he began to make a deliberate use of symbolism, together with other literary devices that he had avoided in the beginning, when he was teaching himself to write "commencing with the simplest things."

Later, in *A Farewell to Arms,* the rain becomes a conscious symbol of disaster. "Things went very badly," the hero tells us in the first chapter. "At the start of the winter came the permanent rain and with the rain came the cholera." Catherine Barkley is afraid of the rain because, she says, "sometimes I see me dead in it." Rain falls all during the retreat from Caporetto; it falls while Catherine is trying to have her baby in a Swiss hospital; and it is still falling when she dies and when Frederic pushes the nurses out of the room to be alone with her. "It wasn't any good," he says. "It was like saying goodbye to a statue. After a while I went out and left the hospital and walked back to the hotel in the rain." On the other hand, it is snow that is used as a symbol of death in "The Snows of Kilimanjaro" (along with other death symbols, like vultures, hyenas, and soaring in an imaginary airplane). And possibly snow has the same value in *For Whom the Bell Tolls,* where a spring snowfall adds to the danger of Robert Jordan's mission and indirectly causes his death.

Even in these later novels and stories, Hemingway almost never makes the error that weakens the effect of most symbolic fiction. Ordinarily we think of it as a type of writing in which the events in the foreground tend to become misty because the author has his eyes fixed on something else. Hawthorne, in *The Marble Faun,* was so preoccupied with inner meanings that he seemed to lose his sense of the real world; but that is almost never the case with Hemingway. It is true that Maria, in *For Whom the Bell Tolls,* is almost more of a dream than she is a woman. When Frederic Henry dives into the flooded Tagliamento, in *A Farewell to Arms,* he is performing a rite of baptism that prepares us for the new life he is about to lead as a deserter from the Italian army; his act is emotionally significant, but it is a little unconvincing on the plane of action. These are perhaps the only two cases in which Hemingway seems to loosen his grip on reality. Elsewhere his eyes are fixed on the foreground; but he gives us a sense of other shadowy meanings that contribute to the force and complexity of his writing.

By the early 1930's Hemingway's technique, apparently simple in the beginning, was becoming more elaborate. He had begun to talk about the possibility of writing what he called fourth-dimensional prose. "The reason everyone now tries to avoid it," he says in *Green Hills of Africa,* "to deny that it is important, to make it seem vain to try to do it, is because it is so difficult. Too many factors must combine to make it possible."

"What is this now?" asks Kandisky, the Austrian in leather breeches who likes to lead the life of the mind. And the author tells him:

"The kind of writing that can be done. How far prose can be carried if anyone is serious enough and has luck. There is a fourth and fifth dimension that can be gotten."

"You believe it?"

"I know it."

"And if a writer can get this?"

"Then nothing else matters. It is more important than anything else he can do. The chances are, of course, that he will fail. But there is a chance that he succeeds."

"But that is poetry you are talking about."

"No. It is much more difficult than poetry. It is a prose that has never been written. But it can be written, without tricks and without cheating. With nothing that will go bad afterwards."

Now, I don't know exactly what Hemingway means by prose with "a fourth and fifth dimension." It would seem to me that any good prose has four dimensions, in the sense of being a solid object that moves through time, whereas the fifth dimension is here a mystical or meaningless figure of speech. But without understanding his choice of words, I do know that Hemingway's prose at its best gives a sense of depth and of moving forward on different levels that is lacking in even the best of his imitators, as it is in almost all the other novelists of our time. Moreover, I have at least a vague notion of how this quality in his work can be explained.

III.

Considering his laborious apprenticeship and the masters with whom he chose to study; considering his theories of writing, which he has often discussed, and how they have developed with the years; considering their subtle and highly conscious application, as well as the very complicated personality they serve to express, it is a little surprising to find that Hemingway is almost always described as a primitive. Yet the word really applies to him, if it is used in what might be called its anthropological sense. The anthropologists tell us that many of the so-called primitive peoples have an extremely elaborate system of beliefs, calling for the almost continual performance of rites and ceremonies; even their drunken orgies are ruled by tradition. Some of the forest-dwelling tribes believe that every rock or tree or animal has its own indwelling spirit. When they kill an animal or chop down a tree, they must beg its forgiveness, repeating a formula of propitiation; otherwise its spirit would haunt them. Living briefly in a world of hostile forces, they preserve themselves—so they believe—only by the exercise of magic lore.

There is something of the same atmosphere in Hemingway's work. His heroes live in a world that is like a hostile forest, full of unseen dangers, not to mention the nightmares that haunt their sleep. Death spies on them from behind every tree. Their only chance of safety lies in the faithful observance of customs they invent for themselves. In an early story like "Big Two-Hearted River," you notice that Nick Adams does everything very slowly, not wishing "to rush his sensations any"; and he pays so much attention to the meaning and rightness of each gesture that his life in the wilderness becomes a series of little ceremonies. "Another hopper poked his face out of the bottle. His antennae wavered. Nick took him by the head and held him while he threaded the hook under his chin, down through his thorax and into the last segments of his abdomen. The grasshopper took hold of the hook with his front feet, spitting tobacco juice on it." The grasshopper is playing its own part in a ritual; so too is the trout that swallows it, then bends the rod in jerks as it pumps against the current. The whole fishing trip, instead of being a mere escape, might be regarded as an incantation, a spell to banish evil spirits. And there are other rituals in Hemingway's work (besides drinking and writing, which I have mentioned already). Without too much difficulty we can recognize rites of animal sacrifice (as in *Death in the Afternoon*), of sexual union (in

For Whom the Bell Tolls), of self-immolation (in "The Snows of Kilimanjaro"), of conversion (in *To Have and Have Not*), and of symbolic death and rebirth (in the Caporetto passage of *A Farewell to Arms*). When one of Hemingway's characters violates his own standards or the just laws of the tribe (as Ole Andreson has done in "The Killers"), he waits for death as stolidly as an Indian. Memories of the Indians he knew in his boyhood play an important part in Hemingway's work; they reappear in *The Torrents of Spring* and in several of his shorter stories. Robert Jordan, in *For Whom the Bell Tolls*, compares his own exploits to Indian warfare, and he strengthens himself during his last moments by thinking about his grandfather, an old Indian fighter. *In Our Time,* Hemingway's first book of stories, starts by telling how Nick Adams' father is called to attend an Indian woman who has been in labor for two days. The woman lies screaming in a bunkhouse, while her husband, with a badly injured foot, lies in the bunk above her smoking his pipe. Dr. Adams performs a Caesarean section without anesthetic, then sews up the wound with fishing leaders. When the operation is finished, he looks at the husband in the upper bunk and finds that he is dead; unable to bear his wife's pain, he has turned his face to the wall and cut his throat. A story Nick Adams later tells is of Trudy Gilby, the Indian girl with whom he used to go squirrel shooting and who, under the big hemlock trees, "did first what no one has ever done better." Most of Hemingway's heroines are in the image of Trudy; they have the obedience to their lovers and the sexual morals of Indian girls. His heroes suffer without complaining and, in one way or another, they destroy themselves like the Indian husband.

But Hemingway feels an even greater kinship with the Spaniards, because they retain a primitive dignity in giving and accepting death. Even when their dignity is transformed into a blind lust for killing, as sometimes happened during their civil war, they continue to hold his respect. Agustín, in *For Whom the Bell Tolls,* sees four of Franco's cavalrymen and breaks out into a sweat that is not the sweat of fear. "When I saw those four there," he says, "and thought that we might kill them I was like a mare in the corral waiting for the stallion." And Robert Jordan thinks to himself: "We do it coldly but they do not, nor ever have. It is their extra sacrament. Their old one that they had before the new religion came from the far end of the Mediterranean, the one they have never abandoned but only suppressed and hidden to bring it out again in wars and inquisitions." Hemingway himself seems to have a feeling for half-forgotten sacraments; his cast of mind is pre-Christian and pre-logical.

Sometimes his stories come close to being adaptations of ancient myths. His first novel, for example, deals in different terms with the same legend that T. S. Eliot was not so much presenting as concealing in *The Waste Land.* When we turn to Eliot's explanatory notes, then read the book to which they refer as a principal source—*From Ritual to Romance,* by Jessie L. Weston—we learn that his poem is largely based on the legend of the Fisher King. The legend tells how the king was wounded in the loins and how he lay wasting in his bed while his whole kingdom became unfruitful; there was thunder but no rain; the rivers dried up, the flocks had no increase, and the women bore no children. *The Sun Also Rises* presents the same situation in terms of Paris after the First World War. It is a less despairing book than critics like to think; at times it is gay, friendly, even exuberant; but the hero has been wounded like the Fisher King, and he lives in a world that is absolutely sterile. I don't mean to imply that Hemingway owes a debt to *The Waste Land.* He had read the poem, which he liked at first, and the notes that followed it, which he didn't like at all; I doubt very much that he bothered to look at Jessie L. Weston's book. He said in 1924, when he was paying tribute to Joseph Conrad: "If I knew that by grinding Mr. Eliot into a fine dry powder and sprinkling that powder over Mr. Conrad's grave Mr. Conrad would shortly appear, looking very annoyed at the forced return, and commence writing, I would leave for London early tomorrow with a sausage grinder." And yet when he wrote his first novel, he dealt with the same legend that Eliot had discovered by scholarship; recovering it for himself, I think, by a sort of instinct for legendary situations.

And it is this instinct for legends, for sacraments, for rituals, for symbols appealing to buried hopes and fears, that helps to explain the power of Hemingway's work and his vast superiority over his imitators. The imitators have learned all his mannerisms as a writer, and in some cases they can tell a story even better than Hemingway himself; but they tell only the story; they communicate with the reader on only one level of experience. Hemingway does more than that. Most of us are also primitive in a sense, for all the machinery that surrounds our lives. We have our private rituals, our little superstitions, our symbols and fears and nightmares; and Hemingway reminds us unconsciously of the hidden worlds in which we live. Reading his best work, we are a little like Nick Adams looking down from the railroad bridge at the trout in Big Two-Hearted River: ". . . many trout in deep, fast-moving water, slightly distorted as he watched far down through the glassy convex surface of the pool, its surface pushing and swelling smooth against the resistance of the log-driven piles of the bridge. At the bottom of the pool were the big trout. Nick did not see them at first. Then he saw them at the bottom of the pool, big trout looking to hold themselves on the gravel bottom in a varying mist of gravel and sand."

During the last few years it has become the fashion to reprimand Hemingway and to point out how much better his work would be (with its undoubted power) if only he were a little more virtuous or reasonable or optimistic, or if he revealed the proper attitude toward progress and democracy. Critics like Maurice Coindreau (in French) and Bernard DeVoto have abused him without bothering to understand what he plainly says, much less what he suggests or implies. Even Maxwell Geismar, who is one of the few professors with a natural feeling for literary values, would like to make him completely over. "What a marvelous teacher Hemingway is," he exclaims, "with all the restrictions of temperament and environment which so far define his work! What could he not show us of living as well as dying, of the positives in our being as well as the destroying forces, of 'grace under pressure' and the grace we need with no pressures, of ordinary life-giving actions along with those superb last gestures of doomed exiles!" Or, to put the matter more plainly, what a great writer Hemingway would be, in Geismar's opinion, if he combined his own work with equal parts of Trollope and Emerson.

And the critics have some justice on their side. It is true that Hemingway has seldom been an affirmative writer; it is true that most of his work is narrow and violent and generally preoccupied with death. But the critics, although they might conceivably change him for the worse, are quite unable to change him for the better. He is one of the novelists who write, not as they should or would, but as they must. Like Poe and Hawthorne and Melville, he listens to his personal demon, which might also be called his intuition or his sense of life. If he listened to the critics instead, he might indeed come to resemble Trollope or Emerson, but the resemblance would be only on the surface and, as he sometimes says of writing that tries hard to meet public requirements, it would all go bad afterwards. Some of his own writing has gone bad, but surprisingly little of it. By now he has earned the right to be taken for what he is, with his great faults and greater virtues; with his narrowness, his power, his always open eyes, his stubborn, chip-on-the-shoulder honesty, his nightmares, his rituals for escaping them, and his sense of an inner and an outer world that for twenty years were moving together toward the same disaster.

MALCOLM COWLEY

THE NOVELS

THE SUN ALSO RISES

EDITOR'S PREFACE

IN the summer of 1924, Hemingway went to Pamplona for the Fiesta of San Fermín and the six bullfights held during the week of the fair. It was the trip described in *The Sun Also Rises*, but with many changes to make it truer than life. Anybody who lived in Paris at the time can recognize many of the characters: Donald Ogden Stewart (the great lover of stuffed animals) and Harold Stearns (the man who was just a little daunted), not to mention Ford Madox Ford and others; their conversation is reported with such complete accuracy that you can hear them talking in their different voices. But it is better not to confuse the people in the novel with those in life, since Hemingway has selected and changed and combined their adventures.

Take the young bullfighter, for example. His name,

Pedro Romero, is that of a famous matador who—I am quoting from *Death in the Afternoon*—"killed 5,600 bulls *recibiendo* between 1771 and 1779 and lived to die in his bed at the age of ninety-five." The character, however, seems to be based on that of Niño de la Palma in his first season as a matador, with a few touches borrowed from Manuel Garcia, known in the bull ring as Maera. Maera died of pneumonia, an occupational disease of bull-fighters. Niño de la Palma was wonderful that first year, but afterwards he was severely gored by a bull and he never regained his courage. It was just as well that Brett didn't marry him. Instead—if she was the woman popularly supposed to be Brett—she married an American and went to live in Mexico. Not long ago she died in a house in Taxco half-way up the mountainside. At the funeral her pallbearers drank a great deal and when they were carrying her downhill they slipped and fell, letting the coffin break. You could put that in a novel too.

The Sun Also Rises, published in October 1926, was Hemingway's first novel. Of course there was *The Torrents of Spring*, which had appeared in May of that year and which was described on the title page as "A Romantic Novel in Honor of the Passing of a Great Race"; but *The Torrents* was simply a satire on American business and American writers, including Sherwood Anderson. It was written in haste, reviewed in brief, and it was a little too quickly forgotten, considering that it has some very funny passages. But *The Sun Also Rises* was serious and accurate and new. It still seems new, after nearly twenty years and more than a hundred passable imitations.

BOOK ONE

CHAPTER I

ROBERT COHN was once middleweight boxing champion of Princeton. Do not think that I am very much impressed by that as a boxing title, but it meant a lot to Cohn. He cared nothing for boxing, in fact he disliked it, but he learned it painfully and thoroughly to counteract the feeling of inferiority and shyness he had felt on being treated as a Jew at Princeton. There was a certain inner comfort in knowing he could knock down anybody who was snooty to him, although, being very shy and a thoroughly nice boy, he never fought except in the gym. He was Spider Kelly's star pupil. Spider Kelly taught all his young gentlemen to box like featherweights, no matter whether they weighed one hundred and five or two hundred and five pounds. But it seemed to fit Cohn. He was really very fast. He was so good that Spider promptly overmatched him and got his nose permanently flattened. This increased Cohn's distaste for boxing, but it gave him a certain satisfaction of some strange sort, and it certainly improved his nose. In his last year at Princeton he read too much and took to wearing spectacles. I never met any one of his class who remembered him. They did not even remember that he was middleweight boxing champion.

I mistrust all frank and simple people, especially when their stories hold together, and I always had a suspicion that perhaps Robert Cohn had never been middleweight boxing champion, and that perhaps a horse had stepped on his face, or that maybe his mother had been frightened or seen something, or that he had, maybe, bumped

into something as a young child, but I finally had somebody verify the story from Spider Kelly. Spider Kelly not
only remembered Cohn. He had often wondered what
had become of him.

Robert Cohn was a member, through his father, of one
of the richest Jewish families in New York, and through
his mother of one of the oldest. At the military school
where he prepped for Princeton, and played a very good
end on the football team, no one had made him race-
conscious. No one had ever made him feel he was a Jew,
and hence any different from anybody else, until he went
to Princeton. He was a nice boy, a friendly boy, and very
shy, and it made him bitter. He took it out in boxing, and
he came out of Princeton with painful self-consciousness
and the flattened nose, and was married by the first girl
who was nice to him. He was married five years, had
three children, lost most of the fifty thousand dollars his
father left him, the balance of the estate having gone to
his mother, hardened into a rather unattractive mould
under domestic unhappiness with a rich wife; and just
when he had made up his mind to leave his wife she left
him and went off with a miniature-painter. As he had
been thinking for months about leaving his wife and had
not done it because it would be too cruel to deprive her
of himself, her departure was a very healthful shock.

The divorce was arranged and Robert Cohn went out
to the Coast. In California he fell among literary people
and, as he still had a little of the fifty thousand left, in a
short time he was backing a review of the Arts. The review commenced publication in Carmel, California, and
finished in Provincetown, Massachusetts. By that time
Cohn, who had been regarded purely as an angel, and
whose name had appeared on the editorial page merely
as a member of the advisory board, had become the sole
editor. It was his money and he discovered he liked the

authority of editing. He was sorry when the magazine became too expensive and he had to give it up.

By that time, though, he had other things to worry about. He had been taken in hand by a lady who hoped to rise with the magazine. She was very forceful, and Cohn never had a chance of not being taken in hand. Also he was sure that he loved her. When this lady saw that the magazine was not going to rise, she became a little disgusted with Cohn and decided that she might as well get what there was to get while there was still something available, so she urged that they go to Europe, where Cohn could write. They came to Europe, where the lady had been educated, and stayed three years. During these three years, the first spent in travel, the last two in Paris, Robert Cohn had two friends, Braddocks and myself. Braddocks was his literary friend. I was his tennis friend.

The lady who had him, her name was Frances, found toward the end of the second year that her looks were going, and her attitude toward Robert changed from one of careless possession and exploitation to the absolute determination that he should marry her. During this time Robert's mother had settled an allowance on him, about three hundred dollars a month. During two years and a half I do not believe that Robert Cohn looked at another woman. He was fairly happy, except that, like many people living in Europe, he would rather have been in America, and he had discovered writing. He wrote a novel, and it was not really such a bad novel as the critics later called it, although it was a very poor novel. He read many books, played bridge, played tennis, and boxed at a local gymnasium.

I first became aware of his lady's attitude toward him one night after the three of us had dined together. We had dined at l'Avenue's and afterward went to the Café de Versailles for coffee. We had several *fines* after the coffee, and I said I must be going. Cohn had been talking about the two of us going off somewhere on a weekend trip. He wanted to get out of town and get in a good walk. I suggested we fly to Strasbourg and walk up to Saint Odile, or somewhere or other in Alsace. "I know a girl in Strasbourg who can show us the town," I said.

Somebody kicked me under the table. I thought it was accidental and went on: "She's been there two years and knows everything there is to know about the town. She's a swell girl."

I was kicked again under the table and, looking, saw Frances, Robert's lady, her chin lifting and her face hardening.

"Hell," I said, "why go to Strasbourg? We could go up to Bruges, or to the Ardennes."

Cohn looked relieved. I was not kicked again. I said good-night and went out. Cohn said he wanted to buy a paper and would walk to the corner with me. "For God's sake," he said, "why did you say that about that girl in Strasbourg for? Didn't you see Frances?"

"No, why should I? If I know an American girl that lives in Strasbourg what the hell is it to Frances?"

"It doesn't make any difference. Any girl. I couldn't go, that would be all."

"Don't be silly."

"You don't know Frances. Any girl at all. Didn't you see the way she looked?"

"Oh, well," I said, "let's go to Senlis."

"Don't get sore."

"I'm not sore. Senlis is a good place and we can stay at the Grand Cerf and take a hike in the woods and come home."

"Good, that will be fine."

"Well, I'll see you to-morrow at the courts," I said.

"Good-night, Jake," he said, and started back to the café.

"You forgot to get your paper," I said.

"That's so." He walked with me up to the kiosque at the corner. "You are not sore, are you, Jake?" He turned with the paper in his hand.

"No, why should I be?"

"See you at tennis," he said. I watched him walk back to the café holding his paper. I rather liked him and evidently she led him quite a life.

CHAPTER II

THAT winter Robert Cohn went over to America with his novel, and it was accepted by a fairly good publisher. His going made an awful row I heard, and I think that was where Frances lost him, because several women were nice to him in New York, and when he came back he was quite changed. He was more enthusiastic about America than ever, and he was not so simple, and he was not so nice. The publishers had praised his novel pretty highly and it rather went to his head. Then several women had put themselves out to be nice to him, and his horizons had all shifted. For four years his horizon had been absolutely limited to his wife. For three years, or almost three years, he had never seen beyond Frances. I am sure he had never been in love in his life.

He had married on the rebound from the rotten time he had in college, and Frances took him on the rebound from his discovery that he had not been everything to his first wife. He was not in love yet but he realized that he was an attractive quantity to women, and that the fact of a woman caring for him and wanting to live with him was not simply a divine miracle. This changed him so that he was not so pleasant to have around. Also, playing for higher stakes than he could afford in some rather steep bridge games with his New York connections, he had held cards and won several hundred dollars. It made him rather vain of his bridge game, and he talked several times of how a man could always make a living at bridge if he were ever forced to.

Then there was another thing. He had been reading W. H. Hudson. That sounds like an innocent occupation, but Cohn had read and reread *The Purple Land*. *The Purple Land* is a very sinister book if read too late in life. It recounts splendid imaginary amorous adventures of a perfect English gentleman in an intensely romantic land, the scenery of which is very well described. For a man to take it at thirty-four as a guidebook to what life holds is about as safe as it would be for a man of the same age to enter Wall Street direct from a French convent, equipped with a complete set of the more practical Alger books. Cohn, I believe, took every word of *The Purple Land* as literally as though it had been an R. G. Dun report. You understand me, he made some reservations, but on the whole the book to him was sound. It was all that was needed to set him off. I did not realize the extent to which it had set him off until one day he came into my office.

"Hello, Robert," I said. "Did you come in to cheer me up?"

"Would you like to go to South America, Jake?" he asked.

"No."

"Why not?"

"I don't know. I never wanted to go. Too expensive. You can see all the South Americans you want in Paris anyway."

"They're not the real South Americans."

"They look awfully real to me."

I had a boat train to catch with a week's mail stories, and only half of them written.

"Do you know any dirt?" I asked.

"No."

"None of your exalted connections getting divorces?"

"No; listen, Jake. If I handled both our expenses, would you go to South America with me?"

"Why me?"

"You can talk Spanish. And it would be more fun with two of us."

"No," I said, "I like this town and I go to Spain in the summer-time."

"All my life I've wanted to go on a trip like that," Cohn said. He sat down. "I'll be too old before I can ever do it."

"Don't be a fool," I said. "You can go anywhere you want. You've got plenty of money."

"I know. But I can't get started."

"Cheer up," I said. "All countries look just like the moving pictures."

But I felt sorry for him. He had it badly.

"I can't stand it to think my life is going so fast and I'm not really living it."

"Nobody ever lives their life all the way up except bull-fighters."

"I'm not interested in bull-fighters. That's an abnormal life. I want to go back in the country in South America. We could have a great trip."

"Did you ever think about going to British East Africa to shoot?"

"No, I wouldn't like that."

"I'd go there with you."

"No; that doesn't interest me."

"That's because you never read a book about it. Go

on and read a book all full of love affairs with the beautiful shiny black princesses."

"I want to go to South America."

He had a hard, Jewish, stubborn streak.

"Come on down-stairs and have a drink."

"Aren't you working?"

"No," I said. We went down the stairs to the café on the ground floor. I had discovered that was the best way to get rid of friends. Once you had a drink all you had to say was: "Well, I've got to get back and get off some cables," and it was done. It is very important to discover graceful exits like that in the newspaper business, where it is such an important part of the ethics that you should never seem to be working. Anyway, we went down-stairs to the bar and had a whiskey and soda. Cohn looked at the bottles in bins around the wall. "This is a good place," he said.

"There's a lot of liquor," I agreed.

"Listen, Jake," he leaned forward on the bar. "Don't you ever get the feeling that all your life is going by and you're not taking advantage of it? Do you realize you've lived nearly half the time you have to live already?"

"Yes, every once in a while."

"Do you know that in about thirty-five years more we'll be dead?"

"What the hell, Robert," I said. "What the hell."

"I'm serious."

"It's one thing I don't worry about," I said.

"You ought to."

"I've had plenty to worry about one time or other. I'm through worrying."

"Well, I want to go to South America."

"Listen, Robert, going to another country doesn't make any difference. I've tried all that. You can't get away from yourself by moving from one place to another. There's nothing to that."

"But you've never been to South America."

"South America hell! If you went there the way you feel now it would be exactly the same. This is a good town. Why don't you start living your life in Paris?"

"I'm sick of Paris, and I'm sick of the Quarter."

"Stay away from the Quarter. Cruise around by yourself and see what happens to you."

"Nothing happens to me. I walked alone all one night and nothing happened except a bicycle cop stopped me and asked to see my papers."

"Wasn't the town nice at night?"

"I don't care for Paris."

So there you were. I was sorry for him, but it was not a thing you could do anything about, because right away you ran up against the two stubbornnesses: South America could fix it and he did not like Paris. He got the first idea out of a book, and I suppose the second came out of a book too.

"Well," I said, "I've got to go up-stairs and get off some cables."

"Do you really have to go?"

"Yes, I've got to get these cables off."

"Do you mind if I come up and sit around the office?"

"No, come on up."

He sat in the outer room and read the papers, and the *Editor and Publisher* and I worked hard for two hours. Then I sorted out the carbons, stamped on a by-line, put the stuff in a couple of big manila envelopes and rang for a boy to take them to the Gare St. Lazare. I went out into the other room and there was Robert Cohn asleep in the big chair. He was asleep with his head on his arms. I did not like to wake him up, but I wanted to lock the office and shove off. I put my hand on his shoulder. He shook his head. "I can't do it," he said, and put his head deeper into his arms. "I can't do it. Nothing will make me do it."

"Robert," I said, and shook him by the shoulder. He looked up. He smiled and blinked.

"Did I talk out loud just then?"

"Something. But it wasn't clear."

"God, what a rotten dream!"

"Did the typewriter put you to sleep?"

"Guess so. I didn't sleep all last night."

"What was the matter?"

"Talking," he said.

I could picture it. I have a rotten habit of picturing the bedroom scenes of my friends. We went out to the Café Napolitain to have an *apéritif* and watch the evening crowd on the Boulevard.

CHAPTER III

IT was a warm spring night and I sat at a table on the terrace of the Napolitain after Robert had gone, watching it get dark and the electric signs come on, and the red and green stop-and-go traffic-signal, and the crowd going by, and the horse-cabs clippety-clopping along at the edge of the solid taxi traffic, and the *poules* going by, singly and in pairs, looking for the evening meal. I watched a good-looking girl walk past the table and watched her go up the street and lost sight of her, and watched another, and then saw the first one coming back again. She went by once more and I caught her eye, and she came over and sat down at the table. The waiter came up.

"Well, what will you drink?" I asked.

"Pernod."

"That's not good for little girls."

"Little girl yourself. Dites garçon, un pernod."

"A pernod for me, too."

"What's the matter?" she asked. "Going on a party?"

"Sure. Aren't you?"

"I don't know. You never know in this town."

"Don't you like Paris?"

"No."

"Why don't you go somewhere else?"

"Isn't anywhere else."

"You're happy, all right."

"Happy, hell!"

Pernod is greenish imitation absinthe. When you add water it turns milky. It tastes like licorice and it has a good uplift, but it drops you just as far. We sat and drank it, and the girl looked sullen.

"Well," I said, "are you going to buy me a dinner?"

She grinned and I saw why she made a point of not laughing. With her mouth closed she was a rather pretty girl. I paid for the saucers and we walked out to the street. I hailed a horse-cab and the driver pulled up at the curb. Settled back in the slow, smoothly rolling *fiacre* we moved up the Avenue de l'Opéra, passed the locked doors of the shops, their windows lighted, the Avenue broad and shiny and almost deserted. The cab passed the New York *Herald* bureau with the window full of clocks.

"What are all the clocks for?" she asked.

"They show the hour all over America."

"Don't kid me."

We turned off the Avenue up the Rue des Pyramides, through the traffic of the Rue de Rivoli, and through a dark gate into the Tuileries. She cuddled against me and

I put my arm around her. She looked up to be kissed. She touched me with one hand and I put her hand away.

"Never mind."

"What's the matter? You sick?"

"Yes."

"Everybody's sick. I'm sick, too."

We came out of the Tuileries into the light and crossed the Seine and then turned up the Rue des Saints Pères.

"You oughtn't to drink pernod if you're sick."

"You neither."

"It doesn't make any difference with me. It doesn't make any difference with a woman."

"What are you called?"

"Georgette. How are you called?"

"Jacob."

"That's a Flemish name."

"American too."

"You're not Flamand?"

"No, American."

"Good, I detest Flamands."

By this time we were at the restaurant. I called to the *cocher* to stop. We got out and Georgette did not like the looks of the place. "This is no great thing of a restaurant."

"No," I said. "Maybe you would rather go to Foyot's. Why don't you keep the cab and go on?"

I had picked her up because of a vague sentimental idea that it would be nice to eat with some one. It was a long time since I had dined with a *poule,* and I had forgotten how dull it could be. We went into the restaurant, passed Madame Lavigne at the desk and into a little room. Georgette cheered up a little under the food.

"It isn't bad here," she said. "It isn't chic, but the food is all right."

"Better than you eat in Liège."

"Brussels, you mean."

We had another bottle of wine and Georgette made a joke. She smiled and showed all her bad teeth, and we touched glasses. "You're not a bad type," she said. "It's a shame you're sick. We get on well. What's the matter with you, anyway?"

"I got hurt in the war," I said.

"Oh, that dirty war."

We would probably have gone on and discussed the war and agreed that it was in reality a calamity for civilization, and perhaps would have been better avoided. I was bored enough. Just then from the other room some one called: "Barnes! I say, Barnes! Jacob Barnes!"

"It's a friend calling me," I explained, and went out.

There was Braddocks at a big table with a party: Cohn, Frances Clyne, Mrs. Braddocks, several people I did not know.

"You're coming to the dance, aren't you?" Braddocks asked.

"What dance?"

"Why, the dancings. Don't you know we've revived them?" Mrs. Braddocks put in.

"You must come, Jake. We're all going," Frances said from the end of the table. She was tall and had a smile.

"Of course, he's coming," Braddocks said. "Come in and have coffee with us, Barnes."

"Right."

"And bring your friend," said Mrs. Braddocks laughing. She was a Canadian and had all their easy social graces.

"Thanks, we'll be in," I said. I went back to the small room.

"Who are your friends?" Georgette asked.

"Writers and artists."

"There are lots of those on this side of the river."

"Too many."

"I think so. Still, some of them make money."

"Oh, yes."

We finished the meal and the wine. "Come on," I said. "We're going to have coffee with the others."

Georgette opened her bag, made a few passes at her face as she looked in the little mirror, re-defined her lips with the lip-stick, and straightened her hat.

"Good," she said.

We went into the room full of people and Braddocks and the men at his table stood up.

"I wish to present my fiancée, Mademoiselle Georgette Leblanc," I said. Georgette smiled that wonderful smile, and we shook hands all round.

"Are you related to Georgette Leblanc, the singer?" Mrs. Braddocks asked.

"Connais pas," Georgette answered.

"But you have the same name," Mrs. Braddocks insisted cordially.

"No," said Georgette. "Not at all. My name is Hobin."

"But Mr. Barnes introduced you as Mademoiselle Georgette Leblanc. Surely he did," insisted Mrs. Braddocks, who in the excitement of talking French was liable to have no idea what she was saying.

"He's a fool," Georgette said.

"Oh, it was a joke, then," Mrs. Braddocks said.

"Yes," said Georgette. "To laugh at."

"Did you hear that, Henry?" Mrs. Braddocks called down the table to Braddocks. "Mr. Barnes introduced his fiancée as Mademoiselle Leblanc, and her name is actually Hobin."

"Of course, darling. Mademoiselle Hobin, I've known her for a very long time."

"Oh, Mademoiselle Hobin," Frances Clyne called, speaking French very rapidly and not seeming so proud

and astonished as Mrs. Braddocks at its coming out really
French. "Have you been in Paris long? Do you like it
here? You love Paris, do you not?"

"Who's she?" Georgette turned to me. "Do I have to
talk to her?"

She turned to Frances, sitting smiling, her hands
folded, her head poised on her long neck, her lips pursed
ready to start talking again.

"No, I don't like Paris. It's expensive and dirty."

"Really? I find it so extraordinarily clean. One of the
cleanest cities in all Europe."

"I find it dirty."

"How strange! But perhaps you have not been here
very long."

"I've been here long enough."

"But it does have nice people in it. One must grant
that."

Georgette turned to me. "You have nice friends."

Frances was a little drunk and would have liked to
have kept it up but the coffee came, and Lavigne with
the liqueurs, and after that we all went out and started
for Braddocks's dancing-club.

The dancing-club was a *bal musette* in the Rue de la
Montagne Sainte Geneviève. Five nights a week the
working people of the Panthéon quarter danced there.
One night a week it was the dancing-club. On Monday
nights it was closed. When we arrived it was quite
empty, except for a policeman sitting near the door, the
wife of the proprietor back of the zinc bar, and the proprietor himself. The daughter of the house came down-
stairs as we went in. There were long benches, and tables
ran across the room, and at the far end a dancing-floor.

"I wish people would come earlier," Braddocks said.
The daughter came up and wanted to know what we
would drink. The proprietor got up on a high stool beside

the dancing-floor and began to play the accordion. He had a string of bells around one of his ankles and beat time with his foot as he played. Every one danced. It was hot and we came off the floor perspiring.

"My God," Georgette said. "What a box to sweat in!"

"It's hot."

"Hot, my God!"

"Take off your hat."

"That's a good idea."

Some one asked Georgette to dance, and I went over to the bar. It was really very hot and the accordion music was pleasant in the hot night. I drank a beer, standing in the doorway and getting the cool breath of wind from the street. Two taxis were coming down the steep street. They both stopped in front of the Bal. A crowd of young men, some in jerseys and some in their shirt-sleeves, got out. I could see their hands and newly washed, wavy hair in the light from the door. The policeman standing by the door looked at me and smiled. They came in. As they went in, under the light I saw white hands, wavy hair, white faces, grimacing, gesturing, talking. With them was Brett. She looked very lovely, and she was very much with them.

One of them saw Georgette and said: "I do declare. There is an actual harlot. I'm going to dance with her, Lett. You watch me."

The tall, dark one, called Lett, said: "Don't you be rash."

The wavy blond one answered: "Don't you worry, dear." And with them was Brett.

I was very angry. Somehow they always made me angry. I know they are supposed to be amusing, and you should be tolerant, but I wanted to swing on one, any one, anything to shatter that superior, simpering composure. Instead, I walked down the street and had a beer at the bar at the next Bal. The beer was not good and I had a worse cognac to take the taste out of my mouth. When I came back to the Bal there was a crowd on the floor and Georgette was dancing with the tall blond youth, who danced big-hippily, carrying his head on one side, his eyes lifted as he danced. As soon as the music stopped another one of them asked her to dance. She had been taken up by them. I knew then that they would all dance with her. They are like that.

I sat down at a table. Cohn was sitting there. Frances was dancing. Mrs. Braddocks brought up somebody and introduced him as Robert Prentiss. He was from New York by way of Chicago, and was a rising new novelist. He had some sort of an English accent. I asked him to have a drink.

"Thanks so much," he said, "I've just had one."

"Have another."

"Thanks, I will then."

We got the daughter of the house over and each had a *fine à l'eau*.

"You're from Kansas City, they tell me," he said.

"Yes."

"Do you find Paris amusing?"

"Yes."

"Really?"

I was a little drunk. Not drunk in any positive sense but just enough to be careless.

"For God's sake," I said, "yes. Don't you?"

"Oh, how charmingly you get angry," he said. "I wish I had that faculty."

I got up and walked over toward the dancing-floor. Mrs. Braddocks followed me. "Don't be cross with Robert," she said. "He's still only a child, you know."

"I wasn't cross," I said. "I just thought perhaps I was going to throw up."

"Your fiancée is having a great success," Mrs. Braddocks looked out on the floor where Georgette was dancing in the arms of the tall, dark one, called Lett.

"Isn't she?" I said.

"Rather," said Mrs. Braddocks.

Cohn came up. "Come on, Jake," he said, "have a drink." We walked over to the bar. "What's the matter with you? You seem all worked up over something?"

"Nothing. This whole show makes me sick is all."

Brett came up to the bar.

"Hello, you chaps."

"Hello, Brett," I said. "Why aren't you tight?"

"Never going to get tight any more. I say, give a chap a brandy and soda."

She stood holding the glass and I saw Robert Cohn looking at her. He looked a great deal as his compatriot must have looked when he saw the promised land. Cohn, of course, was much younger. But he had that look of eager, deserving expectation.

Brett was damned good-looking. She wore a slipover jersey sweater and a tweed skirt, and her hair was brushed back like a boy's. She started all that. She was built with curves like the hull of a racing yacht, and you missed none of it with that wool jersey.

"It's a fine crowd you're with, Brett," I said.

"Aren't they lovely? And you, my dear. Where did you get it?"

"At the Napolitain."

"And have you had a lovely evening?"

"Oh, priceless," I said.

Brett laughed. "It's wrong of you, Jake. It's an insult to all of us. Look at Frances there, and Jo."

This for Cohn's benefit.

"It's in restraint of trade," Brett said. She laughed again.

"You're wonderfully sober," I said.

"Yes. Aren't I? And when one's with the crowd I'm with, one can drink in such safety, too."

The music started and Robert Cohn said: "Will you dance this with me, Lady Brett?"

Brett smiled at him. "I've promised to dance this with Jacob," she laughed. "You've a hell of a biblical name, Jake."

"How about the next?" asked Cohn.

"We're going," Brett said. "We've a date up at Montmartre."

Dancing, I looked over Brett's shoulder and saw Cohn, standing at the bar, still watching her.

"You've made a new one there," I said to her.

"Don't talk about it. Poor chap. I never knew it till just now."

"Oh, well," I said. "I suppose you like to add them up."

"Don't talk like a fool."

"You do."

"Oh, well. What if I do?"

"Nothing," I said. We were dancing to the accordion and some one was playing the banjo. It was hot and I felt happy. We passed close to Georgette dancing with another one of them.

"What possessed you to bring her?"

"I don't know, I just brought her."

"You're getting damned romantic."

"No, bored."

"Now?"

"No, not now."

"Let's get out of here. She's well taken care of."

"Do you want to?"

"Would I ask you if I didn't want to?"

We left the floor and I took my coat off a hanger on the wall and put it on. Brett stood by the bar. Cohn was talking to her. I stopped at the bar and asked them for an envelope. The patronne found one. I took a fifty-franc note from my pocket, put it in the envelope, sealed it, and handed it to the patronne.

"If the girl I came with asks for me, will you give her this?" I said. "If she goes out with one of those gentlemen, will you save this for me?"

"C'est entendu, Monsieur," the patronne said. "You go now? So early?"

"Yes," I said.

We started out the door. Cohn was still talking to Brett. She said good night and took my arm. "Good night, Cohn," I said. Outside in the street we looked for a taxi.

"You're going to lose your fifty francs," Brett said.

"Oh, yes."

"No taxis."

"We could walk up to the Panthéon and get one."

"Come on and we'll get a drink in the pub next door and send for one."

"You wouldn't walk across the street."

"Not if I could help it."

We went into the next bar and I sent a waiter for a taxi.

"Well," I said, "we're out away from them."

We stood against the tall zinc bar and did not talk and looked at each other. The waiter came and said the taxi was outside. Brett pressed my hand hard. I gave the waiter a franc and we went out. "Where should I tell him?" I asked.

"Oh, tell him to drive around."

I told the driver to go to the Parc Montsouris, and got in, and slammed the door. Brett was leaning back in the corner, her eyes closed. I got in and sat beside her. The cab started with a jerk.

"Oh, darling, I've been so miserable," Brett said.

CHAPTER IV

THE taxi went up the hill, passed the lighted square, then on into the dark, still climbing, then levelled out onto a dark street behind St. Etienne du Mont, went smoothly down the asphalt, passed the trees and the standing bus at the Place de la Contrescarpe, then turned onto the cobbles of the Rue Mouffetard. There were lighted bars and late open shops on each side of the street. We were sitting apart and we jolted close together going down the old street. Brett's hat was off. Her head was back. I saw her face in the lights from the open shops, then it was dark, then I saw her face clearly as we came out on the Avenue des Gobelins. The street was torn up and men were working on the car-tracks by the light of acetylene flares. Brett's face was white and the long line of her neck showed in the bright light of the flares. The street was dark again and I kissed her. Our lips were tight together and then she turned away and pressed against the corner of the seat, as far away as she could get. Her head was down.

"Don't touch me," she said. "Please don't touch me."

"What's the matter?"

"I can't stand it."

"Oh, Brett."

"You mustn't. You must know. I can't stand it, that's all. Oh, darling, please understand!"

"Don't you love me?"

"Love you? I simply turn all to jelly when you touch me."

"Isn't there anything we can do about it?"

She was sitting up now. My arm was around her and she was leaning back against me, and we were quite calm. She was looking into my eyes with that way she had of looking that made you wonder whether she really saw out of her own eyes. They would look on and on after every one else's eyes in the world would have stopped looking. She looked as though there were nothing on earth she would not look at like that, and really she was afraid of so many things.

"And there's not a damn thing we could do," I said.

"I don't know," she said. "I don't want to go through that hell again."

"We'd better keep away from each other."

"But, darling, I have to see you. It isn't all that you know."

"No, but it always gets to be."

"That's my fault. Don't we pay for all the things we do, though?"

She had been looking into my eyes all the time. Her eyes had different depths, sometimes they seemed perfectly flat. Now you could see all the way into them.

"When I think of the hell I've put chaps through. I'm paying for it all now."

"Don't talk like a fool," I said. "Besides, what happened to me is supposed to be funny. I never think about it."

"Oh, no. I'll lay you don't."

"Well, let's shut up about it."

"I laughed about it too, myself, once." She wasn't looking at me. "A friend of my brother's came home that way from Mons. It seemed like a hell of a joke. Chaps never know anything, do they?"

"No," I said. "Nobody ever knows anything."

I was pretty well through with the subject. At one time or another I had probably considered it from most of its various angles, including the one that certain injuries or imperfections are a subject of merriment while remaining quite serious for the person possessing them.

"It's funny," I said. "It's very funny. And it's a lot of fun, too, to be in love."

"Do you think so?" her eyes looked flat again.

"I don't mean fun that way. In a way it's an enjoyable feeling."

"No," she said. "I think it's hell on earth."

"It's good to see each other."

"No. I don't think it is."

"Don't you want to?"

"I have to."

We were sitting now like two strangers. On the right was the Parc Montsouris. The restaurant where they have the pool of live trout and where you can sit and look out over the park was closed and dark. The driver leaned his head around.

"Where do you want to go?" I asked. Brett turned her head away.

"Oh, go to the Select."

"Café Select," I told the driver. "Boulevard Montparnasse." We drove straight down, turning around the Lion de Belfort that guards the passing Montrouge trams. Brett looked straight ahead. On the Boulevard Raspail, with the lights of Montparnasse in sight, Brett said: "Would you mind very much if I asked you to do something?"

"Don't be silly."

"Kiss me just once more before we get there."

When the taxi stopped I got out and paid. Brett came out putting on her hat. She gave me her hand as she stepped down. Her hand was shaky. "I say, do I look too much of a mess?" She pulled her man's felt hat down and started in for the bar. Inside, against the bar and at tables, were most of the crowd who had been at the dance.

"Hello, you chaps," Brett said. "I'm going to have a drink."

"Oh, Brett! Brett!" the little Greek portrait-painter who called himself a duke, and whom everybody called Zizi, pushed up to her. "I got something fine to tell you."

"Hello, Zizi," Brett said.

"I want you to meet a friend," Zizi said. A fat man came up.

"Count Mippipopolous, meet my friend Lady Ashley."

"How do you do?" said Brett.

"Well, does your Ladyship have a good time here in Paris?" asked Count Mippipopolous, who wore an elk's tooth on his watch-chain.

"Rather," said Brett.

"Paris is a fine town all right," said the count. "But I guess you have pretty big doings yourself over in London."

"Oh, yes," said Brett. "Enormous."

Braddocks called to me from a table. "Barnes," he said, "have a drink. That girl of yours got in a frightful row."

"What about?"

"Something the patronne's daughter said. A corking row. She was rather splendid, you know. Showed her yellow card and demanded the patronne's daughter's too. I say it was a row."

"What finally happened?"

"Oh, some one took her home. Not a bad-looking girl. Wonderful command of the idiom. Do stay and have a drink."

"No," I said. "I must shove off. Seen Cohn?"

"He went home with Frances," Mrs. Braddocks put in.

"Poor chap, he looks awfully down," Braddocks said.

"I dare say he is," said Mrs. Braddocks.

"I have to shove off," I said. "Good night."

I said good night to Brett at the bar. The count was buying champagne. "Will you take a glass of wine with us, sir?" he asked.

"No. Thanks awfully. I have to go."

"Really going?" Brett asked.

"Yes," I said. "I've got a rotten headache."

"I'll see you to-morrow?"

"Come in at the office."

"Hardly."

"Well, where will I see you?"

"Anywhere around five o'clock."

"Make it the other side of town then."

"Good. I'll be at the Crillon at five."

"Try and be there," I said.

"Don't worry," Brett said. "I've never let you down, have I?"

"Heard from Mike?"

"Letter to-day."

"Good night, sir," said the count.

I went out onto the sidewalk and walked down toward the Boulevard St. Michel, passed the tables of the Rotonde, still crowded, looked across the street at the Dôme, its tables running out to the edge of the pavement. Some one waved at me from a table, I did not see who it was, and went on. I wanted to get home. The Boulevard Montparnasse was deserted. Lavigne's was closed tight, and they were stacking the tables outside the Closerie des Lilas. I passed Ney's statue standing among the new-leaved chestnut-trees in the arc-light. There was a faded purple wreath leaning against the base. I stopped and read the inscription: from the Bonapartist Groups, some date; I forget. He looked very fine, Marshal Ney in his top-boots, gesturing with his sword among the green new horse-chestnut leaves. My flat was just across the street, a little way down the Boulevard St. Michel.

There was a light in the concierge's room and I knocked on the door and she gave me my mail. I wished

her good night and went up-stairs. There were two letters
and some papers. I looked at them under the gas-light in
the dining-room. The letters were from the States. One
was a bank statement. It showed a balance of $2432.60.
I got out my check-book and deducted four checks
drawn since the first of the month, and discovered I
had a balance of $1,832.60. I wrote this on the back of
the statement. The other letter was a wedding announcement. Mr. and Mrs. Aloysius Kirby announce the mar-
riage of their daughter Katherine—I knew neither the
girl nor the man she was marrying. They must be cir-
cularizing the town. It was a funny name. I felt sure I
could remember anybody with a name like Aloysius. It
was a good Catholic name. There was a crest on the
announcement. Like Zizi the Greek duke. And that
count. The count was funny. Brett had a title, too.
Lady Ashley. To hell with Brett. To hell with you, Lady
Ashley.

I lit the lamp beside the bed, turned off the gas, and
opened the wide windows. The bed was far back from
the windows, and I sat with the windows open and undressed by the bed. Outside a night train, running on
the street-car tracks, went by carrying vegetables to the
markets. They were noisy at night when you could not
sleep. Undressing, I looked at myself in the mirror of
the big armoire beside the bed. That was a typically
French way to furnish a room. Practical, too, I suppose.
Of all the ways to be wounded. I suppose it was funny.
I put on my pajamas and got into bed. I had the two
bull-fight papers, and I took their wrappers off. One was
orange. The other yellow. They would both have the
same news, so whichever I read first would spoil the
other. *Le Toril* was the better paper, so I started to read
it. I read it all the way through, including the Petite

Correspondance and the Cornigrams. I blew out the lamp. Perhaps I would be able to sleep.

My head started to work. The old grievance. Well, it was a rotten way to be wounded and flying on a joke front like the Italian. In the Italian hospital we were going to form a society. It had a funny name in Italian. I wonder what became of the others, the Italians. That was in the Ospedale Maggiore in Milano, Padiglione Ponte. The next building was the Padiglione Zonda. There was a statue of Ponte, or maybe it was Zonda. That was where the liaison colonel came to visit me. That was funny. That was about the first funny thing. I was all bandaged up. But they had told him about it. Then he made that wonderful speech: "You, a foreigner, an Englishman (any foreigner was an Englishman), have given more than your life." What a speech! I would like to have it illuminated to hang in the office. He never laughed. He was putting himself in my place, I guess. "Che mala fortuna! Che mala fortuna!"

I never used to realize it, I guess. I try and play it along and just not make trouble for people. Probably I never would have had any trouble if I hadn't run into Brett when they shipped me to England. I suppose she only wanted what she couldn't have. Well, people were that way. To hell with people. The Catholic Church had an awfully good way of handling all that. Good advice, anyway. Not to think about it. Oh, it was swell advice. Try and take it sometime. Try and take it.

I lay awake thinking and my mind jumping around. Then I couldn't keep away from it, and I started to think about Brett and all the rest of it went away. I was thinking about Brett and my mind stopped jumping around and started to go in sort of smooth waves.

Then all of a sudden I started to cry. Then after a while it was better and I lay in bed and listened to the heavy trams go by and way down the street, and then I went to sleep.

I woke up. There was a row going on outside. I listened and I thought I recognized a voice. I put on a dressing-gown and went to the door. The concierge was talking down-stairs. She was very angry. I heard my name and called down the stairs.

"Is that you, Monsieur Barnes?" the concierge called.

"Yes. It's me."

"There's a species of woman here who's waked the whole street up. What kind of dirty business at this time of night! She says she must see you. I've told her you're asleep."

Then I heard Brett's voice. Half asleep I had been sure it was Georgette. I don't know why. She could not have known my address.

"Will you send her up, please?"

Brett came up the stairs. I saw she was quite drunk. "Silly thing to do," she said. "Make an awful row. I say, you weren't asleep, were you?"

"What did you think I was doing?"

"Don't know. What time is it?"

I looked at the clock. It was half-past four. "Had no idea what hour it was," Brett said. "I say, can a chap sit down? Don't be cross, darling. Just left the count. He brought me here."

"What's he like?" I was getting brandy and soda and glasses.

"Just a little," said Brett. "Don't try and make me drunk. The count? Oh, rather. He's quite one of us."

"Is he a count?"

"Here's how. I rather think so, you know. Deserves to be, anyhow. Knows hell's own amount about people.

Don't know where he got it all. Owns a chain of sweet-shops in the States."

She sipped at her glass.

"Think he called it a chain. Something like that. Linked them all up. Told me a little about it. Damned interesting. He's one of us, though. Oh, quite. No doubt. One can always tell."

She took another drink.

"How do I buck on about all this? You don't mind, do you? He's putting up for Zizi, you know."

"Is Zizi really a duke, too?"

"I shouldn't wonder. Greek, you know. Rotten painter. I rather liked the count."

"Where did you go with him?"

"Oh, everywhere. He just brought me here now. Offered me ten thousand dollars to go to Biarritz with him. How much is that in pounds?"

"Around two thousand."

"Lot of money. I told him I couldn't do it. He was awfully nice about it. Told him I knew too many people in Biarritz."

Brett laughed.

"I say, you are slow on the up-take," she said. I had only sipped my brandy and soda. I took a long drink.

"That's better. Very funny," Brett said, "Then he wanted me to go to Cannes with him. Told him I knew too many people in Cannes. Monte Carlo. Told him I knew too many people in Monte Carlo. Told him I knew too many people everywhere. Quite true, too. So I asked him to bring me here."

She looked at me, her hand on the table, her glass raised. "Don't look like that," she said. "Told him I was in love with you. True, too. Don't look like that. He was damn nice about it. Wants to drive us out to dinner to-morrow night. Like to go?"

"Why not?"

"I'd better go now."

"Why?"

"Just wanted to see you. Damned silly idea. Want to get dressed and come down? He's got the car just up the street."

"The count?"

"Himself. And a chauffeur in livery. Going to drive me around and have breakfast in the Bois. Hampers. Got it all at Zelli's. Dozen bottles of Mumms. Tempt you?"

"I have to work in the morning," I said. "I'm too far behind you now to catch up and be any fun."

"Don't be an ass."

"Can't do it."

"Right. Send him a tender message?"

"Anything. Absolutely."

"Good night, darling."

"Don't be sentimental."

"You make me ill."

We kissed good night and Brett shivered. "I'd better go," she said. "Good night, darling."

"You don't have to go."

"Yes."

We kissed again on the stairs and as I called for the cordon the concierge muttered something behind her door. I went back up-stairs and from the open window watched Brett walking up the street to the big limousine drawn up to the curb under the arc-light. She got in and it started off. I turned around. On the table was an empty glass and a glass half-full of brandy and soda. I took them both out to the kitchen and poured the half-full glass down the sink. I turned off the gas in the dining-room, kicked off my slippers sitting on the bed, and got into bed. This was Brett, that I had felt like crying about. Then I thought of her walking up the street and stepping into the car, as I had last seen her, and of course in a little while I felt like hell again. It is awfully easy to be hard-boiled about everything in the daytime, but at night it is another thing.

CHAPTER V

IN the morning I walked down the Boulevard to the Rue Soufflot for coffee and brioche. It was a fine morning. The horse-chestnut trees in the Luxembourg gardens were in bloom. There was the pleasant early-morning feeling of a hot day. I read the papers with the coffee and then smoked a cigarette. The flower-women were coming up from the market and arranging their daily stock. Students went by going up to the law school, or down to the Sorbonne. The Boulevard was busy with trams and people going to work. I got on a S bus and rode down to the Madeleine, standing on the back platform. From the Madeleine I walked along the Boulevard des Capucines to the Opéra, and up to my office. I passed the man with the jumping frogs and the man with the boxer toys. I stepped aside to avoid walking into the thread with which his girl assistant manipulated the boxers. She was standing looking away, the thread in her folded hands. The man was urging two tourists to buy. Three more tourists had stopped and were watching. I walked on behind a man who was pushing a roller that printed the name CINZANO on the sidewalk in damp letters. All along people were going to work. It felt pleasant to be going to work. I walked across the avenue and turned in to my office.

Up-stairs in the office I read the French morning papers, smoked, and then sat at the typewriter and got off a good morning's work. At eleven o'clock I went over to the Quai d'Orsay in a taxi and went in and sat with about a dozen correspondents, while the foreign-office mouthpiece, a young *Nouvelle-Revue-Française* diplomat in horn-rimmed spectacles, talked and answered questions for half an hour. The President of the Council was in Lyons making a speech, or, rather he was on his way back. Several people asked questions to hear themselves talk and there were a couple of questions asked by news service men who wanted to know the answers. There was no news. I shared a taxi back from the Quai d'Orsay with Woolsey and Krum.

"What do you do nights, Jake?" asked Krum. "I never see you around."

"Oh, I'm over in the Quarter."

"I'm coming over some night. The Dingo. That's the great place, isn't it?"

"Yes. That, or this new dive, The Select."

"I've meant to get over," said Krum. "You know how it is, though, with a wife and kids."

"Playing any tennis?" Woolsey asked.

"Well, no," said Krum. "I can't say I've played any this year. I've tried to get away, but Sundays it's always rained, and the courts are so damned crowded."

"The Englishmen all have Saturday off," Woolsey said.

"Lucky beggars," said Krum. "Well, I'll tell you. Some day I'm not going to be working for an agency. Then I'll have plenty of time to get out in the country."

"That's the thing to do. Live out in the country and have a little car."

"I've been thinking some about getting a car next year."

I banged on the glass. The chauffeur stopped. "Here's my street," I said. "Come in and have a drink."

"Thanks, old man," Krum said. Woolsey shook his head. "I've got to file that line he got off this morning."

I put a two-franc piece in Krum's hand.

"You're crazy, Jake," he said. "This is on me."

"It's all on the office, anyway."

"Nope. I want to get it."

I waved good-by. Krum put his head out. "See you at the lunch on Wednesday."

"You bet."

I went to the office in the elevator. Robert Cohn was waiting for me. "Hello, Jake," he said. "Going out to lunch?"

"Yes. Let me see if there is anything new."

"Where will we eat?"

"Anywhere."

I was looking over my desk. "Where do you want to eat?"

"How about Wetzel's? They've got good hors d'œuvres."

In the restaurant we ordered hors d'œuvres and beer. The sommelier brought the beer, tall, beaded on the outside of the steins, and cold. There were a dozen different dishes of hors d'œuvres.

"Have any fun last night?" I asked.

"No. I don't think so."

"How's the writing going?"

"Rotten. I can't get this second book going."

"That happens to everybody."

"Oh, I'm sure of that. It gets me worried, though."

"Thought any more about going to South America?"

"I mean that."

"Well, why don't you start off?"

"Frances."

"Well," I said, "take her with you."

"She wouldn't like it. That isn't the sort of thing she likes. She likes a lot of people around."

"Tell her to go to hell."

"I can't. I've got certain obligations to her."

He shoved the sliced cucumbers away and took a pickled herring.

"What do you know about Lady Brett Ashley, Jake?"

"Her name's Lady Ashley. Brett's her own name. She's a nice girl," I said. "She's getting a divorce and she's going to marry Mike Campbell. He's over in Scotland now. Why?"

"She's a remarkably attractive woman."

"Isn't she?"

"There's a certain quality about her, a certain fineness. She seems to be absolutely fine and straight."

"She's very nice."

"I don't know how to describe the quality," Cohn said. "I suppose it's breeding."

"You sound as though you liked her pretty well."

"I do. I shouldn't wonder if I were in love with her."

"She's a drunk," I said. "She's in love with Mike Campbell, and she's going to marry him. He's going to be rich as hell some day."

"I don't believe she'll ever marry him."

"Why not?"

"I don't know. I just don't believe it. Have you known her a long time?"

"Yes," I said. "She was a V. A. D. in a hospital I was in during the war."

"She must have been just a kid then."

"She's thirty-four now."

"When did she marry Ashley?"

"During the war. Her own true love had just kicked off with the dysentery."

"You talk sort of bitter."

"Sorry. I didn't mean to. I was just trying to give you the facts."

"I don't believe she would marry anybody she didn't love."

"Well," I said. "She's done it twice."

"I don't believe it."

"Well," I said, "don't ask me a lot of fool questions if you don't like the answers."

"I didn't ask you that."

"You asked me what I knew about Brett Ashley."

"I didn't ask you to insult her."

"Oh, go to hell."

He stood up from the table his face white, and stood there white and angry behind the little plates of hors d'œuvres.

"Sit down," I said. "Don't be a fool."

"You've got to take that back."

"Oh, cut out the prep-school stuff."

"Take it back."

"Sure. Anything. I never heard of Brett Ashley. How's that?"

"No. Not that. About me going to hell."

"Oh, don't go to hell," I said. "Stick around. We're just starting lunch."

Cohn smiled again and sat down. He seemed glad to sit down. What the hell would he have done if he hadn't sat down? "You say such damned insulting things, Jake."

"I'm sorry. I've got a nasty tongue. I never mean it when I say nasty things."

"I know it," Cohn said. "You're really about the best friend I have, Jake."

God help you, I thought. "Forget what I said," I said out loud. "I'm sorry."

"It's all right. It's fine. I was just sore for a minute."

"Good. Let's get something else to eat."

After we finished the lunch we walked up to the Café de la Paix and had coffee. I could feel Cohn wanted to bring up Brett again, but I held him off it. We talked about one thing and another, and I left him to come to the office.

CHAPTER VI

AT five o'clock I was in the Hotel Crillon waiting for Brett. She was not there, so I sat down and wrote some letters. They were not very good letters but I hoped their being on Crillon stationery would help them. Brett did not turn up, so about quarter to six I went down to the bar and had a Jack Rose with George the barman. Brett had not been in the bar either, and so I looked for her up-stairs on my way out, and took a taxi to the Café Select. Crossing the Seine I saw a string of barges being towed empty down the current, riding high, the bargemen at the sweeps as they came toward the bridge. The river looked nice. It was always pleasant crossing bridges in Paris.

The taxi rounded the statue of the inventor of the semaphore engaged in doing same, and turned up the Boulevard Raspail, and I sat back to let that part of the ride pass. The Boulevard Raspail always made dull riding. It was like a certain stretch on the P. L. M. between Fontainebleau and Montereau that always made me feel bored and dead and dull until it was over. I suppose it is some association of ideas that makes those dead places in a journey. There are other streets in

Paris as ugly as the Boulevard Raspail. It is a street I
do not mind walking down at all. But I cannot stand to
ride along it. Perhaps I had read something about it
once. That was the way Robert Cohn was about all of
Paris. I wondered where Cohn got that incapacity to
enjoy Paris. Possibly from Mencken. Mencken hates
Paris, I believe. So many young men get their likes and
dislikes from Mencken.

The taxi stopped in front of the Rotonde. No matter
what café in Montparnasse you ask a taxi-driver to bring
you to from the right bank of the river, they always take
you to the Rotonde. Ten years from now it will probably
be the Dôme. It was near enough, anyway. I walked
past the sad tables of the Rotonde to the Select. There
were a few people inside at the bar, and outside, alone,
at Harvey Stone. He had a pile of saucers in front of
him, and he needed a shave.

"Sit down," said Harvey, "I've been looking for you."

"What's the matter?"

"Nothing? Just looking for you."

"Been out to the races?"

"No. Not since Sunday."

"What do you hear from the States?"

"Nothing. Absolutely nothing."

"What's the matter?"

"I don't know. I'm through with them. I'm absolutely
through with them."

He leaned forward and looked me in the eye.

"Do you want to know something, Jake?"

"Yes."

"I haven't had anything to eat for five days."

I figured rapidly back in my mind. It was three days
ago that Harvey had won two hundred francs from me
shaking poker dice in the New York Bar.

"What's the matter?"

"No money. Money hasn't come," he paused. "I tell you it's strange, Jake. When I'm like this I just want to be alone. I want to stay in my own room. I'm like a cat."

I felt in my pocket.

"Would a hundred help you any, Harvey?"

"Yes."

"Come on. Let's go and eat."

"There's no hurry. Have a drink."

"Better eat."

"No. When I get like this I don't care whether I eat or not."

We had a drink. Harvey added my saucer to his own pile.

"Do you know Mencken, Harvey?"

"Yes. Why?"

"What's he like?"

"He's all right. He says some pretty funny things. Last time I had dinner with him we talked about Hoffenheimer. 'The trouble is,' he said, 'he's a garter snapper.' That's not bad."

"That's not bad."

"He's through now," Harvey went on. "He's written about all the things he knows, and now he's on all the things he doesn't know."

"I guess he's all right," I said. "I just can't read him."

"Oh, nobody reads him now," Harvey said, "except the people that used to read the Alexander Hamilton Institute."

"Well," I said. "That was a good thing, too."

"Sure," said Harvey. So we sat and thought deeply for a while.

"Have another port?"

"All right," said Harvey.

"There comes Cohn," I said. Robert Cohn was crossing the street.

"That moron," said Harvey. Cohn came up to our
table.

"Hello, you bums," he said.

"Hello, Robert," Harvey said. "I was just telling
Jake here that you're a moron."

"What do you mean?"

"Tell us right off. Don't think. What would you
rather do if you could do anything you wanted?"

Cohn started to consider.

"Don't think. Bring it right out."

"I don't know," Cohn said. "What's it all about, anyway?"

"I mean what would you rather do. What comes into
your head first. No matter how silly it is."

"I don't know," Cohn said. "I think I'd rather play
football again with what I know about handling myself,
now."

"I misjudged you," Harvey said. "You're not a moron.
You're only a case of arrested development."

"You're awfully funny, Harvey," Cohn said. "Some
day somebody will push your face in."

Harvey Stone laughed. "You think so. They won't,
though. Because it wouldn't make any difference to
me. I'm not a fighter."

"It would make a difference to you if anybody did it."

"No, it wouldn't. That's where you make your big
mistake. Because you're not intelligent."

"Cut it out about me."

"Sure," said Harvey. "It doesn't make any difference to me. You don't mean anything to me."

"Come on, Harvey," I said. "Have another porto."

"No," he said. "I'm going up the street and eat. See
you later, Jake."

He walked out and up the street. I watched him crossing the street through the taxis, small, heavy, slowly sure of himself in the traffic.

"He always gets me sore," Cohn said. "I can't stand him."

"I like him," I said. "I'm fond of him. You don't want to get sore at him."

"I know it," Cohn said. "He just gets on my nerves."

"Write this afternoon?"

"No. I couldn't get it going. It's harder to do than my first book. I'm having a hard time handling it."

The sort of healthy conceit that he had when he returned from America early in the spring was gone. Then he had been sure of his work, only with these personal longings for adventure. Now the sureness was gone. Somehow I feel I have not shown Robert Cohn clearly. The reason is that until he fell in love with Brett, I never heard him make one remark that would, in any way, detach him from other people. He was nice to watch on the tennis-court, he had a good body, and he kept it in shape; he handled his cards well at bridge, and he had a funny sort of undergraduate quality about him. If he were in a crowd nothing he said stood out. He wore what used to be called polo shirts at school, and may be called that still, but he was not professionally youthful. I do not believe he thought about his clothes much. Externally he had been formed at Princeton. Internally he had been moulded by the two women who had trained him. He had a nice, boyish sort of cheerfulness that had never been trained out of him, and I probably have not brought it out. He loved to win at tennis. He probably loved to win as much as Lenglen, for instance. On the other hand, he was not angry at being beaten. When he fell in love with Brett his tennis game went all to pieces. People beat him who had never had a chance with him. He was very nice about it.

Anyhow, we were sitting on the terrace of the Café Select, and Harvey Stone had just crossed the street.

"Come on up to the Lilas," I said.

"I have a date."

"What time?"

"Frances is coming here at seven-fifteen."

"There she is."

Frances Clyne was coming toward us from across the street. She was a very tall girl who walked with a great deal of movement. She waved and smiled. We watched her cross the street.

"Hello," she said, "I'm so glad you're here, Jake. I've been wanting to talk to you."

"Hello, Frances," said Cohn. He smiled.

"Why, hello, Robert. Are you here?" She went on, talking rapidly. "I've had the darndest time. This one" —shaking her head at Cohn—"didn't come home for lunch."

"I wasn't supposed to."

"Oh, I know. But you didn't say anything about it to the cook. Then I had a date myself, and Paula wasn't at her office. I went to the Ritz and waited for her, and she never came, and of course I didn't have enough money to lunch at the Ritz——"

"What did you do?"

"Oh, went out, of course." She spoke in a sort of imitation joyful manner. "I always keep my appointments. No one keeps theirs, nowadays. I ought to know better. How are you, Jake, anyway?"

"Fine."

"That was a fine girl you had at the dance, and then went off with that Brett one."

"Don't you like her?" Cohn asked.

"I think she's perfectly charming. Don't you?"

Cohn said nothing.

"Look, Jake. I want to talk with you. Would you come over with me to the Dôme? You'll stay here, won't you, Robert? Come on, Jake."

We crossed the Boulevard Montparnasse and sat down at a table. A boy came up with the *Paris Times*, and I bought one and opened it.

"What's the matter, Frances?"

"Oh, nothing," she said, "except that he wants to leave me."

"How do you mean?"

"Oh, he told every one that we were going to be married, and I told my mother and every one, and now he doesn't want to do it."

"What's the matter?"

"He's decided he hasn't lived enough. I knew it would happen when he went to New York."

She looked up, very bright-eyed and trying to talk inconsequentially.

"I wouldn't marry him if he doesn't want to. Of course I wouldn't. I wouldn't marry him now for anything. But it does seem to me to be a little late now, after we've waited three years, and I've just gotten my divorce."

I said nothing.

"We were going to celebrate so, and instead we've just had scenes. It's so childish. We have dreadful scenes, and he cries and begs me to be reasonable, but he says he just can't do it."

"It's rotten luck."

"I should say it is rotten luck. I've wasted two years and a half on him now. And I don't know now if any man will ever want to marry me. Two years ago I could have married anybody I wanted, down at Cannes. All the old ones that wanted to marry somebody chic and

settle down were crazy about me. Now I don't thin[k]
could get anybody."

"Sure, you could marry anybody."

"No, I don't believe it. And I'm fond of him,
And I'd like to have children. I always thought
have children."

She looked at me very brightly. "I never liked children much, but I don't want to think I'll never have
them. I always thought I'd have them and then like
them."

"He's got children."

"Oh, yes. He's got children, and he's got money, and
he's got a rich mother, and he's written a book, and nobody will publish my stuff, nobody at all. It isn't bad,
either. And I haven't got any money at all. I could have
had alimony, but I got the divorce the quickest way."

She looked at me again very brightly.

"It isn't right. It's my own fault and it's not, too. I
ought to have known better. And when I tell him he
just cries and says he can't marry. Why can't he marry?
I'd be a good wife. I'm easy to get along with. I leave
him alone. It doesn't do any good."

"It's a rotten shame."

"Yes, it is a rotten shame. But there's no use talking
about it, is there? Come on, let's go back to the café."

"And of course there isn't anything I can do."

"No. Just don't let him know I talked to you. I know
what he wants." Now for the first time she dropped
her bright, terribly cheerful manner. "He wants to go
back to New York alone, and be there when his book
comes out so when a lot of little chickens like it. That's
what he wants."

"Maybe they won't like it. I don't think he's that
way. Really."

"You don't know him like I do, Jake. That's what he wants to do. I know it. I know it. That's why he doesn't want to marry. He wants to have a big triumph fall all by himself."

"Want to go back to the café?"

"Yes. Come on."

We got up from the table—they had never brought us a drink—and started across the street toward the Select, where Cohn sat smiling at us from behind the marble-topped table.

"Well, what are you smiling at?" Frances asked him. "Feel pretty happy?"

"I was smiling at you and Jake with your secrets."

"Oh, what I've told Jake isn't any secret. Everybody will know it soon enough. I only wanted to give Jake a decent version."

"What was it? About your going to England?"

"Yes, about my going to England. Oh, Jake! I forgot to tell you. I'm going to England."

"Isn't that fine!"

"Yes, that's the way it's done in the very best families. Robert's sending me. He's going to give me two hundred pounds and then I'm going to visit friends. Won't it be lovely? The friends don't know about it, yet."

She turned to Cohn and smiled at him. He was not smiling now.

"You were only going to give me a hundred pounds, weren't you, Robert? But I made him give me two hundred. He's really very generous. Aren't you, Robert?"

I do not know how people could say such terrible things to Robert Cohn. There are people to whom you could not say insulting things. They give you a feeling that the world would be destroyed, would actually be destroyed before your eyes, if you said certain things. But here was Cohn taking it all. Here it was, all going on right before me, and I did not even feel an impulse to try and stop it. And this was friendly joking to what went on later.

"How can you say such things, Frances?" Cohn interrupted.

"Listen to him. I'm going to England. I'm going to visit friends. Ever visit friends that didn't want you? Oh, they'll have to take me, all right. 'How do you do, my dear? Such a long time since we've seen you. And how is your dear mother?' Yes, how is my dear mother? She put all her money into French war bonds. Yes, she did. Probably the only person in the world that did. 'And what about Robert?' or else very careful talking around Robert. 'You must be most careful not to mention him, my dear. Poor Frances has had a most unfortunate experience.' Won't it be fun, Robert? Don't you think it will be fun, Jake?"

She turned to me with that terribly bright smile. It was very satisfactory to her to have an audience for this.

"And where are you going to be, Robert? It's my own fault, all right. Perfectly my own fault. When I made you get rid of your little secretary on the magazine I ought to have known you'd get rid of me the same way. Jake doesn't know about that. Should I tell him?"

"Shut up, Frances, for God's sake."

"Yes, I'll tell him. Robert had a little secretary on the magazine. Just the sweetest little thing in the world, and he thought she was wonderful, and then I came along and he thought I was pretty wonderful, too. So I made him get rid of her, and he brought her to Provincetown from Carmel when he moved the magazine, and he didn't even pay her fare back to the coast. All to please me. He thought I was pretty fine, then. Didn't you, Robert?

"You mustn't misunderstand, Jake, it was absolutely platonic with the secretary. Not even platonic. Nothing at all, really. It was just that she was so nice. And he did that just to please me. Well, I suppose that we that live by the sword shall perish by the sword. Isn't that literary, though? You want to remember that for your next book, Robert.

"You know Robert is going to get material for a new book. Aren't you, Robert? That's why he's leaving me. He's decided I don't film well. You see, he was so busy all the time that we were living together, writing on this book, that he doesn't remember anything about us. So now he's going out and get some new material. Well, I hope he gets something frightfully interesting.

"Listen, Robert, dear. Let me tell you something. You won't mind, will you? Don't have scenes with your young ladies. Try not to. Because you can't have scenes without crying, and then you pity yourself so much you can't remember what the other person's said. You'll never be able to remember any conversations that way. Just try and be calm. I know it's awfully hard. But remember, it's for literature. We all ought to make sacrifices for literature. Look at me. I'm going to England without a protest. All for literature. We must all help young writers. Don't you think so, Jake? But you're not a young writer. Are you, Robert? You're thirty-four. Still, I suppose that is young for a great writer. Look at Hardy. Look at Anatole France. He just died a little while ago. Robert doesn't think he's any good, though. Some of his French friends told him. He doesn't read French very well himself. He wasn't a good writer like you are, was he, Robert? Do you think he ever had to go and look for material? What do you suppose he said to his mistresses when he wouldn't marry them. I wonder if he cried, too? Oh, I've just thought of something." She put her gloved hand up to her lips. "I know the real reason why Robert won't marry me, Jake. It's just come to me. They've sent it to me in a vision in the Café Select. Isn't it mystic? Some day they'll put a tablet up. Like at Lourdes. Do you want to hear, Robert? I'll tell you. It's so simple. I wonder why I never thought about it. Why, you see, Robert's always wanted to have a mistress, and if he doesn't marry me, why, then he's had one. She was his mistress for over two years. See how it is? And if he marries me, like he's always promised he would, that would be the end of all the romance. Don't you think that's bright of me to figure that out? It's true, too. Look at him and see if it's not. Where are you going, Jake?"

"I've got to go in and see Harvey Stone a minute."

Cohn looked up as I went in. His face was white. Why did he sit there? Why did he keep on taking it like that?

As I stood against the bar looking out I could see them through the window. Frances was talking on to him, smiling brightly, looking into his face each time she asked: "Isn't it so, Robert?" Or maybe she did not ask that now. Perhaps she said something else. I told the barman I did not want anything to drink and went out through the side door. As I went out the door I looked back through the two thicknesses of glass and saw them sitting there. She was still talking to him. I went down a side street to the Boulevard Raspail. A taxi came along and I got in and gave the driver the address of my flat.

CHAPTER VII

A S I started up the stairs the concierge knocked on
the glass of the door of her lodge, and as I stopped
she came out. She had some letters and a telegram.

"Here is the post. And there was a lady here to see
you."

"Did she leave a card?"

"No. She was with a gentleman. It was the one who
was here last night. In the end I find she is very nice."

"Was she with a friend of mine?"

"I don't know. He was never here before. He was
very large. Very, very large. She was very nice. Very,
very nice. Last night she was, perhaps, a little——" She
put her head on one hand and rocked it up and down.
"I'll speak perfectly frankly, Monsieur Barnes. Last
night I found her not so gentille. Last night I formed another idea of her. But listen to what I tell you. She is
très, très gentille. She is of very good family. It is a
thing you can see."

"They did not leave any word?"

"Yes. They said they would be back in an hour."

"Send them up when they come."

"Yes, Monsieur Barnes. And that lady, that lady
there is some one. An eccentric, perhaps, but quelqu'une,
quelqu'une!"

The concierge, before she became a concierge, had
owned a drink-selling concession at the Paris race-
courses. Her life-work lay in the pelouse, but she kept
an eye on the people of the pesage, and she took great
pride in telling me which of my guests were well brought
up, which were of good family, who were sportsmen, a
French word pronounced with the accent on the men.
The only trouble was that people who did not fall into

any of those three categories were very liable to be told there was no one home, chez Barnes. One of my friends, an extremely underfed-looking painter, who was obviously to Madame Duzinell neither well brought up, of good family, nor a sportsman, wrote me a letter asking if I could get him a pass to get by the concierge so he could come up and see me occasionally in the evenings.

I went up to the flat wondering what Brett had done to the concierge. The wire was a cable from Bill Gorton, saying he was arriving on the *France.* I put the mail on the table, went back to the bedroom, undressed and had a shower. I was rubbing down when I heard the door-bell pull. I put on a bathrobe and slippers and went to the door. It was Brett. Back of her was the count. He was holding a great bunch of roses.

"Hello, darling," said Brett. "Aren't you going to let us in?"

"Come on. I was just bathing."

"Aren't you the fortunate man. Bathing."

"Only a shower. Sit down, Count Mippipopolous. What will you drink?"

"I don't know whether you like flowers, sir," the count said, "but I took the liberty of just bringing these roses."

"Here, give them to me." Brett took them. "Get me some water in this, Jake." I filled the big earthernware jug with water in the kitchen, and Brett put the roses in it, and placed them in the centre of the dining-room table.

"I say. We have had a day."

"You don't remember anything about a date with me at the Crillon?"

"No. Did we have one? I must have been blind."

"You were quite drunk, my dear," said the count.

"Wasn't I, though? And the count's been a brick, absolutely."

"You've got hell's own drag with the concierge now."

"I ought to have. Gave her two hundred francs."

"Don't be a damned fool."

"His," she said, and nodded at the count.

"I thought we ought to give her a little something for last night. It was very late."

"He's wonderful," Brett said. "He remembers everything that's happened."

"So do you, my dear."

"Fancy," said Brett. "Who'd want to? I say, Jake, *do* we get a drink?"

"You get it while I go in and dress. You know where it is."

"Rather."

While I dressed I heard Brett put down glasses and then a siphon, and then heard them talking. I dressed slowly, sitting on the bed. I felt tired and pretty rotten. Brett came in the room, a glass in her hand, and sat on the bed.

"What's the matter, darling? Do you feel rocky?"

She kissed me coolly on the forehead.

"Oh, Brett, I love you so much."

"Darling," she said. Then: "Do you want me to send him away?"

"No. He's nice."

"I'll send him away."

"No, don't."

"Yes, I'll send him away."

"You can't just like that."

"Can't I, though? You stay here. He's mad about me, I tell you."

She was gone out of the room. I lay face down on the

bed. I was having a bad time. I heard them talking but I did not listen. Brett came in and sat on the bed.

"Poor old darling." She stroked my head.

"What did you say to him?" I was lying with my face away from her. I did not want to see her.

"Sent him for champagne. He loves to go for champagne."

Then later: "Do you feel better, darling? Is the head any better?"

"It's better."

Lie quiet. He's gone to the other side of town."

"Couldn't we live together, Brett? Couldn't we just live together?"

"I don't think so. I'd just *tromper* you with everybody. You couldn't stand it."

"I stand it now."

"That would be different. It's my fault, Jake. It's the way I'm made."

"Couldn't we go off in the country for a while?"

"It wouldn't be any good. I'll go if you like. But I couldn't live quietly in the country. Not with my own true love."

"I know."

"Isn't it rotten? There isn't any use my telling you I love you."

"You know I love you."

"Let's not talk. Talking's all bilge. I'm going away from you, and then Michael's coming back."

"Why are you going away?"

"Better for you. Better for me."

"When are you going?"

"Soon as I can."

"Where?"

"San Sebastian."

"Can't we go together?"

"No. That would be a hell of an idea after we'd just talked it out."

"We never agreed."

"Oh, you know as well as I do. Don't be obstinate, darling."

"Oh, sure," I said. "I know you're right. I'm just low, and when I'm low I talk like a fool."

I sat up, leaned over, found my shoes beside the bed and put them on. I stood up.

"Don't look like that, darling."

"How do you want me to look?"

"Oh, don't be a fool. I'm going away to-morrow."

"To-morrow?"

"Yes. Didn't I say so? I am."

"Let's have a drink, then. The count will be back."

"Yes. He should be back. You know he's extraordinary about buying champagne. It means any amount to him."

We went into the dining-room. I took up the brandy bottle and poured Brett a drink and one for myself. There was a ring at the bell-pull. I went to the door and there was the count. Behind him was the chauffeur carrying a basket of champagne.

"Where should I have him put it, sir?" asked the count.

"In the kitchen," Brett said.

"Put it in there, Henry," the count motioned. "Now go down and get the ice." He stood looking after the basket inside the kitchen door. "I think you'll find that's very good wine," he said. "I know we don't get much of a chance to judge good wine in the States now, but I got this from a friend of mine that's in the business."

"Oh, you always have some one in the trade," Brett said.

"This fellow raises the grapes. He's got thousands of acres of them."

"What's his name?" asked Brett. "Veuve Cliquot?"

"No," said the count. "Mumms. He's a baron."

"Isn't it wonderful," said Brett. "We all have titles. Why haven't you a title, Jake?"

"I assure you, sir," the count put his hand on my arm. "It never does a man any good. Most of the time it costs you money."

"Oh, I don't know. It's damned useful sometimes," Brett said.

"I've never known it to do me any good."

"You haven't used it properly. I've had hell's own amount of credit on mine."

"Do sit down, count," I said. "Let me take that stick."

The count was looking at Brett across the table under the gas-light. She was smoking a cigarette and flicking the ashes on the rug. She saw me notice it. "I say, Jake, I don't want to ruin your rugs. Can't you give a chap an ash-tray?"

I found some ash-trays and spread them around. The chauffeur came up with a bucket full of salted ice. "Put two bottles in it, Henry," the count called.

"Anything else, sir?"

"No. Wait down in the car." He turned to Brett and to me. "We'll want to ride out to the Bois for dinner?"

"If you like," Brett said. "I couldn't eat a thing."

"I always like a good meal," said the count.

"Should I bring the wine in, sir?" asked the chauffeur.

"Yes. Bring it in, Henry," said the count. He took out a heavy pigskin cigar-case and offered it to me. "Like to try a real American cigar?"

"Thanks," I said. "I'll finish the cigarette."

He cut off the end of his cigar with a gold cutter he wore on one end of his watch-chain.

"I like a cigar to really draw," said the count. "Half the cigars you smoke don't draw."

He lit the cigar, puffed at it, looking across the table at Brett. "And when you're divorced, Lady Ashley, then you won't have a title."

"No. What a pity."

"No," said the count. "You don't need a title. You got class all over you."

"Thanks. Awfully decent of you."

"I'm not joking you," the count blew a cloud of smoke. "You got the most class of anybody I ever seen. You got it. That's all."

"Nice of you," said Brett. "Mummy would be pleased. Couldn't you write it out, and I'll send it in a letter to her."

"I'd tell her, too," said the count. "I'm not joking you. I never joke people. Joke people and you make enemies. That's what I always say."

"You're right," Brett said. "You're terribly right. I always joke people and I haven't a friend in the world. Except Jake here."

"You don't joke him."

"That's it."

"Do you, now?" asked the count. "Do you joke him?"

Brett looked at me and wrinkled up the corners of her eyes.

"No," she said. "I wouldn't joke him."

"See," said the count. "You don't joke him."

"This is a hell of a dull talk," Brett said. "How about some of that champagne?"

The count reached down and twirled the bottles in

the shiny bucket. "It isn't cold, yet. You're always drinking, my dear. Why don't you just talk?"

"I've talked too ruddy much. I've talked myself all out to Jake."

"I should like to hear you really talk, my dear. When you talk to me you never finish your sentence at all."

"Leave 'em for you to finish. Let any one finish them as they like."

"It is a very interesting system," the count reached down and gave the bottles a twirl. "Still I would like to hear you talk some time."

"Isn't he a fool?" Brett asked.

"Now," the count brought up a bottle. "I think this is cool."

I brought a towel and he wiped the bottle dry and held it up. "I like to drink champagne from magnums. The wine is better but it would have been too hard to cool." He held the bottle, looking at it. I put out the glasses.

"I say. You might open it," Brett suggested.

"Yes, my dear. Now I'll open it."

It was amazing champagne.

"I say that is wine," Brett held up her glass. "We ought to toast something. 'Here's to royalty.'"

"This wine is too good for toast-drinking, my dear. You don't want to mix emotions up with a wine like that. You lose the taste."

Brett's glass was empty.

"You ought to write a book on wines, count," I said.

"Mr. Barnes," answered the count, "all I want out of wines is to enjoy them."

"Let's enjoy a little more of this," Brett pushed her glass forward. The count poured very carefully. "There, my dear. Now you enjoy that slowly, and then you can get drunk."

"Drunk? Drunk?"

"My dear, you are charming when you are drunk."

"Listen to the man."

"Mr. Barnes," the count poured my glass full. "She is the only lady I have ever known who was as charming when she was drunk as when she was sober."

"You haven't been around much, have you?"

"Yes, my dear. I have been around very much. I have been around a very great deal."

"Drink your wine," said Brett. "We've all been around. I dare say Jake here has seen as much as you have."

"My dear, I am sure Mr. Barnes has seen a lot. Don't think I don't think so, sir. I have seen a lot, too."

"Of course you have, my dear," Brett said. "I was only ragging."

"I have been in seven wars and four revolutions," the count said.

"Soldiering?" Brett asked.

"Sometimes, my dear. And I have got arrow wounds. Have you ever seen arrow wounds?"

"Let's have a look at them."

The count stood up, unbuttoned his vest, and opened his shirt. He pulled up the undershirt onto his chest and stood, his chest black, and big stomach muscles bulging under the light.

"You see them?"

Below the line where his ribs stopped were two raised white welts. "See on the back where they come out." Above the small of the back were the same two scars, raised as thick as a finger.

"I say. Those are something."

"Clean through."

The count was tucking in his shirt.

"Where did you get those?" I asked.

"In Abyssinia. When I was twenty-one years old."

"What were you doing?" asked Brett. "Were you in the army?"

"I was on a business trip, my dear."

"I told you he was one of us. Didn't I?" Brett turned to me. "I love you, count. You're a darling."

"You make me very happy, my dear. But it isn't true."

"Don't be an ass."

"You see, Mr. Barnes, it is because I have lived very much that now I can enjoy everything so well. Don't you find it like that?"

"Yes. Absolutely."

"I know," said the count. "That is the secret. You must get to know the values."

"Doesn't anything ever happen to your values?" Brett asked.

"No. Not any more."

"Never fall in love?"

"Always," said the count. "I am always in love."

"What does that do to your values?"

"That, too, has got a place in my values."

"You haven't any values. You're dead, that's all."

"No, my dear. You're not right. I'm not dead at all."

We drank three bottles of the champagne and the count left the basket in my kitchen. We dined at a restaurant in the Bois. It was a good dinner. Food had an excellent place in the count's values. So did wine. The count was in fine form during the meal. So was Brett. It was a good party.

"Where would you like to go?" asked the count after dinner. We were the only people left in the restaurant. The two waiters were standing over against the door. They wanted to go home.

"We might go up on the hill," Brett said. "Haven't we had a splendid party?"

The count was beaming. He was very happy.

"You are very nice people," he said. He was smoking a cigar again. "Why don't you get married, you two?"

"We want to lead our own lives," I said.

"We have our careers," Brett said. "Come on. Let's get out of this."

"Have another brandy," the count said.

"Get it on the hill."

"No. Have it here where it is quiet."

"You and your quiet," said Brett. "What is it men feel about quiet?"

"We like it," said the count. "Like you like noise, my dear."

"All right," said Brett. "Let's have one."

"Sommelier!" the count called.

"Yes, sir."

"What is the oldest brandy you have?"

"Eighteen eleven, sir."

"Bring us a bottle."

"I say. Don't be ostentatious. Call him off, Jake."

"Listen, my dear. I get more value for my money in old brandy than in any other antiquities."

"Got many antiquities?"

"I got a houseful."

Finally we went up to Montmartre. Inside Zelli's it was crowded, smoky, and noisy. The music hit you as you went in. Brett and I danced. It was so crowded we could barely move. The nigger drummer waved at Brett. We were caught in the jam, dancing in one place in front of him.

"Hahre you?"

"Great."

"Thaats good."

He was all teeth and lips.

"He's a great friend of mine," Brett said. "Damn good drummer."

The music stopped and we started toward the table where the count sat. Then the music started again and we danced. I looked at the count. He was sitting at the table smoking a cigar. The music stopped again.

"Let's go over."

Brett started toward the table. The music started and again we danced, tight in the crowd.

"You are a rotten dancer, Jake. Michael's the best dancer I know."

"He's splendid."

"He's got his points."

"I like him," I said. "I'm damned fond of him."

"I'm going to marry him," Brett said. "Funny. I haven't thought about him for a week."

"Don't you write him?"

"Not I. Never write letters."

"I'll bet he writes to you."

"Rather. Damned good letters, too."

"When are you going to get married?"

"How do I know? As soon as we can get the divorce. Michael's trying to get his mother to put up for it."

"Could I help you?"

"Don't be an ass. Michael's people have loads of money."

The music stopped. We walked over to the table. The count stood up.

"Very nice," he said. "You looked very, very nice."

"Don't you dance, count?" I asked.

"No. I'm too old."

"Oh, come off it," Brett said.

"My dear, I would do it if I would enjoy it. I enjoy to watch you dance."

"Splendid," Brett said. "I'll dance again for you some time. I say. What about your little friend, Zizi?"

"Let me tell you. I support that boy, but I don't want to have him around."

"He is rather hard."

"You know I think that boy's got a future. But personally I don't want him around."

"Jake's rather the same way."

"He gives me the willys."

"Well," the count shrugged his shoulders. "About his future you can't ever tell. Anyhow, his father was a great friend of my father."

"Come on. Let's dance," Brett said.

We danced. It was crowded and close.

"Oh, darling," Brett said, "I'm so miserable."

I had that feeling of going through something that has all happened before. "You were happy a minute ago."

The drummer shouted: "You can't two time———"

"It's all gone."

"What's the matter?"

"I don't know. I just feel terribly."

". . . . . ." the drummer chanted. Then turned to his sticks.

"Want to go?"

I had the feeling as in a nightmare of it all being something repeated, something I had been through and that now I must go through again.

". . . . . ." the drummer sang softly.

"Let's go," said Brett. "You don't mind."

". . . . . ." the drummer shouted and grinned at Brett.

"All right," I said. We got out from the crowd. Brett went to the dressing-room.

"Brett wants to go," I said to the count. He nodded.

"Does she? That's fine. You take the car. I'm
stay here for a while, Mr. Barnes."

We shook hands.

"It was a wonderful time," I said. "I wish you would let
me get this." I took a note out of my pocket.

"Mr. Barnes, don't be ridiculous," the count said.

Brett came over with her wrap on. She kissed the count
and put her hand on his shoulder to keep him from standing up. As we went out the door I looked back and there
were three girls at his table. We got into the big car.
Brett gave the chauffeur the address of her hotel.

"No, don't come up," she said at the hotel. She had
rung and the door was unlatched.

"Really?"

"No. Please."

"Good night, Brett," I said. "I'm sorry you feel rotten."

"Good night, Jake. Good night, darling. I won't see
you again." We kissed standing at the door. She pushed
me away. We kissed again. "Oh, don't!" Brett said.

She turned quickly and went into the hotel. The
chauffeur drove me around to my flat. I gave him twenty
francs and he touched his cap and said: "Good night,
sir," and drove off. I rang the bell. The door opened and
I went up-stairs and went to bed.

BOOK TWO

CHAPTER VIII

I DID not see Brett again until she came back from San Sebastian. One card came from her from there. It had a picture of the Concha, and said: "Darling. Very quiet and healthy. Love to all the chaps. BRETT."

Nor did I see Robert Cohn again. I heard Frances had left for England and I had a note from Cohn saying he was going out in the country for a couple of weeks, he did not know where, but that he wanted to hold me to the fishing-trip in Spain we had talked about last winter. I could reach him always, he wrote, through his bankers.

Brett was gone, I was not bothered by Cohn's troubles, I rather enjoyed not having to play tennis, there was plenty of work to do, I went often to the races, dined with friends, and put in some extra time at the office getting things ahead so I could leave it in charge of my secretary when Bill Gorton and I should shove off to Spain the end of June. Bill Gorton arrived, put up a couple of days at the flat and went off to Vienna. He was very cheerful and said the States were wonderful. New York was wonderful. There had been a grand theatrical season and a whole crop of great young light heavyweights. Any one of them was a good prospect to grow up, put on weight and trim Dempsey. Bill was very happy. He had made a lot of money on his last book, and was going to make a lot more. We had a good time while he was in Paris, and then he went off to Vienna. He was coming back in three weeks and we would leave for Spain to get in some fishing and go to the fiesta at Pamplona. He wrote that Vienna was wonderful. Then a card from Budapest:

"Jake, Budapest is wonderful." Then I got a wire: "Back on Monday."

Monday evening he turned up at the flat. I heard his taxi stop and went to the window and called to him; he waved and started up-stairs carrying his bags. I met him on the stairs, and took one of the bags.

"Well," I said, "I hear you had a wonderful trip."

"Wonderful," he said. "Budapest is absolutely wonderful."

"How about Vienna?"

"Not so good, Jake. Not so good. It seemed better than it was."

"How do you mean?" I was getting glasses and a syphon.

"Tight, Jake. I was tight."

"That's strange. Better have a drink."

Bill rubbed his forehead. "Remarkable thing," he said. "Don't know how it happened. Suddenly it happened."

"Last long?"

"Four days, Jake. Lasted just four days."

"Where did you go?"

"Don't remember. Wrote you a post-card. Remember that perfectly."

"Do anything else?"

"Not so sure. Possible."

"Go on. Tell me about it."

"Can't remember. Tell you anything I could remember."

"Go on. Take that drink and remember."

"Might remember a little," Bill said. "Remember something about a prize-fight. Enormous Vienna prize-fight. Had a nigger in it. Remember the nigger perfectly."

"Go on."

"Wonderful nigger. Looked like Tiger Flowers, only four times as big. All of a sudden everybody started to throw things. Not me. Nigger'd just knocked local boy down. Nigger put up his glove. Wanted to make a speech. Then local white boy hit him. Then he knocked white boy cold. Then everybody commenced to throw chairs. Nigger went home with us in our car. Couldn't get his clothes. Wore my coat. Remember the whole thing now. Big sporting evening."

"What happened?"

"Loaned the nigger some clothes and went around with him to try and get his money. Claimed nigger owed them money on account of wrecking hall. Wonder who translated? Was it me?"

"Probably it wasn't you."

"You're all right. Wasn't me at all. Was another fellow. Think we called him the local Harvard man. Remember him now. Studying music."

"How'd you come out?"

"Not so good, Jake. Injustice everywhere. Promoter claimed nigger promised let local boy stay. Claimed nigger violated contract. Can't knock out Vienna boy in Vienna. 'My God, Mister Gorton,' said nigger, 'I didn't do nothing in there for forty minutes but try and let him stay. That white boy musta ruptured himself swinging at me. I never did hit him.'"

"Did you get any money?"

"No money, Jake. All we could get was nigger's clothes. Somebody took his watch, too. Splendid nigger. Big mistake to have come to Vienna. Not so good, Jake. Not so good."

"What became of the nigger?"

"Went back to Cologne. Lives there. Married. Got a family. Going to write me a letter and send me the money I loaned him. Wonderful nigger. Hope I gave him the right address."

"You probably did."

"Well, anyway, let's eat," said Bill. "Unless you want me to tell you some more travel stories."

"Go on."

"Let's eat."

We went down-stairs and out onto the Boulevard St. Michel in the warm June evening.

"Where will we go?"

"Want to eat on the island?"

"Sure."

We walked down the Boulevard. At the juncture of the Rue Denfert-Rochereau with the Boulevard is a statue of two men in flowing robes.

"I know who they are." Bill eyed the monument. "Gentlemen who invented pharmacy. Don't try and fool me on Paris."

We went on.

"Here's a taxidermist's," Bill said. "Want to buy anything? Nice stuffed dog?"

"Come on," I said. "You're pie-eyed."

"Pretty nice stuffed dogs," Bill said. "Certainly brighten up your flat."

"Come on."

"Just one stuffed dog. I can take 'em or leave 'em alone. But listen, Jake. Just one stuffed dog."

"Come on."

"Mean everything in the world to you after you bought it. Simple exchange of values. You give them money. They give you a stuffed dog."

"We'll get one on the way back."

"All right. Have it your own way. Road to hell paved with unbought stuffed dogs. Not my fault."

We went on.

"How'd you feel that way about dogs so sudden?"

"Always felt that way about dogs. Always been a great lover of stuffed animals."

We stopped and had a drink.

"Certainly like to drink," Bill said. "You ought to try it sometimes, Jake."

"You're about a hundred and forty-four ahead of me."

"Ought not to daunt you. Never be daunted. Secret of my success. Never been daunted. Never been daunted in public."

"Where were you drinking?"

"Stopped at the Crillon. George made me a couple of Jack Roses. George's a great man. Know the secret of his success? Never been daunted."

"You'll be daunted after about three more pernods."

"Not in public. If I begin to feel daunted I'll go off by myself. I'm like a cat that way."

"When did you see Harvey Stone?"

"At the Crillon. Harvey was just a little daunted. Hadn't eaten for three days. Doesn't eat any more. Just goes off like a cat. Pretty sad."

"He's all right."

"Splendid. Wish he wouldn't keep going off like a cat, though. Makes me nervous."

"What'll we do to-night?"

"Doesn't make any difference. Only let's not get daunted. Suppose they got any hard-boiled eggs here? If they had hard-boiled eggs here we wouldn't have to go all the way down to the island to eat."

"Nix," I said. "We're going to have a regular meal."

"Just a suggestion," said Bill. "Want to start now?"

"Come on."

We started on again down the Boulevard. A horse-cab passed us. Bill looked at it.

"See that horse-cab? Going to have that horse-cab stuffed for you for Christmas. Going to give all my friends stuffed animals. I'm a nature-writer."

A taxi passed, some one in it waved, then banged for

the driver to stop. The taxi backed up to the curb. In it was Brett.

"Beautiful lady," said Bill. "Going to kidnap us."

"Hullo!" Brett said. "Hullo!"

"This is Bill Gorton. Lady Ashley."

Brett smiled at Bill. "I say I'm just back. Haven't bathed even. Michael comes in to-night."

"Good. Come on and eat with us, and we'll all go to meet him."

"Must clean myself."

"Oh, rot! Come on."

"Must bathe. He doesn't get in till nine."

"Come and have a drink, then, before you bathe."

"Might do that. Now you're not talking rot."

We got in the taxi. The driver looked around.

"Stop at the nearest bistro," I said.

"We might as well go to the Closerie," Brett said. "I can't drink these rotten brandies."

"Closerie des Lilas."

Brett turned to Bill.

"Have you been in this pestilential city long?"

"Just got in to-day from Budapest."

"How was Budapest?"

"Wonderful. Budapest was wonderful."

"Ask him about Vienna."

"Vienna," said Bill, "is a strange city."

"Very much like Paris," Brett smiled at him, wrinkling the corners of her eyes.

"Exactly," Bill said. "Very much like Paris at this moment."

"You *have* a good start."

Sitting out on the terraces of the Lilas Brett ordered a whiskey and soda, I took one, too, and Bill took another pernod.

"How are you, Jake?"

"Great," I said. "I've had a good time."

Brett looked at me. "I was a fool to go away," she said. "One's an ass to leave Paris."

"Did you have a good time?"

"Oh, all right. Interesting. Not frightfully amusing."

"See anybody?"

"No, hardly anybody. I never went out."

"Didn't you swim?"

"No. Didn't do a thing."

"Sounds like Vienna," Bill said.

Brett wrinkled up the corners of her eyes at him.

"So that's the way it was in Vienna."

"It was like everything in Vienna."

Brett smiled at him again.

"You've a nice friend, Jake."

"He's all right," I said. "He's a taxidermist."

"That was in another country," Bill said. "And besides all the animals were dead."

"One more," Brett said, "and I must run. Do send the waiter for a taxi."

"There's a line of them. Right out in front."

"Good."

We had the drink and put Brett into her taxi.

"Mind you're at the Select around ten. Make him come. Michael will be there."

"We'll be there," Bill said. The taxi started and Brett waved.

"Quite a girl," Bill said. "She's damned nice. Who's Michael?"

"The man she's going to marry."

"Well, well," Bill said. "That's always just the stage I meet anybody. What'll I send them? Think they'd like a couple of stuffed race-horses?"

"We better eat."

"Is she really Lady something or other?" Bill asked in the taxi on our way down to the Ile Saint Louis.

"Oh, yes. In the stud-book and everything."

"Well, well."

We ate dinner at Madame Lecomte's restaurant on the far side of the island. It was crowded with Americans and we had to stand up and wait for a place. Some one had put it in the American Women's Club list as a quaint restaurant on the Paris quais as yet untouched by Americans, so we had to wait forty-five minutes for a table. Bill had eaten at the restaurant in 1918, and right after the armistice, and Madame Lecomte made a great fuss over seeing him.

"Doesn't get us a table, though," Bill said. "Grand woman, though."

We had a good meal, a roast chicken, new green beans, mashed potatoes, a salad, and some apple-pie and cheese.

"You've got the world here all right," Bill said to Madame Lecomte. She raised her hand. "Oh, my God!"

"You'll be rich."

"I hope so."

After the coffee and a *fine* we got the bill, chalked up the same as ever on a slate, that was doubtless one of the "quaint" features, paid it, shook hands, and went out.

"You never come here any more, Monsieur Barnes," Madame Lecomte said.

"Too many compatriots."

"Come at lunch-time. It's not crowded then."

"Good. I'll be down soon."

We walked along under the trees that grew out over the river on the Quai d'Orléans side of the island. Across the river were the broken walls of old houses that were being torn down.

"They're going to cut a street through."

"They would," Bill said.

We walked on and circled the island. The river was dark and a bateau mouche went by, all bright with lights, going fast and quiet up and out of sight under the bridge. Down the river was Notre Dame squatting against the night sky. We crossed to the left bank of the Seine by the wooden foot-bridge from the Quai de Béthune, and stopped on the bridge and looked down the river at Notre Dame. Standing on the bridge the island looked dark, the houses were high against the sky, and the trees were shadows.

"It's pretty grand," Bill said. "God, I love to get back."

We leaned on the wooden rail of the bridge and looked up the river to the lights of the big bridges. Below the water was smooth and black. It made no sound against the piles of the bridge. A man and a girl passed us. They were walking with their arms around each other.

We crossed the bridge and walked up the Rue du Cardinal Lemoine. It was steep walking, and we went all the way up to the Place Contrescarpe. The arc-light shone through the leaves of the trees in the square, and underneath the trees was an S bus ready to start. Music came out of the door of the Nègre Joyeux. Through the window of the Café Aux Amateurs I saw the long zinc bar. Outside on the terrace working people were drinking. In the open kitchen of the Amateurs a girl was cooking potato-chips in oil. There was an iron pot of stew. The girl ladled some onto a plate for an old man who stood holding a bottle of red wine in one hand.

"Want to have a drink?"

"No," said Bill. "I don't need it."

We turned to the right off the Place Contrescarpe, walking along smooth narrow streets with high old houses on both sides. Some of the houses jutted out toward the

treet. Others were cut back. We came onto the Rue du
'ot de Fer and followed it along until it brought us to the
igid north and south of the Rue Saint Jacques and then
valked south, past Val de Grâce, set back behind the
ourtyard and the iron fence, to the Boulevard du Port
Royal.

"What do you want to do?" I asked. "Go up to the
afé and see Brett and Mike?"

"Why not?"

We walked along Port Royal until it became Montparnasse, and then on past the Lilas, Lavigne's, and all
he little cafés, Damoy's, crossed the street to the Ro-
onde, past its lights and tables to the Select.

Michael came toward us from the tables. He was
anned and healthy-looking.

"Hel-lo, Jake," he said. "Hel-lo! Hel-lo! How are you,
old lad?"

"You look very fit, Mike."

"Oh, I am. I'm frightfully fit. I've done nothing but
walk. Walk all day long. One drink a day with my mother
at tea."

Bill had gone into the bar. He was standing talking
with Brett, who was sitting on a high stool, her legs
crossed. She had no stockings on.

"It's good to see you, Jake," Michael said. "I'm a little
ight, you know. Amazing, isn't it? Did you see my nose?"

There was a patch of dried blood on the bridge of his
nose.

"An old lady's bags did that," Mike said. "I reached
up to help her with them and they fell on me."

Brett gestured at him from the bar with her cigarette-
holder and wrinkled the corners of her eyes.

"An old lady," said Mike. "Her bags *fell* on me.

"Let's go in and see Brett. I say, she is a piece. You
are a lovely lady, Brett. Where did you get that hat?"

"Chap bought it for me. Don't you like it?"

"It's a dreadful hat. Do get a good hat."

"Oh, we've so much money now," Brett said. "I say, haven't you met Bill yet? You *are* a lovely host, Jake."

She turned to Mike. "This is Bill Gorton. This drunkard is Mike Campbell. Mr. Campbell is an undischarged bankrupt."

"Aren't I, though? You know I met my ex-partner yesterday in London. Chap who did me in."

"What did he say?"

"Bought me a drink. I thought I might as well take it. I say, Brett, you *are* a lovely piece. Don't you think she's beautiful?"

"Beautiful. With this nose?"

"It's a lovely nose. Go on, point it at me. Isn't she a lovely piece?"

"Couldn't we have kept the man in Scotland?"

"I say, Brett, let's turn in early."

"Don't be indecent, Michael. Remember there are ladies at this bar."

"Isn't she a lovely piece? Don't you think so, Jake?"

"There's a fight to-night," Bill said. "Like to go?"

"Fight," said Mike. "Who's fighting?"

"Ledoux and somebody."

"He's very good, Ledoux," Mike said. "I'd like to see it, rather"—he was making an effort to pull himself together—"but I can't go. I have a date with this thing here. I say, Brett, do get a new hat."

Brett pulled the felt hat down far over one eye and smiled out from under it. "You two run along to the fight. I'll have to be taking Mr. Campbell home directly."

"I'm not tight," Mike said. "Perhaps just a little. I say, Brett, you are a lovely piece."

"Go on to the fight," Brett said. "Mr. Campbell's get

ting difficult. What are these outbursts of affection, Michael?"

"I say, you are a lovely piece."

We said good night. "I'm sorry I can't go," Mike said. Brett laughed. I looked back from the door. Mike had one hand on the bar and was leaning toward Brett, talking. Brett was looking at him quite coolly, but the corners of her eyes were smiling.

Outside on the pavement I said: "Do you want to go to the fight?"

"Sure," said Bill. "If we don't have to walk."

"Mike was pretty excited about his girl friend," I said in the taxi.

"Well," said Bill. "You can't blame him such a hell of a lot."

CHAPTER IX

THE Ledoux-Kid Francis fight was the night of the 20th of June. It was a good fight. The morning after the fight I had a letter from Robert Cohn, written from Hendaye. He was having a very quiet time, he said, bathing, playing some golf and much bridge. Hendaye had a splendid beach, but he was anxious to start on the fishing-trip. When would I be down? If I would buy him a double-tapered line he would pay me when I came down.

That same morning I wrote Cohn from the office that Bill and I would leave Paris on the 25th unless I wired him otherwise, and would meet him at Bayonne, where we could get a bus over the mountains to Pamplona. The same evening about seven o'clock I stopped in at the

Select to see Michael and Brett. They were not there, and I went over to the Dingo. They were inside sitting at the bar.

"Hello, darling." Brett put out her hand.

"Hello, Jake," Mike said. "I understand I was tight last night."

"Weren't you, though," Brett said. "Disgraceful business."

"Look," said Mike, "when do you go down to Spain? Would you mind if we came down with you?"

"It would be grand."

"You wouldn't mind, really? I've been at Pamplona, you know. Brett's mad to go. You're sure we wouldn't just be a bloody nuisance?"

"Don't talk like a fool."

"I'm a little tight, you know. I wouldn't ask you like this if I weren't. You're sure you don't mind?"

"Oh, shut up, Michael," Brett said. "How can the man say he'd mind now? I'll ask him later."

"But you don't mind, do you?"

"Don't ask that again unless you want to make me sore. Bill and I go down on the morning of the 25th."

"By the way, where is Bill?" Brett asked.

"He's out at Chantilly dining with some people."

"He's a good chap."

"Splendid chap," said Mike. "He is, you know."

"You don't remember him," Brett said.

"I do. Remember him perfectly. Look, Jake, we'll come down the night of the 25th. Brett can't get up in the morning."

"Indeed not!"

"If our money comes and you're sure you don't mind."

"It will come, all right. I'll see to that."

"Tell me what tackle to send for."

"Get two or three rods with reels, and lines, and some flies."

"I won't fish," Brett put in.

"Get two rods, then, and Bill won't have to buy one."

"Right," said Mike. "I'll send a wire to the keeper."

"Won't it be splendid," Brett said. "Spain! We *will* have fun."

"The 25th. When is that?"

"Saturday."

"We *will* have to get ready."

"I say," said Mike, "I'm going to the barber's."

"I must bathe," said Brett. "Walk up to the hotel with me, Jake. Be a good chap."

"We *have* got the loveliest hotel," Mike said. "I think it's a brothel!"

"We left our bags here at the Dingo when we got in, and they asked us at this hotel if we wanted a room for the afternoon only. Seemed frightfully pleased we were going to stay all night."

"*I* believe it's a brothel," Mike said. "And *I* should know."

"Oh, shut it and go and get your hair cut."

Mike went out. Brett and I sat at the bar.

"Have another?"

"Might."

"I needed that," Brett said.

We walked up the Rue Delambre.

"I haven't seen you since I've been back," Brett said.

"No."

"How *are* you, Jake?"

"Fine."

Brett looked at me. "I say," she said, "is Robert Cohn going on this trip?"

"Yes. Why?"

"Don't you think it will be a bit rough on him?"

"Why should it?"

"Who did you think I went down to San Sebastian with?"

"Congratulations," I said.

We walked along.

"What did you say that for?"

"I don't know. What would you like me to say?"

We walked along and turned a corner.

"He behaved rather well, too. He gets a little dull."

"Does he?"

"I rather thought it would be good for him."

"You might take up social service."

"Don't be nasty."

"I won't."

"Didn't you really know?"

"No," I said. "I guess I didn't think about it."

"Do you think it will be too rough on him?"

"That's up to him," I said. "Tell him you're coming. He can always not come."

"I'll write him and give him a chance to pull out of it."

I did not see Brett again until the night of the 24th of June.

"Did you hear from Cohn?"

"Rather. He's keen about it."

"My God!"

"I thought it was rather odd myself."

"Says he can't wait to see me."

"Does he think you're coming alone?"

"No. I told him we were all coming down together. Michael and all."

"He's wonderful."

"Isn't he?"

They expected their money the next day. We arranged to meet at Pamplona. They would go directly to San

Sebastian and take the train from there. We would all meet at the Montoya in Pamplona. If they did not turn up on Monday at the latest we would go on ahead up to Burguete in the mountains, to start fishing. There was a bus to Burguete. I wrote out an itinerary so they could follow us.

Bill and I took the morning train from the Gare d'Orsay. It was a lovely day, not too hot, and the country was beautiful from the start. We went back into the diner and had breakfast. Leaving the dining-car I asked the conductor for tickets for the first service.

"Nothing until the fifth."

"What's this?"

There were never more than two servings of lunch on that train, and always plenty of places for both of them.

"They're all reserved," the dining-car conductor said. "There will be a fifth service at three-thirty."

"This is serious," I said to Bill.

"Give him ten francs."

"Here," I said. "We want to eat in the first service."

The conductor put the ten francs in his pocket.

"Thank you," he said. "I would advise you gentlemen to get some sandwiches. All the places for the first four services were reserved at the office of the company."

"You'll go a long way, brother," Bill said to him in English. "I suppose if I'd given you five francs you would have advised us to jump off the train."

"Comment?"

"Go to hell!" said Bill. "Get the sandwiches made and a bottle of wine. You tell him, Jake."

"And send it up to the next car." I described where we were.

In our compartment were a man and his wife and their young son.

"I suppose you're Americans, aren't you?" the man asked. "Having a good trip?"

"Wonderful," said Bill.

"That's what you want to do. Travel while you're young. Mother and I always wanted to get over, but we had to wait a while."

"You could have come over ten years ago, if you'd wanted to," the wife said. "What you always said was: 'See America first!' I will say we've seen a good deal, take it one way and another."

"Say, there's plenty of Americans on this train," the husband said. "They've got seven cars of them from Dayton, Ohio. They've been on a pilgrimage to Rome, and now they're going down to Biarritz and Lourdes."

"So, that's what they are. Pilgrims. Goddam Puritans," Bill said.

"What part of the States you boys from?"

"Kansas City," I said. "He's from Chicago."

"You both going to Biarritz?"

"No. We're going fishing in Spain."

"Well, I never cared for it, myself. There's plenty that do out where I come from, though. We got some of the best fishing in the State of Montana. I've been out with the boys, but I never cared for it any."

"Mighty little fishing you did on them trips," his wife said.

He winked at us.

"You know how the ladies are. If there's a jug goes along, or a case of beer, they think it's hell and damnation."

"That's the way men are," his wife said to us. She smoothed her comfortable lap. "I voted against prohibition to please him, and because I like a little beer in the house, and then he talks that way. It's a wonder they ever find any one to marry them."

"Say," said Bill, "do you know that gang of Pilgrim Fathers have cornered the dining-car until half past three this afternoon?"

"How do you mean? They can't do a thing like that."

"You try and get seats."

"Well, Mother, it looks as though we better go back and get another breakfast."

She stood up and straightened her dress.

"Will you boys keep an eye on our things? Come on, Hubert."

They all three went up to the wagon restaurant. A little while after they were gone a steward went through announcing the first service, and pilgrims, with their priests, commenced filing down the corridor. Our friend and his family did not come back. A waiter passed in the corridor with our sandwiches and the bottle of Chablis, and we called him in.

"You're going to work to-day," I said.

He nodded his head. "They start now, at ten-thirty."

"When do we eat?"

"Huh! When do I eat?"

He left two glasses for the bottle, and we paid him for the sandwiches and tipped him.

"I'll get the plates," he said, "or bring them with you."

We ate the sandwiches and drank the Chablis and watched the country out of the window. The grain was just beginning to ripen and the fields were full of poppies. The pastureland was green, and there were fine trees, and sometimes big rivers and châteaux off in the trees.

At Tours we got off and bought another bottle of wine, and when we got back in the compartment the gentleman from Montana and his wife and his son, Hubert, were sitting comfortably.

"Is there good swimming in Biarritz?" asked Hubert.

"That boy's just crazy till he can get in the water,"

his mother said. "It's pretty hard on youngsters travelling."

"There's good swimming," I said. "But it's dangerous when it's rough."

"Did you get a meal?" Bill asked.

"We sure did. We set right there when they started to come in, and they must have just thought we were in the party. One of the waiters said something to us in French, and then they just sent three of them back."

"They thought we were snappers, all right," the man said. "It certainly shows you the power of the Catholic Church. It's a pity you boys ain't Catholics. You could get a meal, then, all right."

"I am," I said. "That's what makes me so sore."

Finally at a quarter past four we had lunch. Bill had been rather difficult at the last. He buttonholed a priest who was coming back with one of the returning streams of pilgrims.

"When do us Protestants gets a chance to eat, Father?"

"I don't know anything about it. Haven't you got tickets?"

"It's enough to make a man join the Klan," Bill said. The priest looked back at him.

Inside the dining-car the waiters served the fifth successive table d'hôte meal. The waiter who served us was soaked through. His white jacket was purple under the arms.

"He must drink a lot of wine."

"Or wear purple undershirts."

"Let's ask him."

"No. He's too tired."

The train stopped for half an hour at Bordeaux and we went out through the station for a little walk. There was not time to get in to the town. Afterward we passed through the Landes and watched the sun set. There were wide fire-gaps cut through the pines, and you could look up them like avenues and see wooded hills way off. About seven-thirty we had dinner and watched the country through the open window in the diner. It was all sandy pine country full of heather. There were little clearings with houses in them, and once in a while we passed a sawmill. It got dark and we could feel the country hot and sandy and dark outside of the window, and about nine o'clock we got into Bayonne. The man and his wife and Hubert all shook hands with us. They were going on to La Nègresse to change to Biarritz.

"Well, I hope you have lots of luck," he said.

"Be careful about those bull-fights."

"Maybe we'll see you at Biarritz," Hubert said.

We got off with our bags and rod-cases and passed through the dark station and out to the lights and the line of cabs and hotel buses. There, standing with the hotel runners, was Robert Cohn. He did not see us at first. Then he started forward.

"Hello, Jake. Have a good trip?"

"Fine," I said. "This is Bill Gorton."

"How are you?"

"Come on," said Robert. "I've got a cab." He was a little near-sighted. I had never noticed it before. He was looking at Bill, trying to make him out. He was shy, too.

"We'll go up to my hotel. It's all right. It's quite nice."

We got into the cab, and the cabman put the bags up on the seat beside him and climbed up and cracked his whip, and we drove over the dark bridge and into the town.

"I'm awfully glad to meet you," Robert said to Bill. "I've heard so much about you from Jake and I've read your books. Did you get my line, Jake?"

The cab stopped in front of the hotel and we all got

out and went in. It was a nice hotel, and the people at
the desk were very cheerful, and we each had a good
small room.

CHAPTER X

IN the morning it was bright, and they were sprinkling
the streets of the town, and we all had breakfast in a
café. Bayonne is a nice town. It is like a very clean Spanish town and it is on a big river. Already, so early in the
morning, it was very hot on the bridge across the river.
We walked out on the bridge and then took a walk
through the town.

I was not at all sure Mike's rods would come from
Scotland in time, so we hunted a tackle store and finally
bought a rod for Bill up-stairs over a drygoods store. The
man who sold the tackle was out, and we had to wait for
him to come back. Finally he came in, and we bought a
pretty good rod cheap, and two landing-nets.

We went out into the street again and took a look at
the cathedral. Cohn made some remark about it being
a very good example of something or other, I forget what.
It seemed like a nice cathedral, nice and dim, like Spanish
churches. Then we went up past the old fort and out to
the local Syndicat d'Initiative office, where the bus was
supposed to start from. There they told us the bus service
did not start until the 1st of July. We found out at the
tourist office what we ought to pay for a motor-car to
Pamplona and hired one at a big garage just around the
corner from the Municipal Theatre for four hundred
francs. The car was to pick us up at the hotel in forty minutes, and we stopped at the café on the square where we
had eaten breakfast, and had a beer. It was hot, but the

town had a cool, fresh, early-morning smell and it was pleasant sitting in the café. A breeze started to blow, and you could feel that the air came from the sea. There were pigeons out in the square, and the houses were a yellow, sun-baked color, and I did not want to leave the café. But we had to go to the hotel to get our bags packed and pay the bill. We paid for the beers, we matched and I think Cohn paid, and went up to the hotel. It was only sixteen francs apiece for Bill and me, with ten per cent added for the service, and we had the bags sent down and waited for Robert Cohn. While we were waiting I saw a cockroach on the parquet floor that must have been at least three inches long. I pointed him out to Bill and then put my shoe on him. We agreed he must have just come in from the garden. It was really an awfully clean hotel.

Cohn came down, finally, and we all went out to the car. It was a big, closed car, with a driver in a white duster with blue collar and cuffs, and we had him put the back of the car down. He piled in the bags and we started off up the street and out of the town. We passed some lovely gardens and had a good look back at the town, and then we were out in the country, green and rolling, and the road climbing all the time. We passed lots of Basques with oxen, or cattle, hauling carts along the road, and nice farmhouses, low roofs, and all white-plastered. In the Basque country the land all looks very rich and green and the houses and villages look well-off and clean. Every village had a pelota court and on some of them kids were playing in the hot sun. There were signs on the walls of the churches saying it was forbidden to play pelota against them, and the houses in the villages had red tiled roofs, and then the road turned off and commenced to climb and we were going way up close along a hillside, with a valley below and hills stretched off back toward the sea. You couldn't see the sea. It was too far away.

You could see only hills and more hills, and you knew where the sea was.

We crossed the Spanish frontier. There was a little stream and a bridge, and Spanish carabineers, with patent-leather Bonaparte hats, and short guns on their backs, on one side, and on the other fat Frenchmen in Képis and mustaches. They only opened one bag and took the passports in and looked at them. There was a general store and inn on each side of the line. The chauffeur had to go in and fill out some papers about the car and we got out and went over to the stream to see if there were any trout. Bill tried to talk some Spanish to one of the carabineers, but it did not go very well. Robert Cohn asked, pointing with his finger, if there were any trout in the stream, and the carabineer said yes, but not many.

I asked him if he ever fished, and he said no, that he didn't care for it.

Just then an old man with long, sunburned hair and beard, and clothes that looked as though they were made of gunny-sacking, came striding up to the bridge. He was carrying a long staff, and he had a kid slung on his back, tied by the four legs, the head hanging down.

The carabineer waved him back with his sword. The man turned without saying anything, and started back up the white road into Spain.

"What's the matter with the old one?" I asked.

"He hasn't got any passport."

I offered the guard a cigarette. He took it and thanked me.

"What will he do?" I asked.

The guard spat in the dust.

"Oh, he'll just wade across the stream."

"Do you have much smuggling?"

"Oh," he said, "they go through."

The chauffeur came out, folding up the papers and

putting them in the inside pocket of his coat. We all got in the car and it started up the white dusty road into Spain. For a while the country was much as it had been; then, climbing all the time, we crossed the top of a Col, the road winding back and forth on itself, and then it was really Spain. There were long brown mountains and a few pines and far-off forests of beech-trees on some of the mountainsides. The road went along the summit of the Col and then dropped down, and the driver had to honk, and slow up, and turn out to avoid running into two donkeys that were sleeping in the road. We came down out of the mountains and through an oak forest, and there were white cattle grazing in the forest. Down below there were grassy plains and clear streams, and then we crossed a stream and went through a gloomy little village, and started to climb again. We climbed up and up and crossed another high Col and turned along it, and the road ran down to the right, and we saw a whole new range of mountains off to the south, all brown and baked-looking and furrowed in strange shapes.

After a while we came out of the mountains, and there were trees along both sides of the road, and a stream and ripe fields of grain, and the road went on, very white and straight ahead, and then lifted to a little rise, and off on the left was a hill with an old castle, with buildings close around it and a field of grain going right up to the walls and shifting in the wind. I was up in front with the driver and I turned around. Robert Cohn was asleep, but Bill looked and nodded his head. Then we crossed a wide plain, and there was a big river off on the right shining in the sun from between the line of trees, and away off you could see the plateau of Pamplona rising out of the plain, and the walls of the city, and the great brown cathedral, and the broken skyline of the other churches. In back of the plateau were the mountains, and every way

you looked there were other mountains, and ahead the
road stretched out white across the plain going toward
Pamplona.

We came into the town on the other side of the plateau,
the road slanting up steeply and dustily with shade-trees
on both sides, and then levelling out through the new
part of town they are building up outside the old walls.
We passed the bull-ring, high and white and concrete-
looking in the sun, and then came into the big square by
a side street and stopped in front of the Hotel Montoya.

The driver helped us down with the bags. There was
a crowd of kids watching the car, and the square was hot,
and the trees were green, and the flags hung on their
staffs, and it was good to get out of the sun and under
the shade of the arcade that runs all the way around the
square. Montoya was glad to see us, and shook hands
and gave us good rooms looking out on the square, and
then we washed and cleaned up and went down-stairs
in the dining-room for lunch. The driver stayed for lunch,
too, and afterward we paid him and he started back to
Bayonne.

There are two dining-rooms in the Montoya. One is
up-stairs on the second floor and looks out on the square.
The other is down one floor below the level of the square
and has a door that opens on the back street that the
bulls pass along when they run through the streets early
in the morning on their way to the ring. It is always cool
in the down-stairs dining-room and we had a very good
lunch. The first meal in Spain was always a shock with
the hors d'œuvres, an egg course, two meat courses,
vegetables, salad, and dessert and fruit. You have to drink
plenty of wine to get it all down. Robert Cohn tried to say
he did not want any of the second meat course, but we
would not interpret for him, and so the waitress brought
him something else as a replacement, a plate of cold

meats, I think. Cohn had been rather nervous ever since we had met at Bayonne. He did not know whether we knew Brett had been with him at San Sebastian, and it made him rather awkward.

"Well," I said, "Brett and Mike ought to get in to-night."

"I'm not sure they'll come," Cohn said.

"Why not?" Bill said. "Of course they'll come."

"They're always late," I said.

"I rather think they're not coming," Robert Cohn said.

He said it with an air of superior knowledge that irritated both of us.

"I'll bet you fifty pesetas they're here to-night," Bill said. He always bets when he is angered, and so he usually bets foolishly.

"I'll take it," Cohn said. "Good. You remember it, Jake. Fifty pesetas."

"I'll remember it myself," Bill said. I saw he was angry and wanted to smooth him down.

"It's a sure thing they'll come," I said. "But maybe not to-night."

"Want to call it off?" Cohn asked.

"No. Why should I? Make it a hundred if you like."

"All right. I'll take that."

"That's enough," I said. "Or you'll have to make a book and give me some of it."

"I'm satisfied," Cohn said. He smiled. "You'll probably win it back at bridge, anyway."

"You haven't got it yet," Bill said.

We went out to walk around under the arcade to the Café Iruña for coffee. Cohn said he was going over and get a shave.

"Say," Bill said to me, "have I got any chance on that bet?"

"You've got a rotten chance. They've never been on

time anywhere. If their money doesn't come it's a cinch they won't get in to-night."

"I was sorry as soon as I opened my mouth. But I had to call him. He's all right, I guess, but where does he get this inside stuff? Mike and Brett fixed it up with us about coming down here."

I saw Cohn coming over across the square.

"Here he comes."

"Well, let him not get superior and Jewish."

"The barber-shop's closed," Cohn said. "It's not open till four."

We had coffee at the Iruña, sitting in comfortable wicker chairs looking out from the cool of the arcade at the big square. After a while Bill went to write some letters and Cohn went over to the barber-shop. It was still closed, so he decided to go up to the hotel and get a bath, and I sat out in front of the café and then went for a walk in the town. It was very hot, but I kept on the shady side of the streets and went through the market and had a good time seeing the town again. I went to the Ayuntamiento and found the old gentleman who subscribes for the bull-fight tickets for me every year, and he had gotten the money I sent him from Paris and renewed my subscriptions, so that was all set. He was the archivist, and all the archives of the town were in his office. That has nothing to do with the story. Anyway, his office had a green baize door and a big wooden door, and when I went out I left him sitting among the archives that covered all the walls, and I shut both the doors, and as I went out of the building into the street the porter stopped me to brush off my coat.

"You must have been in a motor-car," he said.

The back of the collar and the upper part of the shoulders were gray with dust.

"From Bayonne."

"Well, well," he said. "I knew you were in a motor-car from the way the dust was." So I gave him two copper coins.

At the end of the street I saw the cathedral and walked up toward it. The first time I ever saw it I thought the façade was ugly but I liked it now. I went inside. It was dim and dark and the pillars went high up, and there were people praying, and it smelt of incense, and there were some wonderful big windows. I knelt and started to pray and prayed for everybody I thought of, Brett and Mike and Bill and Robert Cohn and myself, and all the bull-fighters, separately for the ones I liked, and lumping all the rest, then I prayed for myself again, and while I was praying for myself I found I was getting sleepy, so I prayed that the bull-fights would be good, and that it would be a fine fiesta, and that we would get some fishing. I wondered if there was anything else I might pray for, and I thought I would like to have some money, so I prayed that I would make a lot of money, and then I started to think how I would make it, and thinking of making money reminded me of the count, and I started wondering about where he was, and regretting I hadn't seen him since that night in Montmartre, and about something funny Brett told me about him, and as all the time I was kneeling with my forehead on the wood in front of me, and was thinking of myself as praying, I was a little ashamed, and regretted that I was such a rotten Catholic, but realized there was nothing I could do about it, at least for a while, and maybe never, but that anyway it was a grand religion, and I only wished I felt religious and maybe I would the next time; and then I was out in the hot sun on the steps of the cathedral, and the fore-fingers and the thumb of my right hand were still damp, and I felt them dry in the sun. The sunlight was hot and hard, and I crossed over beside some buildings, and walked back along side-streets to the hotel.

At dinner that night we found that Robert Cohn had taken a bath, had had a shave and a haircut and a shampoo, and something put on his hair afterward to make it stay down. He was nervous, and I did not try to help him any. The train was due in at nine o'clock from San Sebastian, and, if Brett and Mike were coming, they would be on it. At twenty minutes to nine we were not half through dinner. Robert Cohn got up from the table and said he would go to the station. I said I would go with him, just to devil him. Bill said he would be damned if he would leave his dinner. I said we would be right back.

We walked to the station. I was enjoying Cohn's nervousness. I hoped Brett would be on the train. At the station the train was late, and we sat on a baggage-truck and waited outside in the dark. I have never seen a man in civil life as nervous as Robert Cohn—nor as eager. I was enjoying it. It was lousy to enjoy it, but I felt lousy. Cohn had a wonderful quality of bringing out the worst in anybody.

After a while we heard the train-whistle way off below on the other side of the plateau, and then we saw the headlight coming up the hill. We went inside the station and stood with a crowd of people just back of the gates, and the train came in and stopped, and everybody started coming out through the gates.

They were not in the crowd. We waited till everybody had gone through and out of the station and gotten into buses, or taken cabs, or were walking with their friends or relatives through the dark into the town.

"I knew they wouldn't come," Robert said. We were going back to the hotel.

"I thought they might," I said.

Bill was eating fruit when we came in and finishing a bottle of wine.

"Didn't come, eh?"

"No."

"Do you mind if I give you that hundred pesetas in the morning, Cohn?" Bill asked. "I haven't changed any money here yet."

"Oh, forget about it," Robert Cohn said. "Let's bet on something else. Can you bet on bull-fights?"

"You could," Bill said, "but you don't need to."

"It would be like betting on the war," I said. "You don't need any economic interest."

"I'm very curious to see them," Robert said.

Montoya came up to our table. He had a telegram in his hand. "It's for you." He handed it to me.

It read: "Stopped night San Sebastian."

"It's from them," I said. I put it in my pocket. Ordinarily I should have handed it over.

"They've stopped over in San Sebastian," I said. "Send their regards to you."

Why I felt that impulse to devil him I do not know. Of course I do know. I was blind, unforgivingly jealous of what had happened to him. The fact that I took it as a matter of course did not alter that any. I certainly did hate him. I do not think I ever really hated him until he had that little spell of superiority at lunch—that and when he went through all that barbering. So I put the telegram in my pocket. The telegram came to me, anyway.

"Well," I said. "We ought to pull out on the noon bus for Burguete. They can follow us if they get in to-morrow night."

There were only two trains up from San Sebastian, an early-morning train and the one we had just met.

"That sounds like a good idea," Cohn said.

"The sooner we get on the stream the better."

"It's all one to me when we start," Bill said. "The sooner the better."

We sat in the Iruña for a while and had coffee and then took a little walk out to the bull-ring and across the field and under the trees at the edge of the cliff and looked down at the river in the dark, and I turned in early. Bill and Cohn stayed out in the café quite late, I believe, because I was asleep when they came in.

In the morning I bought three tickets for the bus to Burguete. It was scheduled to leave at two o'clock. There was nothing earlier. I was sitting over at the Iruña reading the papers when I saw Robert Cohn coming across the square. He came up to the table and sat down in one of the wicker chairs.

"This is a comfortable café," he said. "Did you have a good night, Jake?"

"I slept like a log."

"I didn't sleep very well. Bill and I were out late, too."

"Where were you?"

"Here. And after it shut we went over to that other café. The old man there speaks German and English."

"The Café Suizo."

"That's it. He seems like a nice old fellow. I think it's a better café than this one."

"It's not so good in the daytime," I said. "Too hot. By the way, I got the bus tickets."

"I'm not going up to-day. You and Bill go on ahead."

"I've got your ticket."

"Give it to me. I'll get the money back."

"It's five pesetas."

Robert Cohn took out a silver five-peseta piece and gave it to me.

"I ought to stay," he said. "You see I'm afraid there's some sort of misunderstanding."

"Why," I said. "They may not come here for three or four days now if they start on parties at San Sebastian."

"That's just it," said Robert. "I'm afraid they expected to meet me at San Sebastian, and that's why they stopped over."

"What makes you think that?"

"Well, I wrote suggesting it to Brett."

"Why in hell didn't you stay there and meet them, then?" I started to say, but I stopped. I thought that idea would come to him by itself, but I do not believe it ever did.

He was being confidential now and it was giving him pleasure to be able to talk with the understanding that I knew there was something between him and Brett.

"Well, Bill and I will go up right after lunch," I said.

"I wish I could go. We've been looking forward to this fishing all winter." He was being sentimental about it. "But I ought to stay. I really ought. As soon as they come I'll bring them right up."

"Let's find Bill."

"I want to go over to the barber-shop."

"See you at lunch."

I found Bill up in his room. He was shaving.

"Oh, yes, he told me all about it last night," Bill said. "He's a great little confider. He said he had a date with Brett at San Sebastian."

"The lying bastard!"

"Oh, no," said Bill. "Don't get sore. Don't get sore at this stage of the trip. How did you ever happen to know this fellow, anyway?"

"Don't rub it in."

Bill looked around, half-shaved, and then went on talking into the mirror while he lathered his face.

"Didn't you send him with a letter to me in New York last winter? Thank God, I'm a travelling man. Haven't

you got some more Jewish friends you could bring along?"
He rubbed his chin with his thumb, looked at it, and then
started scraping again.

"You've got some fine ones yourself."

"Oh, yes. I've got some darbs. But not alongside of
this Robert Cohn. The funny thing is he's nice, too. I
like him. But he's just so awful."

"He can be damn nice."

"I know it. That's the terrible part."

I laughed.

"Yes. Go on and laugh," said Bill. "You weren't out
with him last night until two o'clock."

"Was he very bad?"

"Awful. What's all this about him and Brett, anyway?
Did she ever have anything to do with him?"

He raised his chin up and pulled it from side to side.

"Sure. She went down to San Sebastian with him."

"What a damn-fool thing to do. Why did she do that?"

"She wanted to get out of town and she can't go anywhere alone. She said she thought it would be good for
him."

"What bloody-fool things people do. Why didn't she
go off with some of her own people? Or you?"—he
slurred that over—"or me? Why not me?" He looked at
his face carefully in the glass, put a big dab of lather on
each cheek-bone. "It's an honest face. It's a face any
woman would be safe with."

"She'd never seen it."

"She should have. All women should see it. It's a face
that ought to be thrown on every screen in the country.
Every woman ought to be given a copy of this face as
she leaves the altar. Mothers should tell their daughters
about his face. My son"—he pointed the razor at me
—"go west with this face and grow up with the country."

He ducked down to the bowl, rinsed his face with cold water, put on some alcohol, and then looked at himself carefully in the glass, pulling down his long upper lip.

"My God!" he said, "isn't it an awful face?"

He looked in the glass.

"And as for this Robert Cohn," Bill said, "he makes me sick, and he can go to hell, and I'm damn glad he's staying here so we won't have him fishing with us."

"You're damn right."

"We're going trout-fishing. We're going trout-fishing in the Irati River, and we're going to get tight now at lunch on the wine of the country, and then take a swell bus ride."

"Come on. Let's go over to the Iruña and start," I said.

CHAPTER XI

IT was baking hot in the square when we came out after lunch with our bags and the rod-case to go to Burguete. People were on top of the bus, and others were climbing up a ladder. Bill went up and Robert sat beside Bill to save a place for me, and I went back in the hotel to get a couple of bottles of wine to take with us. When I came out the bus was crowded. Men and women were sitting on all the baggage and boxes on top, and the women all had their fans going in the sun. It certainly was hot. Robert climbed down and I fitted into the place he had saved on the one wooden seat that ran across the top.

Robert Cohn stood in the shade of the arcade waiting for us to start. A Basque with a big leather wine-bag in his lap lay across the top of the bus in front of our seat,

leaning back against our legs. He offered the wine-skin
to Bill and to me, and when I tipped it up to drink he
imitated the sound of a klaxon motor-horn so well and
so suddenly that I spilled some of the wine, and everybody laughed. He apologized and made me take another
drink. He made the klaxon again a little later, and it
fooled me the second time. He was very good at it. The
Basques liked it. The man next to Bill was talking to
him in Spanish and Bill was not getting it, so he offered
the man one of the bottles of wine. The man waved it
away. He said it was too hot and he had drunk too much
at lunch. When Bill offered the bottle the second time
he took a long drink, and then the bottle went all over
that part of the bus. Every one took a drink very politely,
and then they made us cork it up and put it away. They
all wanted us to drink from their leather wine-bottles.
They were peasants going up into the hills.

Finally, after a couple more false klaxons, the bus
started, and Robert Cohn waved good-by to us, and all
the Basques waved good-by to him. As soon as we started
out on the road outside of town it was cool. It felt nice
riding high up and close under the trees. The bus went
quite fast and made a good breeze, and as we went out
along the road with the dust powdering the trees and
down the hill, we had a fine view, back through the trees,
of the town rising up from the bluff above the river. The
Basque lying against my knees pointed out the view with
the neck of the wine-bottle, and winked at us. He nodded
his head.

"Pretty nice, eh?"

"These Basques are swell people," Bill said.

The Basque lying against my legs was tanned the
color of saddle-leather. He wore a black smock like all
the rest. There were wrinkles in his tanned neck. He
turned around and offered his wine-bag to Bill. Bill

handed him one of our bottles. The Basque wagged a
forefinger at him and handed the bottle back, slapping
in the cork with the palm of his hand. He shoved the
wine-bag up.

"Arriba! Arriba!" he said. "Lift it up."

Bill raised the wine-skin and let the stream of wine
spurt out and into his mouth, his head tipped back. When
he stopped drinking and tipped the leather bottle down
a few drops ran down his chin.

"No! No!" several Basques said. "Not like that." One
snatched the bottle away from the owner, who was himself about to give a demonstration. He was a young fellow
and he held the wine-bottle at full arm's length and
raised it high up, squeezing the leather bag with his hand
so the stream of wine hissed into his mouth. He held the
bag out there, the wine making a flat, hard trajectory into
his mouth, and he kept on swallowing smoothly and regularly.

"Hey!" the owner of the bottle shouted. "Whose wine
is that?"

The drinker waggled his little finger at him and smiled
at us with his eyes. Then he bit the stream off sharp,
made a quick lift with the wine-bag and lowered it down
to the owner. He winked at us. The owner shook the
wine-skin sadly.

We passed through a town and stopped in front of the
posada, and the driver took on several packages. Then
we started on again, and outside the town the road commenced to mount. We were going through farming country with rocky hills that sloped down into the fields. The
grain-fields went up the hillsides. Now as we went higher
there was a wind blowing the grain. The road was white
and dusty, and the dust rose under the wheels and hung
in the air behind us. The road climbed up into the hills
and left the rich grain-fields below. Now there were only

patches of grain on the bare hillsides and on each side of
the water-courses. We turned sharply out to the side of
the road to give room to pass to a long string of six mules,
following one after the other, hauling a high-hooded
wagon loaded with freight. The wagon and the mules
were covered with dust. Close behind was another string
of mules and another wagon. This was loaded with
lumber, and the arriero driving the mules leaned back
and put on the thick wooden brakes as we passed. Up
here the country was quite barren and the hills were
rocky and hard-baked clay furrowed by the rain.

We came around a curve into a town, and on both
sides opened out a sudden green valley. A stream went
through the centre of the town and fields of grapes
touched the houses.

The bus stopped in front of a posada and many of the
passengers got down, and a lot of the baggage was un-
strapped from the roof from under the big tarpaulins
and lifted down. Bill and I got down and went into the
posada. There was a low, dark room with saddles and
harness, and hay-forks made of white wood, and clusters
of canvas rope-soled shoes and hams and slabs of bacon
and white garlics and long sausages hanging from the
roof. It was cool and dusky, and we stood in front of a
long wooden counter with two women behind it serving
drinks. Behind them were shelves stacked with supplies
and goods.

We each had an aguardiente and paid forty centimes
for the two drinks. I gave the woman fifty centimes to
make a tip, and she gave me back the copper piece, thinking I had misunderstood the price.

Two of our Basques came in and insisted on buying a
drink. So they bought a drink and then we bought a
drink, and then they slapped us on the back and bought
another drink. Then we bought, and then we all went

out into the sunlight and the heat, and climbed back
on top of the bus. There was plenty of room now for
every one to sit on the seat, and the Basque who had
been lying on the tin roof now sat between us. The
woman who had been serving drinks came out wiping
her hands on her apron and talked to somebody inside
the bus. Then the driver came out swinging two flat
leather mail-pouches and climbed up, and everybody
waving we started off.

The road left the green valley at once, and we were up
in the hills again. Bill and the wine-bottle Basque were
having a conversation. A man leaned over from the other
side of the seat and asked in English: "You're Americans?"

"Sure."

"I been there," he said. "Forty years ago."

He was an old man, as brown as the others, with the
stubble of a white beard.

"How was it?"

"What you say?"

"How was America?"

"Oh, I was in California. It was fine."

"Why did you leave?"

"What you say?"

"Why did you come back here?"

"Oh! I come back to get married. I was going to go
back but my wife she don't like to travel. Where you
from?"

"Kansas City."

"I been there," he said. "I been in Chicago, St. Louis,
Kansas City, Denver, Los Angeles, Salt Lake City."

He named them carefully.

"How long were you over?"

"Fifteen years. Then I come back and got married."

"Have a drink?"

"All right," he said. "You can't get this in America, eh?"

"There's plenty if you can pay for it."

"What you come over here for?"

"We're going to the fiesta at Pamplona."

"You like the bull-fights?"

"Sure. Don't you?"

"Yes," he said. "I guess I like them."

Then after a little:

"Where you go now?"

"Up to Burguete to fish."

"Well," he said, "I hope you catch something."

He shook hands and turned around to the back seat again. The other Basques had been impressed. He sat back comfortably and smiled at me when I turned around to look at the country. But the effort of talking American seemed to have tired him. He did not say anything after that.

The bus climbed steadily up the road. The country was barren and rocks stuck up through the clay. There was no grass beside the road. Looking back we could see the country spread out below. Far back the fields were squares of green and brown on the hillsides. Making the horizon were the brown mountains. They were strangely shaped. As we climbed higher the horizon kept changing. As the bus ground slowly up the road we could see other mountains coming up in the south. Then the road came over the crest, flattened out, and went into a forest. It was a forest of cork oaks, and the sun came through the trees in patches, and there were cattle grazing back in the trees. We went through the forest and the road came out and turned along a rise of land, and out ahead of us was a rolling green plain, with dark mountains beyond it. These were not like the brown, heat-baked mountains we had left behind. These were wooded nd there were clouds coming down from them. The green plain stretched off. It was cut by fences and the white of the road showed through the trunks of a double ine of trees that crossed the plain toward the north. As we came to the edge of the rise we saw the red roofs and white houses of Burguete ahead strung out on the plain, and away off on the shoulder of the first dark mountain was the gray metal-sheathed roof of the monastery of Roncevalles.

"There's Roncevaux," I said.

"Where?"

"Way off there where the mountain starts."

"It's cold up here," Bill said.

"It's high," I said. "It must be twelve hundred metres."

"It's awful cold," Bill said.

The bus levelled down onto the straight line of road that ran to Burguete. We passed a crossroads and crossed a bridge over a stream. The houses of Burguete were along both sides of the road. There were no side-streets. We passed the church and the school-yard, and the bus stopped. We got down and the driver handed down our bags and the rod-case. A carabineer in his cocked hat and yellow leather cross-straps came up.

"What's in there?" he pointed to the rod-case.

I opened it and showed him. He asked to see our fishing permits and I got them out. He looked at the date and then waved us on.

"Is that all right?" I asked.

"Yes. Of course."

We went up the street, past the whitewashed stone houses, families sitting in their doorways watching us, to the inn.

The fat woman who ran the inn came out from the kitchen and shook hands with us. She took off her spectacles, wiped them, and put them on again. It was cold

in the inn and the wind was starting to blow outside.
The woman sent a girl up-stairs with us to show the
room. There were two beds, a washstand, a clothes-chest,
and a big, framed steel-engraving of Nuestra Señora de
Roncevalles. The wind was blowing against the shutters.
The room was on the north side of the inn. We washed,
put on sweaters, and came down-stairs into the dining-
room. It had a stone floor, low ceiling, and was oak-
panelled. The shutters were all up and it was so cold you
could see your breath.

"My God!" said Bill. "It can't be this cold to-morrow.
I'm not going to wade a stream in this weather."

There was an upright piano in the far corner of the
room beyond the wooden tables and Bill went over and
started to play.

"I got to keep warm," he said.

I went out to find the woman and ask her how much
the room and board was. She put her hands under her
apron and looked away from me.

"Twelve pesetas."

"Why, we only paid that in Pamplona."

She did not say anything, just took off her glasses and
wiped them on her apron.

"That's too much," I said. "We didn't pay more than
that at a big hotel."

"We've put in a bathroom."

"Haven't you got anything cheaper?"

"Not in the summer. Now is the big season."

We were the only people in the inn. Well, I thought,
it's only a few days.

"Is the wine included?"

"Oh, yes."

"Well," I said. "It's all right."

I went back to Bill. He blew his breath at me to show
how cold it was, and went on playing. I sat at one of the

ables and looked at the pictures on the wall. There was
one panel of rabbits, dead, one of pheasants, also dead,
and one panel of dead ducks. The panels were all dark
and smoky-looking. There was a cupboard full of liqueur
bottles. I looked at them all. Bill was still playing. "How
about a hot rum punch?" he said. "This isn't going to
keep me warm permanently."

I went out and told the woman what a rum punch was
and how to make it. In a few minutes a girl brought a
stone pitcher, steaming, into the room. Bill came over
from the piano and we drank the hot punch and listened
to the wind.

"There isn't too much rum in that."

I went over to the cupboard and brought the rum
bottle and poured a half-tumblerful into the pitcher.

"Direct action," said Bill. "It beats legislation."

The girl came in and laid the table for supper.

"It blows like hell up here," Bill said.

The girl brought in a big bowl of hot vegetable soup
and the wine. We had fried trout afterward and some
sort of a stew and a big bowl full of wild strawberries.
We did not lose money on the wine, and the girl was shy
but nice about bringing it. The old woman looked in once
and counted the empty bottles.

After supper we went up-stairs and smoked and read
in bed to keep warm. Once in the night I woke and heard
the wind blowing. It felt good to be warm and in bed.

CHAPTER XII

WHEN I woke in the morning I went to the window and looked out. It had cleared and there
were no clouds on the mountains. Outside under the

window were some carts and an old diligence, the wood
of the roof cracked and split by the weather. It mus
have been left from the days before the motor-buses
A goat hopped up on one of the carts and then to the
roof of the diligence. He jerked his head at the other
goats below and when I waved at him he bounded
down.

Bill was still sleeping, so I dressed, put on my shoe
outside in the hall, and went down-stairs. No one wa
stirring down-stairs, so I unbolted the door and went out
It was cool outside in the early morning and the sun had
not yet dried the dew that had come when the wind died
down. I hunted around in the shed behind the inn and
found a sort of mattock, and went down toward the
stream to try and dig some worms for bait. The stream
was clear and shallow but it did not look trouty. On the
grassy bank where it was damp I drove the mattock into
the earth and loosened a chunk of sod. There were worms
underneath. They slid out of sight as I lifted the sod and
I dug carefully and got a good many. Digging at the edge
of the damp ground I filled two empty tobacco-tins with
worms and sifted dirt onto them. The goats watched me
dig.

When I went back into the inn the woman was down
in the kitchen, and I asked her to get coffee for us, and
that we wanted a lunch. Bill was awake and sitting on
the edge of the bed.

"I saw you out of the window," he said. "Didn't want
to interrupt you. What were you doing? Burying your
money?"

"You lazy bum!"

"Been working for the common good? Splendid.
want you to do that every morning."

"Come on," I said. "Get up."

"What? Get up? I never get up."

He climbed into bed and pulled the sheet up to his chin.

"Try and argue me into getting up."

I went on looking for the tackle and putting it all together in the tackle-bag.

"Aren't you interested?" Bill asked.

"I'm going down and eat."

"Eat? Why didn't you say eat? I thought you just wanted me to get up for fun. Eat? Fine. Now you're reasonable. You go out and dig some more worms and I'll be right down."

"Oh, go to hell!"

"Work for the good of all." Bill stepped into his underclothes. "Show irony and pity."

I started out of the room with the tackle-bag, the nets, and the rod-case.

"Hey! come back!"

I put my head in the door.

"Aren't you going to show a little irony and pity?"

I thumbed my nose.

"That's not irony."

As I went down-stairs I heard Bill singing, "Irony and Pity. When you're feeling . . . Oh, Give them Irony and Give them Pity. Oh, give them Irony. When they're feeling . . . Just a little irony. Just a little pity . . ." He kept on singing until he came down-stairs. The tune was: "The Bells Are Ringing for Me and My Gal." I was reading a week-old Spanish paper.

"What's all this irony and pity?"

"What? Don't you know about Irony and Pity?"

"No. Who got it up?"

"Everybody. They're mad about it in New York. It's just like the Fratellinis used to be."

The girl came in with the coffee and buttered toast. Or, rather it was bread toasted and buttered.

"Ask her if she's got any jam," Bill said. "Be ironical with her."

"Have you got any jam?"

"That's not ironical. I wish I could talk Spanish."

The coffee was good and we drank it out of big bowls. The girl brought in a glass dish of raspberry jam.

"Thank you."

"Hey! that's not the way," Bill said. "Say somethin ironical. Make some crack about Primo de Rivera."

"I could ask her what kind of a jam they think they'v gotten into in the Riff."

"Poor," said Bill. "Very poor. You can't do it. That' all. You don't understand irony. You have no pity. Sa something pitiful."

"Robert Cohn."

"Not so bad. That's better. Now why is Cohn pitiful Be ironic."

He took a big gulp of coffee.

"Aw, hell!" I said. "It's too early in the morning."

"There you go. And you claim you want to be a writer too. You're only a newspaper man. An expatriated news paper man. You ought to be ironical the minute you ge out of bed. You ought to wake up with your mouth fu of pity."

"Go on," I said. "Who did you get this stuff from?"

"Everybody. Don't you read? Don't you ever see any body? You know what you are? You're an expatriate Why don't you live in New York? Then you'd know thes things. What do you want me to do? Come over her and tell you every year?"

"Take some more coffee," I said.

"Good. Coffee is good for you. It's the caffeine in i Caffeine, we are here. Caffeine puts a man on her hors and a woman in his grave. You know what's the troubl with you? You're an expatriate. One of the worst type

Haven't you heard that? Nobody that ever left their own country ever wrote anything worth printing. Not even in the newspapers."

He drank the coffee.

"You're an expatriate. You've lost touch with the soil. You get precious. Fake European standards have ruined you. You drink yourself to death. You become obsessed by sex. You spend all your time talking, not working. You are an expatriate, see? You hang around cafés."

"It sounds like a swell life," I said. "When do I work?"

"You don't work. One group claims women support you. Another group claims you're impotent."

"No," I said. "I just had an accident."

"Never mention that," Bill said. "That's the sort of thing that can't be spoken of. That's what you ought to work up into a mystery. Like Henry's bicycle."

He had been going splendidly, but he stopped. I was afraid he thought he had hurt me with that crack about being impotent. I wanted to start him again.

"It wasn't a bicycle," I said. "He was riding horse-back."

"I heard it was a tricycle."

"Well," I said. "A plane is sort of like a tricycle. The joystick works the same way."

"But you don't pedal it."

"No," I said, "I guess you don't pedal it."

"Let's lay off that," Bill said.

"All right. I was just standing up for the tricycle."

"I think he's a good writer, too," Bill said. "And you're a hell of a good guy. Anybody ever tell you you were a good guy?"

"I'm not a good guy."

"Listen. You're a hell of a good guy, and I'm fonder of you than anybody on earth. I couldn't tell you that in New York. It'd mean I was a faggot. That was what the Civil War was about. Abraham Lincoln was a faggot. He was in love with General Grant. So was Jefferson Davis. Lincoln just freed the slaves on a bet. The Dred Scott case was framed by the Anti-Saloon League. Sex explains it all. The Colonel's Lady and Judy O'Grady are Lesbians under their skin."

He stopped.

"Want to hear some more?"

"Shoot," I said.

"I don't know any more. Tell you some more at lunch."

"Old Bill," I said.

"You bum!"

We packed the lunch and two bottles of wine in the rucksack, and Bill put it on. I carried the rod-case and the landing-nets slung over my back. We started up the road and then went across a meadow and found a path that crossed the fields and went toward the woods on the slope of the first hill. We walked across the fields on the sandy path. The fields were rolling and grassy and the grass was short from the sheep grazing. The cattle were up in the hills. We heard their bells in the woods.

The path crossed a stream on a foot-log. The log was surfaced off, and there was a sapling bent across for a rail. In the flat pool beside the stream tadpoles spotted the sand. We went up a steep bank and across the rolling fields. Looking back we saw Burguete, white houses and red roofs, and the white road with a truck going along it and the dust rising.

Beyond the fields we crossed another faster-flowing stream. A sandy road led down to the ford and beyond into the woods. The path crossed the stream on another foot-log below the ford, and joined the road, and we went into the woods.

It was a beech wood and the trees were very old. Their roots bulked above the ground and the branches were twisted. We walked on the road between the thick trunks of the old beeches and the sunlight came through the leaves in light patches on the grass. The trees were big, and the foliage was thick but it was not gloomy. There was no undergrowth, only the smooth grass, very green and fresh, and the big gray trees well spaced as though it were a park.

"This is country," Bill said.

The road went up a hill and we got into thick woods, and the road kept on climbing. Sometimes it dipped down but rose again steeply. All the time we heard the cattle in the woods. Finally, the road came out on the top of the hills. We were on the top of the height of land that was the highest part of the range of wooded hills we had seen from Burguete. There were wild strawberries growing on the sunny side of the ridge in a little clearing in the trees.

Ahead the road came out of the forest and went along the shoulder of the ridge of hills. The hills ahead were not wooded, and there were great fields of yellow gorse. Way off we saw the steep bluffs, dark with trees and jutting with gray stone, that marked the course of the Irati River.

"We have to follow this road along the ridge, cross these hills, go through the woods on the far hills, and come down to the Irati valley," I pointed out to Bill.

"That's a hell of a hike."

"It's too far to go and fish and come back the same day, comfortably."

"Comfortably. That's a nice word. We'll have to go like hell to get there and back and have any fishing at all."

It was a long walk and the country was very fine, but we were tired when we came down the steep road that led out of the wooded hills into the valley of the Rio de la Fabrica.

The road came out from the shadow of the woods into the hot sun. Ahead was a river-valley. Beyond the river was a steep hill. There was a field of buckwheat on the hill. We saw a white house under some trees on the hillside. It was very hot and we stopped under some trees beside a dam that crossed the river.

Bill put the pack against one of the trees and we jointed up the rods, put on the reels, tied on leaders, and got ready to fish.

"You're sure this thing has trout in it?" Bill asked.

"It's full of them."

"I'm going to fish a fly. You got any McGintys?"

"There's some in there."

"You going to fish bait?"

"Yeah. I'm going to fish the dam here."

"Well, I'll take the fly-book, then." He tied on a fly. "Where'd I better go? Up or down?"

"Down is the best. They're plenty up above, too."

Bill went down the bank.

"Take a worm can."

"No, I don't want one. If they won't take a fly I'll just flick it around."

Bill was down below watching the stream.

"Say," he called up against the noise of the dam. "How about putting the wine in that spring up the road?"

"All right," I shouted. Bill waved his hand and started down the stream. I found the two wine-bottles in the pack, and carried them up the road to where the water of a spring flowed out of an iron pipe. There was a board over the spring and I lifted it and, knocking the corks firmly into the bottles, lowered them down into the water. It was so cold my hand and wrist felt numbed. I put back the slab of wood, and hoped nobody would find the wine.

I got my rod that was leaning against the tree, took

the bait-can and landing-net, and walked out onto the
dam. It was built to provide a head of water for driving
logs. The gate was up, and I sat on one of the squared
timbers and watched the smooth apron of water before
the river tumbled into the falls. In the white water at
the foot of the dam it was deep. As I baited up, a trout
shot up out of the white water into the falls and was
carried down. Before I could finish baiting, another
trout jumped at the falls, making the same lovely arc and
disappearing into the water that was thundering down.
I put on a good-sized sinker and dropped into the white
water close to the edge of the timbers of the dam.

I did not feel the first trout strike. When I started to
pull up I felt that I had one and brought him, fighting
and bending the rod almost double, out of the boiling
water at the foot of the falls, and swung him up and onto
the dam. He was a good trout, and I banged his head
against the timber so that he quivered out straight, and
then slipped him into my bag.

While I had him on, several trout had jumped at the
falls. As soon as I baited up and dropped in again I
hooked another and brought him in the same way. In
a little while I had six. They were all about the same
size. I laid them out, side by side, all their heads pointing the same way, and looked at them. They were beautifully colored and firm and hard from the cold water.
It was a hot day, so I slit them all and shucked out the
insides, gills and all, and tossed them over across the
river. I took the trout ashore, washed them in the cold,
smoothly heavy water above the dam, and then picked
some ferns and packed them all in the bag, three trout
on a layer of ferns, then another layer of ferns, then three
more trout, and then covered them with ferns. They
looked nice in the ferns, and now the bag was bulky, and
I put it in the shade of the tree.

It was very hot on the dam, so I put my worm-can in the shade with the bag, and got a book out of the pack and settled down under the tree to read until Bill should come up for lunch.

It was a little past noon and there was not much shade, but I sat against the trunk of two of the trees that grew together, and read. The book was something by A. E. W. Mason, and I was reading a wonderful story about a man who had been frozen in the Alps and then fallen into a glacier and disappeared, and his bride was going to wait twenty-four years exactly for his body to come out on the moraine, while her true love waited too, and they were still waiting when Bill came up.

"Get any?" he asked. He had his rod and his bag and his net all in one hand, and he was sweating. I hadn't heard him come up, because of the noise from the dam.

"Six. What did you get?"

Bill sat down, opened up his bag, laid a big trout on the grass. He took out three more, each one a little bigger than the last, and laid them side by side in the shade from the tree. His face was sweaty and happy.

"How are yours?"

"Smaller."

"Let's see them."

"They're packed."

"How big are they really?"

"They're all about the size of your smallest."

"You're not holding out on me?"

"I wish I were."

"Get them all on worms?"

"Yes."

"You lazy bum!"

Bill put the trout in the bag and started for the river, swinging the open bag. He was wet from the waist down and I knew he must have been wading the stream.

I walked up the road and got out the two bottles of wine. They were cold. Moisture beaded on the bottles as I walked back to the trees. I spread the lunch on a newspaper, and uncorked one of the bottles and leaned the other against a tree. Bill came up drying his hands, his bag plump with ferns.

"Let's see that bottle," he said. He pulled the cork and tipped up the bottle and drank. "Whew! That makes my eyes ache."

"Let's try it."

The wine was icy cold and tasted faintly rusty.

"That's not such filthy wine," Bill said.

"The cold helps it," I said.

We unwrapped the little parcels of lunch.

"Chicken."

"There's hard-boiled eggs."

"Find any salt?"

"First the egg," said Bill. "Then the chicken. Even Bryan could see that."

"He's dead. I read it in the paper yesterday."

"No. Not really?"

"Yes. Bryan's dead."

Bill laid down the egg he was peeling.

"Gentlemen," he said, and unwrapped a drumstick from a piece of newspaper. "I reverse the order. For Bryan's sake. As a tribute to the Great Commoner. First the chicken; then the egg."

"Wonder what day God created the chicken?"

"Oh," said Bill, sucking the drumstick, "how should we know? We should not question. Our stay on earth is not for long. Let us rejoice and believe and give thanks."

"Eat an egg."

Bill gestured with the drumstick in one hand and the bottle of wine in the other.

"Let us rejoice in our blessings. Let us utilize the fowls of the air. Let us utilize the product of the vine. Will you utilize a little, brother?"

"After you, brother."

Bill took a long drink.

"Utilize a little, brother," he handed me the bottle. "Let us not doubt, brother. Let us not pry into the holy mysteries of the hen-coop with simian fingers. Let us accept on faith and simply say—I want you to join with me in saying— What shall we say, brother?" He pointed the drumstick at me and went on. "Let me tell you. We will say, and I for one am proud to say—and I want you to say with me, on your knees, brother. Let no man be ashamed to kneel here in the great out-of-doors. Remember the woods were God's first temples. Let us kneel and say: 'Don't eat that Lady—that's Mencken.'"

"Here," I said. "Utilize a little of this."

We uncorked the other bottle.

"What's the matter?" I said. "Didn't you like Bryan?"

"I loved Bryan," said Bill. "We were like brothers."

"Where did you know him?"

"He and Mencken and I all went to Holy Cross together."

"And Frankie Frisch."

"It's a lie. Frankie Frisch went to Fordham."

"Well," I said, "I went to Loyola with Bishop Manning."

"It's a lie," Bill said. "I went to Loyola with Bishop Manning myself."

"You're cock-eyed," I said.

"On wine?"

"Why not?"

"It's the humidity," Bill said. "They ought to take this damn humidity away."

"Have another shot."

"Is this all we've got?"

"Only the two bottles."

"Do you know what you are?" Bill looked at the bottle affectionately.

"No," I said.

"You're in the pay of the Anti-Saloon League."

"I went to Notre Dame with Wayne B. Wheeler."

"It's a lie," said Bill. "I went to Austin Business College with Wayne B. Wheeler. He was class president."

"Well," I said, "the saloon must go."

"You're right there, old classmate," Bill said. "The saloon must go, and I will take it with me."

"You're cock-eyed."

"On wine?"

"On wine."

"Well, maybe I am."

"Want to take a nap?"

"All right."

We lay with our heads in the shade and looked up into the trees.

"You asleep?"

"No," Bill said. "I was thinking."

I shut my eyes. It felt good lying on the ground.

"Say," Bill said, "what about this Brett business?"

"What about it?"

"Were you ever in love with her?"

"Sure."

"For how long?"

"Off and on for a hell of a long time."

"Oh, hell!" Bill said. "I'm sorry, fella."

"It's all right," I said. "I don't give a damn any more."

"Really?"

"Really. Only I'd a hell of a lot rather not talk about it."

"You aren't sore I asked you?"

"Why the hell should I be?"

"I'm going to sleep," Bill said. He put a newspaper over his face.

"Listen, Jake," he said, "are you really a Catholic?"

"Technically."

"What does that mean?"

"I don't know."

"All right, I'll go to sleep now," he said. "Don't keep me awake by talking so much."

I went to sleep, too. When I woke up Bill was packing the rucksack. It was late in the afternoon and the shadow from the trees was long and went out over the dam. I was stiff from sleeping on the ground.

"What did you do? Wake up?" Bill asked. "Why didn't you spend the night?" I stretched and rubbed my eyes.

"I had a lovely dream," Bill said. "I don't remember what it was about, but it was a lovely dream."

"I don't think I dreamt."

"You ought to dream," Bill said. "All our biggest business men have been dreamers. Look at Ford. Look at President Coolidge. Look at Rockefeller. Look at Jo Davidson."

I disjointed my rod and Bill's and packed them in the rod-case. I put the reels in the tackle-bag. Bill had packed the rucksack and we put one of the trout-bags in. I carried the other.

"Well," said Bill, "have we got everything?"

"The worms."

"Your worms. Put them in there."

He had the pack on his back and I put the worm-cans in one of the outside flap pockets.

"You got everything now?"

I looked around on the grass at the foot of the elm-trees.

"Yes."

We started up the road into the woods. It was a long walk home to Burguete, and it was dark when we came down across the fields to the road, and along the road between the houses of the town, their windows lighted, to the inn.

We stayed five days at Burguete and had good fishing. The nights were cold and the days were hot, and there was always a breeze even in the heat of the day. It was hot enough so that it felt good to wade in a cold stream, and the sun dried you when you came out and sat on the bank. We found a stream with a pool deep enough to swim in. In the evenings we played three-handed bridge with an Englishman named Harris, who had walked over from Saint Jean Pied de Port and was stopping at the inn for the fishing. He was very pleasant and went with us twice to the Irati River. There was no word from Robert Cohn nor from Brett and Mike.

CHAPTER XIII

ONE morning I went down to breakfast and the Englishman, Harris, was already at the table. He was reading the paper through spectacles. He looked up and smiled.

"Good morning," he said. "Letter for you. I stopped at the post and they gave it me with mine."

The letter was at my place at the table, leaning against a coffee-cup. Harris was reading the paper again. I opened the letter. It had been forwarded from Pamplona. It was dated San Sebastian, Sunday:

Dear Jake,

We got here Friday, Brett passed out on the train, so brought her here for 3 days' rest with old friends of ours. We go to Montoya Hotel Pamplona Tuesday, arriving at I don't know what hour. Will you send a note by the bus to tell us what to do to rejoin you all on Wednesday. All our love and sorry to be late, but Brett was really done in and will be quite all right by Tues. and is practically so now. I know her so well and try to look after her but its not so easy. Love to all the chaps,

Michael.

"What day of the week is it?" I asked Harris.

"Wednesday, I think. Yes, quite. Wednesday. Wonderful how one loses track of the days up here in the mountains."

"Yes. We've been here nearly a week."

"I hope you're not thinking of leaving?"

"Yes. We'll go in on the afternoon bus, I'm afraid."

"What a rotten business. I had hoped we'd all have another go at the Irati together."

"We have to go into Pamplona. We're meeting people there."

"What rotten luck for me. We've had a jolly time here at Burguete."

"Come on in to Pamplona. We can play some bridge there, and there's going to be a damned fine fiesta."

"I'd like to. Awfully nice of you to ask me. I'd best stop on here, though. I've not much more time to fish."

"You want those big ones in the Irati."

"I say, I do, you know. They're enormous trout there."

"I'd like to try them once more."

"Do. Stop over another day. Be a good chap."

"We really have to get into town," I said.

"What a pity."

After breakfast Bill and I were sitting warming in the sun on a bench out in front of the inn and talking it over. I saw a girl coming up the road from the centre of the town. She stopped in front of us and took a telegram out of the leather wallet that hung against her skirt.

"Por ustedes?"

I looked at it. The address was: "Barnes, Burguete."

"Yes. It's for us."

She brought out a book for me to sign, and I gave her a couple of coppers. The telegram was in Spanish: "Vengo jueves Cohn."

I handed it to Bill.

"What does the word Cohn mean?" he asked.

"What a lousy telegram!" I said. "He could send ten words for the same price. 'I come Thursday'. That gives you a lot of dope, doesn't it?"

"It gives you all the dope that's of interest to Cohn."

"We're going in, anyway," I said. "There's no use trying to move Brett and Mike out here and back before the fiesta. Should we answer it?"

"We might as well," said Bill. "There's no need for us to be snooty."

We walked up to the post-office and asked for a telegraph blank.

"What will we say?" Bill asked.

" 'Arriving to-night.' That's enough."

We paid for the message and walked back to the inn. Harris was there and the three of us walked up to Roncevalles. We went through the monastery.

"It's a remarkable place," Harris said, when we came out. "But you know I'm not much on those sort of places."

"Me either," Bill said.

"It's a remarkable place, though," Harris said. "I wouldn't not have seen it. I'd been intending coming up each day."

"It isn't the same as fishing, though, is it?" Bill asked. He liked Harris.

"I say not."

We were standing in front of the old chapel of the monastery.

"Isn't that a pub across the way?" Harris asked. "Or do my eyes deceive me?"

"It has the look of a pub," Bill said.

"It looks to me like a pub," I said.

"I say," said Harris, "let's utilize it." He had taken up utilizing from Bill.

We had a bottle of wine apiece. Harris would not let us pay. He talked Spanish quite well, and the inn-keeper would not take our money.

"I say. You don't know what it's meant to me to have you chaps up here."

"We've had a grand time, Harris."

Harris was a little tight.

"I say. Really you don't know how much it means. I've not had much fun since the war."

"We'll fish together again, some time. Don't you forget it, Harris."

"We must. We *have* had such a jolly good time."

"How about another bottle around?"

"Jolly good idea," said Harris.

"This is mine," said Bill. "Or we don't drink it."

"I wish you'd let me pay for it. It *does* give me pleasure, you know."

"This is going to give me pleasure," Bill said.

The innkeeper brought in the fourth bottle. We had kept the same glasses. Harris lifted his glass.

"I say. You know this does utilize well."

Bill slapped him on the back.

"Good old Harris."

"I say. You know my name isn't really Harris. It's Wilson-Harris. All one name. With a hyphen, you know."

"Good old Wilson-Harris," Bill said. "We call you Harris because we're so fond of you."

"I say, Barnes. You don't know what this all means to me."

"Come on and utilize another glass," I said.

"Barnes. Really, Barnes, you can't know. That's all."

"Drink up, Harris."

We walked back down the road from Roncevalles with Harris between us. We had lunch at the inn and Harris went with us to the bus. He gave us his card, with his address in London and his club and his business address, and as we got on the bus he handed us each an envelope. I opened mine and there were a dozen flies in it. Harris had tied them himself. He tied all his own flies.

"I say, Harris—" I began.

"No, no!" he said. He was climbing down from the bus. "They're not first-rate flies at all. I only thought if you fished them some time it might remind you of what a good time we had."

The bus started. Harris stood in front of the post-office. He waved. As we started along the road he turned and walked back toward the inn.

"Say, wasn't that Harris nice?" Bill said.

"I think he really did have a good time."

"Harris? You bet he did."

"I wish he'd come into Pamplona."

"He wanted to fish."

"Yes. You couldn't tell how English would mix with each other, anyway."

"I suppose not."

We got into Pamplona late in the afternoon and the
bus stopped in front of the Hotel Montoya. Out in the
plaza they were stringing electric-light wires to light
the plaza for the fiesta. A few kids came up when the
bus stopped, and a custom officer for the town made all
the people getting down from the bus open their bundles
on the sidewalk. We went into the hotel and on the
stairs I met Montoya. He shook hands with us, smiling
in his embarrassed way.

"Your friends are here," he said.

"Mr. Campbell?"

"Yes. Mr. Cohn and Mr. Campbell and Lady Ashley."

He smiled as though there were something I would
hear about.

"When did they get in?"

"Yesterday. I've saved you the rooms you had."

"That's fine. Did you give Mr. Campbell the room on
the plaza?"

"Yes. All the rooms we looked at."

"Where are our friends now?"

"I think they went to the pelota."

"And how about the bulls?"

Montoya smiled. "To-night," he said. "To-night at
seven o'clock they bring in the Villar bulls, and to-morrow come the Miuras. Do you all go down?"

"Oh, yes. They've never seen a desencajonada."

Montoya put his hand on my shoulder.

"I'll see you there."

He smiled again. He always smiled as though bull-
fighting were a very special secret between the two of
us; a rather shocking but really very deep secret that
we knew about. He always smiled as though there were
something lewd about the secret to outsiders, but that

it was something that we understood. It would not do to expose it to people who would not understand.

"Your friend, is he aficionado, too?" Montoya smiled at Bill.

"Yes. He came all the way from New York to see the San Fermines."

"Yes?" Montoya politely disbelieved. "But he's not aficionado like you."

He put his hand on my shoulder again embarrassedly.

"Yes," I said. "He's a real aficionado."

"But he's not aficionado like you are."

Aficion means passion. An aficionado is one who is passionate about the bull-fights. All the good bull-fighters stayed at Montoya's hotel; that is, those with aficion stayed there. The commercial bull-fighters stayed once, perhaps, and then did not come back. The good ones came each year. In Montoya's room were their photographs. The photographs were dedicated to Juanito Montoya or to his sister. The photographs of bull-fighters Montoya had really believed in were framed. Photographs of bull-fighters who had been without aficion Montoya kept in a drawer of his desk. They often had the most flattering inscriptions. But they did not mean anything. One day Montoya took them all out and dropped them in the waste-basket. He did not want them around.

We often talked about bulls and bull-fighters. I had stopped at the Montoya for several years. We never talked for very long at a time. It was simply the pleasure of discovering what we each felt. Men would come in from distant towns and before they left Pamplona stop and talk for a few minutes with Montoya about bulls. These men were aficionados. Those who were aficionados could always get rooms even when the hotel was full. Montoya introduced me to some of them. They were always very polite at first, and it amused them very much that I should be an American. Somehow it was taken for granted that an American could not have aficion. He might simulate it or confuse it with excitement, but he could not really have it. When they saw that I had aficion, and there was no password, no set questions that could bring it out, rather it was a sort of oral spiritual examination with the questions always a little on the defensive and never apparent, there was this same embarrassed putting the hand on the shoulder, or a "Buen hombre." But nearly always there was the actual touching. It seemed as though they wanted to touch you to make it certain.

Montoya could forgive anything of a bull-fighter who had aficion. He could forgive attacks of nerves, panic, bad unexplainable actions, all sorts of lapses. For one who had aficion he could forgive anything. At once he forgave me all my friends. Without his ever saying anything they were simply a little something shameful between us, like the spilling open of the horses in bull-fighting.

Bill had gone up-stairs as we came in, and I found him washing and changing in his room.

"Well," he said, "talk a lot of Spanish?"

"He was telling me about the bulls coming in to-night."

"Let's find the gang and go down."

"All right. They'll probably be at the café."

"Have you got tickets?"

"Yes. I got them for all the unloadings."

"What's it like?" He was pulling his cheek before the glass, looking to see if there were unshaved patches under the line of the jaw.

"It's pretty good," I said. "They let the bulls out of the cages one at a time, and they have steers in the corral to receive them and keep them from fighting, and the bulls tear in at the steers and the steers run around like old maids trying to quiet them down."

"Do they ever gore the steers?"

"Sure. Sometimes they go right after them and kill them."

"Can't the steers do anything?"

"No. They're trying to make friends."

"What do they have them in for?"

"To quiet down the bulls and keep them from breaking their horns against the stone walls, or goring each other."

"Must be swell being a steer."

We went down the stairs and out of the door and walked across the square toward the Café Iruña. There were two lonely looking ticket-houses standing in the square. Their windows, marked SOL, SOL Y SOMBRA, and SOMBRA, were shut. They would not open until the day before the fiesta.

Across the square the white wicker tables and chairs of the Iruña extended out beyond the arcade to the edge of the street. I looked for Brett and Mike at the tables. There they were. Brett and Mike and Robert Cohn. Brett was wearing a Basque beret. So was Mike. Robert Cohn was bare-headed and wearing his spectacles. Brett saw us coming and waved. Her eyes crinkled up as we came up to the table.

"Hello, you chaps!" she called.

Brett was happy. Mike had a way of getting an intensity of feeling into shaking hands. Robert Cohn shook hands because we were back.

"Where the hell have you been?" I asked.

"I brought them up here," Cohn said.

"What rot," Brett said. "We'd have gotten here earlier if you hadn't come."

"You'd never have gotten here."

"What rot! You chaps are brown. Look at Bill."

"Did you get good fishing?" Mike asked. "We wanted to join you."

"It wasn't bad. We missed you."

"I wanted to come," Cohn said, "but I thought I ought to bring them."

"You bring us. What rot."

"Was it really good?" Mike asked. "Did you take many?"

"Some days we took a dozen apiece. There was an Englishman up there."

"Named Harris," Bill said. "Ever know him, Mike? He was in the war, too."

"Fortunate fellow," Mike said. "What times we had. How I wish those dear days were back."

"Don't be an ass."

"Were you in the war, Mike?" Cohn asked.

"Was I not."

"He was a very distinguished soldier," Brett said. "Tell them about the time your horse bolted down Piccadilly."

"I'll not. I've told that four times."

"You never told me," Robert Cohn said.

"I'll not tell that story. It reflects discredit on me."

"Tell them about your medals."

"I'll not. That story reflects great discredit on me."

"What story's that?"

"Brett will tell you. She tells all the stories that reflect discredit on me."

"Go on. Tell it, Brett."

"Should I?"

"I'll tell it myself."

"What medals have you got, Mike?"

"I haven't got any medals."

"You must have some."

"I suppose I've the usual medals. But I never sent in for them. One time there was this wopping big dinner and the Prince of Wales was to be there, and the cards said medals will be worn. So naturally I had no medals, and I stopped at my tailor's and he was impressed by the invitation, and I thought that's a good piece of business, and I said to him: 'You've got to fix me up with some medals.' He said: 'What medals, sir?' And I said: 'Oh, any medals. Just give me a few medals.' So he said: 'What medals *have* you, sir?' And I said: 'How should I know?' Did he think I spent all my time reading the bloody gazette? 'Just give me a good lot. Pick them out yourself.' So he got me some medals, you know, miniature medals, and handed me the box, and I put it in my pocket and forgot it. Well, I went to the dinner, and it was the night they'd shot Henry Wilson, so the Prince didn't come and the King didn't come, and no one wore any medals, and all these coves were busy taking off their medals, and I had mine in my pocket."

He stopped for us to laugh.

"Is that all?"

"That's all. Perhaps I didn't tell it right."

"You didn't," said Brett. "But no matter."

We were all laughing.

"Ah, yes," said Mike. "I know now. It was a damn dull dinner, and I couldn't stick it, so I left. Later on in the evening I found the box in my pocket. What's this? I said. Medals? Bloody military medals? So I cut them all off their backing—you know, they put them on a strip—and gave them all around. Gave one to each girl. Form of souvenir. They thought I was hell's own shakes of a soldier. Give away medals in a night club. Dashing fellow."

"Tell the rest," Brett said.

"Don't you think that was funny?" Mike asked. We were all laughing. "It was. I swear it was. Any rate, my tailor wrote me and wanted the medals back. Sent a man around. Kept on writing for months. Seems some chap had left them to be cleaned. Frightfully military cove. Set hell's own store by them." Mike paused. "Rotten luck for the tailor," he said.

"You don't mean it," Bill said. "I should think it would have been grand for the tailor."

"Frightfully good tailor. Never believe it to see me now," Mike said. "I used to pay him a hundred pounds a year just to keep him quiet. So he wouldn't send me any bills. Frightful blow to him when I went bankrupt. It was right after the medals. Gave his letters rather a bitter tone."

"How did you go bankrupt?" Bill asked.

"Two ways," Mike said. "Gradually and then suddenly."

"What brought it on?"

"Friends," said Mike. "I had a lot of friends. False friends. Then I had creditors, too. Probably had more creditors than anybody in England."

"Tell them about in the court," Brett said.

"I don't remember," Mike said. "I was just a little tight."

"Tight!" Brett exclaimed. "You were blind!"

"Extraordinary thing," Mike said. "Met my former partner the other day. Offered to buy me a drink."

"Tell them about your learned counsel," Brett said.

"I will not," Mike said. "My learned counsel was blind, too. I say this is a gloomy subject. Are we going down and see these bulls unloaded or not?"

"Let's go down."

We called the waiter, paid, and started to walk through the town. I started off walking with Brett, but Robert Cohn came up and joined her on the other side. The three of us walked along, past the Ayuntamiento with the banners hung from the balcony, down past the market and down past the steep street that led to the bridge across the Arga. There were many people walking to go and see the bulls, and carriages drove down the hill and across the bridge, the drivers, the horses, and the whips rising above the walking people in the street. Across the bridge we turned up a road to the corrals. We passed a wine-shop with a sign in the window: Good Wine 30 Centimes A Liter.

"That's where we'll go when funds get low," Brett said.

The woman standing in the door of the wine-shop looked at us as we passed. She called to some one in the house and three girls came to the window and stared. They were staring at Brett.

At the gate of the corrals two men took tickets from the people that went in. We went in through the gate. There were trees inside and a low, stone house. At the far end was the stone wall of the corrals, with apertures in the stone that were like loopholes running all along the face of each corral. A ladder led up to the top of the wall, and people were climbing up the ladder and spreading down to stand on the walls that separated the two corrals. As we came up the ladder, walking across the grass under the trees, we passed the big, gray painted cages with the bulls in them. There was one bull in each travelling-box. They had come by train from a bull-breeding ranch in Castile, and had been unloaded off flat-cars at the station and brought up here to be let out of their cages into the corrals. Each cage was stencilled with the name and the brand of the bullbreeder.

We climbed up and found a place on the wall looking down into the corral. The stone walls were whitewashed, and there was straw on the ground and wooden feedboxes and water-troughs set against the wall.

"Look up there," I said.

Beyond the river rose the plateau of the town. All along the old walls and ramparts people were standing. The three lines of fortifications made three black lines of people. Above the walls there were heads in the windows of the houses. At the far end of the plateau boys had climbed into the trees.

"They must think something is going to happen," Brett said.

"They want to see the bulls."

Mike and Bill were on the other wall across the pit of the corral. They waved to us. People who had come late were standing behind us, pressing against us when other people crowded them.

"Why don't they start?" Robert Cohn asked.

A single mule was hitched to one of the cages and dragged it up against the gate in the corral wall. The men shoved and lifted it with crowbars into position against the gate. Men were standing on the wall ready to pull up the gate of the corral and then the gate of the cage. At the other end of the corral a gate opened and two steers came in, swaying their heads and trotting, their lean flanks swinging. They stood together at the far end, their heads toward the gate where the bull would enter.

"They don't look happy," Brett said.

The men on top of the wall leaned back and pulled up the door of the corral. Then they pulled up the door of the cage.

I leaned way over the wall and tried to see into the cage. It was dark. Some one rapped on the cage with an iron bar. Inside something seemed to explode. The bull, striking into the wood from side to side with his horns, made a great noise. Then I saw a dark muzzle and the shadow of horns, and then, with a clattering on the wood in the hollow box, the bull charged and came out into the corral, skidding with his forefeet in the straw as he stopped, his head up, the great hump of muscle on his neck swollen tight, his body muscles quivering as he looked up at the crowd on the stone walls. The two steers backed away against the wall, their heads sunken, their eyes watching the bull.

The bull saw them and charged. A man shouted from behind one of the boxes and slapped his hat against the planks, and the bull, before he reached the steer, turned, gathered himself and charged where the man had been, trying to reach him behind the planks with a half-dozen quick, searching drives with the right horn.

"My God, isn't he beautiful?" Brett said. We were looking right down on him.

"Look how he knows how to use his horns," I said. "He's got a left and a right just like a boxer."

"Not really?"

"You watch."

"It goes too fast."

"Wait. There'll be another one in a minute."

They had backed up another cage into the entrance. In the far corner a man, from behind one of the plank shelters, attracted the bull, and while the bull was facing away the gate was pulled up and a second bull came out into the corral.

He charged straight for the steers and two men ran out from behind the planks and shouted, to turn him. He did not change his direction and the men shouted: "Hah! Hah! Toro!" and waved their arms; the two steers turned sideways to take the shock, and the bull drove into one of the steers.

"Don't look," I said to Brett. She was watching, fascinated.

"Fine," I said. "If it doesn't buck you."

"I saw it," she said. "I saw him shift from his left to his right horn."

"Damn good!"

The steer was down now, his neck stretched out, his head twisted, he lay the way he had fallen. Suddenly the bull left off and made for the other steer which had been standing at the far end, his head swinging, watching it all. The steer ran awkwardly and the bull caught him, hooked him lightly in the flank, and then turned away and looked up at the crowd on the walls, his crest of muscle rising. The steer came up to him and made as though to nose at him and the bull hooked perfunctorily. The next time he nosed at the steer and then the two of them trotted over to the other bull.

When the next bull came out, all three, the two bulls and the steer, stood together, their heads side by side, their horns against the newcomer. In a few minutes the steer picked the new bull up, quieted him down, and made him one of the herd. When the last two bulls had been unloaded the herd were all together.

The steer who had been gored had gotten to his feet and stood against the stone wall. None of the bulls came near him, and he did not attempt to join the herd.

We climbed down from the wall with the crowd, and

had a last look at the bulls through the loopholes in the wall of the corral. They were all quiet now, their heads down. We got a carriage outside and rode up to the café. Mike and Bill came in half an hour later. They had stopped on the way for several drinks.

We were sitting in the café.

"That's an extraordinary business," Brett said.

"Will those last ones fight as well as the first?" Robert Cohn asked. "They seemed to quiet down awfully fast.".

"They all know each other," I said. "They're only dangerous when they're alone, or only two or three of them together."

"What do you mean, dangerous?" Bill said. "They all looked dangerous to me."

"They only want to kill when they're alone. Of course, if you went in there you'd probably detach one of them from the herd, and he'd be dangerous."

"That's too complicated," Bill said. "Don't you ever detach me from the herd, Mike."

"I say," Mike said, "they *were* fine bulls, weren't they? Did you see their horns?"

"Did I not," said Brett. "I had no idea what they were like."

"Did you see the one hit that steer?" Mike asked. "That was extraordinary."

"It's no life being a steer," Robert Cohn said.

"Don't you think so?" Mike said. "I would have thought you'd loved being a steer, Robert."

"What do you mean, Mike?"

"They lead such a quiet life. They never say anything and they're always hanging about so."

We were embarrassed. Bill laughed. Robert Cohn was angry. Mike went on talking.

"I should think you'd love it. You'd never have to

say a word. Come on, Robert. Do say something. Don't just sit there."

"I said something, Mike. Don't you remember? About the steers."

"Oh, say something more. Say something funny. Can't you see we're all having a good time here?"

"Come off it, Michael. You're drunk," Brett said.

"I'm not drunk. I'm quite serious. *Is* Robert Cohn going to follow Brett around like a steer all the time?"

"Shut up, Michael. Try and show a little breeding."

"Breeding be damned. Who has any breeding, anyway, except the bulls? Aren't the bulls lovely? Don't you like them, Bill? Why don't you say something, Robert? Don't sit there looking like a bloody funeral. What if Brett did sleep with you? She's slept with lots of better people than you."

"Shut up," Cohn said. He stood up. "Shut up, Mike."

"Oh, don't stand up and act as though you were going to hit me. That won't make any difference to me. Tell me, Robert. Why do you follow Brett around like a poor bloody steer? Don't you know you're not wanted? I know when I'm not wanted. Why don't you know when you're not wanted? You came down to San Sebastian where you weren't wanted, and followed Brett around like a bloody steer. Do you think that's right?"

"Shut up. You're drunk."

"Perhaps I am drunk. Why aren't you drunk? Why don't you ever get drunk, Robert? You know you didn't have a good time at San Sebastian because none of our friends would invite you on any of the parties. You can't blame them hardly. Can you? I asked them to. They wouldn't do it. You can't blame them, now. Can you? Now, answer me. Can you blame them?"

"Go to hell, Mike."

"I can't blame them. Can you blame them? Why

do you follow Brett around? Haven't you any manners? How do you think it makes *me* feel?"

"You're a splendid one to talk about manners," Brett said. "You've such lovely manners."

"Come on, Robert," Bill said.

"What do you follow her around for?"

Bill stood up and took hold of Cohn.

"Don't go," Mike said. "Robert Cohn's going to buy a drink."

Bill went off with Cohn. Cohn's face was sallow. Mike went on talking. I sat and listened for a while. Brett looked disgusted.

"I say, Michael, you might not be such a bloody ass," she interrupted. "I'm not saying he's not right, you know." She turned to me.

The emotion left Mike's voice. We were all friends together.

"I'm not so damn drunk as I sounded," he said.

"I know you're not," Brett said.

"We're none of us sober," I said.

"I didn't say anything I didn't mean."

"But you put it so badly," Brett laughed.

"He was an ass, though. He came down to San Sebastian where he damn well wasn't wanted. He hung around Brett and just *looked* at her. It made me damned well sick."

"He did behave very badly," Brett said.

"Mark you. Brett's had affairs with men before. She tells me all about everything. She gave me this chap Cohn's letters to read. I wouldn't read them."

"Damned noble of you."

"No, listen, Jake. Brett's gone off with men. But they weren't ever Jews, and they didn't come and hang about afterward."

"Damned good chaps," Brett said. "It's all rot to

talk about it. Michael and I understand each other."

"She gave me Robert Cohn's letters. I wouldn't read them."

"You wouldn't read any letters, darling. You wouldn't read mine."

"I can't read letters," Mike said. "Funny, isn't it?"

"You can't read anything."

"No. You're wrong there. I read quite a bit. I read when I'm at home."

"You'll be writing next," Brett said. "Come on, Michael. Do buck up. You've got to go through with this thing now. He's here. Don't spoil the fiesta."

"Well, let him behave, then."

"He'll behave. I'll tell him."

"You tell him, Jake. Tell him either he must behave or get out."

"Yes," I said, "it would be nice for me to tell him."

"Look, Brett. Tell Jake what Robert calls you. That *is* perfect, you know."

"Oh, no. I can't."

"Go on. We're all friends. Aren't we all friends, Jake?"

"I can't tell him. It's too ridiculous."

"I'll tell him."

"You won't, Michael. Don't be an ass."

"He calls her Circe," Mike said. "He claims she turns men into swine. Damn good. I wish I were one of these literary chaps."

"He'd be good, you know," Brett said. "He writes a good letter."

"I know," I said. "He wrote me from San Sebastian."

"That was nothing," Brett said. "He can write a damned amusing letter."

"She made me write that. She was supposed to be ill."

"I damned well was, too."

"Come on," I said, "we must go in and eat."

"How should I meet Cohn?" Mike said.

"Just act as though nothing had happened."

"It's quite all right with me," Mike said. "I'm not embarrassed."

"If he says anything, just say you were tight."

"Quite. And the funny thing is I think I was tight."

"Come on," Brett said. "Are these poisonous things paid for? I must bathe before dinner."

We walked across the square. It was dark and all around the square were the lights from the cafés under the arcades. We walked across the gravel under the trees to the hotel.

They went up-stairs and I stopped to speak with Montoya.

"Well, how did you like the bulls?" he asked.

"Good. They were nice bulls."

"They're all right"—Montoya shook his head—"but they're not too good."

"What didn't you like about them?"

"I don't know. They just didn't give me the feeling that they were so good."

"I know what you mean."

"They're all right."

"Yes. They're all right."

"How did your friends like them?"

"Fine."

"Good," Montoya said.

I went up-stairs. Bill was in his room standing on the balcony looking out at the square. I stood beside him.

"Where's Cohn?"

"Up-stairs in his room."

"How does he feel?"

"Like hell, naturally. Mike was awful. He's terrible when he's tight."

"He wasn't so tight."

"The hell he wasn't. I know what we had before we came to the café."

"He sobered up afterward."

"Good. He was terrible. I don't like Cohn, God knows, and I think it was a silly trick for him to go down to San Sebastian, but nobody has any business to talk like Mike."

"How'd you like the bulls?"

"Grand. It's grand the way they bring them out."

"To-morrow come the Miuras."

"When does the fiesta start?"

"Day after to-morrow."

"We've got to keep Mike from getting so tight. That kind of stuff is terrible."

"We'd better get cleaned up for supper."

"Yes. That will be a pleasant meal."

"Won't it?"

As a matter of fact, supper was a pleasant meal. Brett wore a black, sleeveless evening dress. She looked quite beautiful. Mike acted as though nothing had happened. I had to go up and bring Robert Cohn down. He was reserved and formal, and his face was still taut and sallow, but he cheered up finally. He could not stop looking at Brett. It seemed to make him happy. It must have been pleasant for him to see her looking so lovely and know he had been away with her and that every one knew it. They could not take that away from him. Bill was very funny. So was Michael. They were good together.

It was like certain dinners I remember from the war. There was much wine, an ignored tension, and a feeling of things coming that you could not prevent happening. Under the wine I lost the disgusted feeling and was happy. It seemed they were all such nice people.

CHAPTER XIV

I DO not know what time I got to bed. I remember undressing, putting on a bathrobe, and standing out on the balcony. I knew I was quite drunk, and when I came in I put on the light over the head of the bed and started to read. I was reading a book by Turgenieff. Probably I read the same two pages over several times. It was one of the stories in *A Sportsman's Sketches*. I had read it before, but it seemed quite new. The country became very clear and the feeling of pressure in my head seemed to loosen. I was very drunk and I did not want to shut my eyes because the room would go round and round. If I kept on reading that feeling would pass.

I heard Brett and Robert Cohn come up the stairs. Cohn said good night outside the door and went on up to his room. I heard Brett go into the room next door. Mike was already in bed. He had come in with me an hour before. He woke as she came in, and they talked together. I heard them laugh. I turned off the light and tried to go to sleep. It was not necessary to read any more. I could shut my eyes without getting the wheeling sensation. But I could not sleep. There is no reason why because it is dark you should look at things differently from when it is light. The hell there isn't!

I figured that all out once, and for six months I never slept with the electric light off. That was another bright idea. To hell with women, anyway. To hell with you, Brett Ashley.

Women made such swell friends. Awfully swell. In the first place, you had to be in love with a woman to have a basis of friendship. I had been having Brett for a friend. I had not been thinking about her side of it. I had been getting something for nothing. That only delayed the presentation of the bill. The bill always came. That was one of the swell things you could count on.

I thought I had paid for everything. Not like the woman pays and pays and pays. No idea of retribution or punishment. Just exchange of values. You gave up something and got something else. Or you worked for something. You paid some way for everything that was any good. I paid my way into enough things that I liked, so that I had a good time. Either you paid by learning about them, or by experience, or by taking chances, or by money. Enjoying living was learning to get your money's worth and knowing when you had it. You could get your money's worth. The world was a good place to buy in. It seemed like a fine philosophy. In five years, I thought, it will seem just as silly as all the other fine philosophies I've had.

Perhaps that wasn't true, though. Perhaps as you went along you did learn something. I did not care what it was all about. All I wanted to know was how to live in it. Maybe if you found out how to live in it you learned from that what it was all about.

I wished Mike would not behave so terribly to Cohn, though. Mike was a bad drunk. Brett was a good drunk. Bill was a good drunk. Cohn was never drunk. Mike was unpleasant after he passed a certain point. I liked to see him hurt Cohn. I wished he would not do it, though, because afterward it made me disgusted at myself. That was morality; things that made you disgusted afterward. No, that must be immorality. That was a large statement. What a lot of bilge I could think up at night. What rot, I could hear Brett say it. What rot! When you were with English you got into the habit of using English expressions in your thinking. The English spoken language—the upper classes, anyway—

must have fewer words than the Eskimo. Of course I
didn't know anything about the Eskimo. Maybe the
Eskimo was a fine language. Say the Cherokee. I didn't
know anything about the Cherokee, either. The English
talked with inflected phrases. One phrase to mean everything. I like them, though. I liked the way they talked.
Take Harris. Still Harris was not the upper classes.

I turned on the light again and read. I read the Turgenieff. I knew that now, reading it in the oversensi-
tized state of mind after much too much brandy, I
would remember it somewhere, and afterward it would
seem as though it had really happened to me. I would
always have it. That was another good thing you paid
for and then had. Some time along toward daylight I
went to sleep.

The next two days in Pamplona were quiet, and there
were no more rows. The town was getting ready for the
fiesta. Workmen put up the gate-posts that were to
shut off the side streets when the bulls were released
from the corrals and came running through the streets
in the morning on their way to the ring. The workmen
dug holes and fitted in the timbers, each timber num-
bered for its regular place. Out on the plateau beyond
the town employees of the bull-ring exercised picador
horses, galloping them stiff-legged on the hard, sun-baked
fields behind the bull-ring. The big gate of the bull-ring
was open, and inside the amphitheatre was being swept.
The ring was rolled and sprinkled, and carpenters replaced weakened or cracked planks in the barrera.
Standing at the edge of the smooth rolled sand you could
look up in the empty stands and see old women sweeping
out the boxes.

Outside, the fence that led from the last street of the
town to the entrance of the bull-ring was already in

place and made a long pen; the crowd would come running down with the bulls behind them on the morning of the day of the first bull-fight. Out across the plain, where the horse and cattle fair would be, some gypsies had camped under the trees. The wine and aguardiente sellers were putting up their booths. One booth advertised ANIS DEL TORO. The cloth sign hung against the planks in the hot sun. In the big square that was the centre of the town there was no change yet. We sat in the white wicker chairs on the terrasse of the café and watched the motor-buses come in and unload peasants from the country coming in to the market, and we watched the buses fill up and start out with peasants sitting with their saddle-bags full of the things they had bought in the town. The tall gray motor-buses were the only life of the square except for the pigeons and the man with a hose who sprinkled the gravelled square and watered the streets.

In the evening was the paseo. For an hour after dinner every one, all the good-looking girls, the officers from the garrison, all the fashionable people of the town, walked in the street on one side of the square while the café tables filled with the regular after-dinner crowd.

During the morning I usually sat in the café and read the Madrid papers and then walked in the town or out into the country. Sometimes Bill went along. Sometimes he wrote in his room. Robert Cohn spent the mornings studying Spanish or trying to get a shave at the barber-shop. Brett and Mike never got up until noon. We all had a vermouth at the café. It was a quiet life and no one was drunk. I went to church a couple of times, once with Brett. She said she wanted to hear me go to confession, but I told her that not only was it impossible but it was not as interesting as it sounded, and, besides, it would be in a language she did not know. We met Cohn as we came out of church, and although it was obvious he had followed us, yet he was very pleasant and nice, and we all three went for a walk out to the gypsy camp, and Brett had her fortune told.

It was a good morning, there were high white clouds above the mountains. It had rained a little in the night and it was fresh and cool on the plateau, and there was a wonderful view. We all felt good and we felt healthy, and 1 felt quite friendly to Cohn. You could not be upset about anything on a day like that.

That was the last day before the fiesta.

CHAPTER XV

AT noon of Sunday, the 6th of July, the fiesta exploded. There is no other way to describe it. People had been coming in all day from the country, but they were assimilated in the town and you did not notice them. The square was as quiet in the hot sun as on any other day. The peasants were in the outlying wineshops. There they were drinking, getting ready for the fiesta. They had come in so recently from the plains and the hills that it was necessary that they make their shifting in values gradually. They could not start in paying café prices. They got their money's worth in the wine-shops. Money still had a definite value in hours worked and bushels of grain sold. Late in the fiesta it would not matter what they paid, nor where they bought.

Now on the day of the starting of the fiesta of San Fermin they had been in the wine-shops of the narrow streets of the town since early morning. Going down the streets in the morning on the way to mass in the cathedral, I heard them singing through the open doors of the shops. They were warming up. There were many people at the eleven o'clock Mass. San Fermin is also a religious festival.

I walked down the hill from the cathedral and up the street to the café on the square. It was a little before noon. Robert Cohn and Bill were sitting at one of the tables. The marble-topped tables and the white wicker chairs were gone. They were replaced by cast-iron tables and severe folding chairs. The café was like a battleship stripped for action. To-day the waiters did not leave you alone all morning to read without asking if you wanted to order something. A waiter came up as soon as I sat down.

"What are you drinking?" I asked Bill and Robert.

"Sherry," Cohn said.

"Jerez," I said to the waiter.

Before the waiter brought the sherry the rocket that announced the fiesta went up in the square. It burst and there was a gray ball of smoke high up above the Theatre Gayarre, across on the other side of the plaza. The ball of smoke hung in the sky like a shrapnel burst, and as I watched, another rocket came up to it, trickling smoke in the bright sunlight. I saw the bright flash as it burst and another little cloud of smoke appeared. By the time the second rocket had burst there were so many people in the arcade, that had been empty a minute before, that the waiter, holding the bottle high up over his head, could hardly get through the crowd to our table. People were coming into the square from all sides, and down the street we heard the pipes and the fifes and the drums coming. They were playing the *riau-riau* music, the pipes shrill and the drums pounding, and behind them came the men and boys dancing. When the fifers stopped they all crouched down in the street, and when the reed-pipes and the fifes shrilled, and the flat, dry, hollow drums tapped it out again, they all went up in the air dancing. In the crowd you saw only the heads and shoulders of the dancers going up and down.

In the square a man, bent over, was playing on a reed-pipe, and a crowd of children were following him shouting, and pulling at his clothes. He came out of the square, the children following him, and piped them past the café and down a side street. We saw his blank pockmarked face as he went by, piping, the children close behind him shouting and pulling at him.

"He must be the village idiot," Bill said. "My God! look at that!"

Down the street came dancers. The street was solid with dancers, all men. They were all dancing in time behind their own fifers and drummers. They were a club of some sort, and all wore workmen's blue smocks, and red handkerchiefs around their necks, and carried a great banner on two poles. The banner danced up and down with them as they came down surrounded by the crowd.

"Hurray for Wine! Hurray for the Foreigners!" was painted on the banner.

"Where are the foreigners?" Robert Cohn asked.

"We're the foreigners," Bill said.

All the time rockets were going up. The café tables were all full now. The square was emptying of people and the crowd was filling the cafés.

"Where's Brett and Mike?" Bill asked.

"I'll go and get them," Cohn said.

"Bring them here."

The fiesta was really started. It kept up day and night for seven days. The dancing kept up, the drinking kept up, the noise went on. The things that happened could only have happened during a fiesta. Every-

thing became quite unreal finally and it seemed as
though nothing could have any consequences. It seemed
out of place to think of consequences during the fiesta.
All during the fiesta you had the feeling, even when it
was quiet, that you had to shout any remark to make it
heard. It was the same feeling about any action. It
was a fiesta and it went on for seven days.

That afternoon was the big religious procession. San
Fermin was translated from one church to another. In
the procession were all the dignitaries, civil and religious.
We could not see them because the crowd was too great.
Ahead of the formal procession and behind it danced the
riau-riau dancers. There was one mass of yellow shirts
dancing up and down in the crowd. All we could see of
the procession through the closely pressed people that
crowded all the side streets and curbs were the great
giants, cigar-store Indians, thirty feet high, Moors, a
King and Queen, whirling and waltzing solemnly to the
riau-riau.

They were all standing outside the chapel where San
Fermin and the dignitaries had passed in leaving a
guard of soldiers, the giants, with the men who danced
in them standing beside their resting frames, and the
dwarfs moving with their whacking bladders through the
crowd. We started inside and there was a smell of incense and people filing back into the church, but Brett
was stopped just inside the door because she had no
hat, so we went out again and along the street that ran
back from the chapel into town. The street was lined
on both sides with people keeping their place at the curb
for the return of the procession. Some dancers formed a
circle around Brett and started to dance. They wore
big wreaths of white garlics around their necks. They
took Bill and me by the arms and put us in the circle.
Bill started to dance, too. They were all chanting. Brett

wanted to dance but they did not want her to. They
wanted her as an image to dance around. When the
song ended with the sharp *riau-riau!* they rushed us
into a wine-shop.

We stood at the counter. They had Brett seated on
a wine-cask. It was dark in the wine-shop and full of
men singing, hard-voiced singing. Back of the counter
they drew the wine from casks. I put down money for
the wine, but one of the men picked it up and put it
back in my pocket.

"I want a leather wine-bottle," Bill said.

"There's a place down the street," I said. "I'll go
get a couple."

The dancers did not want me to go out. Three of them
were sitting on the high wine-cask beside Brett, teaching
her to drink out of the wine-skins. They had hung a
wreath of garlics around her neck. Some one insisted
on giving her a glass. Somebody was teaching Bill a
song. Singing it into his ear. Beating time on Bill's
back.

I explained to them that I would be back. Outside in
the street I went down the street looking for the shop
that made leather wine-bottles. The crowd was packed
on the sidewalks and many of the shops were shuttered,
and I could not find it. I walked as far as the church,
looking on both sides of the street. Then I asked a man
and he took me by the arm and led me to it. The shutters were up but the door was open.

Inside it smelled of fresh tanned leather and hot tar.
A man was stencilling completed wine-skins. They hung
from the roof in bunches. He took one down, blew it up,
screwed the nozzle tight, and then jumped on it.

"See! It doesn't leak."

"I want another one, too. A big one."

He took down a big one that would hold a gallon or

more, from the roof. He blew it up, his cheeks puffing ahead of the wine-skin, and stood on the bota holding on to a chair.

"What are you going to do? Sell them in Bayonne?"

"No. Drink out of them."

He slapped me on the back.

"Good man. Eight pesetas for the two. The lowest price."

The man who was stencilling the new ones and tossing them into a pile stopped.

"It's true," he said. "Eight pesetas is cheap."

I paid and went out and along the street back to the wine-shop. It was darker than ever inside and very crowded. I did not see Brett and Bill, and some one said they were in the back room. At the counter the girl filled the two wine-skins for me. One held two litres. The other held five litres. Filling them both cost three pesetas sixty céntimos. Some one at the counter, that I had never seen before, tried to pay for the wine, but I finally paid for it myself. The man who had wanted to pay then bought me a drink. He would not let me buy one in return, but said he would take a rinse of the mouth from the new wine-bag. He tipped the big six-litre bag up and squeezed it so the wine hissed against the back of his throat.

"All right," he said, and handed back the bag.

In the back room Brett and Bill were sitting on barrels surrounded by the dancers. Everybody had his arms on everybody else's shoulders, and they were all singing. Mike was sitting at a table with several men in their shirt-sleeves, eating from a bowl of tuna fish, chopped onions and vinegar. They were all drinking wine and mopping up the oil and vinegar with pieces of bread.

"Hello, Jake. Hello!" Mike called. "Come here. I want you to meet my friends. We're all having an hors-d'œuvre."

I was introduced to the people at the table. They supplied their names to Mike and sent for a fork for me.

"Stop eating their dinner, Michael," Brett shouted from the wine-barrels.

"I don't want to eat up your meal," I said when some one handed me a fork.

"Eat," he said. "What do you think it's here for?"

I unscrewed the nozzle of the big wine-bottle and handed it around. Every one took a drink, tipping the wine-skin at arm's length.

Outside, above the singing, we could hear the music of the procession going by.

"Isn't that the procession?" Mike asked.

"Nada," some one said. "It's nothing. Drink up. Lift the bottle."

"Where did they find you?" I asked Mike.

"Some one brought me here," Mike said. "They said you were here."

"Where's Cohn?"

"He's passed out," Brett called. "They've put him away somewhere."

"Where is he?"

"I don't know."

"How should we know," Bill said. "I think he's dead."

"He's not dead," Mike said. "I know he's not dead. He's just passed out on Anis del Mono."

As he said Anis del Mono one of the men at the table looked up, brought out a bottle from inside his smock, and handed it to me.

"No," I said. "No, thanks!"

"Yes. Yes. Arriba! Up with the bottle!"

I took a drink. It tasted of licorice and warmed all the way. I could feel it warming in my stomach.

"Where the hell is Cohn?"

"I don't know," Mike said. "I'll ask. Where is the drunken comrade?" he asked in Spanish.

"You want to see him?"

"Yes," I said.

"Not me," said Mike. "This gent."

The Anis del Mono man wiped his mouth and stood up.

"Come on."

In a back room Robert Cohn was sleeping quietly on some wine-casks. It was almost too dark to see his face. They had covered him with a coat and another coat was folded under his head. Around his neck and on his chest was a big wreath of twisted garlics.

"Let him sleep," the man whispered. "He's all right."

Two hours later Cohn appeared. He came into the front room still with the wreath of garlics around his neck. The Spaniards shouted when he came in. Cohn wiped his eyes and grinned.

"I must have been sleeping," he said.

"Oh, not at all," Brett said.

"You were only dead," Bill said.

"Aren't we going to go and have some supper?" Cohn asked.

"Do you want to eat?"

"Yes. Why not? I'm hungry."

"Eat those garlics, Robert," Mike said. "I say. Do eat those garlics."

Cohn stood there. His sleep had made him quite all right.

"Do let's go and eat," Brett said. "I must get a bath."

"Come on," Bill said. "Let's translate Brett to the hotel."

We said good-bye to many people and shook hands with many people and went out. Outside it was dark.

"What time is it do you suppose?" Cohn asked.

"It's to-morrow," Mike said. "You've been asleep two days."

"No," said Cohn, "what time is it?"

"It's ten o'clock."

"What a lot we've drunk."

"You mean what a lot *we've* drunk. You went to sleep."

Going down the dark streets to the hotel we saw the sky-rockets going up in the square. Down the side streets that led to the square we saw the square solid with people, those in the centre all dancing.

It was a big meal at the hotel. It was the first meal of the prices being doubled for the fiesta, and there were several new courses. After the dinner we were out in the town. I remember resolving that I would stay up all night to watch the bulls go through the streets at six o'clock in the morning, and being so sleepy that I went to bed around four o'clock. The others stayed up.

My own room was locked and I could not find the key, so I went up-stairs and slept on one of the beds in Cohn's room. The fiesta was going on outside in the night, but I was too sleepy for it to keep me awake. When I woke it was the sound of the rocket exploding that announced the release of the bulls from the corrals at the edge of town. They would race through the streets and out to the bull-ring. I had been sleeping heavily and I woke feeling I was too late. I put on a coat of Cohn's and went out on the balcony. Down below the narrow street was empty. All the balconies were crowded with people.

Suddenly a crowd came down the street. They were all running, packed close together. They passed along and up the street toward the bull-ring and behind them came more men running faster, and then some stragglers who were really running. Behind them was a little bare space, and then the bulls, galloping, tossing their heads up and down. It all went out of sight around the corner. One man fell, rolled to the gutter, and lay quiet. But the bulls went right on and did not notice him. They were all running together.

After they went out of sight a great roar came from the bull-ring. It kept on. Then finally the pop of the rocket that meant the bulls had gotten through the people in the ring and into the corrals. I went back in the room and got into bed. I had been standing on the stone balcony in bare feet. I knew our crowd must have all been out at the bull-ring. Back in bed, I went to sleep.

Cohn woke me when he came in. He started to undress and went over and closed the window because the people on the balcony of the house just across the street were looking in.

"Did you see the show?" I asked.

"Yes. We were all there."

"Anybody get hurt?"

"One of the bulls got into the crowd in the ring and tossed six or eight people."

"How did Brett like it?"

"It was all so sudden there wasn't any time for it to bother anybody."

"I wish I'd been up."

"We didn't know where you were. We went to your room but it was locked."

"Where did you stay up?"

"We danced at some club."

"I got sleepy," I said.

"My gosh! I'm sleepy now," Cohn said. "Doesn't this thing ever stop?"

"Not for a week."

Bill opened the door and put his head in.

"Where were you, Jake?"

"I saw them go through from the balcony. How was it?"

"Grand."

"Where you going?"

"To sleep."

No one was up before noon. We ate at tables set out under the arcade. The town was full of people. We had to wait for a table. After lunch we went over to the Iruña. It had filled up, and as the time for the bull-fight came it got fuller, and the tables were crowded closer. There was a close, crowded hum that came every day before the bull-fight. The café did not make this same noise at any other time, no matter how crowded it was. This hum went on, and we were in it and a part of it.

I had taken six seats for all the fights. Three of them were barreras, the first row at the ring-side, and three were sobrepuertos, seats with wooden backs, half-way up the amphitheatre. Mike thought Brett had best sit high up for her first time, and Cohn wanted to sit with them. Bill and I were going to sit in the barreras, and I gave the extra ticket to a waiter to sell. Bill said something to Cohn about what to do and how to look so he would not mind the horses. Bill had seen one season of bull-fights.

"I'm not worried about how I'll stand it. I'm only afraid I may be bored," Cohn said.

"You think so?"

"Don't look at the horses, after the bull hits them,"

I said to Brett. "Watch the charge and see the picador try and keep the bull off, but then don't look again until the horse is dead if it's been hit."

"I'm a little nervy about it," Brett said. "I'm worried whether I'll be able to go through with it all right."

"You'll be all right. There's nothing but that horse part that will bother you, and they're only in for a few minutes with each bull. Just don't watch when it's bad."

"She'll be all right," Mike said. "I'll look after her."

"I don't think you'll be bored," Bill said.

"I'm going over to the hotel to get the glasses and the wine-skin," I said. "See you back here. Don't get cock-eyed."

"I'll come along," Bill said. Brett smiled at us.

We walked around through the arcade to avoid the heat of the square.

"That Cohn gets me," Bill said. "He's got this Jewish superiority so strong that he thinks the only emotion he'll get out of the fight will be being bored."

"We'll watch him with the glasses," I said.

"Oh, to hell with him!"

"He spends a lot of time there."

"I want him to stay there."

In the hotel on the stairs we met Montoya.

"Come on," said Montoya. "Do you want to meet Pedro Romero?"

"Fine," said Bill. "Let's go see him."

We followed Montoya up a flight and down the corridor.

"He's in room number eight," Montoya explained. "He's getting dressed for the bull-fight."

Montoya knocked on the door and opened it. It was a gloomy room with a little light coming in from the window on the narrow street. There were two beds separated by a monastic partition. The electric light was on. The

boy stood very straight and unsmiling in his bull-fighting
clothes. His jacket hung over the back of a chair. They
were just finishing winding his sash. His black hair shone
under the electric light. He wore a white linen shirt and
the sword-handler finished his sash and stood up and
stepped back. Pedro Romero nodded, seeming very far
away and dignified when we shook hands. Montoya said
something about what great aficionados we were, and
that we wanted to wish him luck. Romero listened very
seriously. Then he turned to me. He was the best-looking
boy I have ever seen.

"You go to the bull-fight," he said in English.

"You know English," I said, feeling like an idiot.

"No," he answered, and smiled.

One of three men who had been sitting on the beds
came up and asked us if we spoke French. "Would you
like me to interpret for you? Is there anything you would
like to ask Pedro Romero?"

We thanked him. What was there that you would like
to ask? The boy was nineteen years old, alone except for
his sword-handler, and the three hangers-on, and the
bull-fight was to commence in twenty minutes. We
wished him "Mucha suerte," shook hands, and went out.
He was standing, straight and handsome and altogether
by himself, alone in the room with the hangers-on as we
shut the door.

"He's a fine boy, don't you think so?" Montoya asked.

"He's a good-looking kid," I said.

"He looks like a torero," Montoya said. "He has the
type."

"He's a fine boy."

"We'll see how he is in the ring," Montoya said.

We found the big leather wine-bottle leaning against
the wall in my room, took it and the field-glasses, locked
the door, and went down-stairs.

It was a good bull-fight. Bill and I were very excited about Pedro Romero. Montoya was sitting about ten places away. After Romero had killed his first bull Montoya caught my eye and nodded his head. This was a real one. There had not been a real one for a long time. Of the other two matadors, one was very fair and the other was passable. But there was no comparison with Romero, although neither of his bulls was much.

Several times during the bull-fight I looked up at Mike and Brett and Cohn, with the glasses. They seemed to be all right. Brett did not look upset. All three were leaning forward on the concrete railing in front of them.

"Let me take the glasses," Bill said.

"Does Cohn look bored?" I asked.

"That kike!"

Outside the ring, after the bull-fight was over, you could not move in the crowd. We could not make our way through but had to be moved with the whole thing, slowly, as a glacier, back to town. We had that disturbed emotional feeling that always comes after a bull-fight, and the feeling of elation that comes after a good bull-fight. The fiesta was going on. The drums pounded and the pipe music was shrill, and everywhere the flow of the crowd was broken by patches of dancers. The dancers were in a crowd, so you did not see the intricate play of the feet. All you saw was the heads and shoulders going up and down, up and down. Finally, we got out of the crowd and made for the café. The waiter saved chairs for the others, and we each ordered an absinthe and watched the crowd in the square and the dancers.

"What do you suppose that dance is?" Bill asked.

"It's a sort of jota."

"They're not all the same," Bill said. "They dance differently to all the different tunes."

"It's swell dancing."

In front of us on a clear part of the street a company
of boys were dancing. The steps were very intricate and
their faces were intent and concentrated. They all looked
down while they danced. Their rope-soled shoes tapped
and spatted on the pavement. The toes touched. The
heels touched. The balls of the feet touched. Then the
music broke wildly and the step was finished and they
were all dancing on up the street.

"Here come the gentry," Bill said.

They were crossing the street.

"Hello, men," I said.

"Hello, gents!" said Brett. "You saved us seats? How
nice."

"I say," Mike said, "that Romero what'shisname is
somebody. Am I wrong?"

"Oh, isn't he lovely," Brett said. "And those green
trousers."

"Brett never took her eyes off them."

"I say, I must borrow your glasses to-morrow."

"How did it go?"

"Wonderfully! Simply perfect. I say, it is a spectacle!"

"How about the horses?"

"I couldn't help looking at them."

"She couldn't take her eyes off them," Mike said. "She's
an extraordinary wench."

"They do have some rather awful things happen to
them," Brett said. "I couldn't look away, though."

"Did you feel all right?"

"I didn't feel badly at all."

"Robert Cohn did," Mike put in. "You were quite
green, Robert."

"The first horse did bother me," Cohn said.

"You weren't bored, were you?" asked Bill.

Cohn laughed.

"No. I wasn't bored. I wish you'd forgive me that."

"It's all right," Bill said, "so long as you weren't bored."

"He didn't look bored," Mike said. "I thought he was going to be sick."

"I never felt that bad. It was just for a minute."

"*I* thought he was going to be sick. You weren't bored, were you, Robert?"

"Let up on that, Mike. I said I was sorry I said it."

"He was, you know. He was positively green."

"Oh, shove it along, Michael."

"You mustn't ever get bored at your first bull-fight, Robert," Mike said. "It might make such a mess."

"Oh, shove it along, Michael," Brett said.

"He said Brett was a sadist," Mike said. "Brett's not a sadist. She's just a lovely, healthy wench."

"Are you a sadist, Brett?" I asked.

"Hope not."

"He said Brett was a sadist just because she has a good, healthy stomach."

"Won't be healthy long."

Bill got Mike started on something else than Cohn. The waiter brought the absinthe glasses.

"Did you really like it?" Bill asked Cohn.

"No, I can't say I liked it. I think it's a wonderful show."

"Gad, yes! What a spectacle!" Brett said.

"I wish they didn't have the horse part," Cohn said.

"They're not important," Bill said. "After a while you never notice anything disgusting."

"It is a bit strong just at the start," Brett said. "There's a dreadful moment for me just when the bull starts for the horse."

"The bulls were fine," Cohn said.

"They were very good," Mike said.

"I want to sit down below, next time." Brett drank from her glass of absinthe.

"She wants to see the bull-fighters close by," Mike said.

"They are something," Brett said. "That Romero lad is just a child."

"He's a damned good-looking boy," I said. "When we were up in his room I never saw a better-looking kid."

"How old do you suppose he is?"

"Nineteen or twenty."

"Just imagine it."

The bull-fight on the second day was much better than on the first. Brett sat between Mike and me at the barrera, and Bill and Cohn went up above. Romero was the whole show. I do not think Brett saw any other bull-fighter. No one else did either, except the hard-shelled technicians. It was all Romero. There were two other matadors, but they did not count. I sat beside Brett and explained to Brett what it was all about. I told her about watching the bull, not the horse, when the bulls charged the picadors, and got her to watching the picador place the point of his pic so that she saw what it was all about, so that it became more something that was going on with a definite end, and less of a spectacle with unexplained horrors. I had her watch how Romero took the bull away from a fallen horse with his cape, and how he held him with the cape and turned him, smoothly and suavely, never wasting the bull. She saw how Romero avoided every brusque movement and saved his bulls for the last when he wanted them, not winded and discomposed but smoothly worn down. She saw how close Romero always worked to the bull, and I pointed out to her the tricks the other bull-fighters used to make it look as though they were working closely. She saw why she liked Romero's cape-work and why she did not like the others.

Romero never made any contortions, always it was

straight and pure and natural in line. The others twisted themselves like corkscrews, their elbows raised, and leaned against the flanks of the bull after his horns had passed, to give a faked look of danger. Afterward, all that was faked turned bad and gave an unpleasant feeling. Romero's bull-fighting gave real emotion, because he kept the absolute purity of line in his movements and always quietly and calmly let the horns pass him close each time. He did not have to emphasize their closeness. Brett saw how something that was beautiful done close to the bull was ridiculous if it were done a little way off. I told her how since the death of Joselito all the bull-fighters had been developing a technic that simulated this appearance of danger in order to give a fake emotional feeling, while the bull-fighter was really safe. Romero had the old thing, the holding of his purity of line through the maximum of exposure, while he dominated the bull by making him realize he was unattainable, while he prepared him for the killing.

"I've never seen him do an awkward thing," Brett said.

"You won't until he gets frightened," I said.

"He'll never be frightened," Mike said. "He knows too damned much."

"He knew everything when he started. The others can't ever learn what he was born with."

"And God, what looks," Brett said.

"I believe, you know, that she's falling in love with this bull-fighter chap," Mike said.

"I wouldn't be surprised."

"Be a good chap, Jake. Don't tell her anything more about him. Tell her how they beat their old mothers."

"Tell me what drunks they are."

"Oh, frightful," Mike said. "Drunk all day and spend all their time beating their poor old mothers."

"He looks that way," Brett said.

"Doesn't he?" I said.

They had hitched the mules to the dead bull and then the whips cracked, the men ran, and the mules, straining forward, their legs pushing, broke into a gallop, and the bull, one horn up, his head on its side, swept a swath smoothly across the sand and out the red gate.

"This next is the last one."

"Not really," Brett said. She leaned forward on the barrera. Romero waved his picadors to their places, then stood, his cape against his chest, looking across the ring to where the bull would come out.

After it was over we went out and were pressed tight in the crowd.

"These bull-fights are hell on one," Brett said. "I'm limp as a rag."

"Oh, you'll get a drink," Mike said.

The next day Pedro Romero did not fight. It was Miura bulls, and a very bad bull-fight. The next day there was no bull-fight scheduled. But all day and all night the fiesta kept on.

CHAPTER XVI

IN the morning it was raining. A fog had come over the mountains from the sea. You could not see the tops of the mountains. The plateau was dull and gloomy, and the shapes of the trees and the houses were changed. I walked out beyond the town to look at the weather. The bad weather was coming over the mountains from the sea.

The flags in the square hung wet from the white poles and the banners were wet and hung damp against the front of the houses, and in between the steady drizzle the rain came down and drove every one under the arcades and made pools of water in the square, and the streets wet and dark and deserted; yet the fiesta kept up without any pause. It was only driven under cover.

The covered seats of the bull-ring had been crowded with people sitting out of the rain watching the concourse of Basque and Navarrais dancers and singers, and afterward the Val Carlos dancers in their costumes danced down the street in the rain, the drums sounding hollow and damp, and the chiefs of the bands riding ahead on their big, heavy-footed horses, their costumes wet, the horses' coats wet in the rain. The crowd was in the cafés and the dancers came in, too, and sat, their tight-wound white legs under the tables, shaking the water from their belled caps, and spreading their red and purple jackets over the chairs to dry. It was raining hard outside.

I left the crowd in the café and went over to the hotel to get shaved for dinner. I was shaving in my room when there was a knock on the door.

"Come in," I called.

Montoya walked in.

"How are you?" he said.

"Fine," I said.

"No bulls to-day."

"No," I said, "nothing but rain."

"Where are your friends?"

"Over at the Iruña."

Montoya smiled his embarrassed smile.

"Look," he said. "Do you know the American ambassador?"

"Yes," I said. "Everybody knows the American ambassador."

"He's here in town, now."

"Yes," I said. "Everybody's seen them."

"I've seen them, too," Montoya said. He didn't say anything. I went on shaving.

"Sit down," I said. "Let me send for a drink."

"No, I have to go."

I finished shaving and put my face down into the bowl and washed it with cold water. Montoya was standing there looking more embarrassed.

"Look," he said. "I've just had a message from them at the Grand Hotel that they want Pedro Romero and Marcial Lalanda to come over for coffee to-night after dinner."

"Well," I said, "it can't hurt Marcial any."

"Marcial has been in San Sebastian all day. He drove over in a car this morning with Marquez. I don't think they'll be back to-night."

Montoya stood embarrassed. He wanted me to say something.

"Don't give Romero the message," I said.

"You think so?"

"Absolutely."

Montoya was very pleased.

"I wanted to ask you because you were an American," he said.

"That's what I'd do."

"Look," said Montoya. "People take a boy like that. They don't know what he's worth. They don't know what he means. Any foreigner can flatter him. They start this Grand Hotel business, and in one year they're through."

"Like Algabeno," I said.

"Yes, like Algabeno."

"They're a fine lot," I said. "There's one American woman down here now that collects bull-fighters."

"I know. They only want the young ones."

"Yes," I said. "The old ones get fat."

"Or crazy like Gallo."

"Well," I said, "it's easy. All you have to do is not give him the message."

"He's such a fine boy," said Montoya. "He ought to stay with his own people. He shouldn't mix in that stuff."

"Won't you have a drink?" I asked.

"No," said Montoya, "I have to go." He went out.

I went down-stairs and out the door and took a walk around through the arcades around the square. It was still raining. I looked in at the Iruña for the gang and they were not there, so I walked on around the square and back to the hotel. They were eating dinner in the down-stairs dining-room.

They were well ahead of me and it was no use trying to catch them. Bill was buying shoe-shines for Mike. Bootblacks opened the street door and each one Bill called over and started to work on Mike.

"This is the eleventh time my boots have been polished," Mike said. "I say, Bill is an ass."

The bootblacks had evidently spread the report. Another came in.

"Limpia botas?" he said to Bill.

"No," said Bill. "For this Señor."

The bootblack knelt down beside the one at work and started on Mike's free shoe that shone already in the electric light.

"Bill's a yell of laughter," Mike said.

I was drinking red wine, and so far behind them that I felt a little uncomfortable about all this shoe-shining. I looked around the room. At the next table was Pedro Romero. He stood up when I nodded, and asked me to come over and meet a friend. His table was beside ours, almost touching. I met the friend, a Madrid bull-fight

critic, a little man with a drawn face. I told Romero how
much I liked his work, and he was very pleased. We
talked Spanish and the critic knew a little French. I
reached to our table for my wine-bottle, but the critic
took my arm. Romero laughed.

"Drink here," he said in English.

He was very bashful about his English, but he was
really very pleased with it, and as we went on talking
he brought out words he was not sure of, and asked me
about them. He was anxious to know the English for
Corrida de toros, the exact translation. Bull-fight he was
suspicious of. I explained that bull-fight in Spanish was
the *lidia* of a *toro*. The Spanish word *corrida* means in
English the running of bulls—the French translation is
Course de taureaux. The critic put that in. There is no
Spanish word for bull-fight.

Pedro Romero said he had learned a little English in
Gibraltar. He was born in Ronda. That is not far above
Gibraltar. He started bull-fighting in Malaga in the bull-
fighting school there. He had only been at it three years.
The bull-fight critic joked him about the number of
Malagueño expressions he used. He was nineteen years
old, he said. His older brother was with him as a bander-
llero, but he did not live in this hotel. He lived in a
smaller hotel with the other people who worked for
Romero. He asked me how many times I had seen him
in the ring. I told him only three. It was really only two,
but I did not want to explain after I had made the mistake.

"Where did you see me the other time? In Madrid?"

"Yes," I lied. I had read the accounts of his two ap-
pearances in Madrid in the bull-fight papers, so I was all
right.

"The first or the second time?"

"The first."

"I was very bad," he said. "The second time I wa
better. You remember?" He turned to the critic.

He was not at all embarrassed. He talked of his wor'
as something altogether apart from himself. There wa
nothing conceited or braggartly about him.

"I like it very much that you like my work," he said
"But you haven't seen it yet. To-morrow, if I get a good
bull, I will try and show it to you."

When he said this he smiled, anxious that neither the
bull-fight critic nor I would think he was boasting.

"I am anxious to see it," the critic said. "I would lik
to be convinced."

"He doesn't like my work much." Romero turned t
me. He was serious.

The critic explained that he liked it very much, bu
that so far it had been incomplete.

"Wait till to-morrow, if a good one comes out."

"Have you seen the bulls for to-morrow?" the criti
asked me.

"Yes. I saw them unloaded."

Pedro Romero leaned forward.

"What did you think of them?"

"Very nice," I said. "About twenty-six arrobas. Very
short horns. Haven't you seen them?"

"Oh, yes," said Romero.

"They won't weigh twenty-six arrobas," said the critic

"No," said Romero.

"They've got bananas for horns," the critic said.

"You call them bananas?" asked Romero. He turned
to me and smiled. "*You* wouldn't call them bananas?"

"No," I said. "They're horns all right."

"They're very short," said Pedro Romero. "Very, very
short. Still, they aren't bananas."

"I say, Jake," Brett called from the next table, "you *have* deserted us."

"Just temporarily," I said. "We're talking bulls."

"You *are* superior."

"Tell him that bulls have no horns," Mike shouted. He was drunk.

Romero looked at me inquiringly.

"Drunk," I said. "Borracho! Muy borracho!"

"You might introduce your friends," Brett said. She had not stopped looking at Pedro Romero. I asked them if they would like to have coffee with us. They both stood up. Romero's face was very brown. He had very nice manners.

I introduced them all around and they started to sit down, but there was not enough room, so we all moved over to the big table by the wall to have coffee. Mike ordered a bottle of Fundador and glasses for everybody. There was a lot of drunken talking.

"Tell him I think writing is lousy," Bill said. "Go on, tell him. Tell him I'm ashamed of being a writer."

Pedro Romero was sitting beside Brett and listening to her.

"Go on. Tell him!" Bill said.

Romero looked up smiling.

"This gentleman," I said, "is a writer."

Romero was impressed. "This other one, too," I said, pointing at Cohn.

"He looks like Villalta," Romero said, looking at Bill. "Rafael, doesn't he look like Villalta?"

"I can't see it," the critic said.

"Really," Romero said in Spanish. "He looks a lot like Villalta. What does the drunken one do?"

"Nothing."

"Is that why he drinks?"

"No. He's waiting to marry this lady."

"Tell him bulls have no horns!" Mike shouted, very drunk, from the other end of the table.

"What does he say?"

"He's drunk."

"Jake," Mike called. "Tell him bulls have no horns!"

"You understand?" I said.

"Yes."

I was sure he didn't, so it was all right.

"Tell him Brett wants to see him put on those green pants."

"Pipe down, Mike."

"Tell him Brett is dying to know how he can get into those pants."

"Pipe down."

During this Romero was fingering his glass and talking with Brett. Brett was talking French and he was talking Spanish and a little English, and laughing.

Bill was filling the glasses.

"Tell him Brett wants to come into——"

"Oh, pipe down, Mike, for Christ's sake!"

Romero looked up smiling. "Pipe down! I know that," he said.

Just then Montoya came into the room. He started to smile at me, then he saw Pedro Romero with a big glass of cognac in his hand, sitting laughing between me and a woman with bare shoulders, at a table full of drunks. He did not even nod.

Montoya went out of the room. Mike was on his feet proposing a toast. "Let's all drink to——" he began. "Pedro Romero," I said. Everybody stood up. Romero took very seriously, and we touched glasses and drank it down, I rushing it a little because Mike was trying to make it clear that that was not at all what he was going to drink to. But it went off all right, and Pedro Romero shook hands with every one and he and the critic went out together.

"My God! he's a lovely boy," Brett said. "And how I would love to see him get into those clothes. He must use a shoe-horn."

"I started to tell him," Mike began. "And Jake kept interrupting me. Why do you interrupt me? Do you think you talk Spanish better than I do?"

"Oh, shut up, Mike! Nobody interrupted you."

"No, I'd like to get this settled." He turned away from me. "Do you think you amount to something, Cohn? Do you think you belong here among us? People who are out to have a good time? For God's sake don't be so noisy, Cohn!"

"Oh, cut it out, Mike," Cohn said.

"Do you think Brett wants you here? Do you think you add to the party? Why don't you say something?"

"I said all I had to say the other night, Mike."

"I'm not one of you literary chaps." Mike stood shakily and leaned against the table. "I'm not clever. But I do know when I'm not wanted. Why don't you see when you're not wanted, Cohn? Go away. Go away, for God's sake. Take that sad Jewish face away. Don't you think I'm right?"

He looked at us.

"Sure," I said. "Let's all go over to the Iruña."

"No. Don't you think I'm right? I love that woman."

"Oh, don't start that again. Do shove it along, Michael," Brett said.

"Don't you think I'm right, Jake?"

Cohn still sat at the table. His face had the sallow, yellow look it got when he was insulted, but somehow he seemed to be enjoying it. The childish, drunken heroics of it. It was his affair with a lady of title.

"Jake," Mike said. He was almost crying. "You know

I'm right. Listen, you!" He turned to Cohn: "Go away.
Go away now!"

"But I won't go, Mike," said Cohn.

"Then I'll make you!" Mike started toward him around
the table. Cohn stood up and took off his glasses. He
stood waiting, his face sallow, his hands fairly low,
proudly and firmly waiting for the assault, ready to do
battle for his lady love.

I grabbed Mike. "Come on to the café," I said. "You
can't hit him here in the hotel."

"Good!" said Mike. "Good idea!"

We started off. I looked back as Mike stumbled up the
stairs and saw Cohn putting his glasses on again. Bill
was sitting at the table pouring another glass of Fundador. Brett was sitting looking straight ahead at nothing.

Outside on the square it had stopped raining and the
moon was trying to get through the clouds. There was
a wind blowing. The military band was playing and the
crowd was massed on the far side of the square where
the fireworks specialist and his son were trying to send
up fire balloons. A balloon would start up jerkily, on a
great bias, and be torn by the wind or blown against the
houses of the square. Some fell into the crowd. The
magnesium flared and the fireworks exploded and chased
about in the crowd. There was no one dancing in the
square. The gravel was too wet.

Brett came out with Bill and joined us. We stood in
the crowd and watched Don Manuel Orquito, the fireworks king, standing on a little platform, carefully starting the balloons with sticks, standing above the heads
of the crowd to launch the balloons off into the wind. The
wind brought them all down, and Don Manuel Orquito's
face was sweaty in the light of his complicated fireworks
that fell into the crowd and charged and chased, sputter-
ing and cracking, between the legs of the people. The

people shouted as each new luminous paper bubble careened, caught fire, and fell.

"They're razzing Don Manuel," Bill said.

"How do you know he's Don Manuel?" Brett said.

"His name's on the programme. Don Manuel Orquito, the pirotecnico of esta ciudad."

"Globos illuminados," Mike said. "A collection of globos illuminados. That's what the paper said."

The wind blew the band music away.

"I say, I wish one would go up," Brett said. "That Don Manuel chap is furious."

"He's probably worked for weeks fixing them to go off, spelling out 'Hail to San Fermin,'" Bill said.

"Globos illuminados," Mike said. "A bunch of bloody globos illuminados."

"Come on," said Brett. "We can't stand here."

"Her ladyship wants a drink," Mike said.

"How you know things," Brett said.

Inside, the café was crowded and very noisy. No one noticed us come in. We could not find a table. There was a great noise going on.

"Come on, let's get out of here," Bill said.

Outside the paseo was going in under the arcade. There were some English and Americans from Biarritz in sport clothes scattered at the tables. Some of the women stared at the people going by with lorgnons. We had acquired, at some time, a friend of Bill's from Biarritz. She was staying with another girl at the Grand Hotel. The other girl had a headache and had gone to bed.

"Here's the pub," Mike said. It was the Bar Milano, a small, tough bar where you could get food and where they danced in the back room. We all sat down at a table and ordered a bottle of Fundador. The bar was not full. There was nothing going on.

"This is a hell of a place," Bill said.

"It's too early."

"Let's take the bottle and come back later," Bill said. "I don't want to sit here on a night like this."

"Let's go and look at the English," Mike said. "I love to look at the English."

"They're awful," Bill said. "Where did they all come from?"

"They come from Biarritz," Mike said. "They come to see the last day of the quaint little Spanish festa."

"I'll festa them," Bill said.

"You're an extraordinarily beautiful girl." Mike turned to Bill's friend. "When did you come here?"

"Come off it, Michael."

"I say, she *is* a lovely girl. Where have I been? Where have I been looking all this while? You're a lovely thing. *Have* we met? Come along with me and Bill. We're going to festa the English."

"I'll festa them," Bill said. "What the hell are they doing at this fiesta?"

"Come on," Mike said. "Just us three. We're going to fiesta the bloody English. I hope you're not English? I'm Scotch. I hate the English. I'm going to festa them. Come on, Bill."

Through the window we saw them, all three arm in arm, going toward the café. Rockets were going up in the square.

"I'm going to sit here," Brett said.

"I'll stay with you," Cohn said.

"Oh, don't!" Brett said. "For God's sake, go off somewhere. Can't you see Jake and I want to talk?"

"I didn't," Cohn said. "I thought I'd sit here because I felt a little tight."

"What a hell of a reason for sitting with any one. If you're tight, go to bed. Go on to bed."

"Was I rude enough to him?" Brett asked. Cohn was gone. "My God! I'm so sick of him!"

"He doesn't add much to the gayety."

"He depresses me so."

"He's behaved very badly."

"Damned badly. He had a chance to behave so well."

"He's probably waiting just outside the door now."

"Yes. He would. You know I do know how he feels. He can't believe it didn't mean anything."

"I know."

"Nobody else would behave as badly. Oh, I'm so sick of the whole thing. And Michael. Michael's been lovely, too."

"It's been damned hard on Mike."

"Yes. But he didn't need to be a swine."

"Everybody behaves badly," I said. "Give them the proper chance."

"You wouldn't behave badly." Brett looked at me.

"I'd be as big an ass as Cohn," I said.

"Darling, don't let's talk a lot of rot."

"All right. Talk about anything you like."

"Don't be difficult. You're the only person I've got, and I feel rather awful to-night."

"You've got Mike."

"Yes, Mike. Hasn't he been pretty?"

"Well," I said, "it's been damned hard on Mike, having Cohn around and seeing him with you."

"Don't I know it, darling? Please don't make me feel any worse than I do."

Brett was nervous as I had never seen her before. She kept looking away from me and looking ahead at the wall.

"Want to go for a walk?"

"Yes. Come on."

I corked up the Fundador bottle and gave it to the bartender.

"Let's have one more drink of that," Brett said. "My nerves are rotten."

We each drank a glass of the smooth amontillado brandy.

"Come on," said Brett.

As we came out the door I saw Cohn walk out from under the arcade.

"He *was* there," Brett said.

"He can't be away from you."

"Poor devil!"

"I'm not sorry for him. I hate him, myself."

"I hate him, too," she shivered. "I hate his damned suffering."

We walked arm in arm down the side street away from the crowd and the lights of the square. The street was dark and wet, and we walked along it to the fortifications at the edge of town. We passed wine-shops with light coming out from their doors onto the black, wet street, and sudden bursts of music.

"Want to go in?"

"No."

We walked out across the wet grass and onto the stone wall of the fortifications. I spread a newspaper on the stone and Brett sat down. Across the plain it was dark, and we could see the mountains. The wind was high up and took the clouds across the moon. Below us were the dark pits of the fortifications. Behind were the trees and the shadow of the cathedral, and the town silhouetted against the moon.

"Don't feel bad," I said.

"I feel like hell," Brett said. "Don't let's talk."

We looked out at the plain. The long lines of trees were

dark in the moonlight. There were the lights of a car on the road climbing the mountain. Up on the top of the mountain we saw the lights of the fort. Below to the left was the river. It was high from the rain, and black and smooth. Trees were dark along the banks. We sat and looked out. Brett stared straight ahead. Suddenly she shivered.

"It's cold."

"Want to walk back?"

"Through the park."

We climbed down. It was clouding over again. In the park it was dark under the trees.

"Do you still love me, Jake?"

"Yes," I said.

"Because I'm a goner," Brett said.

"How?"

"I'm a goner. I'm mad about the Romero boy. I'm in love with him, I think."

"I wouldn't be if I were you."

"I can't help it. I'm a goner. It's tearing me all up inside."

"Don't do it."

"I can't help it. I've never been able to help anything."

"You ought to stop it."

"How can I stop it? I can't stop things. Feel that?"

Her hand was trembling.

"I'm like that all through."

"You oughtn't to do it."

"I can't help it. I'm a goner now, anyway. Don't you see the difference?"

"No."

"I've got to do something. I've got to do something I really want to do. I've lost my self-respect."

"You don't have to do that."

"Oh, darling, don't be difficult. What do you think it's meant to have that damned Jew about, and Mike the way he's acted?"

"Sure."

"I can't just stay tight all the time."

"No."

"Oh, darling, please stay by me. Please stay by me and see me through this."

"Sure."

"I don't say it's right. It is right though for me. God knows, I've never felt such a bitch."

"What do you want me to do?"

"Come on," Brett said. "Let's go and find him."

Together we walked down the gravel path in the park in the dark, under the trees and then out from under the trees and past the gate into the street that led into town.

Pedro Romero was in the café. He was at a table with other bull-fighters and bull-fight critics. They were smoking cigars. When we came in they looked up. Romero smiled and bowed. We sat down at a table half-way down the room.

"Ask him to come over and have a drink."

"Not yet. He'll come over."

"I can't look at him."

"He's nice to look at," I said.

"I've always done just what I wanted."

"I know."

"I do feel such a bitch."

"Well," I said.

"My God!" said Brett, "the things a woman goes through."

"Yes?"

"Oh, I do feel such a bitch."

I looked across at the table. Pedro Romero smiled. He

said something to the other people at his table, and stood up. He came over to our table. I stood up and we shook hands.

"Won't you have a drink?"

"You must have a drink with me," he said. He seated himself, asking Brett's permission without saying anything. He had very nice manners. But he kept on smoking his cigar. It went well with his face.

"You like cigars?" I asked.

"Oh, yes. I always smoke cigars."

It was part of his system of authority. It made him seem older. I noticed his skin. It was clear and smooth and very brown. There was a triangular scar on his cheek-bone. I saw he was watching Brett. He felt there was something between them. He must have felt it when Brett gave him her hand. He was being very careful. I think he was sure, but he did not want to make any mistake.

"You fight to-morrow?" I said.

"Yes," he said. "Algabeno was hurt to-day in Madrid. Did you hear?"

"No," I said. "Badly?"

He shook his head.

"Nothing. Here," he showed his hand. Brett reached out and spread the fingers apart.

"Oh!" he said in English, "you tell fortunes?"

"Sometimes. Do you mind?"

"No. I like it." He spread his hand flat on the table. "Tell me I live for always, and be a millionaire."

He was still very polite, but he was surer of himself. "Look," he said, "do you see any bulls in my hand?"

He laughed. His hand was very fine and the wrist was small.

"There are thousands of bulls," Brett said. She was not at all nervous now. She looked lovely.

"Good," Romero laughed. "At a thousand duros apiece," he said to me in Spanish. "Tell me some more."

"It's a good hand," Brett said. "I think he'll live a long time."

"Say it to me. Not to your friend."

"I said you'd live a long time."

"I know it," Romero said. "I'm never going to die."

I tapped with my finger-tips on the table. Romero saw it. He shook his head.

"No. Don't do that. The bulls are my best friends."

I translated to Brett.

"You kill your friends?" she asked.

"Always," he said in English, and laughed. "So they don't kill me." He looked at her across the table.

"You know English well."

"Yes," he said. "Pretty well, sometimes. But I must not let anybody know. It would be very bad, a torero who speaks English."

"Why?" asked Brett.

"It would be bad. The people would not like it. Not yet."

"Why not?"

"They would not like it. Bull-fighters are not like that."

He laughed and tipped his hat down over his eyes and changed the angle of his cigar and the expression of his face.

"Like at the table," he said. I glanced over. He had mimicked exactly the expression of Nacional. He smiled, his face natural again. "No. I must forget English."

"Don't forget it, yet," Brett said.

"No?"

"No."

"All right."

He laughed again.

"I would like a hat like that," Brett said.

"Good. I'll get you one."

"Right. See that you do."

"I will. I'll get you one to-night."

I stood up. Romero rose, too.

"Sit down," I said. "I must go and find our friends and bring them here."

He looked at me. It was a final look to ask if it were understood. It was understood all right.

"Sit down," Brett said to him. "You must teach me Spanish."

He sat down and looked at her across the table. I went out. The hard-eyed people at the bull-fighter table watched me go. It was not pleasant. When I came back and looked in the café, twenty minutes later, Brett and Pedro Romero were gone. The coffee-glasses and our three empty cognac-glasses were on the table. A waiter came with a cloth and picked up the glasses and mopped off the table.

CHAPTER XVII

OUTSIDE the Bar Milano I found Bill and Mike and Edna. Edna was the girl's name.

"We've been thrown out," Edna said.

"By the police," said Mike. "There's some people in here that don't like me."

"I've kept them out of four fights," Edna said. "You've got to help me."

Bill's face was red.

"Come back in, Edna," he said. "Go on in there and dance with Mike."

"It's silly," Edna said. "There'll just be another row."

"Damned Biarritz swine," Bill said.

"Come on," Mike said. "After all, it's a pub. They can't occupy a whole pub."

"Good old Mike," Bill said. "Damned English swine come here and insult Mike and try and spoil the fiesta."

"They're so bloody," Mike said. "I hate the English."

"They can't insult Mike," Bill said. "Mike is a swell fellow. They can't insult Mike. I won't stand it. Who cares if he is a damn bankrupt?" His voice broke.

"Who cares?" Mike said. "I don't care. Jake doesn't care. Do *you* care?"

"No," Edna said. "Are you a bankrupt?"

"Of course I am. You don't care, do you, Bill?"

Bill put his arm around Mike's shoulder.

"I wish to hell I was a bankrupt. I'd show those bastards."

"They're just English," Mike said. "It never makes any difference what the English say."

"The dirty swine," Bill said. "I'm going to clean them out."

"Bill," Edna looked at me. "Please don't go in again, Bill. They're so stupid."

"That's it," said Mike. "They're stupid. I knew that was what it was."

"They can't say things like that about Mike," Bill said.

"Do you know them?" I asked Mike.

"No. I never saw them. They say they know me."

"I won't stand it," Bill said.

"Come on. Let's go over to the Suizo," I said.

"They're a bunch of Edna's friends from Biarritz," Bill said.

"They're simply stupid," Edna said.

"One of them's Charley Blackman, from Chicago," Bill said.

"I was never in Chicago," Mike said.

Edna started to laugh and could not stop.

"Take me away from here," she said, "you bankrupts."

"What kind of a row was it?" I asked Edna. We were walking across the square to the Suizo. Bill was gone.

"I don't know what happened, but some one had the police called to keep Mike out of the back room. There were some people that had known Mike at Cannes. What's the matter with Mike?"

"Probably he owes them money," I said. "That's what people usually get bitter about."

In front of the ticket-booths out in the square there were two lines of people waiting. They were sitting on chairs or crouched on the ground with blankets and newspapers around them. They were waiting for the wickets to open in the morning to buy tickets for the bull-fight. The night was clearing and the moon was out. Some of the people in the line were sleeping.

At the Café Suizo we had just sat down and ordered Fundador when Robert Cohn came up.

"Where's Brett?" he asked.

"I don't know."

"She was with you."

"She must have gone to bed."

"She's not."

"I don't know where she is."

His face was sallow under the light. He was standing up.

"Tell me where she is."

"Sit down," I said. "I don't know where she is."

"The hell you don't!"

"You can shut your face."

"Tell me where Brett is."

"I'll not tell you a damn thing."

"You know where she is."

"If I did I wouldn't tell you."

"Oh, go to hell, Cohn," Mike called from the table. "Brett's gone off with the bull-fighter chap. They're on their honeymoon."

"You shut up."

"Oh, go to hell!" Mike said languidly.

"Is that where she is?" Cohn turned to me.

"Go to hell!"

"She was with you. Is that where she is?"

"Go to hell!"

"I'll make you tell me"—he stepped forward—"you damned pimp."

I swung at him and he ducked. I saw his face duck sideways in the light. He hit me and I sat down on the pavement. As I started to get on my feet he hit me twice. I went down backward under a table. I tried to get up and felt I did not have any legs. I felt I must get on my feet and try and hit him. Mike helped me up. Some one poured a carafe of water on my head. Mike had an arm around me, and I found I was sitting on a chair. Mike was pulling at my ears.

"I say, you were cold," Mike said.

"Where the hell were you?"

"Oh, I was around."

"You didn't want to mix in it?"

"He knocked Mike down, too," Edna said.

"He didn't knock me out," Mike said. "I just lay there."

"Does this happen every night at your fiestas?" Edna asked. "Wasn't that Mr. Cohn?"

"I'm all right," I said. "My head's a little wobbly."

There were several waiters and a crowd of people standing around.

"Vaya!" said Mike. "Get away. Go on."

The waiters moved the people away.

"It was quite a thing to watch," Edna said. "He must be a boxer."

"He is."

"I wish Bill had been here," Edna said. "I'd like to have seen Bill knocked down, too. I've always wanted to see Bill knocked down. He's so big."

"I was hoping he would knock down a waiter," Mike said, "and get arrested. I'd like to see Mr. Robert Cohn in jail."

"No," I said.

"Oh, no," said Edna. "You don't mean that."

"I do, though," Mike said. "I'm not one of these chaps likes being knocked about. I never play games, even."

Mike took a drink.

"I never liked to hunt, you know. There was always the danger of having a horse fall on you. How do you feel, Jake?"

"All right."

"You're nice," Edna said to Mike. "Are you really a bankrupt?"

"I'm a tremendous bankrupt," Mike said. "I owe money to everybody. Don't you owe any money?"

"Tons."

"I owe everybody money," Mike said. "I borrowed a hundred pesetas from Montoya to-night."

"The hell you did," I said.

"I'll pay it back," Mike said. "I always pay everything back."

"That's why you're a bankrupt, isn't it?" Edna said.

I stood up. I had heard them talking from a long way away. It seemed like some bad play.

"I'm going over to the hotel," I said. Then I heard them talking about me.

"Is he all right?" Edna asked.

"We'd better walk with him."

"I'm all right," I said. "Don't come. I'll see you all later."

I walked away from the café. They were sitting at the table. I looked back at them and at the empty tables. There was a waiter sitting at one of the tables with his head in his hands.

Walking across the square to the hotel everything looked new and changed. I had never seen the trees before. I had never seen the flagpoles before, nor the front of the theatre. It was all different. I felt as I felt once coming home from an out-of-town football game. I was carrying a suitcase with my football things in it, and I walked up the street from the station in the town I had lived in all my life and it was all new. They were raking the lawns and burning leaves in the road, and I stopped for a long time and watched. It was all strange. Then I went on, and my feet seemed to be a long way off, and everything seemed to come from a long way off, and I could hear my feet walking a great distance away. I had been kicked in the head early in the game. It was like that crossing the square. It was like that going up the stairs in the hotel. Going up the stairs took a long time, and I had the feeling that I was carrying my suitcase. There was a light in the room. Bill came out and met me in the hall.

"Say," he said, "go up and see Cohn. He's been in a jam, and he's asking for you."

"The hell with him."

"Go on. Go on up and see him."

I did not want to climb another flight of stairs.

"What are you looking at me that way for?"

"I'm not looking at you. Go on up and see Cohn. He's in bad shape."

"You were drunk a little while ago," I said.

"I'm drunk now," Bill said. "But you go up and see Cohn. He wants to see you."

"All right," I said. It was just a matter of climbing more stairs. I went on up the stairs carrying my phantom suitcase. I walked down the hall to Cohn's room. The door was shut and I knocked.

"Who is it?"

"Barnes."

"Come in, Jake."

I opened the door and went in, and set down my suitcase. There was no light in the room. Cohn was lying, face down, on the bed in the dark.

"Hello, Jake."

"Don't call me Jake."

I stood by the door. It was just like this that I had come home. Now it was a hot bath that I needed. A deep, hot bath, to lie back in.

"Where's the bathroom?" I asked.

Cohn was crying. There he was, face down on the bed, crying. He had on a white polo shirt, the kind he'd worn at Princeton.

"I'm sorry, Jake. Please forgive me."

"Forgive you, hell."

"Please forgive me, Jake."

I did not say anything. I stood there by the door.

"I was crazy. You must see how it was."

"Oh, that's all right."

"I couldn't stand it about Brett."

"You called me a pimp."

I did not care. I wanted a hot bath. I wanted a hot bath in deep water.

"I know. Please don't remember it. I was crazy."

"That's all right."

He was crying. His voice was funny. He lay there in

his white shirt on the bed in the dark. His polo shirt.

"I'm going away in the morning."

He was crying without making any noise.

"I just couldn't stand it about Brett. I've been through hell, Jake. It's been simply hell. When I met her down here Brett treated me as though I were a perfect stranger. I just couldn't stand it. We lived together at San Sebastian. I suppose you know it. I can't stand it any more."

He lay there on the bed.

"Well," I said, "I'm going to take a bath."

"You were the only friend I had, and I loved Brett so."

"Well," I said, "so long."

"I guess it isn't any use," he said. "I guess it isn't any damn use."

"What?"

"Everything. Please say you forgive me, Jake."

"Sure," I said. "It's all right."

"I felt so terribly. I've been through such hell, Jake. Now everything's gone. Everything."

"Well," I said, "so long. I've got to go."

He rolled over, sat on the edge of the bed, and then stood up.

"So long, Jake," he said. "You'll shake hands, won't you?"

"Sure. Why not?"

We shook hands. In the dark I could not see his face very well.

"Well," I said, "see you in the morning."

"I'm going away in the morning."

"Oh, yes," I said.

I went out. Cohn was standing in the door of the room.

"Are you all right, Jake?" he asked.

"Oh, yes," I said. "I'm all right."

I could not find the bathroom. After a while I found it. There was a deep stone tub. I turned on the taps and the water would not run. I sat down on the edge of the bath-tub. When I got up to go I found I had taken off my shoes. I hunted for them and found them and carried them down-stairs. I found my room and went inside and undressed and got into bed.

I woke with a headache and the noise of the bands going by in the street. I remembered I had promised to take Bill's friend Edna to see the bulls go through the street and into the ring. I dressed and went down-stairs and out into the cold early morning. People were crossing the square, hurrying toward the bull-ring. Across the square were the two lines of men in front of the ticket-booths. They were still waiting for the tickets to go on sale at seven o'clock. I hurried across the street to the café. The waiter told me that my friends had been there and gone.

"How many were they?"

"Two gentlemen and a lady."

That was all right. Bill and Mike were with Edna. She had been afraid last night they would pass out. That was why I was to be sure to take her. I drank the coffee and hurried with the other people toward the bull-ring. I was not groggy now. There was only a bad headache. Everything looked sharp and clear, and the town smelt of the early morning.

The stretch of ground from the edge of the town to the bull-ring was muddy. There was a crowd all along the fence that led to the ring, and the outside balconies and the top of the bull-ring were solid with people. I heard the rocket and I knew I could not get into the ring in time to see the bulls come in, so I shoved through the crowd to the fence. I was pushed close against the planks of the fence. Between the two fences of the run-way the police were clearing the crowd along. They walked or trotted on into the bull-ring. Then people commenced to come running. A drunk slipped and fell. Two policemen grabbed him and rushed him over to the fence. The crowd were running fast now. There was a great shout from the crowd, and putting my head through between the boards I saw the bulls just coming out of the street into the long running pen. They were going fast and gaining on the crowd. Just then another drunk started out from the fence with a blouse in his hands. He wanted to do capework with the bulls. The two policemen tore out, collared him, one hit him with a club, and they dragged him against the fence and stood flattened out against the fence as the last of the crowd and the bulls went by. There were so many people running ahead of the bulls that the mass thickened and slowed up going through the gate into the ring, and as the bulls passed, galloping together, heavy, muddy-sided, horns swinging, one shot ahead, caught a man in the running crowd in the back and lifted him in the air. Both the man's arms were by his sides, his head went back as the horn went in, and the bull lifted him and then dropped him. The bull picked another man running in front, but the man disappeared into the crowd, and the crowd was through the gate and into the ring with the bulls behind them. The red door of the ring went shut, the crowd on the outside balconies of the bull-ring were pressing through to the inside, there was a shout, then another shout.

The man who had been gored lay face down in the trampled mud. People climbed over the fence, and I could not see the man because the crowd was so thick around him. From inside the ring came the shouts. Each shout meant a charge by some bull into the crowd. You could tell by the degree of intensity in the shout how bad a thing it was that was happening. Then the rocket went up that meant the steers had gotten the bulls out of the ring and into the corrals. I left the fence and started back toward the town.

Back in the town I went to the café to have a second coffee and some buttered toast. The waiters were sweeping out the café and mopping off the tables. One came over and took my order.

"Anything happen at the encierro?"

"I didn't see it all. One man was badly cogido."

"Where?"

"Here." I put one hand on the small of my back and the other on my chest, where it looked as though the horn must have come through. The waiter nodded his head and swept the crumbs from the table with his cloth.

"Badly cogido," he said. "All for sport. All for pleasure."

He went away and came back with the long-handled coffee and milk pots. He poured the milk and coffee. It came out of the long spouts in two streams into the big cup. The waiter nodded his head.

"Badly cogido through the back," he said. He put the pots down on the table and sat down in the chair at the table. "A big horn wound. All for fun. Just for fun. What do you think of that?"

"I don't know."

"That's it. All for fun. Fun, you understand."

"You're not an aficionado?"

"Me? What are bulls? Animals. Brute animals." He stood up and put his hand on the small of his back. "Right through the back. A cornada right through the back. For fun—you understand."

He shook his head and walked away, carrying the coffee-pots. Two men were going by in the street. The waiter shouted to them. They were grave-looking. One shook his head. "Muerto!" he called.

The waiter nodded his head. The two men went on. They were on some errand. The waiter came over to my table.

"You hear? Muerto. Dead. He's dead. With a horn through him. All for morning fun. Es muy flamenco."

"It's bad."

"Not for me," the waiter said. "No fun in that for me."

Later in the day we learned that the man who was killed was named Vicente Girones, and came from near Tafalla. The next day in the paper we read that he was twenty-eight years old, and had a farm, a wife, and two children. He had continued to come to the fiesta each year after he was married. The next day his wife came in from Tafalla to be with the body, and the day after there was a service in the chapel of San Fermin, and the coffin was carried to the railway-station by members of the dancing and drinking society of Tafalla. The drums marched ahead, and there was music on the fifes, and behind the men who carried the coffin walked the wife and two children. . . . Behind them marched all the members of the dancing and drinking societies of Pamplona, Estella, Tafalla, and Sanguesa who could stay over for the funeral. The coffin was loaded into the baggage-car of the train, and the widow and the two children rode, sitting all three together, in an open third-class railway-carriage. The train started with a jerk, and then ran smoothly, going down grade around the edge of the plateau and out into the fields of grain that blew in the wind on the plain on the way to Tafalla.

The bull who killed Vicente Girones was named Bocanegra, was Number 118 of the bull-breeding establishment of Sanchez Taberno, and was killed by Pedro Romero as the third bull of that same afternoon. His ear was cut by popular acclamation and given to Pedro Romero, who, in turn, gave it to Brett, who wrapped it in a handkerchief belonging to myself, and left both ear and hand-kerchief, along with a number of Muratti cigarette-stubs, shoved far back in the drawer of the bed-table that stood beside her bed in the Hotel Montoya, in Pamplona.

Back in the hotel, the night watchman was sitting on a bench inside the door. He had been there all night and was very sleepy. He stood up as I came in. Three of the waitresses came in at the same time. They had been to the morning show at the bull-ring. They went up-stairs laughing. I followed them up-stairs and went into my room. I took off my shoes and lay down on the bed. The window was open onto the balcony and the sunlight was bright in the room. I did not feel sleepy. It must have been half past three o'clock when I had gone to bed and the bands had waked me at six. My jaw was sore on both sides. I felt it with my thumb and fingers. That damn Cohn. He should have hit somebody the first time he was insulted, and then gone away. He was so sure that Brett loved him. He was going to stay, and true love would conquer all. Some one knocked on the door.

"Come in."

It was Bill and Mike. They sat down on the bed.

"Some encierro," Bill said. "Some encierro."

"I say, weren't you there?" Mike asked. "Ring for some beer, Bill."

"What a morning!" Bill said. He mopped off his face. "My God! what a morning! And here's old Jake. Old Jake, the human punching-bag."

"What happened inside?"

"Good God!" Bill said, "what happened, Mike?"

"There were these bulls coming in," Mike said. "Just ahead of them was the crowd, and some chap tripped and brought the whole lot of them down."

"And the bulls all came in right over them," Bill said.

"I heard them yell."

"That was Edna," Bill said.

"Chaps kept coming out and waving their shirts."

"One bull went along the barrera and hooked everybody over."

"They took about twenty chaps to the infirmary," Mike said.

"What a morning!" Bill said. "The damn police kept arresting chaps that wanted to go and commit suicide with the bulls."

"The steers took them in, in the end," Mike said.

"It took about an hour."

"It was really about a quarter of an hour," Mike objected.

"Oh, go to hell," Bill said. "You've been in the war. It was two hours and a half for me."

"Where's that beer?" Mike asked.

"What did you do with the lovely Edna?"

"We took her home just now. She's gone to bed."

"How did she like it?"

"Fine. We told her it was just like that every morning."

"She was impressed," Mike said.

"She wanted us to go down in the ring, too," Bill said. "She likes action."

"I said it wouldn't be fair to my creditors," Mike said.

"What a morning," Bill said. "And what a night!"

"How's your jaw, Jake?" Mike asked.

"Sore," I said.

Bill laughed.

"Why didn't you hit him with a chair?"

"You can talk," Mike said. "He'd have knocked you out, too. I never saw him hit me. I rather think I saw him just before, and then quite suddenly I was sitting down in the street, and Jake was lying under a table."

"Where did he go afterward?" I asked.

"Here she is," Mike said. "Here's the beautiful lady with the beer."

The chambermaid put the tray with the beer-bottles and glasses down on the table.

"Now bring up three more bottles," Mike said.

"Where did Cohn go after he hit me?" I asked Bill.

"Don't you know about that?" Mike was opening a beer-bottle. He poured the beer into one of the glasses, holding the glass close to the bottle.

"Really?" Bill asked.

"Why he went in and found Brett and the bull-fighter chap in the bull-fighter's room, and then he massacred the poor, bloody bull-fighter."

"No."

"Yes."

"What a night!" Bill said.

"He nearly killed the poor, bloody bull-fighter. Then Cohn wanted to take Brett away. Wanted to make an honest woman of her, I imagine. Damned touching scene."

He took a long drink of the beer.

"He is an ass."

"What happened?"

"Brett gave him what for. She told him off. I think she was rather good."

"I'll bet she was," Bill said.

"Then Cohn broke down and cried, and wanted to shake hands with the bull-fighter fellow. He wanted to shake hands with Brett, too."

"I know. He shook hands with me."

"Did he? Well, they weren't having any of it. The bull-fighter fellow was rather good. He didn't say much, but he kept getting up and getting knocked down again. Cohn couldn't knock him out. It must have been damned funny."

"Where did you hear all this?"

"Brett. I saw her this morning."

"What happened finally?"

"It seems the bull-fighter fellow was sitting on the bed. He'd been knocked down about fifteen times, and he wanted to fight some more. Brett held him and wouldn't let him get up. He was weak, but Brett couldn't hold him, and he got up. Then Cohn said he wouldn't hit him again. Said he couldn't do it. Said it would be wicked. So the bull-fighter chap sort of rather staggered over to him. Cohn went back against the wall.

" 'So you won't hit me?'

" 'No,' said Cohn. 'I'd be ashamed to.'

"So the bull-fighter fellow hit him just as hard as he could in the face, and then sat down on the floor. He couldn't get up, Brett said. Cohn wanted to pick him up and carry him to the bed. He said if Cohn helped him he'd kill him, and he'd kill him anyway this morning if Cohn wasn't out of town. Cohn was crying, and Brett had told him off, and he wanted to shake hands. I've told you that before."

"Tell the rest," Bill said.

"It seems the bull-fighter chap was sitting on the floor. He was waiting to get strength enough to get up and hit Cohn again. Brett wasn't having any shaking hands, and Cohn was crying and telling her how much he loved her, and she was telling him not to be a ruddy ass. Then Cohn leaned down to shake hands with the bull-fighter fellow. No hard feelings, you know. All for forgiveness. And the bull-fighter chap hit him in the face again."

"That's quite a kid," Bill said.

"He ruined Cohn," Mike said. "You know I don't think Cohn will ever want to knock people about again."

"When did you see Brett?"

"This morning. She came in to get some things. She's looking after this Romero lad."

He poured out another bottle of beer.

"Brett's rather cut up. But she loves looking after people. That's how we came to go off together. She was looking after me."

"I know," I said.

"I'm rather drunk," Mike said. "I think I'll *stay* rather drunk. This is all awfully amusing, but it's not too pleasant. It's not too pleasant for me."

He drank off the beer.

"I gave Brett what for, you know. I said if she would go about with Jews and bull-fighters and such people, she must expect trouble." He leaned forward. "I say, Jake, do you mind if I drink that bottle of yours? She'll bring you another one."

"Please," I said. "I wasn't drinking it, anyway."

Mike started to open the bottle. "Would you mind opening it?" I pressed up the wire fastener and poured it for him.

"You know," Mike went on, "Brett was rather good. She's always rather good. I gave her a fearful hiding about Jews and bull-fighters, and all those sort of people, and do you know what she said: 'Yes. I've had such a hell of a happy life with the British aristocracy!'"

He took a drink.

"That was rather good. Ashley, chap she got the title from, was a sailor, you know. Ninth baronet. When he came home he wouldn't sleep in a bed. Always made Brett sleep on the floor. Finally, when he got really bad, he used to tell her he'd kill her. Always slept with a loaded service revolver. Brett used to take the shells out when he'd gone to sleep. She hasn't had an absolutely happy life, Brett. Damned shame, too. She enjoys things so."

He stood up. His hand was shaky.

"I'm going in the room. Try and get a little sleep."

He smiled.

"We go too long without sleep in these fiestas. I'm going to start now and get plenty of sleep. Damn bad thing not to get sleep. Makes you frightfully nervy."

"We'll see you at noon at the Iruña," Bill said.

Mike went out the door. We heard him in the next room.

He rang the bell and the chambermaid came and knocked at the door.

"Bring up half a dozen bottles of beer and a bottle of Fundador," Mike told her.

"Si, Señorito."

"I'm going to bed," Bill said. "Poor old Mike. I had a hell of a row about him last night."

"Where? At that Milano place?"

"Yes. There was a fellow there that had helped pay Brett and Mike out of Cannes, once. He was damned nasty."

"I know the story."

"I didn't. Nobody ought to have a right to say things about Mike."

"That's what makes it bad."

"They oughtn't to have any right. I wish to hell they didn't have any right. I'm going to bed."

"Was anybody killed in the ring?"

"I don't think so. Just badly hurt."

"A man was killed outside in the runway."

"Was there?" said Bill.

CHAPTER XVIII

A T noon we were all at the café. It was crowded. We were eating shrimps and drinking beer. The town was crowded. Every street was full. Big motor-cars from Biarritz and San Sebastian kept driving up and parking around the square. They brought people for the bull-fight. Sight-seeing cars came up, too. There was one with twenty-five Englishwomen in it. They sat in the big, white car and looked through their glasses at the fiesta. The dancers were all quite drunk. It was the last day of the fiesta.

The fiesta was solid and unbroken, but the motor-cars and tourist-cars made little islands of onlookers. When the cars emptied, the onlookers were absorbed into the crowd. You did not see them again except as sport clothes, odd-looking at a table among the closely packed peasants in black smocks. The fiesta absorbed even the Biarritz English so that you did not see them unless you passed close to a table. All the time there was music in the street. The drums kept on pounding and the pipes were going. Inside the cafés men with their hands gripping the table, or on each other's shoulders, were singing the hard-voiced singing.

"Here comes Brett," Bill said.

I looked and saw her coming through the crowd in the square, walking, her head up, as though the fiesta were being staged in her honor, and she found it pleasant and amusing.

"Hello, you chaps!" she said. "I say, I *have* a thirst."

"Get another big beer," Bill said to the waiter.

"Shrimps?"

"Is Cohn gone?" Brett asked.

"Yes," Bill said. "He hired a car."

The beer came. Brett started to lift the glass mug and her hand shook. She saw it and smiled, and leaned forward and took a long sip.

"Good beer."

"Very good," I said. I was nervous about Mike. I did not think he had slept. He must have been drinking all the time, but he seemed to be under control.

"I heard Cohn had hurt you, Jake," Brett said.

"No. Knocked me out. That was all."

"I say, he did hurt Pedro Romero," Brett said. "He hurt him most badly."

"How is he?"

"He'll be all right. He won't go out of the room."

"Does he look badly?"

"Very. He was really hurt. I told him I wanted to pop out and see you chaps for a minute."

"Is he going to fight?"

"Rather. I'm going with you, if you don't mind."

"How's your boy friend?" Mike asked. He had not listened to anything that Brett had said.

"Brett's got a bull-fighter," he said. "She had a Jew named Cohn, but he turned out badly."

Brett stood up.

"I am not going to listen to that sort of rot from you, Michael."

"How's your boy friend?"

"Damned well," Brett said. "Watch him this afternoon."

"Brett's got a bull-fighter," Mike said. "A beautiful bloody bull-fighter."

"Would you mind walking over with me? I want to talk to you, Jake."

"Tell him all about your bull-fighter," Mike said. "Oh to hell with your bull-fighter!" He tipped the table so that all the beers and the dish of shrimps went over in a crash.

"Come on," Brett said. "Let's get out of this."

In the crowd crossing the square I said: "How is it?"

"I'm not going to see him after lunch until the fight. His people come in and dress him. They're very angry about me, he says."

Brett was radiant. She was happy. The sun was out and the day was bright.

"I feel altogether changed," Brett said. "You've no idea, Jake."

"Anything you want me to do?"

"No, just go to the fight with me."

"We'll see you at lunch?"

"No. I'm eating with him."

We were standing under the arcade at the door of the hotel. They were carrying tables out and setting them up under the arcade.

"Want to take a turn out to the park?" Brett asked. "I don't want to go up yet. I fancy he's sleeping."

We walked along past the theatre and out of the square and along through the barracks of the fair, moving with the crowd between the lines of booths. We came out on a cross-street that led to the Paseo de Sarasate. We could see the crowd walking there, all the fashionably dressed people. They were making the turn at the upper end of the park.

"Don't let's go there," Brett said. "I don't want staring at just now."

We stood in the sunlight. It was hot and good after the rain and the clouds from the sea.

"I hope the wind goes down," Brett said. "It's very bad for him."

"So do I."

"He says the bulls are all right."

"Is that San Fermin's?"

Brett looked at the yellow wall of the chapel.

"Yes. Where the show started on Sunday."

"Let's go in. Do you mind? I'd rather like to pray a little for him or something."

We went in through the heavy leather door that moved very lightly. It was dark inside. Many people were praying. You saw them as your eyes adjusted themselves to the half-light. We knelt at one of the long wooden benches. After a little I felt Brett stiffen beside me, and saw she was looking straight ahead.

"Come on," she whispered throatily. "Let's get out of here. Makes me damned nervous."

Outside in the hot brightness of the street Brett looked up at the tree-tops in the wind. The praying had not been much of a success.

"Don't know why I get so nervy in church," Brett said. "Never does me any good."

We walked along.

"I'm damned bad for a religious atmosphere," Brett said. "I've the wrong type of face."

"You know," Brett said, "I'm not worried about him at all. I just feel happy about him."

"Good."

"I wish the wind would drop, though."

"It's liable to go down by five o'clock."

"Let's hope."

"You might pray," I laughed.

"Never does me any good. I've never gotten anything I prayed for. Have you?"

"Oh, yes."

"Oh, rot," said Brett. "Maybe it works for some people, though. You don't look very religious, Jake."

"I'm pretty religious."

"Oh, rot," said Brett. "Don't start proselyting to-day. To-day's going to be bad enough as it is."

It was the first time I had seen her in the old happy, careless way since before she went off with Cohn. We were back again in front of the hotel. All the tables were set now, and already several were filled with people eating.

"Do look after Mike," Brett said. "Don't let him get too bad."

"Your frients haff gone up-stairs," the German maître d'hôtel said in English. He was a continual eavesdropper. Brett turned to him:

"Thank you, so much. Have you anything else to say?"

"No, ma'am."

"Good," said Brett.

"Save us a table for three," I said to the German. He smiled his dirty little pink-and-white smile.

"Iss madam eating here?"

"No," Brett said.

"Den I think a tabul for two will be enuff."

"Don't talk to him," Brett said. "Mike must have been in bad shape," she said on the stairs. We passed Montoya on the stairs. He bowed and did not smile.

"I'll see you at the café," Brett said. "Thank you, so much, Jake."

We had stopped at the floor our rooms were on. She went straight down the hall and into Romero's room. She did not knock. She simply opened the door, went in, and closed it behind her.

I stood in front of the door of Mike's room and knocked. There was no answer. I tried the knob and it opened. Inside the room was in great disorder. All the bags were opened and clothing was strewn around.

There were empty bottles beside the bed. Mike lay on
the bed looking like a death mask of himself. He opened
his eyes and looked at me.

"Hello, Jake," he said very slowly. "I'm getting a
lit tle sleep. I've want ed a lit tle sleep for a long time."

"Let me cover you over."

"No. I'm quite warm."

"Don't go. I have n't got ten to sleep yet."

"You'll sleep, Mike. Don't worry, boy."

"Brett's got a bull-fighter," Mike said. "But her Jew
has gone away."

He turned his head and looked at me.

"Damned good thing, what?"

"Yes. Now go to sleep, Mike. You ought to get some
sleep."

"I'm just start ing. I'm go ing to get a lit tle sleep."

He shut his eyes. I went out of the room and turned
the door to quietly. Bill was in my room reading the
paper.

"See Mike?"

"Yes."

"Let's go and eat."

"I won't eat down-stairs with that German head
waiter. He was damned snotty when I was getting Mike
up-stairs."

"He was snotty to us, too."

"Let's go out and eat in the town."

We went down the stairs. On the stairs we passed a
girl coming up with a covered tray.

"There goes Brett's lunch," Bill said.

"And the kid's," I said.

Outside on the terrace under the arcade the German
head waiter came up. His red cheeks were shiny. He
was being polite.

"I haff a tabul for two for you gentlemen," he said.

"Go sit at it," Bill said. We went on out across the street.

We ate at a restaurant in a side street off the square. They were all men eating in the restaurant. It was full of smoke and drinking and singing. The food was good and so was the wine. We did not talk much. Afterward we went to the café and watched the fiesta come to the boiling-point. Brett came over soon after lunch. She said she had looked in the room and that Mike was asleep.

When the fiesta boiled over and toward the bull-ring we went with the crowd. Brett sat at the ringside between Bill and me. Directly below us was the callejon, the passageway between the stands and the red fence of the barrera. Behind us the concrete stands filled solidly. Out in front, beyond the red fence, the sand of the ring was smooth-rolled and yellow. It looked a little heavy from the rain, but it was dry in the sun and firm and smooth. The sword-handlers and bull-ring servants came down the callejon carrying on their shoulders the wicker baskets of fighting capes and muletas. They were blood-stained and compactly folded and packed in the baskets. The sword-handlers opened the heavy leather sword-cases so the red wrapped hilts of the sheaf of swords showed as the leather case leaned against the fence. They unfolded the dark-stained red flannel of the muletas and fixed batons in them to spread the stuff and give the matador something to hold. Brett watched it all. She was absorbed in the professional details.

"He's his name stencilled on all the capes and muletas," she said. "Why do they call them muletas?"

"I don't know."

"I wonder if they ever launder them."

"I don't think so. It might spoil the color."

"The blood must stiffen them," Bill said.

"Funny," Brett said. "How one doesn't mind the blood."

Below in the narrow passage of the callejon the sword-handlers arranged everything. All the seats were full. Above, all the boxes were full. There was not an empty seat except in the President's box. When he came in the fight would start. Across the smooth sand, in the high doorway that led into the corrals, the bull-fighters were standing, their arms furled in their capes, talking, waiting for the signal to march in across the arena. Brett was watching them with the glasses.

"Here, would you like to look?"

I looked through the glasses and saw the three matadors. Romero was in the centre, Belmonte on his left, Marcial on his right. Back of them were their people, and behind the banderilleros, back in the passageway and in the open space of the corral I saw, the picadors. Romero was wearing a black suit. His tricornered hat was low down over his eyes. I could not see his face clearly under the hat, but it looked badly marked. He was looking straight ahead. Marcial was smoking a cigarette guardedly, holding it in his hand. Belmonte looked ahead, his face wan and yellow, his long wolf jaw out. He was looking at nothing. Neither he nor Romero seemed to have anything in common with the others. They were all alone. The President came in; there was handclapping above us in the grand stand, and I handed the glasses to Brett. There was applause. The music started. Brett looked through the glasses.

"Here, take them," she said.

Through the glasses I saw Belmonte speak to Romero. Marcial straightened up and dropped his cigarette, and, looking straight ahead, their heads back, their free arms swinging, the three matadors walked out. Behind them came all the procession, opening out, all striding in step, all the capes furled, everybody with free arms swinging, and behind rode the picadors, their pics rising like lances. Behind all came the two trains of mules and the bull-ring servants. The matadors bowed, holding their hats on, before the President's box, and then came over to the barrera below us. Pedro Romero took off his heavy gold-brocaded cape and handed it over the fence to his sword-handler. He said something to the sword-handler. Close below us we saw Romero's lips were puffed, both eyes were discolored. His face was discolored and swollen. The sword-handler took the cape, looked up at Brett, and came over to us and handed up the cape.

"Spread it out in front of you," I said.

Brett leaned forward. The cape was heavy and smoothly stiff with gold. The sword-handler looked back, shook his head, and said something. A man beside me leaned over toward Brett.

"He doesn't want you to spread it," he said. "You should fold it and keep it in your lap."

Brett folded the heavy cape.

Romero did not look up at us. He was speaking to Belmonte. Belmonte had sent his formal cape over to some friends. He looked across at them and smiled, his wolf smile that was only with the mouth. Romero leaned over the barrera and asked for the water-jug. The sword-handler brought it and Romero poured water over the percale of his fighting-cape, and then scuffed the lower folds in the sand with his slippered foot.

"What's that for?" Brett asked.

"To give it weight in the wind."

"His face looks bad," Bill said.

"He feels very badly," Brett said. "He should be in bed."

The first bull was Belmonte's. Belmonte was very good.

But because he got thirty thousand pesetas and people had stayed in line all night to buy tickets to see him, the crowd demanded that he should be more than very good. Belmonte's great attraction is working close to the bull. In bull-fighting they speak of the terrain of the bull and the terrain of the bull-fighter. As long as a bull-fighter stays in his own terrain he is comparatively safe. Each time he enters into the terrain of the bull he is in great danger. Belmonte, in his best days, worked always in the terrain of the bull. This way he gave the sensation of coming tragedy. People went to the corrida to see Belmonte, to be given tragic sensations, and perhaps to see the death of Belmonte. Fifteen years ago they said if you wanted to see Belmonte you should go quickly, while he was still alive. Since then he has killed more than a thousand bulls. When he retired the legend grew up about how his bull-fighting had been, and when he came out of retirement the public were disappointed because no real man could work as close to the bulls as Belmonte was supposed to have done not, of course, even Belmonte.

Also Belmonte imposed conditions and insisted that his bulls should not be too large, nor too dangerously armed with horns, and so the element that was necessary to give the sensation of tragedy was not there, and the public, who wanted three times as much from Belmonte, who was sick with a fistula, as Belmonte had ever been able to give, felt defrauded and cheated, and Belmonte's jaw came further out in contempt, and his face turned yellower, and he moved with greater difficulty as his pain increased, and finally the crowd were actively against him, and he was utterly contemptuous and indifferent. He had meant to have a great afternoon, and instead it was an afternoon of sneers, shouted insults, and finally a volley of cushions and pieces of bread and vegetables, thrown down at him in the plaza where he had had his greatest triumphs. His jaw only went further out. Sometimes he turned to smile that toothed, long-jawed, lipless smile when he was called something particularly insulting, and always the pain that any movement produced grew stronger and stronger, until finally his yellow face was parchment color, and after his second bull was dead and the throwing of bread and cushions was over, after he had saluted the President with the same wolf-jawed smile and contemptuous eyes, and handed his sword over the barrera to be wiped, and put back in its case, he passed through into the callejon and leaned on the barrera below us, his head on his arms, not seeing, not hearing anything, only going through his pain. When he looked up, finally, he asked for a drink of water. He swallowed a little, rinsed his mouth, spat the water, took his cape, and went back into the ring.

Because they were against Belmonte the public were for Romero. From the moment he left the barrera and went toward the bull they applauded him. Belmonte watched Romero, too, watched him always without seeming to. He paid no attention to Marcial. Marcial was the sort of thing he knew all about. He had come out of retirement to compete with Marcial, knowing it was a competition gained in advance. He had expected to compete with Marcial and the other stars of the decadence of bull-fighting, and he knew that the sincerity of his own bull-fighting would be so set off by the false æsthetics of the bull-fighters of the decadent period that he would only have to be in the ring. His return from retirement had been spoiled by Romero. Romero did always, smoothly, calmly, and beautifully, what he, Belmonte, could only bring himself to do now sometimes. The crowd felt it, even the people from Biarritz, even the American ambassador saw it, finally. It was a competition that Belmonte would not enter because it would lead only to a bad horn wound or death. Belmonte was no longer well enough. He no longer had his greatest moments in the bull-ring. He was not sure that there were any great moments. Things were not the same and now life only came in flashes. He had flashes of the old greatness with his bulls, but they were not of value because he had discounted them in advance when he had picked the bulls out for their safety, getting out of a motor and leaning on a fence, looking over at the herd on the ranch of his friend the bull-breeder. So he had two small, manageable bulls without much horns, and when he felt the greatness again coming, just a little of it through the pain that was always with him, it had been discounted and sold in advance, and it did not give him a good feeling. It was the greatness, but it did not make bull-fighting wonderful to him any more.

Pedro Romero had the greatness. He loved bull-fighting, and I think he loved the bulls, and I think he loved Brett. Everything of which he could control the locality he did in front of her all that afternoon. Never once did he look up. He made it stronger that way, and did it for himself, too, as well as for her. Because he did not look up to ask if it pleased he did it all for himself inside, and it strengthened him, and yet he did it for her, too. But he did not do it for her at any loss to himself. He gained by it all through the afternoon.

His first "quite" was directly below us. The three matadors take the bull in turn after each charge he makes at a picador. Belmonte was the first. Marcial was the second. Then came Romero. The three of them were standing at the left of the horse. The picador, his hat down over his eyes, the shaft of his pic angling sharply toward the bull, kicked in the spurs and held them and with the reins in his left hand walked the horse forward toward the bull. The bull was watching. Seemingly he watched the white horse, but really he watched the triangular steel point of the pic. Romero, watching, saw the bull start to turn his head. He did not want to charge. Romero flicked his cape so the color caught the bull's eye. The bull charged with the reflex, charged, and found not the flash of color but a white horse, and a man leaned far over the horse, shot the steel point of the long hickory shaft into the hump of muscle on the bull's shoulder, and pulled his horse sideways as he pivoted on the pic, making a wound, enforcing the iron into the bull's shoulder, making him bleed for Belmonte.

The bull did not insist under the iron. He did not really want to get at the horse. He turned and the group broke apart and Romero was taking him out with his cape. He took him out softly and smoothly, and then stopped and, standing squarely in front of the bull, offered him the cape. The bull's tail went up and he charged, and Romero moved his arms ahead of the bull, wheeling, his feet firmed. The dampened, mud-weighted cape swung open and full as a sail fills, and Romero pivoted with it just ahead of the bull. At the end of the pass they were facing each other again. Romero smiled. The bull wanted it again, and Romero's cape filled again, this time on the other side. Each time he let the bull pass so close that the man and the bull and the cape that filled and pivoted ahead of the bull were all one sharply etched mass. It was all so slow and so controlled. It was as though he were rocking the bull to sleep. He made four veronicas like that, and finished with a half-veronica that turned his back on the bull and came away toward the applause, his hand on his hip, his cape on his arm, and the bull watching his back going away.

In his own bulls he was perfect. His first bull did not see well. After the first two passes with the cape Romero knew exactly how bad the vision was impaired. He worked accordingly. It was not brilliant bull-fighting. It was only perfect bull-fighting. The crowd wanted the bull changed. They made a great row. Nothing very fine could happen with a bull that could not see the lures, but the President would not order him replaced.

"Why don't they change him?" Brett asked.

"They've paid for him. They don't want to lose their money."

"It's hardly fair to Romero."

"Watch how he handles a bull that can't see the color."

"It's the sort of thing I don't like to see."

It was not nice to watch if you cared anything about the person who was doing it. With the bull who could not see the colors of the capes, or the scarlet flannel of the muleta, Romero had to make the bull consent with his body. He had to get so close that the bull saw his body, and would start for it, and then shift the bull's charge to the flannel and finish out the pass in the classic manner. The Biarritz crowd did not like it. They thought Romero was afraid, and that was why he gave that little sidestep each time as he transferred the bull's charge from his own body to the flannel. They preferred Belmonte's imitation of himself or Marcial's imitation of Belmonte. There were three of them in the row behind us.

"What's he afraid of the bull for? The bull's so dumb he only goes after the cloth."

"He's just a young bull-fighter. He hasn't learned it yet."

"But I thought he was fine with the cape before."

"Probably he's nervous now."

Out in the centre of the ring, all alone, Romero was going on with the same thing, getting so close that the bull could see him plainly, offering the body, offering it again a little closer, the bull watching dully, then so close that the bull thought he had him, offering again and finally drawing the charge and then, just before the horns came, giving the bull the red cloth to follow with that little, almost imperceptible, jerk that so offended the critical judgment of the Biarritz bull-fight experts.

"He's going to kill now," I said to Brett. "The bull's still strong. He wouldn't wear himself out."

Out in the centre of the ring Romero profiled in front of the bull, drew the sword out from the folds of the muleta, rose on his toes, and sighted along the blade. The bull charged as Romero charged. Romero's left hand dropped the muleta over the bull's muzzle to blind him, his left shoulder went forward between the horns as the sword went in and for just an instant he and the bull were one, Romero way out over the bull, the right arm extended high up to where the hilt of the sword had gone in between the bull's shoulders. Then the figure was broken. There was a little jolt as Romero came clear, and then he was standing, one hand up, facing the bull, his shirt ripped out from under his sleeve, the white blowing in the wind, and the bull, the red sword hilt tight between his shoulders, his head going down and his legs settling.

"There he goes," Bill said.

Romero was close enough so the bull could see him. His hand still up, he spoke to the bull. The bull gathered himself, then his head went forward and he went over slowly, then all over, suddenly, four feet in the air.

They handed the sword to Romero, and carrying it blade down, the muleta in his other hand, he walked over to in front of the President's box, bowed, straightened, and came over to the barrera and handed over the sword and muleta.

"Bad one," said the sword-handler.

"He made me sweat," said Romero. He wiped off his face. The sword-handler handed him the water-jug. Romero wiped his lips. It hurt him to drink out of the jug. He did not look up at us.

Marcial had a big day. They were still applauding him when Romero's last bull came in. It was the bull that had sprinted out and killed the man in the morning running.

During Romero's first bull his hurt face had been very noticeable. Everything he did showed it. All the concentration of the awkwardly delicate working with the bull that could not see well brought it out. The fight with Cohn had not touched his spirit but his face had been smashed and his body hurt. He was wiping all that out now. Each thing that he did with this bull wiped that out a little cleaner. It was a good bull, a big bull, and with horns, and it turned and recharged easily and surely. He was what Romero wanted in bulls.

When he had finished his work with the muleta and was ready to kill, the crowd made him go on. They did not want the bull killed yet, they did not want it to be over. Romero went on. It was like a course in bull-fighting. All the passes he linked up, all completed, all slow, templed and smooth. There were no tricks and no mystifications. There was no brusqueness. And each pass as it reached the summit gave you a sudden ache inside. The crowd did not want it ever to be finished.

The bull was squared on all four feet to be killed, and Romero killed directly below us. He killed not as he had been forced to by the last bull, but as he wanted to. He profiled directly in front of the bull, drew the sword out of the folds of the muleta and sighted along

the blade. The bull watched him. Romero spoke to the
bull and tapped one of his feet. The bull charged and
Romero waited for the charge, the muleta held low, sighting along the blade, his feet firm. Then without taking
a step forward, he became one with the bull, the sword
was in high between the shoulders, the bull had followed
the low-swung flannel, that disappeared as Romero
lurched clear to the left, and it was over. The bull tried
to go forward, his legs commenced to settle, he swung
from side to side, hesitated, then went down on his
knees, and Romero's older brother leaned forward behind him and drove a short knife into the bull's neck at
the base of the horns. The first time he missed. He drove
the knife in again, and the bull went over, twitching and
rigid. Romero's brother, holding the bull's horn in one
hand, the knife in the other, looked up at the President's
box. Handkerchiefs were waving all over the bull-ring.
The President looked down from the box and waved his
handkerchief. The brother cut the notched black ear from
the dead bull and trotted over with it to Romero. The
bull lay heavy and black on the sand, his tongue out. Boys
were running toward him from all parts of the arena,
making a little circle around him. They were starting to
dance around the bull.

Romero took the ear from his brother and held it up
toward the President. The President bowed and Romero,
running to get ahead of the crowd, came toward us. He
leaned up against the barrera and gave the ear to Brett. He
nodded his head and smiled. The crowd were all
about him. Brett held down the cape.

"You liked it?" Romero called.

Brett did not say anything. They looked at each other
and smiled. Brett had the ear in her hand.

"Don't get bloody," Romero said, and grinned. The
crowd wanted him. Several boys shouted at Brett. The

crowd was the boys, the dancers, and the drunks. Romero turned and tried to get through the crowd. They were all around him trying to lift him and put him on their shoulders. He fought and twisted away, and started running, in the midst of them, toward the exit. He did not want to be carried on people's shoulders. But they held him and lifted him. It was uncomfortable and his legs were spraddled and his body was very sore. They were lifting him and all running toward the gate. He had his hand on somebody's shoulder. He looked around at us apologetically. The crowd, running, went out the gate with him.

We all three went back to the hotel. Brett went upstairs. Bill and I sat in the down-stairs dining-room and ate some hard-boiled eggs and drank several bottles of beer. Belmonte came down in his street clothes with his manager and two other men. They sat at the next table and ate. Belmonte ate very little. They were leaving on the seven o'clock train for Barcelona. Belmonte wore a blue-striped shirt and a dark suit, and ate soft-boiled eggs. The others ate a big meal. Belmonte did not talk. He only answered questions.

Bill was tired after the bull-fight. So was I. We both took a bull-fight very hard. We sat and ate the eggs and I watched Belmonte and the people at his table. The men with him were tough-looking and businesslike.

"Come on over to the café," Bill said. "I want an absinthe."

It was the last day of the fiesta. Outside it was beginning to be cloudy again. The square was full of people and the fireworks experts were making up their set pieces for the night and covering them over with beech branches. Boys were watching. We passed stands of rockets with long bamboo stems. Outside the café there was a great crowd. The music and the dancing were going on. The giants and the dwarfs were passing.

"Where's Edna?" I asked Bill.

"I don't know."

We watched the beginning of the evening of the last night of the fiesta. The absinthe made everything seem better. I drank it without sugar in the dripping glass, and it was pleasantly bitter.

"I feel sorry about Cohn," Bill said. "He had an awful time."

"Oh, to hell with Cohn," I said.

"Where do you suppose he went?"

"Up to Paris."

"What do you suppose he'll do?"

"Oh, to hell with him."

"What do you suppose he'll do?"

"Pick up with his old girl, probably."

"Who was his old girl?"

"Somebody named Frances."

We had another absinthe.

"When do you go back?" I asked.

"To-morrow."

After a little while Bill said: "Well, it was a swell fiesta."

"Yes," I said; "something doing all the time."

"You wouldn't believe it. It's like a wonderful nightmare."

"Sure," I said. "I'd believe anything. Including nightmares."

"What's the matter? Feel low?"

"Low as hell."

"Have another absinthe. Here, waiter! Another absinthe for this señor."

"I feel like hell," I said.

"Drink that," said Bill. "Drink it slow."

It was beginning to get dark. The fiesta was going on. I began to feel drunk but I did not feel any better.

"How do you feel?"

"I feel like hell."

"Have another?"

"It won't do any good."

"Try it. You can't tell; maybe this is the one that gets it. Hey, waiter! Another absinthe for this señor!"

I poured the water directly into it and stirred it instead of letting it drip. Bill put in a lump of ice. I stirred the ice around with a spoon in the brownish, cloudy mixture.

"How is it?"

"Fine."

"Don't drink it fast that way. It will make you sick."

I set down the glass. I had not meant to drink it fast.

"I feel tight."

"You ought to."

"That's what you wanted, wasn't it?"

"Sure. Get tight. Get over your damn depression."

"Well, I'm tight. Is that what you want?"

"Sit down."

"I won't sit down," I said. "I'm going over to the hotel."

I was very drunk. I was drunker than I ever remembered having been. At the hotel I went up-stairs. Brett's door was open. I put my head in the room. Mike was sitting on the bed. He waved a bottle.

"Jake," he said. "Come in, Jake."

I went in and sat down. The room was unstable unless I looked at some fixed point.

"Brett, you know. She's gone off with the bull-fighter chap."

"No."

"Yes. She looked for you to say good-bye. They went on the seven o'clock train."

"Did they?"

"Bad thing to do," Mike said. "She shouldn't have done it."

"No."

"Have a drink? Wait while I ring for some beer."

"I'm drunk," I said. "I'm going in and lie down."

"Are you blind? I was blind myself."

"Yes," I said, "I'm blind."

"Well, bung-o," Mike said. "Get some sleep, old Jake."

I went out the door and into my own room and lay on the bed. The bed went sailing off and I sat up in bed and looked at the wall to make it stop. Outside in the square the fiesta was going on. It did not mean anything. Later Bill and Mike came in to get me to go down and eat with them. I pretended to be asleep.

"He's asleep. Better let him alone."

"He's blind as a tick," Mike said. They went out.

I got up and went to the balcony and looked out at the dancing in the square. The world was not wheeling any more. It was just very clear and bright, and inclined to blur at the edges. I washed, brushed my hair. I looked strange to myself in the glass, and went down-stairs to the dining-room.

"Here he is!" said Bill. "Good old Jake! I knew you wouldn't pass out."

"Hello, you old drunk," Mike said.

"I got hungry and woke up."

"Eat some soup," Bill said.

The three of us sat at the table, and it seemed as though about six people were missing.

BOOK THREE

CHAPTER XIX

IN the morning it was all over. The fiesta was finished. I woke about nine o'clock, had a bath, dressed, and went down-stairs. The square was empty and there were no people on the streets. A few children were picking up rocket-sticks in the square. The cafés were just opening and the waiters were carrying out the comfortable white wicker chairs and arranging them around the marble-topped tables in the shade of the arcade. They were sweeping the streets and sprinkling them with a hose.

I sat in one of the wicker chairs and leaned back comfortably. The waiter was in no hurry to come. The white-paper announcements of the unloading of the bulls and the big schedules of special trains were still up on the pillars of the arcade. A waiter wearing a blue apron came out with a bucket of water and a cloth, and commenced to tear down the notices, pulling the paper off in strips and washing and rubbing away the paper that stuck to the stone. The fiesta was over.

I drank a coffee and after a while Bill came over. I watched him come walking across the square. He sat down at the table and ordered a coffee.

"Well," he said, "it's all over."

"Yes," I said. "When do you go?"

"I don't know. We better get a car, I think. Aren't you going back to Paris?"

"No. I can stay away another week. I think I'll go to San Sebastian."

"I want to get back."

"What's Mike going to do?"

"He's going to Saint Jean de Luz."

"Let's get a car and all go as far as Bayonne. You can get the train up from there to-night."

"Good. Let's go after lunch."

"All right. I'll get the car."

We had lunch and paid the bill. Montoya did not come near us. One of the maids brought the bill. The car was outside. The chauffeur piled and strapped the bags on top of the car and put them in beside him in the front seat and we got in. The car went out of the square, along through the side streets, out under the trees and down the hill and away from Pamplona. It did not seem like a very long ride. Mike had a bottle of Fundador. I only took a couple of drinks. We came over the mountains and out of Spain and down the white roads and through the overfoliaged, wet, green, Basque country, and finally into Bayonne. We left Bill's baggage at the station, and he bought a ticket to Paris. His train left at seven-ten. We came out of the station. The car was standing out in front.

"What shall we do about the car?" Bill asked.

"Oh, bother the car," Mike said. "Let's just keep the car with us."

"All right," Bill said. "Where shall we go?"

"Let's go to Biarritz and have a drink."

"Old Mike the spender," Bill said.

We drove in to Biarritz and left the car outside a very Ritz place. We went into the bar and sat on high stools and drank a whiskey and soda.

"That drink's mine," Mike said.

"Let's roll for it."

So we rolled poker dice out of a deep leather dice-cup. Bill was out first roll. Mike lost to me and handed the bartender a hundred-franc note. The whiskeys were twelve francs apiece. We had another round and Mike lost again. Each time he gave the bartender a good tip. In a room off the bar there was a good jazz band playing. It was a pleasant bar. We had another round. I went out on the first roll with four kings. Bill and Mike rolled. Mike won the first roll with four jacks. Bill won the second. On the final roll Mike had three kings and let them stay. He handed the dice-cup to Bill. Bill rattled them and rolled, and there were three kings, an ace, and a queen.

"It's yours, Mike," Bill said. "Old Mike, the gambler."

"I'm so sorry," Mike said. "I can't get it."

"What's the matter?"

"I've no money," Mike said. "I'm stony. I've just twenty francs. Here, take twenty francs."

Bill's face sort of changed.

"I just had enough to pay Montoya. Damned lucky to have it, too."

"I'll cash you a check," Bill said.

"That's damned nice of you, but you see I can't write checks."

"What are you going to do for money?"

"Oh, some will come through. I've two weeks allowance should be here. I can live on tick at this pub in Saint Jean."

"What do you want to do about the car?" Bill asked me. "Do you want to keep it on?"

"It doesn't make any difference. Seems sort of idiotic."

"Come on, let's have another drink," Mike said.

"Fine. This one is on me," Bill said. "Has Brett any money?" He turned to Mike.

"I shouldn't think so. She put up most of what I gave to old Montoya."

"She hasn't any money with her?" I asked.

"I shouldn't think so. She never has any money. She gets five hundred quid a year and pays three hundred and fifty of it in interest to Jews."

"I suppose they get it at the source," said Bill.

"Quite. They're not really Jews. We just call them Jews. They're Scotsmen, I believe."

"Hasn't she any at all with her?" I asked.

"I hardly think so. She gave it all to me when she left."

"Well," Bill said, "we might as well have another drink."

"Damned good idea," Mike said. "One never gets anywhere by discussing finances."

"No," said Bill. Bill and I rolled for the next two rounds. Bill lost and paid. We went out to the car.

"Anywhere you'd like to go, Mike?" Bill asked.

"Let's take a drive. It might do my credit good. Let's drive about a little."

"Fine. I'd like to see the coast. Let's drive down toward Hendaye."

"I haven't any credit along the coast."

"You can't ever tell," said Bill.

We drove out along the coast road. There was the green of the headlands, the white, red-roofed villas, patches of forest, and the ocean very blue with the tide out and the water curling far out along the beach. We drove through Saint Jean de Luz and passed through villages farther down the coast. Back of the rolling country we were going through we saw the mountains we had come over from Pamplona. The road went on ahead. Bill looked at his watch. It was time for us to go back. He knocked on the glass and told the driver to turn around. The driver backed the car out into the grass to turn it. In back of us were the woods, below a stretch of meadow, then the sea.

At the hotel where Mike was going to stay in Saint Jean we stopped the car and he got out. The chauffeur carried in his bags. Mike stood by the side of the car.

"Good-bye, you chaps," Mike said. "It was a damned fine fiesta."

"So long, Mike," Bill said.

"I'll see you around," I said.

"Don't worry about money," Mike said. "You can pay for the car, Jake, and I'll send you my share."

"So long, Mike."

"So long, you chaps. You've been damned nice."

We all shook hands. We waved from the car to Mike. He stood in the road watching. We got to Bayonne just before the train left. A porter carried Bill's bags in from the consigne. I went as far as the inner gate to the tracks.

"So long, fella," Bill said.

"So long, kid!"

"It was swell. I've had a swell time."

"Will you be in Paris?"

"No. I have to sail on the 17th. So long, fella!"

"So long, old kid!"

He went in through the gate to the train. The porter went ahead with the bags. I watched the train pull out. Bill was at one of the windows. The window passed, the rest of the train passed, and the tracks were empty. I went outside to the car.

"How much do we owe you?" I asked the driver. The price to Bayonne had been fixed at a hundred and fifty pesetas.

"Two hundred pesetas."

"How much more will it be if you drive me to San Sebastian on your way back?"

"Fifty pesetas."

"Don't kid me."

"Thirty-five pesetas."

"It's not worth it," I said. "Drive me to the Hotel Panier Fleuri."

At the hotel I paid the driver and gave him a tip. The car was powdered with dust. I rubbed the rod-case through the dust. It seemed the last thing that connected me with Spain and the fiesta. The driver put the car in gear and went down the street. I watched it turn off to take the road to Spain. I went into the hotel and they gave me a room. It was the same room I had slept in when Bill and Cohn and I were in Bayonne. That seemed a very long time ago. I washed, changed my shirt, and went out in the town.

At a newspaper kiosque I bought a copy of the New York *Herald* and sat in a café to read it. It felt strange to be in France again. There was a safe, suburban feeling. I wished I had gone up to Paris with Bill, except that Paris would have meant more fiesta-ing. I was through with fiestas for a while. It would be quiet in San Sebastian. The season does not open there until August. I could get a good hotel room and read and swim. There was a fine beach there. There were wonderful trees along the promenade above the beach, and there were many children sent down with their nurses before the season opened. In the evening there would be band concerts under the trees across from the Café Marinas. I could sit in the Marinas and listen.

"How does one eat inside?" I asked the waiter. Inside the café was a restaurant.

"Well. Very well. One eats very well."

"Good."

I went in and ate dinner. It was a big meal for France but it seemed very carefully apportioned after Spain. I drank a bottle of wine for company. It was a Château Margaux. It was pleasant to be drinking slowly and to be tasting the wine and to be drinking alone. A bottle of wine was good company. Afterward I had coffee. The waiter recommended a Basque liqueur called Izzarra. He brought in the bottle and poured a liqueur-glass full. He said Izzarra was made of the flowers of the Pyrenees. The veritable flowers of the Pyrenees. It looked like hair-oil and smelled like Italian *strega*. I told him to take the flowers of the Pyrenees away and bring me a *vieux marc*. The *marc* was good. I had a second *marc* after the coffee.

The waiter seemed a little offended about the flowers of the Pyrenees, so I overtipped him. That made him happy. It felt comfortable to be in a country where it is so simple to make people happy. You can never tell whether a Spanish waiter will thank you. Everything is on such a clear financial basis in France. It is the simplest country to live in. No one makes things complicated by becoming your friend for any obscure reason. If you want people to like you you have only to spend a little money. I spent a little money and the waiter liked me. He appreciated my valuable qualities. He would be glad to see me back. I would dine there again some time and he would be glad to see me, and would want me at his table. It would be a sincere liking because it would have a sound basis. I was back in France.

Next morning I tipped every one a little too much at the hotel to make more friends, and left on the morning train for San Sebastian. At the station I did not tip the porter more than I should because I did not think I would ever see him again. I only wanted a few good

French friends in Bayonne to make me welcome in case I should come back there again. I knew that if they remembered me their friendship would be loyal.

At Irun we had to change trains and show passports. I hated to leave France. Life was so simple in France. I felt I was a fool to be going back into Spain. In Spain you could not tell about anything. I felt like a fool to be going back into it, but I stood in line with my passport, opened my bags for the customs, bought a ticket, went through a gate, climbed onto the train, and after forty minutes and eight tunnels I was at San Sebastian.

Even on a hot day San Sebastian has a certain early-morning quality. The trees seem as though their leaves were never quite dry. The streets feel as though they had just been sprinkled. It is always cool and shady on certain streets on the hottest day. I went to a hotel in the town where I had stopped before, and they gave me a room with a balcony that opened out above the roofs of the town. There was a green mountainside beyond the roofs.

I unpacked my bags and stacked my books on the table beside the head of the bed, put out my shaving things, hung up some clothes in the big armoire, and made up a bundle for the laundry. Then I took a shower in the bathroom and went down to lunch. Spain had not changed to summer-time, so I was early. I set my watch again. I had recovered an hour by coming to San Sebastian.

As I went into the dining-room the concierge brought me a police bulletin to fill out. I signed it and asked him for two telegraph forms, and wrote a message to the Hotel Montoya, telling them to forward all mail and telegrams for me to this address. I calculated how many days I would be in San Sebastian and then wrote out a wire to the office asking them to hold mail, but forward all wires for me to San Sebastian for six days. Then I went in and had lunch.

After lunch I went up to my room, read a while, and went to sleep. When I woke it was half past four. I found my swimming-suit, wrapped it with a comb in a towel, and went down-stairs and walked up the street to the Concha. The tide was about half-way out. The beach was smooth and firm, and the sand yellow. I went into a bathing-cabin, undressed, put on my suit, and walked across the smooth sand to the sea. The sand was warm under bare feet. There were quite a few people in the water and on the beach. Out beyond where the headlands of the Concha almost met to form the harbor there was a white line of breakers and the open sea. Although the tide was going out, there were a few slow rollers. They came in like undulations in the water, gathered weight of water, and then broke smoothly on the warm sand. I waded out. The water was cold. As a roller came I dove, swam out under water, and came to the surface with all the chill gone. I swam out to the raft, pulled myself up, and lay on the hot planks. A boy and girl were at the other end. The girl had undone the top strap of her bathing-suit and was browning her back. The boy lay face downward on the raft and talked to her. She laughed at things he said, and turned her brown back in the sun. I lay on the raft in the sun until I was dry. Then I tried several dives. I dove deep once, swimming down to the bottom. I swam with my eyes open and it was green and dark. The raft made a dark shadow. I came out of water beside the raft, pulled up, dove once more, holding it for length, and then swam ashore. I lay on the beach until I was dry, then went into the bathing-cabin, took off my suit, sloshed myself with fresh water, and rubbed dry.

I walked around the harbor under the trees to
the casino, and then up one of the cool streets to the
Café Marinas. There was an orchestra playing inside
the café and I sat out on the terrace and enjoyed the
fresh coolness in the hot day, and had a glass of
lemon-juice and shaved ice and then a long whiskey
and soda. I sat in front of the Marinas for a long time
and read and watched the people, and listened to the
music.

Later when it began to get dark, I walked around
the harbor and out along the promenade, and finally back
to the hotel for supper. There was a bicycle-race on, the
Tour du Pays Basque, and the riders were stopping that
night in San Sebastian. In the dining-room, at one side,
there was a long table of bicycle-riders, eating with their
trainers and managers. They were all French and Bel-
gians, and paid close attention to their meal, but they
were having a good time. At the head of the table were
two good-looking French girls, with much Rue du Fau-
bourg Montmartre chic. I could not make out whom they
belonged to. They all spoke in slang at the long table
and there were many private jokes and some jokes at the
far end that were not repeated when the girls asked to
hear them. The next morning at five o'clock the race
resumed with the last lap, San Sebastian-Bilbao. The
bicycle-riders drank much wine, and were burned and
browned by the sun. They did not take the race seriously
except among themselves. They had raced among themselves so often that it did not make much difference who
won. Especially in a foreign country. The money could
be arranged.

The man who had a matter of two minutes lead in the
race had an attack of boils, which were very painful.
He sat on the small of his back. His neck was very red
and the blond hairs were sunburned. The other riders

joked him about his boils. He tapped on the table with his fork.

"Listen," he said, "to-morrow my nose is so tight on the handle-bars that the only thing touches those boils is a lovely breeze."

One of the girls looked at him down the table, and he grinned and turned red. The Spaniards, they said, did not know how to pedal.

I had coffee out on the terrasse with the team manager of one of the big bicycle manufacturers. He said it had been a very pleasant race, and would have been worth watching if Bottechia had not abandoned it at Pamplona. The dust had been bad, but in Spain the roads were better than in France. Bicycle road-racing was the only sport in the world, he said. Had I ever followed the Tour de France? Only in the papers. The Tour de France was the greatest sporting event in the world. Following and organizing the road races had made him know France. Few people know France. All spring and all summer and all fall he spent on the road with bicycle road-racers. Look at the number of motor-cars now that followed the riders from town to town in a road race. It was a rich country and more *sportif* every year. It would be the most *sportif* country in the world. It was bicycle road-racing did it. That and football. He knew France. *La France Sportive.* He knew road-racing. We had a cognac. After all, though, it wasn't bad to get back to Paris. There is only one Paname. In all the world, that is. Paris is the town the most *sportif* in the world. Did I know the *Chope de Nègre*? Did I not. I would see him there some time. I certainly would. We would drink another *fine* together. We certainly would. They started at six o'clock less a quarter in the morning. Would I be up for the depart? I would certainly try to. Would I like him to call me? It was very interesting. I would leave a call at the desk. He would not mind calling me. I could not let him take the trouble. I would leave a call at the desk. We said good-bye until the next morning.

In the morning when I awoke the bicycle-riders and their following cars had been on the road for three hours. I had coffee and the papers in bed and then dressed and took my bathing-suit down to the beach. Everything was fresh and cool and damp in the early morning. Nurses in uniform and in peasant costume walked under the trees with children. The Spanish children were beautiful. Some bootblacks sat together under a tree talking to a soldier. The soldier had only one arm. The tide was in and there was a good breeze and a surf on the beach.

I undressed in one of the bath-cabins, crossed the narrow line of beach and went into the water. I swam out, trying to swim through the rollers, but having to dive sometimes. Then in the quiet water I turned and floated. Floating I saw only the sky, and felt the drop and lift of the swells. I swam back to the surf and coasted in, face down, on a big roller, then turned and swam, try-ing to keep in the trough and not have a wave break over me. It made me tired, swimming in the trough, and I turned and swam out to the raft. The water was buoyant and cold. It felt as though you could never sink. I swam slowly, it seemed like a long swim with the high tide, and then pulled up on the raft and sat, dripping, on the boards that were becoming hot in the sun. I looked round at the bay, the old town, the casino, the line of trees along the promenade, and the big hotels with their white porches and gold-lettered names. Off on the right, almost closing the harbor, was a green hill with a castle. The raft rocked with the motion of the water. On the other side of the narrow gap that led into the open sea was another high headland. I thought I would like to swim across the bay but I was afraid of cramp.

I sat in the sun and watched the bathers on the beach.
They looked very small. After a while I stood up, gripped
with my toes on the edge of the raft as it tipped with
my weight, and dove cleanly and deeply, to come up
through the lightening water, blew the salt water out
of my head, and swam slowly and steadily in to shore.

After I was dressed and had paid for the bath-cabin, I
walked back to the hotel. The bicycle-racers had left
several copies of *L'Auto* around, and I gathered them up
in the reading-room and took them out and sat in an easy
chair in the sun to read about and catch up on French
sporting life. While I was sitting there the concierge came
out with a blue envelope in his hand.

"A telegram for you, sir."

I poked my finger along under the fold that was fastened down, spread it open, and read it. It had been forwarded from Paris:

COULD YOU COME HOTEL MONTANA
MADRID AM RATHER IN TROUBLE BRETT.

I tipped the concierge and read the message again. A
postman was coming along the sidewalk. He turned in the
hotel. He had a big moustache and looked very military.
He came out of the hotel again. The concierge was just
behind him.

"Here's another telegram for you, sir."

"Thank you," I said.

I opened it. It was forwarded from Pamplona.

COULD YOU COME HOTEL MONTANA
MADRID AM RATHER IN TROUBLE BRETT.

The concierge stood there waiting for another tip
probably.

"What time is there a train for Madrid?"

"It left at nine this morning. There is a slow train at eleven, and the Sud Express at ten to-night."

"Get me a berth on the Sud Express. Do you want the money now?"

"Just as you wish," he said. "I will have it put on the bill."

"Do that."

Well, that meant San Sebastian all shot to hell. I suppose, vaguely, I had expected something of the sort. I saw the concierge standing in the doorway.

"Bring me a telegram form, please."

He brought it and I took out my fountain-pen and printed:

LADY ASHLEY HOTEL MONTANA MADRID
ARRIVING SUD EXPRESS TOMORROW LOVE
JAKE.

That seemed to handle it. That was it. Send a girl off with one man. Introduce her to another to go off with him. Now go and bring her back. And sign the wire with love. That was it all right. I went in to lunch.

I did not sleep much that night on the Sud Express. In the morning I had breakfast in the dining-car and watched the rock and pine country between Avila and Escorial. I saw the Escorial out of the window, gray and long and cold in the sun, and did not give a damn about it. I saw Madrid come up over the plain, a compact white sky-line on the top of a little cliff away off across the sun-hardened country.

The Norte station in Madrid is the end of the line. All trains finish there. They don't go on anywhere. Outside were cabs and taxis and a line of hotel runners. It was like a country town. I took a taxi and we climbed up

through the gardens, by the empty palace and the u‐
finished church on the edge of the cliff, and on up un‐
we were in the high, hot, modern town. The taxi coaste‐
down a smooth street to the Puerta del Sol, and the‐
through the traffic and out into the Carrera San Jeronim‐
All the shops had their awnings down against the hea‐
The windows on the sunny side of the street were shu‐
tered. The taxi stopped at the curb. I saw the sign HOTE‐
MONTANA on the second floor. The taxi-driver carrie‐
the bags in and left them by the elevator. I could n‐
make the elevator work, so I walked up. On the secor‐
floor up was a cut brass sign: HOTEL MONTANA. I rar‐
and no one came to the door. I rang again and a ma‐
with a sullen face opened the door.

"Is Lady Ashley here?" I asked.

She looked at me dully.

"Is an Englishwoman here?"

She turned and called some one inside. A very f‐
woman came to the door. Her hair was gray and stif‐
oiled in scallops around her face. She was short ar‐
commanding.

"Muy buenos," I said. "Is there an Englishwoma‐
here? I would like to see this English lady."

"Muy buenos. Yes, there is a female English. Ce‐
tainly you can see her if she wishes to see you."

"She wishes to see me."

"The chica will ask her."

"It is very hot."

"It is very hot in the summer in Madrid."

"And how cold in winter."

"Yes, it is very cold in winter."

Did I want to stay myself in person in the Hot‐
Montana?

Of that as yet I was undecided, but it would give n‐

easure if my bags were brought up from the ground
oor in order that they might not be stolen. Nothing
as ever stolen in the Hotel Montana. In other fondas,
es. Not here. No. The personages of this establishment
ere rigidly selectioned. I was happy to hear it. Never-
eless I would welcome the upbringal of my bags.

The maid came in and said that the female English
anted to see the male English now, at once.

"Good," I said. "You see. It is as I said."

"Clearly."

I followed the maid's back down a long, dark corridor.
t the end she knocked on a door.

"Hello," said Brett. "Is it you, Jake?"

"It's me."

"Come in. Come in."

I opened the door. The maid closed it after me. Brett
as in bed. She had just been brushing her hair and held
e brush in her hand. The room was in that disorder
oduced only by those who have always had servants.

"Darling!" Brett said.

I went over to the bed and put my arms around her.
e kissed me, and while she kissed me I could feel she
as thinking of something else. She was trembling in my
ms. She felt very small.

"Darling! I've had such a hell of a time."

"Tell me about it."

"Nothing to tell. He only left yesterday. I made him
."

"Why didn't you keep him?"

"I don't know. It isn't the sort of thing one does. I
n't think I hurt him any."

"You were probably damn good for him."

"He shouldn't be living with any one. I realized that
ght away."

"No."

"Oh, hell!" she said, "let's not talk about it. Let
never talk about it."

"All right."

"It was rather a knock his being ashamed of me. H
was ashamed of me for a while, you know."

"No."

"Oh, yes. They ragged him about me at the café,
guess. He wanted me to grow my hair out. Me, with lon
hair. I'd look so like hell."

"It's funny."

"He said it would make me more womanly. I'd loc
a fright."

"What happened?"

"Oh, he got over that. He wasn't ashamed of me long

"What was it about being in trouble?"

"I didn't know whether I could make him go, and
didn't have a sou to go away and leave him. He trie
to give me a lot of money, you know. I told him I ha
scads of it. He knew that was a lie. I couldn't take h
money, you know."

"No."

"Oh, let's not talk about it. There were some funn
things, though. Do give me a cigarette."

I lit the cigarette.

"He learned his English as a waiter in Gib."

"Yes."

"He wanted to marry me, finally."

"Really?"

"Of course. I can't even marry Mike."

"Maybe he thought that would make him Lor
Ashley."

"No. It wasn't that. He really wanted to marry m
So I couldn't go away from him, he said. He wanted t

"We'll have two more Martinis."

"As they were before, sir?"

"They were very good." Brett smiled at him.

"Thank you, ma'am."

"Well, bung-o," Brett said.

"Bung-o!"

"You know," Brett said, "he'd only been with two women before. He never cared about anything but bullfighting."

"He's got plenty of time."

"I don't know. He thinks it was me. Not the show in general."

"Well, it was you."

"Yes. It was me."

"I thought you weren't going to ever talk about it."

"How can I help it?"

"You'll lose it if you talk about it."

"I just talk around it. You know I feel rather damned good, Jake."

"You should."

"You know it makes one feel rather good deciding not to be a bitch."

"Yes."

"It's sort of what we have instead of God."

"Some people have God," I said. "Quite a lot."

"He never worked very well with me."

"Should we have another Martini?"

The barman shook up two more Martinis and poured them out into fresh glasses.

"Where will we have lunch?" I asked Brett. The bar was cool. You could feel the heat outside through the window.

"Here?" asked Brett.

"It's rotten here in the hotel. Do you know a place called Botin's?" I asked the barman.

"Yes, sir. Would you like to have me write out the address?"

"Thank you."

We lunched up-stairs at Botin's. It is one of the best restaurants in the world. We had roast young suckling pig and drank *rioja alta*. Brett did not eat much. She never ate much. I ate a very big meal and drank three bottles of *rioja alta*.

"How do you feel, Jake?" Brett asked. "My God! what a meal you've eaten."

"I feel fine. Do you want a dessert?"

"Lord, no."

Brett was smoking.

"You like to eat, don't you?" she said.

"Yes," I said. "I like to do a lot of things."

"What do you like to do?"

"Oh," I said, "I like to do a lot of things. Don't you want a dessert?"

"You asked me that once," Brett said.

"Yes," I said. "So I did. Let's have another bottle of *rioja alta*."

"It's very good."

"You haven't drunk much of it," I said.

"I have. You haven't seen."

"Let's get two bottles," I said. The bottles came. I poured a little in my glass, then a glass for Brett, then filled my glass. We touched glasses.

"Bung-o!" Brett said. I drank my glass and poured out another. Brett put her hand on my arm.

"Don't get drunk, Jake," she said. "You don't have to."

"How do you know?"

"Don't," she said. "You'll be all right."

"I'm not getting drunk," I said. "I'm just drinking a little wine. I like to drink wine."

"Don't get drunk," she said. "Jake, don't get drunk."

"Want to go for a ride?" I said. "Want to ride through the town?"

"Right," Brett said. "I haven't seen Madrid. I should see Madrid."

"I'll finish this," I said.

Down-stairs we came out through the first-door dining-room to the street. A waiter went for a taxi. It was hot and bright. Up the street was a little square with trees and grass where there were taxis parked. A taxi came up the street, the waiter hanging out at the side. I tipped him and told the driver where to drive, and got in beside Brett. The driver started up the street. I settled back. Brett moved close to me. We sat close against each other. I put my arm around her and she rested against me comfortably. It was very hot and bright, and the houses looked sharply white. We turned out onto the Gran Via.

"Oh, Jake," Brett said, "we could have had such a damned good time together."

Ahead was a mounted policeman in khaki directing traffic. He raised his baton. The car slowed suddenly pressing Brett against me.

"Yes," I said. "Isn't it pretty to think so?"

A FAREWELL TO ARMS

CAPORETTO

EDITOR'S PREFACE

A *Farewell to Arms* is more purely fictional than
Hemingway's first novel. Although the author served
with an ambulance section in Italy; although he later
enlisted in the Italian shock troops, the Arditi; and although he was seriously wounded and received a silver
medal like his hero, Frederic Henry, he did not take
part in the Caporetto retreat, nor did he ever flee into
Switzerland with his beloved. For the germ of the war
story, see Chapter VI of *In Our Time*, reprinted in this
volume. It tells how Nick Adams, sitting wounded
against the wall of a church, turns his head to look down
at Rinaldi. "Senta Rinaldo; Senta," he says. "You and me
we've made a separate peace." For the germ of the love
story, see "A Very Short Story," in the same book.

But there is more to be said about *A Farewell to Arms*.

If you think of Hemingway's four novels as telling a more
or less connected story, a legend of war and peace, then
this would be the first volume, even though it was written
three years after *The Sun Also Rises*. You might say that
the author goes back to explain how Lady Brett and
Jake Barnes became the sort of people they were. Brett
can't be Catherine Barkley, for Catherine is dead; but
she might be Catherine's sister, or her ghost, and she has
been molded by almost the same experiences. Jake is
what Frederic Henry might have become six years after
the war. When we read the story of the Caporetto
retreat—a great story, here reprinted in full—we learn
that the real nature of his wound was moral rather than
physical. What he lost at the crossing of the Tagliamento
was not his manhood but his faith in organized society.

A Farewell to Arms was serialized in *Scribner's Magazine* before being published in September 1929. It had
a sale in the trade edition of 93,000 copies, very large for
that year when people were reading nothing but the
ticker tape. Later it appeared in cheaper editions and was
translated into I don't know how many languages. It
was dramatized by Laurence Stallings (the play had a
short run) and was also sold to the movies, although
when Hemingway saw what they had done with it, he
tried to buy it back again.

CAPORETTO

CHAPTER I

NOW in the fall the trees were all bare and the roads were muddy. I rode to Gorizia from Udine on a camion. We passed other camions on the road and I looked at the country. The mulberry trees were bare and the fields were brown. There were wet dead leaves on the road from the rows of bare trees and men were working on the road, tamping stone in the ruts from piles of crushed stone along the side of the road between the trees. We saw the town with a mist over it that cut off the mountains. We crossed the river and I saw that it was running high. It had been raining in the mountains. We came into the town past the factories and then the houses and villas and I saw that many more houses had been hit. On a narrow street we passed a British Red Cross ambulance. The driver wore a cap and his face was thin and very tanned. I did not know him. I got down from the camion in the big square in front of the Town Major's house, the driver handed down my rucksack and I put it on and swung on the two musettes and walked to our villa. It did not feel like a homecoming.

I walked down the damp gravel driveway looking at the villa through the trees. The windows were all shut but the door was open. I went in and found the major sitting at a table in the bare room with maps and typed sheets of paper on the wall.

"Hello," he said. "How are you?" He looked older and drier.

"I'm good," I said. "How is everything?"

"It's all over," he said. "Take off your kit and sit down." I put my pack and the two musettes on the floor and my cap on the pack. I brought the other chair over from the wall and sat down by the desk.

"It's been a bad summer," the major said. "Are you strong now?"

"Yes."

"Did you ever get the decorations?"

"Yes. I got them fine. Thank you very much."

"Let's see them."

I opened my cape so he could see the two ribbons.

"Did you get the boxes with the medals?"

"No. Just the papers."

"The boxes will come later. That takes more time."

"What do you want me to do?"

"The cars are all away. There are six up north at Caporetto. You know Caporetto?"

"Yes," I said. I remembered it as a little white town with a campanile in a valley. It was a clean little town and there was a fine fountain in the square.

"They are working from there. There are many sick now. The fighting is over."

"Where are the others?"

"There are two up in the mountains and four still on the Bainsizza. The other two ambulance sections are in the Carso with the third army."

"What do you wish me to do?"

"You can go and take over the four cars on the Bainsizza if you like. Gino has been up there a long time. You haven't seen it up there, have you?"

"No."

"It was very bad. We lost three cars."

"I heard about it."

"Yes, Rinaldi wrote you."

"Where is Rinaldi?"

"He is here at the hospital. He has had a summer and fall of it."

"I believe it."

"It has been bad," the major said. "You couldn't believe how bad it's been. I've often thought you were lucky to be hit when you were."

"I know I was."

"Next year will be worse," the major said. "Perhaps they will attack now. They say they are to attack but I can't believe it. It is too late. You saw the river?"

"Yes. It's high already."

"I don't believe they will attack now that the rains have started. We will have the snow soon. What about your countrymen? Will there be other Americans besides yourself?"

"They are training an army of ten million."

"I hope we get some of them. But the French will hog them all. We'll never get any down here. All right. You stay here to-night and go out to-morrow with the little car and send Gino back. I'll send somebody with you that knows the road. Gino will tell you everything. They are shelling quite a little still but it is all over. You will want to see the Bainsizza."

"I'm glad to see it. I am glad to be back with you again, Signor Maggiore."

He smiled. "You are very good to say so. I am very tired of this war. If I was away I do not believe I would come back."

"Is it so bad?"

"Yes. It is so bad and worse. Go get cleaned up and find your friend Rinaldi."

I went out and carried my bags up the stairs. Rinaldi was not in the room but his things were there and I sat down on the bed and unwrapped my puttees and took the shoe off my right foot. Then I lay back on the bed. I was tired and my right foot hurt. It seemed silly to lie on the bed with one shoe off, so I sat up and unlaced the other shoe and dropped it on the floor, then lay back on the blanket again. The room was stuffy with the window closed but I was too tired to get up and open it. I saw my things were all in one corner of the room. Outside it was getting dark. I lay on the bed and thought about Catherine and waited for Rinaldi. I was going to try not to think about Catherine except at night before I went to sleep. But now I was tired and there was nothing to do, so I lay and thought about her. I was thinking about her when Rinaldi came in. He looked just the same. Perhaps he was a little thinner.

"Well, baby," he said. I sat up on the bed. He came over, sat down and put his arm around me. "Good old baby." He whacked me on the back and I held both his arms.

"Old baby," he said. "Let me see your knee."

"I'll have to take off my pants."

"Take off your pants, baby. We're all friends here. I want to see what kind of a job they did." I stood up, took off the breeches and pulled off the knee-brace. Rinaldi sat on the floor and bent the knee gently back and forth. He ran his finger along the scar; put his thumbs together over the kneecap and rocked the knee gently with his fingers.

"Is that all the articulation you have?"

"Yes."

"It's a crime to send you back. They ought to get complete articulation."

"It's a lot better than it was. It was stiff as a board."

Rinaldi bent it more. I watched his hands. He had fine surgeon's hands. I looked at the top of his head, his hair shiny and parted smoothly. He bent the knee too far.

"Ouch!" I said.

"You ought to have more treatment on it with the machines," Rinaldi said.

"It's better than it was."

"I see that, baby. This is something I know more about than you." He stood up and sat down on the bed. "The knee itself is a good job." He was through with the knee. "Tell me all about everything."

"There's nothing to tell," I said. "I've led a quiet life."

"You act like a married man," he said. "What's the matter with you?"

"Nothing," I said. "What's the matter with you?"

"This war is killing me," Rinaldi said, "I am very depressed by it." He folded his hands over his knee.

"Oh," I said.

"What's the matter? Can't I even have human impulses?"

"No. I can see you've been having a fine time. Tell me."

"All summer and all fall I've operated. I work all the time. I do everybody's work. All the hard ones they leave to me. By God, baby, I am becoming a lovely surgeon."

"That sounds better."

"I never think. No, by God, I don't think; I operate."

"That's right."

"But now, baby, it's all over. I don't operate now and I feel like hell. This is a terrible war, baby. You believe me when I say it. Now you cheer me up. Did you bring the phonograph records?"

"Yes."

They were wrapped in paper in a cardboard box in my rucksack. I was too tired to get them out.

"Don't you feel good yourself, baby?"

"I feel like hell."

"This war is terrible," Rinaldi said. "Come on. We'll both get drunk and be cheerful. Then we'll go get the ashes dragged. Then we'll feel fine."

"I've had the jaundice," I said, "and I can't get drunk."

"Oh, baby, how you've come back to me. You come back serious and with a liver. I tell you this war is a bad thing. Why did we make it anyway?"

"We'll have a drink. I don't want to get drunk but we'll have a drink."

Rinaldi went across the room to the washstand and brought back two glasses and a bottle of cognac.

"It's Austrian cognac," he said. "Seven stars. It's all they captured on San Gabriele."

"Were you up there?"

"No. I haven't been anywhere. I've been here all the time operating. Look, baby, this is your old tooth-brushing glass. I kept it all the time to remind me of you."

"To remind you to brush your teeth."

"No. I have my own too. I kept this to remind me of you trying to brush away the Villa Rossa from your teeth in the morning, swearing and eating aspirin and cursing harlots. Every time I see that glass I think of you trying to clean your conscience with a toothbrush." He came over to the bed. "Kiss me once and tell me you're not serious."

"I never kiss you. You're an ape."

"I know, you are the fine good Anglo-Saxon boy. I know. You are the remorse boy, I know. I will wait till I see the Anglo-Saxon brushing away harlotry with a toothbrush."

"Put some cognac in the glass."

We touched glasses and drank. Rinaldi laughed at me.

"I will get you drunk and take out your liver and put you in a good Italian liver and make you a man again."

I held the glass for some more cognac. It was dark outside now. Holding the glass of cognac, I went over and opened the window. The rain had stopped falling. It was colder outside and there was a mist in the trees.

"Don't throw the cognac out the window," Rinaldi said. "If you can't drink it give it to me."

"Go something yourself," I said. I was glad to see Rinaldi again. He had spent two years teasing me and I had always liked it. We understood each other very well.

"Are you married?" he asked from the bed. I was standing against the wall by the window.

"Not yet."

"Are you in love?"

"Yes."

"With that English girl?"

"Yes."

"Poor baby. Is she good to you?"

"Of course."

"I mean is she good to you practically speaking?"

"Shut up."

"I will. You will see I am a man of extreme delicacy. Does she——?"

"Rinin," I said. "Please shut up. If you want to be my friend, shut up."

"I don't *want* to be your friend, baby. I *am* your friend."

"Then shut up."

"All right."

I went over to the bed and sat down beside Rinaldi. He was holding his glass and looking at the floor.

"You see how it is, Rinin?"

"Oh, yes. All my life I encounter sacred subjects. But very few with you. I suppose you must have them too." He looked at the floor.

"You haven't any?"

"No."

"Not any?"

"No."

"I can say this about your mother and that about your sister?"

"And that about *your sister*," Rinaldi said swiftly. We both laughed.

"The old superman," I said.

"I am jealous maybe," Rinaldi said.

"No, you're not."

"I don't mean like that. I mean something else. Have you any married friends?"

"Yes," I said.

"I haven't," Rinaldi said. "Not if they love each other."

"Why not?"

"They don't like me."

"Why not?"

"I am the snake. I am the snake of reason."

"You're getting it mixed. The apple was reason."

"No, it was the snake." He was more cheerful.

"You are better when you don't think so deeply," I said.

"I love you, baby," he said. "You puncture me when I become a great Italian thinker. But I know many things I can't say. I know more than you."

"Yes. You do."

"But you will have a better time. Even with remorse you will have a better time."

"I don't think so."

"Oh, yes. That is true. Already I am only happy when I am working." He looked at the floor again.

"You'll get over that."

"No. I only like two other things; one is bad for my work and the other is over in half an hour or fifteen minutes. Sometimes less."

"Sometimes a good deal less."

"Perhaps I have improved, baby. You do not know. But there are only the two things and my work."

"You'll get other things."

"No. We never get anything. We are born with all we have and we never learn. We never get anything new. We all start complete. You should be glad not to be a Latin."

"There's no such thing as a Latin. That is 'Latin' thinking. You are so proud of your defects." Rinaldi looked up and laughed.

"We'll stop, baby. I am tired from thinking so much." He had looked tired when he came in "It's nearly time to eat. I'm glad you're back. You are my best friend and my war brother."

"When do the war brothers eat?" I asked.

"Right away. We'll drink once more for your liver's sake."

"Like Saint Paul."

"You are inaccurate. That was wine and the stomach. Take a little wine for your stomach's sake."

"Whatever you have in the bottle," I said. "For any sake you mention."

"To your girl," Rinaldi said. He held out his glass.

"All right."

"I'll never say a dirty thing about her."

"Don't strain yourself."

He drank off the cognac. "I am pure," he said. "I am like you, baby. I will get an English girl too. As a matter of fact I knew your girl first but she was a little tall for me. A tall girl for a sister," he quoted.

"You have a lovely pure mind," I said.

"Haven't I? That's why they call me Rinaldo Purissimo."

"Rinaldo Sporchissimo."

"Come on, baby, we'll go down to eat while my mind is still pure."

I washed, combed my hair and we went down the stairs. Rinaldi was a little drunk. In the room where we ate, the meal was not quite ready.

"I'll go get the bottle," Rinaldi said. He went off up the stairs. I sat at the table and he came back with the bottle and poured us each a half tumbler of cognac.

"Too much," I said and held up the glass and sighted at the lamp on the table.

"Not for an empty stomach. It is a wonderful thing. It burns out the stomach completely. Nothing is worse for you."

"All right."

"Self-destruction day by day," Rinaldi said. "It ruins the stomach and makes the hand shake. Just the thing for a surgeon."

"You recommend it?"

"Heartily. I use no other. Drink it down, baby, and look forward to being sick."

I drank half the glass. In the hall I could hear the orderly calling. "Soup! Soup is ready!"

The major came in, nodded to us and sat down. He seemed very small at table.

"Is this all we are?" he asked. The orderly put the soup bowl down and he ladled out a plate full.

"We are all," Rinaldi said. "Unless the priest comes. If he knew Federico was here he would be here."

"Where is he?" I asked.

"He's at 307," the major said. He was busy with his

soup. He wiped his mouth, wiping his upturned gray mustache carefully. "He will come I think. I called them and left word to tell him you were here."

"I miss the noise of the mess," I said.

"Yes, it's quiet," the major said.

"I will be noisy," said Rinaldi.

"Drink some wine, Enrico," said the major. He filled my glass. The spaghetti came in and we were all busy. We were finishing the spaghetti when the priest came in. He was the same as ever, small and brown and compact looking. I stood up and we shook hands. He put his hand on my shoulder.

"I came as soon as I heard," he said.

"Sit down," the major said. "You're late."

"Good-evening, priest," Rinaldi said, using the English word. They had taken that up from the priest-baiting captain, who spoke a little English. "Good-evening, Rinaldo," the priest said. The orderly brought him soup but he said he would start with the spaghetti.

"How are you?" he asked me.

"Fine," I said. "How have things been?"

"Drink some wine, priest," Rinaldi said. "Take a little wine for your stomach's sake. That's Saint Paul, you know."

"Yes I know," said the priest politely. Rinaldi filled his glass.

"That Saint Paul," said Rinaldi. "He's the one who makes all the trouble." The priest looked at me and smiled. I could see that the baiting did not touch him now.

"That Saint Paul," Rinaldi said. "He was a rounder and a chaser and then when he was no longer hot he said it was no good. When he was finished he made the rules for us who are still hot. Isn't it true, Federico?"

The major smiled. We were eating meat stew now.

"I never discuss a Saint after dark," I said. The priest looked up from the stew and smiled at me.

"There he is, gone over with the priest," Rinaldi said. "Where are all the good old priest-baiters? Where is Cavalcanti? Where is Brundi? Where is Cesare? Do I have to bait this priest alone without support?"

"He is a good priest," said the major.

"He is a good priest," said Rinaldi. "But still a priest. I try to make the mess like the old days. I want to make Federico happy. To hell with you, priest!"

I saw the major look at him and notice that he was drunk. His thin face was white. The line of his hair was very black against the white of his forehead.

"It's all right, Rinaldo," said the priest. "It's all right."

"To hell with you," said Rinaldi. "To hell with the whole damn business." He sat back in his chair.

"He's been under a strain and he's tired," the major said to me. He finished his meat and wiped up the gravy with a piece of bread.

"I don't give a damn," Rinaldi said to the table. "To hell with the whole business." He looked defiantly around the table, his eyes flat, his face pale.

"All right," I said. "To hell with the whole damn business."

"No, no," said Rinaldi. "You can't do it. You can't do it. I say you can't do it. You're dry and you're empty and there's nothing else. There's nothing else I tell you. Not a damned thing. I know, when I stop working."

The priest shook his head. The orderly took away the stew dish.

"What are you eating meat for?" Rinaldi turned to the priest. "Don' you know it's Friday?"

"It's Thursday," the priest said.

"It's a lie. It's Friday. You're eating the body of our Lord. It's God-meat. I know. It's dead Austrian. That's what you're eating."

"The white meat is from officers," I said, completing the old joke.

Rinaldi laughed. He filled his glass.

"Don't mind me," he said. "I'm just a little crazy."

"You ought to have a leave," the priest said.

The major shook his head at him. Rinaldi looked at the priest.

"You think I ought to have a leave?"

The major shook his head at the priest. Rinaldi was looking at the priest.

"Just as you like," the priest said. "Not if you don't want."

"To hell with you," Rinaldi said. "They try to get rid of me. Every night they try to get rid of me. I fight them off. What if I have it. Everybody has it. The whole world's got it. First," he went on, assuming the manner of a lecturer, "it's a little pimple. Then we notice a rash between the shoulders. Then we notice nothing at all. We put our faith in mercury."

"Or salvarsan," the major interrupted quietly.

"A mercurial product," Rinaldi said. He acted very elated now. "I know something worth two of that. Good old priest," he said. "You'll never get it. Baby will get it. It's an industrial accident. It's a simple industrial accident."

The orderly brought in the sweet and coffee. The dessert was a sort of black bread pudding with hard sauce. The lamp was smoking; the black smoke going close up inside the chimney.

"Bring two candles and take away the lamp," the major said. The orderly brought two lighted candles each in a saucer, and took out the lamp blowing it out. Rinaldi was quiet now. He seemed all right. We talked and after the coffee we all went out into the hall.

"You want to talk to the priest. I have to go in the town," Rinaldi said. "Good-night, priest."

"Good-night, Rinaldo," the priest said.

"I'll see you Fredi," Rinaldi said.

"Yes," I said. "Come in early." He made a face and went out the door. The major was standing with us. "He's very tired and overworked," he said. "He thinks too he has syphilis. I don't believe it but he may have. He is treating himself for it. Good-night. You will leave before daylight, Enrico?"

"Yes."

"Good-by then," he said. "Good luck. Peduzzi will wake you and go with you."

"Good-by, Signor Maggiore."

"Good-by. They talk about an Austrian offensive but I don't believe it. I hope not. But anyway it won't be here. Gino will tell you everything. The telephone works well now."

"I'll call regularly."

"Please do. Good-night. Don't let Rinaldi drink so much brandy."

"I'll try not to."

"Good-night, priest."

"Good-night, Signor Maggiore."

He went off into his office.

CHAPTER II

I WENT to the door and looked out. It had stopped raining but there was a mist.

"Should we go upstairs?" I asked the priest.

"I can only stay a little while."

"Come on up."

We climbed the stairs and went into my room. I lay down on Rinaldi's bed. The priest sat on my cot that the orderly had set up. It was dark in the room.

"Well," he said, "how are you really?"

"I'm all right. I'm tired to-night."

"I'm tired too, but from no cause."

"What about the war?"

"I think it will be over soon. I don't know why, but I feel it."

"How do you feel it?"

"You know how your major is? Gentle? Many people are like that now."

"I feel that way myself," I said.

"It has been a terrible summer," said the priest. He was surer of himself now than when I had gone away. "You cannot believe how it has been. Except that you have been there and you know how it can be. Many people have realized the war this summer. Officers whom I thought could never realize it realize it now."

"What will happen?" I stroked the blanket with my hand.

"I do not know but I do not think it can go on much longer."

"What will happen?"

"They will stop fighting."

"Who?"

"Both sides."

"I hope so," I said.

"You don't believe it?"

"I don't believe both sides will stop fighting at once."

"I suppose not. It is too much to expect. But when I see the changes in men I do not think it can go on."

"Who won the fighting this summer?"

"No one."

"The Austrians won," I said. "They kept them from taking San Gabriele. They've won. They won't stop fighting."

"If they feel as we feel they may stop. They have gone through the same thing."

"No one ever stopped when they were winning."

"You discourage me."

"I can only say what I think."

"Then you think it will go on and on? Nothing will ever happen?"

"I don't know. I only think the Austrians will not stop when they have won a victory. It is in defeat that we become Christian."

"The Austrians are Christians—except for the Bosnians."

"I don't mean technically Christian. I mean like Our Lord."

He said nothing.

"We are all gentler now because we are beaten. How would Our Lord have been if Peter had rescued him in the Garden?"

"He would have been just the same."

"I don't think so," I said.

"You discourage me," he said. "I believe and I pray that something will happen. I have felt it very close."

"Something may happen," I said. "But it will happen only to us. If they felt the way we do, it would be all right. But they have beaten us. They feel another way."

"Many of the soldiers have always felt this way. It is not because they were beaten."

"They were beaten to start with. They were beaten when they took them from their farms and put them in the army. That is why the peasant has wisdom, because he is defeated from the start. Put him in power and see how wise he is."

He did not say anything. He was thinking.

"Now I am depressed myself," I said. "That's why I never think about these things. I never think and yet when I begin to talk I say the things I have found out in my mind without thinking."

"I had hoped for something."

"Defeat?"

"No. Something more."

"There isn't anything more. Except victory. It may be worse."

"I hoped for a long time for victory."

"Me too."

"Now I don't know."

"It has to be one or the other."

"I don't believe in victory any more."

"I don't. But I don't believe in defeat. Though it may be better."

"What do you believe in?"

"In sleep," I said. He stood up.

"I am very sorry to have stayed so long. But I like so to talk with you."

"It is very nice to talk again. I said that about sleeping, meaning nothing."

We stood up and shook hands in the dark.

"I sleep at 307 now," he said.

"I go out on post early to-morrow."

"I'll see you when you come back."

"We'll have a walk and talk together." I walked with him to the door.

"Don't go down," he said. "It is very nice that you are back. Though not so nice for you." He put his hand on my shoulder.

"It's all right for me," I said. "Good-night."

"Good-night. Ciaou!"

"Ciaou!" I said. I was deadly sleepy.

CHAPTER III

I WOKE when Rinaldi came in but he did not talk and I went back to sleep again. In the morning I was dressed and gone before it was light. Rinaldi did not wake when I left.

I had not seen the Bainsizza before and it was strange to go up the slope where the Austrians had been, beyond the place on the river where I had been wounded. There was a steep new road and many trucks. Beyond, the road flattened out and I saw woods and steep hills in the mist. There were woods that had been taken quickly and not smashed. Then beyond where the road was not protected by the hills it was screened by matting on the sides and over the top. The road ended in a wrecked village. The lines were up beyond. There was much artillery around. The houses were badly smashed but things were very well organized and there were signboards everywhere. We found Gino and he got us some coffee and later I went with him and met various people and saw the posts. Gino said the British cars were working further down the Bainsizza at Ravne. He had great admiration for the British. There was still a certain amount of shelling, he said, but not many wounded. There would be many sick now the rains had started. The Austrians were supposed to attack but he did not believe it. We were supposed to attack too, but they had not brought up any new troops so he thought that was

off too. Food was scarce and he would be glad to get a
full meal in Gorizia. What kind of supper had I had? I
told him and he said that would be wonderful. He was
especially impressed by the *dolce*. I did not describe it
in detail, only said it was a *dolce*, and I think he believed
it was something more elaborate than bread pudding.

Did I know where he was going to go? I said I didn't
but that some of the other cars were at Caporetto. He
hoped he would go up that way. It was a nice little place
and he liked the high mountain hauling up beyond. He
was a nice boy and every one seemed to like him. He
said where it really had been hell was at San Gabriele
and the attack beyond Lom that had gone bad. He said
the Austrians had a great amount of artillery in the woods
along Ternova ridge beyond and above us, and shelled
the roads badly at night. There was a battery of naval
guns that had gotten on his nerves. I would recognize
them because of their flat trajectory. You heard the report and then the shriek commenced almost instantly.
They usually fired two guns at once, one right after the
other, and the fragments from the burst were enormous.
He showed me one, a smoothly jagged piece of metal over
a foot long. It looked like babbiting metal.

"I don't suppose they are so effective," Gino said.
"But they scare me. They all sound as though they came
directly for you. There is the boom, then instantly the
shriek and burst. What's the use of not being wounded if
they scare you to death?"

He said there were Croats in the lines opposite us
now and some Magyars. Our troops were still in the
attacking positions. There was no wire to speak of and
no place to fall back to if there should be an Austrian
attack. There were fine positions for defense along the
low mountains that came up out of the plateau but

nothing had been done about organizing them for defense. What did I think about the Bainsizza anyway?

I had expected it to be flatter, more like a plateau. I had not realized it was so broken up.

"Alto piano," Gino said, "but no piano."

We went back to the cellar of the house where he lived. I said I thought a ridge that flattened out on top and had a little depth would be easier and more practical to hold than a succession of small mountains. It was no harder to attack up a mountain than on the level, I argued. "That depends on the mountains," he said. "Look at San Gabriele."

"Yes," I said, "but where they had trouble was at the top where it was flat. They got up to the top easy enough."

"Not so easy," he said.

"Yes," I said, "but that was a special case because it was a fortress rather than a mountain, anyway. The Austrians had been fortifying it for years." I meant tactically speaking in a war where there was some movement a succession of mountains were nothing to hold as a line because it was too easy to turn them. You should have possible mobility and a mountain is not very mobile. Also, people always over-shoot down hill. If the flank were turned, the best men would be left on the highest mountains. I did not believe in a war in mountains. I had thought about it a lot, I said. You pinched off one mountain and they pinched off another but when something really started every one had to get down off the mountains.

What were you going to do if you had a mountain frontier? he asked.

I had not worked that out yet, I said, and we both laughed. "But," I said, "in the old days the Austrians were always whipped in the quadrilateral around Ve

na. They let them come down onto the plain and
hipped them there."

"Yes," said Gino. "But those were Frenchmen and
ou can work out military problems clearly when you
e fighting in somebody else's country."

"Yes," I agreed, "when it is your own country you
annot use it so scientifically."

"The Russians did, to trap Napoleon."

"Yes, but they had plenty of country. If you tried to
etreat to trap Napoleon in Italy you would find yourself
Brindisi."

"A terrible place," said Gino. "Have you ever been
ere?"

"Not to stay."

"I am a patriot," Gino said. "But I cannot love Brindisi
Taranto."

"Do you love the Bainsizza?" I asked.

"The soil is sacred," he said. "But I wish it grew more
otatoes. You know when we came here we found fields
potatoes the Austrians had planted."

"Has the food really been short?"

"I myself have never had enough to eat but I am a
g eater and I have not starved. The mess is average.
he regiments in the line get pretty good food but those
support don't get so much. Something is wrong some-
here. There should be plenty of food."

"The dogfish are selling it somewhere else."

"Yes, they give the battalions in the front line as much
they can but the ones in back are very short. They
ave eaten all the Austrians' potatoes and chestnuts from
e woods. They ought to feed them better. We are big
ters. I am sure there is plenty of food. It is very bad for
e soldiers to be short of food. Have you ever noticed
e difference it makes in the way you think?"

"Yes," I said. "It can't win a war but it can lose one."

"We won't talk about losing. There is enough tall
about losing. What has been done this summer canno
have been done in vain."

I did not say anything. I was always embarrassed by
the words sacred, glorious, and sacrifice and the expres
sion in vain. We had heard them, sometimes standing i
the rain almost out of earshot, so that only the shouted
words came through, and had read them, on proclama
tions that were slapped up by billposters over othe
proclamations, now for a long time, and I had seen noth
ing sacred, and the things that were glorious had no glory
and the sacrifices were like the stockyards at Chicago i
nothing was done with the meat except to bury it. Ther
were many words that you could not stand to hear and
finally only the names of places had dignity. Certain
numbers were the same way and certain dates and these
with the names of the places were all you could say and
have them mean anything. Abstract words such as glory
honor, courage, or hallow were obscene beside the con
crete names of villages, the numbers of roads, the name
of rivers, the numbers of regiments and the dates. Gin
was a patriot, so he said things that separated us some
times, but he was also a fine boy and I understood hi
being a patriot. He was born one. He left with Peduzz
in the car to go back to Gorizia.

It stormed all that day. The wind drove down the
rain and everywhere there was standing water and mud
The plaster of the broken houses was gray and wet. Lat
in the afternoon the rain stopped and from out numbe
two post I saw the bare wet autumn country with cloud
over the tops of the hills and the straw screening ove
the roads wet and dripping. The sun came out once be
fore it went down and shone on the bare woods beyond
the ridge. There were many Austrian guns in the wood
on that ridge but only a few fired. I watched the sudde

ound puffs of shrapnel smoke in the sky above a broken
armhouse near where the line was; soft puffs with a
ellow white flash in the centre. You saw the flash, then
eard the crack, then saw the smoke ball distort and
hin in the wind. There were many iron shrapnel balls
n the rubble of the houses and on the road beside the
roken house where the post was, but they did not shell
ear the post that afternoon. We loaded two cars and
rove down the road that was screened with wet mats
nd the last of the sun came through in the breaks be-
veen the strips of mattings. Before we were out on the
lear road behind the hill the sun was down. We went
n down the clear road and as it turned a corner into
he open and went into the square arched tunnel of mat-
ng the rain started again.

The wind rose in the night and at three o'clock in the
norning with the rain coming in sheets there was a
ombardment and the Croatians came over across the
nountain meadows and through patches of woods and
nto the front line. They fought in the dark in the rain
nd a counter-attack of scared men from the second line
rove them back. There was much shelling and many
ockets in the rain and machine-gun and rifle fire all along
he line. They did not come again and it was quieter
nd between the gusts of wind and rain we could hear
he sound of a great bombardment far to the north.

The wounded were coming into the post, some were
arried on stretchers, some walking and some were
rought on the backs of men that came across the field.
hey were wet to the skin and all were scared. We filled
vo cars with stretcher cases as they came up from the
ellar of the post and as I shut the door of the second car
nd fastened it I felt the rain on my face turn to snow.
he flakes were coming heavy and fast in the rain.

When daylight came the storm was still blowing but

the snow had stopped. It had melted as it fell on th
wet ground and now it was raining again. There wa
another attack just after daylight but it was unsuccess
ful. We expected an attack all day but it did not com
until the sun was going down. The bombardment starte
to the south below the long wooded ridge where th
Austrian guns were concentrated. We expected a bom
bardment but it did not come. It was getting dark. Gun
were firing from the field behind the village and th
shells, going away, had a comfortable sound.

We heard that the attack to the south had been un
successful. They did not attack that night but we hear
that they had broken through to the north. In the nigh
word came that we were to prepare to retreat. The cap
tain at the post told me this. He had it from the Brigade
A little while later he came from the telephone and sai
it was a lie. The Brigade had received orders that th
line of the Bainsizza should be held no matter what hap
pened. I asked about the break through and he said tha
he had heard at the Brigade that the Austrians ha
broken through the twenty-seventh army corps up to
ward Caporetto. There had been a great battle in th
north all day.

"If those bastards let them through we are cooked,
he said.

"It's Germans that are attacking," one of the medica
officers said. The word Germans was something to b
frightened of. We did not want to have anything to d
with the Germans.

"There are fifteen divisions of Germans," the medi
cal officer said. "They have broken through and we wil
be cut off."

"At the Brigade, they say this line is to be held. The
say they have not broken through badly and that w

will hold a line across the mountains from Monte Maggiore."

"Where do they hear this?"

"From the Division."

"The word that we were to retreat came from the Division."

"We work under the Army Corps," I said. "But here I work under you. Naturally when you tell me to go I will go. But get the orders straight."

"The orders are that we stay here. You clear the wounded from here to the clearing station."

"Sometimes we clear from the clearing station to the field hospitals too," I said. "Tell me, I have never seen a retreat—if there is a retreat how are all the wounded evacuated?"

"They are not. They take as many as they can and leave the rest."

"What will I take in the cars?"

"Hospital equipment."

"All right," I said.

The next night the retreat started. We heard that Germans and Austrians had broken through in the north and were coming down the mountain valleys toward Cividale and Udine. The retreat was orderly, wet and sullen. In the night, going slowly along the crowded roads we passed troops marching under the rain, guns, horses pulling wagons, mules, motor trucks, all moving away from the front. There was no more disorder than in an advance.

That night we helped empty the field hospitals that had been set up in the least ruined villages of the plateau, taking the wounded down to Plava on the riverbed: and the next day hauled all day in the rain to evacuate the hospitals and clearing station at Plava. It rained steadily and the army of the Bainsizza moved down off the plateau in the October rain and across the river where the great victories had commenced in the spring of that year. We came into Gorizia in the middle of the next day. The rain had stopped and the town was nearly empty. As we came up the street they were loading the girls from the soldiers' whorehouse into a truck. There were seven girls and they had on their hats and coats and carried small suitcases. Two of them were crying. Of the others one smiled at us and put out her tongue and fluttered it up and down. She had thick full lips and black eyes.

I stopped the car and went over and spoke to the matron. The girls from the officers' house had left early that morning, she said. Where were they going? To Conegliano, she said. The truck started. The girl with thick lips put out her tongue again at us. The matron waved. The two girls kept on crying. The others looked interestedly out at the town. I got back in the car.

"We ought to go with them," Bonello said. "That would be a good trip."

"We'll have a good trip," I said.

"We'll have a hell of a trip."

"That's what I mean," I said. We came up the drive to the villa.

"I'd like to be there when some of those tough babies climb in and try and hop them."

"You think they will?"

"Sure. Everybody in the Second Army knows that matron."

We were outside the villa.

"They call her the Mother Superior," Bonello said. "The girls are new but everybody knows her. They must have brought them up just before the retreat."

"They'll have a time."

"I'll say they'll have a time. I'd like to have a crack at them for nothing. They charge too much at that house anyway. The government gyps us."

"Take the car out and have the mechanics go over it," I said. "Change the oil and check the differential. Fill it up and then get some sleep."

"Yes, Signor Tenente."

The villa was empty. Rinaldi was gone with the hospital. The major was gone taking hospital personnel in the staff car. There was a note on the window for me to fill the cars with the material piled in the hall and to proceed to Pordenone. The mechanics were gone already. I went out back to the garage. The other two cars came in while I was there and their drivers got down. It was starting to rain again.

"I'm so ———— sleepy I went to sleep three times coming here from Plava," Piani said. "What are we going to do, Tenente?"

"We'll change the oil, grease them, fill them up, then take them around in front and load up the junk they've left."

"Then do we start?"

"No, we'll sleep for three hours."

"Christ I'm glad to sleep," Bonello said. "I couldn't keep awake driving."

"How's your car, Aymo?" I asked.

"It's all right."

"Get me a monkey suit and I'll help you with the oil."

"Don't you do that, Tenente," Aymo said. "It's nothing to do. You go and pack your things."

"My things are all packed," I said. "I'll go and carry out the stuff that they left for us. Bring the cars around as soon as they're ready."

They brought the cars around to the front of the villa and we loaded them with the hospital equipment which was piled in the hallway. When it was all in, the three cars stood in line down the driveway under the trees in the rain. We went inside.

"Make a fire in the kitchen and dry your things," I said.

"I don't care about dry clothes," Piani said. "I want to sleep."

"I'm going to sleep on the major's bed," Bonello said. "I'm going to sleep where the old man corks off."

"I don't care where I sleep," Piani said.

"There are two beds in here." I opened the door.

"I never knew what was in that room," Bonello said.

"That was old fish-face's room," Piani said.

"You two sleep in there," I said. "I'll wake you."

"The Austrians will wake us if you sleep too long, Tenente," Bonello said.

"I won't oversleep," I said. "Where's Aymo?"

"He went out in the kitchen."

"Get to sleep," I said.

"I'll sleep," Piani said. "I've been asleep sitting up all day. The whole top of my head kept coming down over my eyes."

"Take your boots off," Bonello said. "That's old fish-face's bed."

"Fish-face is nothing to me." Piani lay on the bed, his muddy boots straight out, his head on his arm. I went out to the kitchen. Aymo had a fire in the stove and a kettle of water on.

"I thought I'd start some *pasta asciutta*," he said. "We'll be hungry when we wake up."

"Aren't you sleepy, Bartolomeo?"

"Not so sleepy. When the water boils I'll leave it. The fire will go down."

"You'd better get some sleep," I said. "We can eat cheese and monkey meat."

"This is better," he said. "Something hot will be good for those two anarchists. You go to sleep, Tenente."

"There's a bed in the major's room."

"You sleep there."

"No, I'm going up to my old room. Do you want a drink, Bartolomeo?"

"When we go, Tenente. Now it wouldn't do me any good."

"If you wake in three hours and I haven't called you, wake me, will you?"

"I haven't any watch, Tenente."

"There's a clock on the wall in the major's room."

"All right."

I went out then through the dining-room and the hall and up the marble stairs to the room where I had lived with Rinaldi. It was raining outside. I went to the window and looked out. It was getting dark and I saw the three cars standing in line under the trees. The trees were dripping in the rain. It was cold and the drops hung to the branches. I went back to Rinaldi's bed and lay down and let sleep take me.

We ate in the kitchen before we started. Aymo had a basin of spaghetti with onions and tinned meat chopped up in it. We sat around the table and drank two bottles of the wine that had been left in the cellar of the villa. It was dark outside and still raining. Piani sat at the table very sleepy.

"I like a retreat better than an advance," Bonello said. "On a retreat we drink barbera."

"We drink it now. To-morrow maybe we drink rain-water," Aymo said.

"To-morrow we'll be in Udine. We'll drink champagne. That's where the slackers live. Wake up, Piani! We'll drink champagne to-morrow in Udine!"

"I'm awake," Piani said. He filled his plate with the

spaghetti and meat. "Couldn't you find tomato sauce, Barto?"

"There wasn't any," Aymo said.

"We'll drink champagne in Udine," Bonello said He filled his glass with the clear red barbera.

"We may drink ——— before Udine," Piani said.

"Have you eaten enough, Tenente?" Aymo asked.

"I've got plenty. Give me the bottle, Bartolomeo."

"I have a bottle apiece to take in the cars," Aymo said.

"Did you sleep at all?"

"I don't need much sleep. I slept a little."

"To-morrow we'll sleep in the king's bed," Bonello said. He was feeling very good.

"To-morrow maybe we'll sleep in ———," Piani said.

"I'll sleep with the queen," Bonello said. He looked to see how I took the joke.

"You'll sleep with ———," Piani said sleepily.

"That's treason, Tenente," Bonello said. "Isn't that treason?"

"Shut up," I said. "You get too funny with a little wine." Outside it was raining hard. I looked at my watch. It was half-past nine.

"It's time to roll," I said and stood up.

"Who are you going to ride with, Tenente?" Bonello asked.

"With Aymo. Then you come. Then Piani. We'll start out on the road for Cormons."

"I'm afraid I'll go to sleep," Piani said.

"All right. I'll ride with you. Then Bonello. Then Aymo."

"That's the best way," Piani said. "Because I'm so sleepy."

"I'll drive and you sleep awhile."

"No. I can drive just so long as I know somebody will wake me up if I go to sleep."

"I'll wake you up. Put out the lights, Barto."

"You might as well leave them," Bonello said. "We've got no more use for this place."

"I have a small locker trunk in my room," I said. "Will you help take it down, Piani?"

"We'll take it," Piani said. "Come on, Aldo." He went off into the hall with Bonello. I heard them going upstairs.

"This was a fine place," Bartolomeo Aymo said. He put two bottles of wine and half a cheese into his haversack. "There won't be a place like this again. Where will they retreat to, Tenente?"

"Beyond the Tagliamento, they say. The hospital and the sector are to be at Pordenone."

"This is a better town than Pordenone."

"I don't know Pordenone," I said. "I've just been through there."

"It's not much of a place," Aymo said.

CHAPTER IV

A S we moved out through the town it was empty in the rain and the dark except for columns of troops and guns that were going through the main street. There were many trucks too and some carts going through on other streets and converging on the main road. When we were out past the tanneries onto the main road the troops, the motor trucks, the horse-drawn carts and the guns were in one wide slow-moving column. We moved slowly but steadily in the rain, the radiator cap of our car almost against the tailboard of a truck that was loaded high, the load covered with wet canvas. Then the truck stopped. The whole column was stopped. It started again and we went a little farther, then stopped. I got out and walked ahead, going between the trucks and carts and under the wet necks of the horses. The block was farther ahead. I left the road, crossed the ditch on a footboard and walked along the field beyond the ditch. I could see the stalled column between the trees in the rain as I went forward across from it in the field. I went about a mile. The column did not move, although, on the other side beyond the stalled vehicles I could see the troops moving. I went back to the cars. This block might extend as far as Udine. Piani was asleep over the wheel. I climbed up beside him and went to sleep too. Several hours later I heard the truck ahead of us grinding into gear. I woke Piani and we started, moving a few yards, then stopping, then going on again. It was still raining.

The column stalled again in the night and did not start. I got down and went back to see Aymo and Bonello. Bonello had two sergeants of engineers on the seat of his car with him. They stiffened when I came up.

"They were left to do something to a bridge," Bonello said. "They can't find their unit so I gave them a ride."

"With the Sir Lieutenant's permission."

"With permission," I said.

"The lieutenant is an American," Bonello said. "He'll give anybody a ride."

One of the sergeants smiled. The other asked Bonello if I was an Italian from North or South America.

"He's not an Italian. He's North American English."

The sergeants were polite but did not believe it. I left them and went back to Aymo. He had two girls on the seat with him and was sitting back in the corner and smoking.

"Barto, Barto," I said. He laughed.

"Talk to them, Tenente," he said. "I can't understand

them. Hey!" he put his hand on the girl's thigh and squeezed it in a friendly way. The girl drew her shawl tight around her and pushed his hand away. "Hey!" he said. "Tell the Tenente your name and what you're doing here."

The girl looked at me fiercely. The other girl kept her eyes down. The girl who looked at me said something in a dialect I could not understand a word of. She was plump and dark and looked about sixteen.

"Sorella?" I asked and pointed at the other girl.

She nodded her head and smiled.

"All right," I said and patted her knee. I felt her stiffen away when I touched her. The sister never looked up. She looked perhaps a year younger. Aymo put his hand on the elder girl's thigh and she pushed it away. He laughed at her.

"Good man," he pointed at himself. "Good man," he pointed at me. "Don't you worry." The girl looked at him fiercely. The pair of them were like two wild birds.

"What does she ride with me for if she doesn't like me?" Aymo asked. "They got right up in the car the minute I motioned to them." He turned to the girl. "Don't worry," he said. "No danger of ————," using the vulgar word. "No place for ————." I could see she understood the word and that was all. Her eyes looked at him very scared. She pulled the shawl tight. "Car all full," Aymo said. "No danger of ————. No place for ————." Every time he said the word the girl stiffened a little. Then sitting stiffly and looking at him she began to cry. I saw her lips working and then tears came down her plump cheeks. Her sister, not looking up, took her hand and they sat there together. The older one, who had been so fierce, began to sob.

"I guess I scared her," Aymo said. "I didn't mean to scare her."

Bartolomeo brought out his knapsack and cut off two pieces of cheese. "Here," he said. "Stop crying."

The older girl shook her head and still cried, but the younger girl took the cheese and commenced to eat. After a while the younger girl gave her sister the second piece of cheese and they both ate. The older sister still sobbed a little.

"She'll be all right after a while," Aymo said.

An idea came to him. "Virgin?" he asked the girl next to him. She nodded her head vigorously. "Virgin too?" he pointed to the sister. Both the girls nodded their heads and the elder said something in dialect.

"That's all right," Bartolomeo said. "That's all right."

Both the girls seemed cheered.

I left them sitting together with Aymo sitting back in the corner and went back to Piani's car. The column of vehicles did not move but the troops kept passing alongside. It was still raining hard and I thought some of the stops in the movement of the column might be from cars with wet wiring. More likely they were from horses or men going to sleep. Still, traffic could tie up in cities when every one was awake. It was the combination of horse and motor vehicles. They did not help each other any. The peasants' carts did not help much either. Those were a couple of fine girls with Barto. A retreat was no place for two virgins. Real virgins. Probably very religious. If there were no war we would probably all be in bed. In bed I lay me down my head. Bed and board. Stiff as a board in bed. Catherine was in bed now between two sheets, over her and under her. Which side did she sleep on? Maybe she wasn't asleep. Maybe she was lying thinking about me. Blow, blow, ye western wind. Well, it blew and it wasn't the small rain but the big rain down that rained. It rained all night. You knew it rained down that rained. Look at it. Christ, that my love were in my arms and I in my bed again. That my love Catherine. That my sweet love Catherine down might rain. Blow her again to me. Well, we were in it. Every one was caught in it and the small rain would not quiet it. "Good-night, Catherine," I said out loud. "I hope you sleep well. If it's too uncomfortable, darling, lie on the other side," I said. "I'll get you some cold water. In a little while it will be morning and then it won't be so bad. I'm sorry he makes you so uncomfortable. Try and go to sleep, sweet."

I was asleep all the time, she said. You've been talking in your sleep. Are you all right?

Are you really there?

Of course I'm here. I wouldn't go way. This doesn't make any difference between us.

You're so lovely and sweet. You wouldn't go away in the night, would you?

Of course I wouldn't go away. I'm always here. I come whenever you want me.

"————," Piani said. "They've started again."

"I was dopey," I said. I looked at my watch. It was three o'clock in the morning. I reached back behind the seat for a bottle of the barbera.

"You talked out loud," Piani said.

"I was having a dream in English," I said.

The rain was slacking and we were moving along. Before daylight we were stalled again and when it was light we were at a little rise in the ground and I saw the road of the retreat stretched out far ahead, everything stationary except for the infantry filtering through. We started to move again but seeing the rate of progress in the daylight, I knew we were going to have to get off that main road some way and go across country if we ever hoped to reach Udine.

In the night many peasants had joined the column

from the roads of the country and in the column there were carts loaded with household goods; there were mirrors projecting up between mattresses, and chickens and ducks tied to carts. There was a sewing-machine on the cart ahead of us in the rain. They had saved the most valuable things. On some carts the women sat huddled from the rain and others walked beside the carts keeping as close to them as they could. There were dogs now in the column, keeping under the wagons as they moved along. The road was muddy, the ditches at the side were high with water and beyond the trees that lined the road the fields looked too wet and too soggy to try to cross. I got down from the car and worked up the road a way, looking for a place where I could see ahead to find a side-road we could take across country. I knew there were many side-roads but did not want one that would lead to nothing. I could not remember them because we had always passed them bowling along in the car on the main road and they all looked much alike. Now I knew we must find one if we hoped to get through. No one knew where the Austrians were nor how things were going but I was certain that if the rain should stop and planes come over and get to work on that column that it would be all over. All that was needed was for a few men to leave their trucks or a few horses be killed to tie up completely the movement on the road.

The rain was not falling so heavily now and I thought it might clear. I went ahead along the edge of the road and when there was a small road that led off to the north between two fields with a hedge of trees on both sides, I thought that we had better take it and hurried back to the cars. I told Piani to turn off and went back to tell Bonello and Aymo.

"If it leads nowhere we can turn around and cut back in," I said.

"What about these?" Bonello asked. His two sergeants were beside him on the seat. They were unshaven but still military looking in the early morning.

"They'll be good to push," I said. I went back to Aymo and told him we were going to try it across country.

"What about my virgin family?" Aymo asked. The two girls were asleep.

"They won't be very useful," I said. "You ought to have some one that could push."

"They could go back in the car," Aymo said. "There's room in the car."

"All right if you want them," I said. "Pick up somebody with a wide back to push."

"Bersaglieri," Aymo smiled. "They have the widest backs. They measure them. How do you feel, Tenente?"

"Fine. How are you?"

"Fine. But very hungry."

"There ought to be something up that road and we will stop and eat."

"How's your leg, Tenente?"

"Fine," I said. Standing on the step and looking up ahead I could see Piani's car pulling out onto the little side-road and starting up it, his car showing through the hedge of bare branches. Bonello turned off and followed him and then Piani worked his way out and we followed the two ambulances ahead along the narrow road between hedges. It led to a farmhouse. We found Piani and Bonello stopped in the farmyard. The house was low and long with a trellis with a grape-vine over the door. There was a well in the yard and Piani was getting up water to fill his radiator. So much going in low gear had boiled it out. The farmhouse was deserted. I looked back down the road, the farmhouse was on a slight elevation above the plain, and we could see over the country, and saw the road, the hedges, the fields and the line of trees along the main road where the retreat was passing. The two sergeants were looking through the house. The girls were awake and looking at the courtyard, the well and the two big ambulances in front of the farmhouse, with three drivers at the well. One of the sergeants came out with a clock in his hand.

"Put it back," I said. He looked at me, went in the house and came back without the clock.

"Where's your partner?" I asked.

"He's gone to the latrine." He got up on the seat of the ambulance. He was afraid we would leave him.

"What about breakfast, Tenente?" Bonello asked. "We could eat something. It wouldn't take very long."

"Do you think this road going down on the other side will lead to anything?"

"Sure."

"All right. Let's eat." Piani and Bonello went in the house.

"Come on," Aymo said to the girls. He held his hand to help them down. The older sister shook her head. They were not going into any deserted house. They looked after us.

"They are difficult," Aymo said. We went into the farmhouse together. It was large and dark, an abandoned feeling. Bonello and Piani were in the kitchen.

"There's not much to eat," Piani said. "They've cleaned it out."

Bonello sliced a big white cheese on the heavy kitchen table.

"Where was the cheese?"

"In the cellar. Piani found wine too and apples."

"That's a good breakfast."

Piani was taking the wooden cork out of a big wicker-covered wine jug. He tipped it and poured a copper pan full.

"It smells all right," he said. "Find some beakers, Barto."

The two sergeants came in.

"Have some cheese, sergeants," Bonello said.

"We should go," one of the sergeants said, eating his cheese and drinking a cup of wine.

"We'll go. Don't worry," Bonello said.

"An army travels on its stomach," I said.

"What?" asked the sergeant.

"It's better to eat."

"Yes. But time is precious."

"I believe the bastards have eaten already," Piani said. The sergeants looked at him. They hated the lot of us.

"You know the road?" one of them asked me.

"No," I said. They looked at each other.

"We would do best to start," the first one said.

"We are starting," I said. I drank another cup of the red wine. It tasted very good after the cheese and apple.

"Bring the cheese," I said and went out. Bonello came out carrying the great jug of wine.

"That's too big," I said. He looked at it regretfully.

"I guess it is," he said. "Give me the canteens to fill." He filled the canteens and some of the wine ran out on the stone paving of the courtyard. Then he picked up the wine jug and put it just inside the door.

"The Austrians can find it without breaking the door down," he said.

"We'll roll," I said. "Piani and I will go ahead." The two engineers were already on the seat beside Bonello. The girls were eating cheese and apples. Aymo was smoking. We started off down the narrow road. I looked back at the two cars coming and the farmhouse. It was a fine, low, solid stone house and the ironwork of the well was very good. Ahead of us the road was narrow and muddy and there was a high hedge on either side. Behind, the cars were following closely.

CHAPTER V

AT noon we were stuck in a muddy road about as nearly as we could figure, ten kilometres from Udine. The rain had stopped during the forenoon and three times we had heard planes coming, seen them pass overhead, watched them go far to the left and heard them bombing on the main highroad. We had worked through a network of secondary roads and had taken many roads that were blind, but had always, by backing up and finding another road, gotten closer to Udine. Now, Aymo's car, in backing so that we might get out of a blind road, had gotten into the soft earth at the side and the wheels, spinning, had dug deeper and deeper until the car rested on its differential. The thing to do now was to dig out in front of the wheels, put in brush so that the chains could grip, and then push until the car was on the road. We were all down on the road around the car. The two sergeants looked at the car and examined the wheels. Then they started off down the road without a word. I went after them.

"Come on," I said. "Cut some brush."

"We have to go," one said.

"Get busy," I said, "and cut brush."

"We have to go," one said. The other said nothing. They were in a hurry to start. They would not look at me.

"I order you to come back to the car and cut brush,"

I said. The one sergeant turned. "We have to go on. In a little while you will be cut off. You can't order us. You're not our officer."

"I order you to cut brush," I said. They turned and started down the road.

"Halt," I said. They kept on down the muddy road, the hedge on either side. "I order you to halt," I called. They went a little faster. I opened up my holster, took the pistol, aimed at the one who had talked the most, and fired. I missed and they both started to run. I shot three times and dropped one. The other went through the hedge and was out of sight. I fired at him through the hedge as he ran across the field. The pistol clicked empty and I put in another clip. I saw it was too far to shoot at the second sergeant. He was far across the field, running, his head held low. I commenced to reload the empty clip. Bonello came up.

"Let me go finish him," he said. I handed him the pistol and he walked down to where the sergeant of engineers lay face down across the road. Bonello leaned over, put the pistol against the man's head and pulled the trigger. The pistol did not fire.

"You have to cock it," I said. He cocked it and fired twice. He took hold of the sergeant's legs and pulled him to the side of the road so he lay beside the hedge. He came back and handed me the pistol.

"The son of a bitch," he said. He looked toward the sergeant. "You see me shoot him, Tenente?"

"We've got to get the brush quickly," I said. "Did I hit the other one at all?"

"I don't think so," Aymo said. "He was too far away to hit with a pistol."

"The dirty scum," Piani said. We were all cutting twigs and branches. Everything had been taken out of the car. Bonello was digging out in front of the wheels. When we were ready Aymo started the car and put it into gear. The wheels spun round throwing brush and mud. Bonello and I pushed until we could feel our joints crack. The car would not move.

"Rock her back and forth, Barto," I said.

He drove the engine in reverse, then forward. The wheels only dug in deeper. Then the car was resting on the differential again, and the wheels spun freely in the holes they had dug. I straightened up.

"We'll try her with a rope," I said.

"I don't think it's any use, Tenente. You can't get a straight pull."

"We have to try it," I said. "She won't come out any other way."

Piani's and Bonello's cars could only move straight ahead down the narrow road. We roped both cars together and pulled. The wheels only pulled sideways against the ruts.

"It's no good," I shouted. "Stop it."

Piani and Bonello got down from their cars and came back. Aymo got down. The girls were up the road about forty yards sitting on a stone wall.

"What do you say, Tenente?" Bonello asked.

"We'll dig out and try once more with the brush," I said. I looked down the road. It was my fault. I had led them up here. The sun was almost out from behind the clouds and the body of the sergeant lay beside the hedge.

"We'll put his coat and cape under," I said. Bonello went to get them. I cut brush and Aymo and Piani dug out in front and between the wheels. I cut the cape, then ripped it in two, and laid it under the wheel in the mud, then piled brush for the wheels to catch. We were ready to start and Aymo got up on the seat and started the car.

The wheels spun and we pushed and pushed. But it wasn't any use.

"It's ———ed," I said. "Is there anything you want in the car, Barto?"

Aymo climbed up with Bonello, carrying the cheese and two bottles of wine and his cape. Bonello, sitting behind the wheel, was looking through the pockets of the sergeant's coat.

"Better throw the coat away," I said. "What about Barto's virgins?"

"They can get in the back," Piani said. "I don't think we are going far."

I opened the back door of the ambulance.

"Come on," I said. "Get in." The two girls climbed in and sat in the corner. They seemed to have taken no notice of the shooting. I looked back up the road. The sergeant lay in his dirty long-sleeved underwear. I got up with Piani and we started. We were going to try to cross the field. When the road entered the field I got down and walked ahead. If we could get across, there was a road on the other side. We could not get across. It was too soft and muddy for the cars. When they were finally and completely stalled, the wheels dug in to the hubs, we left them in the field and started on foot for Udine.

When we came to the road which led back toward the main highway I pointed down it to the two girls.

"Go down there," I said. "You'll meet people." They looked at me. I took out my pocket-book and gave them each a ten-lira note. "Go down there," I said, pointing. "Friends! Family!"

They did not understand but they held the money tightly and started down the road. They looked back as though they were afraid I might take the money back.

I watched them go down the road, their shawls close around them, looking back apprehensively at us. The three drivers were laughing.

"How much will you give me to go in that direction, Tenente?" Bonello asked.

"They're better off in a bunch of people than alone if they catch them," I said.

"Give me two hundred lire and I'll walk straight back toward Austria," Bonello said.

"They'd take it away from you," Piani said.

"Maybe the war will be over," Aymo said. We were going up the road as fast as we could. The sun was trying to come through. Beside the road were mulberry trees. Through the trees I could see our two big moving-vans of cars stuck in the field. Piani looked back too.

"They'll have to build a road to get them out," he said.

"I wish to Christ we had bicycles," Bonello said.

"Do they ride bicycles in America?" Aymo asked.

"They used to."

"Here it is a great thing," Aymo said. "A bicycle is a splendid thing."

"I wish to Christ we had bicycles," Bonello said. "I'm no walker."

"Is that firing?" I asked. I thought I could hear firing a long way away.

"I don't know," Aymo said. He listened.

"I think so," I said.

"The first thing we will see will be the cavalry," Piani said.

"I don't think they've got any cavalry."

"I hope to Christ not," Bonello said. "I don't want to be stuck on a lance by any ———— cavalry."

"You certainly shot that sergeant, Tenente," Piani said. We were walking fast.

"I killed him," Bonello said. "I never killed anybody

in this war, and all my life I've wanted to kill a sergeant."

"You killed him on the sit all right," Piani said. "He wasn't flying very fast when you killed him."

"Never mind. That's one thing I can always remember. I killed that ———— of a sergeant."

"What will you say in confession?" Aymo asked.

"I'll say, 'Bless me, Father, I killed a sergeant.'" They all laughed.

"He's an anarchist," Piani said. "He doesn't go to church."

"Piani's an anarchist too," Bonello said.

"Are you really anarchists?" I asked.

"No, Tenente. We're socialists. We come from Imola."

"Haven't you ever been there?"

"No."

"By Christ it's a fine place, Tenente. You come there after the war and we'll show you something."

"Are you all socialists?"

"Everybody."

"Is it a fine town?"

"Wonderful. You never saw a town like that."

"How did you get to be socialists?"

"We're all socialists. Everybody is a socialist. We've always been socialists."

"You come, Tenente. We'll make you a socialist too."

Ahead the road turned off to the left and there was a little hill and, beyond a stone wall, an apple orchard. As the road went uphill they ceased talking. We walked along together all going fast against time.

CHAPTER VI

LATER we were on a road that led to a river. There was a long line of abandoned trucks and carts on the road leading up to the bridge. No one was in sight. The river was high and the bridge had been blown up in the centre; the stone arch was fallen into the river and the brown water was going over it. We went on up the bank looking for a place to cross. Up ahead I knew there was a railway bridge and I thought we might be able to get across there. The path was wet and muddy. We did not see any troops; only abandoned trucks and stores. Along the river bank there was nothing and no one but the wet brush and muddy ground. We went up to the bank and finally we saw the railway bridge.

"What a beautiful bridge," Aymo said. It was a long plain iron bridge across what was usually a dry river-bed.

"We better hurry and get across before they blow it up," I said.

"There's nobody to blow it up," Piani said. "They're all gone."

"It's probably mined," Bonello said. "You cross first, Tenente."

"Listen to the anarchist," Aymo said. "Make him go first."

"I'll go," I said. "It won't be mined to blow up with one man."

"You see," Piani said. "That is brains. Why haven't you brains, anarchist?"

"If I had brains I wouldn't be here," Bonello said.

"That's pretty good, Tenente," Aymo said.

"That's pretty good," I said. We were close to the bridge now. The sky had clouded over again and it was

raining a little. The bridge looked long and solid. We
climbed up the embankment.

"Come one at a time," I said and started across the
bridge. I watched the ties and the rails for any trip-wires
or signs of explosive but I saw nothing. Down below the
gaps in the ties the river ran muddy and fast. Ahead
across the wet countryside I could see Udine in the rain.
Across the bridge I looked back. Just up the river was another bridge. As I watched, a yellow mud-colored motor
car crossed it. The sides of the bridge were high and the
body of the car, once on, was out of sight. But I saw the
heads of the driver, the man on the seat with him, and
the two men on the rear seat. They all wore German helmets. Then the car was over the bridge and out of sight
behind the trees and the abandoned vehicles on the road.
I waved to Aymo who was crossing and to the others to
come on. I climbed down and crouched beside the railway embankment. Aymo came down with me.

"Did you see the car?" I asked.

"No. We were watching you."

"A German staff car crossed on the upper bridge."

"A staff car?"

"Yes."

"Holy Mary."

The others came and we all crouched in the mud behind the embankment, looking across the rails at the
bridge, the line of trees, the ditch and the road.

"Do you think we're cut off then, Tenente?"

"I don't know. All I know is a German staff car went
along that road."

"You don't feel funny, Tenente? You haven't got
strange feelings in the head?"

"Don't be funny, Bonello."

"What about a drink?" Piani asked. "If we're cut off

we might as well have a drink." He unhooked his canteen
and uncorked it.

"Look! Look!" Aymo said and pointed toward the road.
Along the top of the stone bridge we could see German
helmets moving. They were bent forward and moved
smoothly, almost supernaturally, along. As they came off
the bridge we saw them. They were bicycle troops. I saw
the faces of the first two. They were ruddy and healthy-
looking. Their helmets came low down over their fore-
heads and the side of their faces. Their carbines were
clipped to the frame of the bicycles. Stick bombs hung
handle down from their belts. Their helmets and their
gray uniforms were wet and they rode easily, looking
ahead and to both sides. There were two—then four in
line, then two, then almost a dozen; then another dozen—
then one alone. They did not talk but we could not have
heard them because of the noise from the river. They
were gone out of sight up the road.

"Holy Mary," Aymo said.

"They were Germans," Piani said. "Those weren't
Austrians."

"Why isn't there somebody here to stop them?" I said.
"Why haven't they blown the bridge up? Why aren't
there machine-guns along this embankment?"

"You tell us, Tenente," Bonello said.

I was very angry.

"The whole bloody thing is crazy. Down below they
blow up a little bridge. Here they leave a bridge on
the main road. Where is everybody? Don't they try and
stop them at all?"

"You tell us, Tenente," Bonello said. I shut up. It was
none of my business; all I had to do was to get to Pordenone with three ambulances. I had failed at that. All I
had to do now was get to Pordenone. I probably could

not even get to Udine. The hell I couldn't. The thing to
do was to be calm and not get shot or captured.

"Didn't you have a canteen open?" I asked Piani. He
handed it to me. I took a long drink. "We might as well
start," I said. "There's no hurry though. Do you want to
eat something?"

"This is no place to stay," Bonello said.

"All right. We'll start."

"Should we keep on this side—out of sight?"

"We'll be better off on top. They may come along this
bridge too. We don't want them on top of us before we
see them."

We walked along the railroad track. On both sides of
us stretched the wet plain. Ahead across the plain was
the hill of Udine. The roofs fell away from the castle on
the hill. We could see the campanile and the clock-tower.
There were many mulberry trees in the fields. Ahead I
saw a place where the rails were torn up. The ties had
been dug out too and thrown down the embankment.

"Down! down!" Aymo said. We dropped down beside
the embankment. There was another group of bicyclists
passing along the road. I looked over the edge and saw
them go on.

"They saw us but they went on," Aymo said.

"We'll get killed up there, Tenente," Bonello said.

"They don't want us," I said. "They're after something
else. We're in more danger if they should come on us
suddenly."

"I'd rather walk here out of sight," Bonello said.

"All right. We'll walk along the tracks."

"Do you think we can get through?" Aymo asked.

"Sure. There aren't very many of them yet. We'll go
through in the dark."

"What was that staff car doing?"

"Christ knows," I said. We kept on up the tracks. Bonello tired of walking in the mud of the embankment and came up with the rest of us. The railway moved south away from the highway now and we could not see what passed along the road. A short bridge over a canal was blown up but we climbed across on what was left of the span. We heard firing ahead of us.

We came up on the railway beyond the canal. It went on straight toward the town across the low fields. We could see the line of the other railway ahead of us. To the north was the main road where we had seen the cyclists; to the south there was a small branch-road across the fields with thick trees on each side. I thought we had better cut to the south and work around the town that way and across country toward Campoformio and the main road to the Tagliamento. We could avoid the main line of the retreat by keeping to the secondary roads beyond Udine. I knew there were plenty of sideroads across the plain. I started down the embankment.

"Come on," I said. We would make for the side-road and work to the south of the town. We all started down the embankment. A shot was fired at us from the sideroad. The bullet went into the mud of the embankment.

"Go on back," I shouted. I started up the embankment, slipping in the mud. The drivers were ahead of me. I went up the embankment as fast as I could go. Two more shots came from the thick brush and Aymo, as he was crossing the tracks, lurched, tripped and fell face down. We pulled him down on the other side and turned him over. "His head ought to be uphill," I said. Piani moved him around. He lay in the mud on the side of the embankment, his feet pointing downhill, breathing blood irregularly. The three of us squatted over him in the rain. He was hit low in the back of the neck and the bullet had ranged upward and come out under the right eye.

He died while I was stopping up the two holes. Piani laid his head down, wiped at his face, with a piece of the emergency dressing, then let it alone.

"The———," he said.

"They weren't Germans," I said. "There can't be any Germans over there."

"Italians," Piani said, using the word as an epithet, "Italiani!" Bonello said nothing. He was sitting beside Aymo, not looking at him. Piani picked up Aymo's cap where it had rolled down the embankment and put it over his face. He took out his canteen.

"Do you want a drink?" Piani handed Bonello the canteen.

"No," Bonello said. He turned to me. "That might have happened to us any time on the railway tracks."

"No," I said. "It was because we started across the field."

Bonello shook his head. "Aymo's dead," he said. "Who's dead next, Tenente? Where do we go now?"

"Those were Italians that shot," I said. "They weren't Germans."

"I suppose if they were Germans they'd have killed all of us," Bonello said.

"We are in more danger from Italians than Germans," I said. "The rear guard are afraid of everything. The Germans know what they're after."

"You reason it out, Tenente," Bonello said.

"Where do we go now?" Piani asked.

"We better lie up some place till it's dark. If we could get south we'd be all right."

"They'd have to shoot us all to prove they were right the first time," Bonello said. "I'm not going to try them."

"We'll find a place to lie up as near to Udine as we can get and then go through when it's dark."

"Let's go then," Bonello said. We went down the north

side of the embankment. I looked back. Aymo lay in
the mud with the angle of the embankment. He was
quite small and his arms were by his side, his puttee-
wrapped legs and muddy boots together, his cap over
his face. He looked very dead. It was raining. I had liked
him as well as any one I ever knew. I had his papers in
my pocket and would write to his family. Ahead across
the fields was a farmhouse. There were trees around it
and the farm buildings were built against the house.
There was a balcony along the second floor held up by
columns.

"We better keep a little way apart," I said. "I'll go
ahead." I started toward the farmhouse. There was a
path across the field.

Crossing the field, I did not know but that some one
would fire on us from the trees near the farmhouse or
from the farmhouse itself. I walked toward it, seeing it
very clearly. The balcony of the second floor merged into
the barn and there was hay coming out between the
columns. The courtyard was of stone blocks and all the
trees were dripping with the rain. There was a big
empty two-wheeled cart, the shafts tipped high up in
the rain. I came to the courtyard, crossed it, and stood
under the shelter of the balcony. The door of the house
was open and I went in. Bonello and Piani came in after
me. It was dark inside. I went back to the kitchen. There
were ashes of a fire on the big open hearth. The pots
hung over the ashes, but they were empty. I looked
around but I could not find anything to eat.

"We ought to lie up in the barn," I said. "Do you
think you could find anything to eat, Piani, and bring
it up there?"

"I'll look," Piani said.

"I'll look too," Bonello said.

"All right," I said. "I'll go up and look at the barn." I

found a stone stairway that went up from the stable
underneath. The stable smelt dry and pleasant in the
rain. The cattle were all gone, probably driven off when
they left. The barn was half full of hay. There were two
windows in the roof, one was blocked with boards, the
other was a narrow dormer window on the north side.
There was a chute so that hay might be pitched down to
the cattle. Beams crossed the opening down into the main
floor where the haycarts drove in when the hay was
hauled in to be pitched up. I heard the rain on the roof
and smelled the hay and, when I went down, the clean
smell of dried dung in the stable. We could pry a board
loose and see out of the south window down into the
courtyard. The other window looked out on the field
toward the north. We could get out of either window onto
the roof and down, or go down the hay chute if the
stairs were impractical. It was a big barn and we could
hide in the hay if we heard any one. It seemed like a good
place. I was sure we could have gotten through to the
south if they had not fired on us. It was impossible that
there were Germans there. They were coming from the
north and down the road from Cividale. They could not
have come through from the south. The Italians were
even more dangerous. They were frightened and firing
on anything they saw. Last night on the retreat we had
heard that there had been many Germans in Italian uniforms mixing with the retreat in the north. I did not
believe it. That was one of those things you always heard
in the war. It was one of the things the enemy always did
to you. You did not know any one who went over in
German uniform to confuse them. Maybe they did but it
sounded difficult. I did not believe the Germans did it.
I did not believe they had to. There was no need to confuse our retreat. The size of the army and the fewness of
the roads did that. Nobody gave any orders, let alone

Germans. Still, they would shoot us for Germans. They shot Aymo. The hay smelled good and lying in a barn in the hay took away all the years in between. We had lain in hay and talked and shot sparrows with an air-rifle when they perched in the triangle cut high up in the wall of the barn. The barn was gone now and one year they had cut the hemlock woods and there were only stumps, dried tree-tops, branches and fireweed where the woods had been. You could not go back. If you did not go forward what happened? You never got back to Milan. And if you got back to Milan what happened? I listened to the firing to the north toward Udine. I could hear machine-gun firing. There was no shelling. That was something. They must have gotten some troops along the road. I looked down in the half-light of the hay-barn and saw Piani standing on the hauling floor. He had a long sausage, a jar of something and two bottles of wine under his arm.

"Come up," I said. "There is the ladder." Then I realized that I should help him with the things and went down. I was vague in the head from lying in the hay. I had been nearly asleep.

"Where's Bonello?" I asked.

"I'll tell you," Piani said. We went up the ladder. Up on the hay we set the things down. Piani took out his knife with the corkscrew and drew the cork on a wine bottle.

"They have sealing-wax on it," he said. "It must be good." He smiled.

"Where's Bonello?" I asked.

Piani looked at me.

"He went away, Tenente," he said. "He wanted to be a prisoner."

I did not say anything.

"He was afraid we would get killed."

I held the bottle of wine and did not say anything.

"You see we don't believe in the war anyway, Tenente."

"Why didn't you go?" I asked.

"I did not want to leave you."

"Where did he go?"

"I don't know, Tenente. He went away."

"All right," I said. "Will you cut the sausage?"

Piani looked at me in the half-light.

"I cut it while we were talking," he said. We sat in the hay and ate the sausage and drank the wine. It must have been wine they had saved for a wedding. It was so old that it was losing its color.

"You look out of this window, Luigi," I said. "I'll go look out the other window."

We had each been drinking out of one of the bottles and I took my bottle with me and went over and lay flat on the hay and looked out the narrow window at the wet country. I do not know what I expected to see but I did not see anything except the fields and the bare mulberry trees and the rain falling. I drank the wine and it did not make me feel good. They had kept it too long and it had gone to pieces and lost its quality and color. I watched it get dark outside; the darkness came very quickly. It would be a black night with the rain. When it was dark there was no use watching any more, so I went over to Piani. He was lying asleep and I did not wake him but sat down beside him for a while. He was a big man and he slept heavily. After a while I woke him and we started.

That was a very strange night. I do not know what I had expected, death perhaps and shooting in the dark and running, but nothing happened. We waited, lying flat beyond the ditch along the main road while a German battalion passed, then when they were gone we crossed the road and went on to the north. We were very close to Germans twice in the rain but they did not see us. We got past the town to the north without seeing any Italians, then after a while came on the main channels of the retreat and walked all night toward the Tagliamento. I had not realized how gigantic the retreat was. The whole country was moving, as well as the army. We walked all night, making better time than the vehicles. My leg ached and I was tired but we made good time. It seemed so silly for Bonello to have decided to be taken prisoner. There was no danger. We had walked through two armies without incident. If Aymo had not been killed there would never have seemed to be any danger. No one had bothered us when we were in plain sight along the railway. The killing came suddenly and unreasonably. I wondered where Bonello was.

"How do you feel, Tenente?" Piani asked. We were going along the side of a road crowded with vehicles and troops.

"Fine."

"I'm tired of this walking."

"Well, all we have to do is walk now. We don't have to worry."

"Bonello was a fool."

"He was a fool all right."

"What will you do about him, Tenente?"

"I don't know."

"Can't you just put him down as taken prisoner?"

"I don't know."

"You see if the war went on they would make bad trouble for his family."

"The war won't go on," a soldier said. "We're going home. The war is over."

"Everybody's going home."

"We're all going home."

'Come on, Tenente," Piani said. He wanted to get past them.

"Tenente? Who's a Tenente? *A basso gli ufficiali!* Down with the officers!"

Piani took me by the arm. "I better call you by your name," he said. "They might try and make trouble. They've shot some officers." We worked up past them.

"I won't make a report that will make trouble for his family." I went on with our conversation.

"If the war is over it makes no difference," Piani said. "But I don't believe it's over. It's too good that it should be over."

"We'll know pretty soon," I said.

"I don't believe it's over. They all think it's over but I don't believe it."

"*Viva la Pace!*" a soldier shouted out. "We're going home!"

"It would be fine if we all went home," Piani said. "Wouldn't you like to go home?"

"Yes."

"We'll never go. I don't think it's over."

"*Andiamo a casa!*" a soldier shouted.

"They throw away their rifles," Piani said. "They take them off and drop them down while they're marching. Then they shout."

"They ought to keep their rifles."

"They think if they throw away their rifles they can't make them fight."

In the dark and the rain, making our way along the side of the road I could see that many of the troops still had their rifles. They stuck up above the capes.

"What brigade are you?" an officer called out.

"*Brigata di Pace,*" some one shouted. "Peace Brigade!" The officer said nothing.

"What does he say? What does the officer say?"

"Down with the officer. *Viva la Pace!*"

"Come on," Piani said. We passed two British ambulances, abandoned in the block of vehicles.

"They're from Gorizia," Piani said. "I know the cars."

"They got further than we did."

"They started earlier."

"I wonder where the drivers are?"

"Up ahead probably."

"The Germans have stopped outside Udine," I said. "These people will all get across the river."

"Yes," Piani said. "That's why I think the war will go on."

"The Germans could come on," I said. "I wonder why they don't come on."

"I don't know. I don't know anything about this kind of war."

"They have to wait for their transport I suppose."

"I don't know," Piani said. Alone he was much gentler. When he was with the others he was a very rough talker.

"Are you married, Luigi?"

"You know I am married."

"Is that why you did not want to be a prisoner?"

"That is one reason. Are you married, Tenente?"

"No."

"Neither is Bonello."

"You can't tell anything by a man's being married. But I should think a married man would want to get back to his wife," I said. I would be glad to talk about wives.

"Yes."

"How are your feet?"

"They're sore enough."

Before daylight we reached the bank of the Tagliamento and followed down along the flooded river to the bridge where all the traffic was crossing.

"They ought to be able to hold at this river," Piani said. In the dark the flood looked high. The water swirled and it was wide. The wooden bridge was nearly three-quarters of a mile across, and the river, that usually ran in narrow channels in the wide stony bed far below the bridge, was close under the wooden planking. We went along the bank and then worked our way into the crowd that were crossing the bridge. Crossing slowly in the rain a few feet above the flood, pressed tight in the crowd, the box of an artillery caisson just ahead, I looked over the side and watched the river. Now that we could not go our own pace I felt very tired. There was no exhilaration in crossing the bridge. I wondered what it would be like if a plane bombed it in the daytime.

"Piani," I said.

"Here I am, Tenente." He was a little ahead in the jam. No one was talking. They were all trying to get across as soon as they could: thinking only of that. We were almost across. At the far end of the bridge there were officers and carabinieri standing on both sides flashing lights. I saw them silhouetted against the sky-line. As we came close to them I saw one of the officers point to a man in the column. A carabiniere went in after him and came out holding the man by the arm. He took him away from the road. We came almost opposite them. The officers were scrutinizing every one in the column, sometimes speaking to each other, going forward to flash a light in some one's face. They took some one else out just before we came opposite. I saw the man. He was a lieutenant-colonel. I saw the stars in the box on his sleeve as they flashed a light on him. His hair was gray and he was short and fat. The carabiniere pulled him in behind the line of officers. As we came opposite I saw one or two of them look at me. Then one pointed at me and spoke to a carabiniere. I saw the carabiniere start for me, come through the edge of the column toward me, then felt him take me by the collar.

"What's the matter with you?" I said and hit him in the face. I saw the face under the hat, upturned mustaches and blood coming down his cheek. Another one dove in toward us.

"What's the matter with you?" I said. He did not answer. He was watching a chance to grab me. I put my arm behind me to loosen my pistol.

"Don't you know you can't touch an officer?"

The other one grabbed me from behind and pulled my arm up so that it twisted in the socket. I turned with him and the other one grabbed me around the neck. I kicked his shins and got my left knee into his groin.

"Shoot him if he resists," I heard some one say.

"What's the meaning of this?" I tried to shout but my voice was not very loud. They had me at the side of the road now.

"Shoot him if he resists," an officer said. "Take him over back."

"Who are you?"

"You'll find out."

"Who are you?"

"Battle police," another officer said.

"Why don't you ask me to step over instead of having one of these airplanes grab me?"

They did not answer. They did not have to answer. They were battle police.

"Take him back there with the others," the first officer said. "You see. He speaks Italian with an accent."

"So do you, you ——————," I said.

"Take him back with the others," the first officer said. They took me down behind the line of officers below the road toward a group of people in a field by the river

bank. As we walked toward them shots were fired. I
saw flashes of the rifles and heard the reports. We came
up to the group. There were four officers standing together, with a man in front of them with a carabiniere on
each side of him. A group of men were standing guarded
by carabinieri. Four other carabinieri stood near the
questioning officers, leaning on their carbines. They
were wide-hatted carabinieri. The two who had me
shoved me in with the group waiting to be questioned. I
looked at the man the officers were questioning. He was
the fat gray-haired little lieutenant-colonel they had
taken out of the column. The questioners had all the
efficiency, coldness and command of themselves of
Italians who are firing and are not being fired on.

"Your brigade?"

He told them.

"Regiment?"

He told them.

"Why are you not with your regiment?"

He told them.

"Do you not know that an officer should be with his
troops?"

He did.

That was all. Another officer spoke.

"It is you and such as you that have let the barbar-
ians onto the sacred soil of the fatherland."

"I beg your pardon," said the lieutenant-colonel.

"It is because of treachery such as yours that we have
lost the fruits of victory."

"Have you ever been in a retreat?" the lieutenant-
colonel asked.

"Italy should never retreat."

We stood there in the rain and listened to this. We
were facing the officers and the prisoner stood in front
and a little to one side of us.

"If you are going to shoot me," the lieutenant-colonel said, "please shoot me at once without further questioning. The questioning is stupid." He made the sign of the cross. The officers spoke together. One wrote something on a pad of paper.

"Abandoned his troops, ordered to be shot," he said.

Two carabinieri took the lieutenant-colonel to the river bank. He walked in the rain, an old man with his hat off, a carabiniere on either side. I did not watch them shoot him but I heard the shots. They were questioning some one else. This officer too was separated from his troops. He was not allowed to make an explanation. He cried when they read the sentence from the pad of paper, and they were questioning another when they shot him. They made a point of being intent on questioning the next man while the man who had been questioned before was being shot. In this way there was obviously nothing they could do about it. I did not know whether I should wait to be questioned or make a break now. I was obviously a German in Italian uniform. I saw how their minds worked; if they had minds and if they worked. They were all young men and they were saving their country. The second army was being re-formed beyond the Tagliamento. They were executing officers of the rank of major and above who were separated from their troops. They were also dealing summarily with German agitators in Italian uniform. They wore steel helmets. Only two of us had steel helmets. Some of the carabinieri had them. The other carabinieri wore the wide hat. Airplanes we called them. We stood in the rain and were taken out one at a time to be questioned and shot. So far they had shot every one they had questioned. The questioners had that beautiful detachment and devotion to stern justice of men dealing in death without being in any danger of it. They were questioning a full colonel of a line regiment. Three more officers had just been put in with us.

"Where was his regiment?"

I looked at the carabinieri. They were looking at the newcomers. The others were looking at the colonel. I ducked down, pushed between two men, and ran for the river, my head down. I tripped at the edge and went in with a splash. The water was very cold and I stayed under as long as I could. I could feel the current swirl me and I stayed under until I thought I could never come up. The minute I came up I took a breath and went down again. It was easy to stay under with so much clothing and my boots. When I came up the second time I saw a piece of timber ahead of me and reached it and held on with one hand. I kept my head behind it and did not even look over it. I did not want to see the bank. There were shots when I ran and shots when I came up the first time. I heard them when I was almost above water. There were no shots now. The piece of timber swung in the current and I held it with one hand. I looked at the bank. It seemed to be going by very fast. There was much wood in the stream. The water was very cold. We passed the brush of an island above the water. I held onto the timber with both hands and let it take me along. The shore was out of sight now.

CHAPTER VII

YOU do not know how long you are in a river when the current moves swiftly. It seems a long time and it may be very short. The water was cold and in flood and many things passed that had been floated off the banks when the river rose. I was lucky to have a heavy timber to hold on to, and I lay in the icy water with my chin on the wood, holding as easily as I could with both hands. I was afraid of cramps and I hoped we would move toward the shore. We went down the river in a long curve. It was beginning to be light enough so I could see the bushes along the shore-line. There was a brush island ahead and the current moved toward the shore. I wondered if I should take off my boots and clothes and try to swim ashore, but decided not to. I had never thought of anything but that I would reach the shore some way, and I would be in a bad position if I landed barefoot. I had to get to Mestre some way.

I watched the shore come close, then swing away, then come closer again. We were floating more slowly. The shore was very close now. I could see twigs on the willow bush. The timber swung slowly so that the bank was behind me and I knew we were in an eddy. We went slowly around. As I saw the bank again, very close now, I tried holding with one arm and kicking and swimming the timber toward the bank with the other, but I did not bring it any closer. I was afraid we would move out of the eddy and, holding with one hand, I drew up my feet so they were against the side of the timber and shoved hard toward the bank. I could see the brush, but even with my momentum and swimming as hard as I could, the current was taking me away. I thought then I would drown because of my boots, but I thrashed and fought through the water, and when I looked up the bank was coming toward me, and I kept thrashing and swimming in a heavy-footed panic until I reached it. I hung to the willow branch and did not have strength to pull myself up but I knew I would not drown now. It had never occurred to me on the timber that I might drown. I felt hollow and sick in my stomach and chest from the effort, and I held to the branches and waited. When the sick feeling was gone I pulled into the willow bushes and rested again, my arms around some brush, holding tight with my hands to the branches. Then I crawled out, pushed on through the willows and onto the bank. It was half-daylight and I saw no one. I lay flat on the bank and heard the river and the rain.

After a while I got up and started along the bank. I knew there was no bridge across the river until Latisana. I thought I might be opposite San Vito. I began to think out what I should do. Ahead there was a ditch running into the river. I went toward it. So far I had seen no one and I sat down by some bushes along the bank of the ditch and took off my shoes and emptied them of water. I took off my coat, took my wallet with my papers and my money all wet in it out of the inside pocket and then wrung the coat out. I took off my trousers and wrung them too, then my shirt and underclothing. I slapped and rubbed myself and then dressed again. I had lost my cap.

Before I put on my coat I cut the cloth stars off my sleeves and put them in the inside pocket with my money. My money was wet but was all right. I counted it. There were three thousand and some lire. My clothes felt wet and clammy and I slapped my arms to keep the circulation going. I had woven underwear and I did not think I would catch cold if I kept moving. They had taken my pistol at the road and I put the holster under my coat. I had no cape and it was cold in the rain. I started up the bank of the canal. It was daylight and the country was wet, low and dismal looking. The fields were bare and wet; a long way away I could see a campanile rising out of the plain. I came up onto a road. Ahead I saw some troops coming down the road. I limped along the side of the road and they passed me and paid no attention to me. They were a machine-gun detachment going up toward the river. I went on down the road.

That day I crossed the Venetian plain. It is a low level country and under the rain it is even flatter. Toward the sea there are salt marshes and very few roads. The roads all go along the river mouths to the sea and to cross the country you must go along the paths beside the canals. I was working across the country from the north to the south and had crossed two railway lines and many roads and finally I came out at the end of a path onto a railway line where it ran beside a marsh. It was the main line from Venice to Trieste, with a high solid embankment, a solid roadbed and double track. Down the tracks a way was a flag-station and I could see soldiers on guard. Up the line there was a bridge over a stream that flowed into the marsh. I could see a guard too at the bridge. Crossing the fields to the north I had seen a train pass on this rail-road, visible a long way across the flat plain, and I thought a train might come from Portogruaro. I watched the guards and lay down on the embankment so that I could see both ways along the track. The guard at the bridge walked a way up the line toward where I lay, then turned and went back toward the bridge. I lay, and was hungry, and waited for the train. The one I had seen was so long that the engine moved it very slowly and I was sure I could get aboard it. After I had almost given up hoping for one I saw a train coming. The en-gine, coming straight on, grew larger slowly. I looked at the guard at the bridge. He was walking on the near side of the bridge but on the other side of the tracks. That would put him out of sight when the train passed. I watched the engine come nearer. It was working hard. I could see there were many cars. I knew there would be guards on the train, and I tried to see where they were, but, keeping out of sight, I could not. The engine was almost to where I was lying. When it came opposite, working and puffing even on the level, and I saw the engineer pass, I stood up and stepped up close to the passing cars. If the guards were watching I was a less suspicious object standing beside the track. Several closed freight-cars passed. Then I saw a low open car of the sort they call gondolas coming, covered with canvas. I stood until it had almost passed, then jumped and caught the rear hand-rods and pulled up. I crawled down between the gondola and the shelter of the high freight-car behind. I did not think any one had seen me. I was holding to the hand-rods and crouching low, my feet on the coupling. We were almost opposite the bridge. I remembered the guard. As we passed him he looked at me. He was a boy and his helmet was too big for him. I stared at him contemptuously and he looked away. He thought I had something to do with the train.

We were past. I saw him still looking uncomfortable, watching the other cars pass and I stooped to see how the canvas was fastened. It had grummets and was laced down at the edge with cord. I took out my knife, cut the cord and put my arm under. There were hard bulges under the canvas that tightened in the rain. I looked up and ahead. There was a guard on the freight-car ahead but he was looking forward. I let go of the hand-rails and ducked under the canvas. My forehead hit something that gave me a violent bump and I felt blood on my face but I crawled on in and lay flat. Then I turned around and fastened down the canvas.

I was in under the canvas with guns. They smelled cleanly of oil and grease. I lay and listened to the rain on the canvas and the clicking of the car over the rails. There was a little light came through and I lay and looked at the guns. They had their canvas jackets on.

I thought they must have been sent ahead from the third army. The bump on my forehead was swollen and I stopped the bleeding by lying still and letting it coagulate, then picked away the dried blood except over the cut. It was nothing. I had no handkerchief, but feeling with my fingers I washed away where the dried blood had been, with rain-water that dripped from the canvas, and wiped it clean with the sleeve of my coat. I did not want to look conspicuous. I knew I would have to get out before they got to Mestre because they would be taking care of these guns. They had no guns to lose or forget about. I was terrifically hungry.

CHAPTER VIII

LYING on the floor of the flat-car with the guns beside me under the canvas I was wet, cold and very hungry. Finally I rolled over and lay flat on my stomach with my head on my arms. My knee was stiff, but it had been very satisfactory. Valentini had done a fine job. I had done half the retreat on foot and swum part of the Tagliamento with his knee. It was his knee all right. The other knee was mine. Doctors did things to you and then it was not your body any more. The head was mine, and the inside of the belly. It was very hungry in there. I could feel it turn over on itself. The head was mine, but not to use, not to think with; only to remember and not too much remember.

I could remember Catherine but I knew I would get crazy if I thought about her when I was not sure yet I would see her, so I would not think about her, only about her a little, only about her with the car going slowly and clickingly, and some light through the canvas and my lying with Catherine on the floor of the car. Hard as the floor of the car to lie not thinking only feeling, having been away too long, the clothes wet and the floor moving only a little each time and lonesome inside and alone with wet clothing and hard floor for a wife.

You did not love the floor of a flat-car nor guns with canvas jackets and the smell of vaselined metal or a canvas that rain leaked through, although it is very fine under a canvas and pleasant with guns; but you loved some one else whom now you knew was not even to be pretended there; you seeing now very clearly and coldly —not so coldly as clearly and emptily. You saw emptily, lying on your stomach, having been present when one army moved back and another came forward. You had lost your cars and your men as a floorwalker loses the stock of his department in a fire. There was, however, no insurance. You were out of it now. You had no more obligation. If they shot floorwalkers after a fire in the department store because they spoke with an accent they had always had, then certainly the floorwalkers would not be expected to return when the store opened again for business. They might seek other employment; if there was any other employment and the police did not get them.

Anger was washed away in the river along with any obligation. Although that ceased when the carabiniere put his hand on my collar. I would like to have had the uniform off although I did not care much about the outward forms. I had taken off the stars, but that was for convenience. It was no point of honor. I was not against them. I was through. I wished them all the luck. There were the good ones, and the brave ones, and the calm ones and the sensible ones, and they deserved it.

But it was not my show any more and I wished this bloody train would get to Mestre and I would eat and stop thinking. I would have to stop.

Piani would tell them they had shot me. They went through the pockets and took the papers of the people they shot. They would not have my papers. They might call me drowned. I wondered what they would hear in the States. Dead from wounds and other causes. Good Christ I was hungry. I wondered what had become of the priest at the mess. And Rinaldi. He was probably at Pordenone. If they had not gone further back. Well, I would never see him now. I would never see any of them now. That life was over. I did not think he had syphilis. It was not a serious disease anyway if you took it in time, they said. But he would worry. I would worry too if I had it. Any one would worry.

I was not made to think. I was made to eat. My God, yes. Eat and drink and sleep with Catherine. To-night maybe. No that was impossible. But to-morrow night, and a good meal and sheets and never going away again except together. Probably have to go damned quickly. She would go. I knew she would go. When would we go? That was something to think about. It was getting dark. I lay and thought where we would go. There were many places.

TO HAVE
AND HAVE NOT

A BOATLOAD FOR CUBA

EDITOR'S PREFACE

APPARENTLY Harry Morgan, in *To Have and Have Not,* bears no relation to the other Hemingway heroes, who are tough because they are wounded and lonely and because they want to hide their apprehensiveness from themselves as well as from others. This Florida fisherman and outlaw is tough all the way through. Yet Harry in one sense is a development out of Frederic Henry and Jake Barnes. If you carry their distrust of society to its logical extreme, you finally reach a man like Harry Morgan (named after the great buccaneer), who lives by instinct, hunts alone, feels no loyalty even to his shipmates, and has no virtues except self-discipline and animal fortitude. But that is not the end, as the author is careful to explain.

To Have and Have Not is a loosely constructed novel,

but it contains a number of memorable passages: for example, the first long section, with its fishing in the Gulf Stream and its murdered revolutionists in the streets of Havana; and the dialogue between Richard Gordon and his wife (the one where she says, "I'm through with you and I'm through with love. Your kind of pick-nose love. You writer."); and the Walpurgisnacht with the punch-drunk veterans in Freddy's bar. The chapter printed here is the climax of Harry Morgan's adventures and perhaps the best of Hemingway's battle scenes (excepting El Sordo's last fight in *For Whom the Bell Tolls*). It is afterwards, when Harry lies dying with two Coast Guardsmen bending above him to hear his story, that he murmurs, "No matter how a man alone ain't got no bloody f—— chance."—"It had taken him a long time to get it out," the author says, "and it had taken him all of his life to learn it."

The first long section of the novel, "Harry Morgan: Spring," was printed as a story in the *Cosmopolitan,* as was also the second brief section, "Harry Morgan: Fall." The book appeared in the autumn of 1937, when the author was in Madrid. Most of the critics said that it was Hemingway's weakest novel, but they also said that it showed a broadening of his sympathies and made them feel that he was beginning a new stage in his career.

A BOATLOAD FOR CUBA

ALBERT was on board the boat and the gas was loaded.

"I'll start her up and try how those two cylinders hit," Harry said. "You got the things stowed?"

"Yes."

"Cut some baits then."

"You want a wide bait?"

"That's right. For tarpon."

Albert was on the stern cutting baits and Harry was at the wheel warming up the motors when he heard a noise like a motor backfiring. He looked down the street and saw a man come out of the bank. He had a gun in his hand and he came running. Then he was out of sight. Two more men came out carrying leather brief cases and guns in their hands and ran in the same direction. Harry looked at Albert busy cutting baits. The fourth man, the big one, came out of the bank door as he watched, holding a Thompson gun in front of him, and as he backed out of the door the siren in the bank rose in a long breath-holding shriek and Harry saw the gun muzzle jump-jump-jump-jump and heard the bop-bop-bop-bop, small and hollow sounding in the wail of the siren. The man turned and ran, stopping to fire once more at the bank door, and as Albert stood up in the stern saying, "Christ, they're robbing the bank. Christ, what can we do?" Harry heard the Ford taxi coming out of the side street and saw it careening up onto the dock.

There were three Cubans in the back and one beside the driver.

"Where's the boat?" yelled one in Spanish.

"There, you fool," said another.

319

"That's not the boat."

"That's the captain."

"Come on. Come on for Christ sake."

"Get out," said the Cuban to the driver. "Get your hands up."

As the driver stood beside the car he put a knife inside his belt and ripping it toward him cut the belt and slit his pants almost to the knee. He yanked the trousers down. "Stand still," he said. The two Cubans with the valises tossed them into the cockpit of the launch and they all came tumbling aboard.

"Geta going," said one. The big one with the machine-gun poked it into Harry's back.

"Come on, Cappie," he said. "Let's go."

"Take it easy," said Harry. "Point that some place else."

"Cast off those lines," the big one said. "You!" to Albert.

"Wait a minute," Albert said. "Don't start her. These are the bank robbers."

The biggest Cuban turned and swung the Thompson gun and held it on Albert. "Hey, don't! Don't!" Albert said. "Don't!"

The burst was so close to his chest that the bullets whocked like three slaps. Albert slid down on his knees, his eyes wide, his mouth open. He looked like he was still trying to say, "Don't!"

"You don't need no mate," the big Cuban said. "You one-armed son-of-a-bitch." Then in Spanish, "Cut those lines with that fish knife." And in English, "Come on. Let's go."

Then in Spanish, "Put a gun against his back!" and in English, "Come on. Let's go. I'll blow your head off."

"We'll go," said Harry.

One of the Indian-looking Cubans was holding a pistol

against the side his bad arm was on. The muzzle almost touched the hook.

As he swung her out, spinning the wheel with his good arm, he looked astern to watch the clearance past the piling, and saw Albert on his knees in the stern, his head slipped sidewise now, in a pool of it. On the dock was the Ford taxi, and the fat driver in his underdrawers, his trousers around his ankles, his hands above his head, his mouth open as wide as Albert's. There was still no one coming down the street.

The pilings of the dock went past as she came out of the basin and then he was in the channel passing the lighthouse dock.

"Come on. Hook her up," the big Cuban said. "Make some time."

"Take that gun away," Harry said. He was thinking, I could run her on Crawfish bar, but sure as hell that Cuban would plug me.

"Make her go," said the big Cuban. Then, in Spanish, "Lie down flat, everybody. Keep the captain covered." He lay down himself in the stern, pulling Albert flat down into the cockpit. The other three all lay flat in the cockpit now. Harry sat on the steering seat. He was looking ahead steering out the channel, past the opening into the sub-base now, with the notice board to yachts and the green blinker, out away from the jetty, past the fort now, past the red blinker; he looked back. The big Cuban had a green box of shells out of his pocket and was filling clips. The gun lay by his side and he was filling clips without looking at them, filling by feel, looking back over the stern. The others were all looking astern except the one that was watching him. This one, one of the two Indian-looking ones, motioned with his pistol for him to look ahead. No boat had started after them yet. The engines were running smoothly and they were going with the tide. He noticed the heavy slant seawards of the buoy he passed, with the current swirling at its base.

There are two speedboats that could catch us, Harry was thinking. One, Ray's, is running the mail from Matecumbe. Where is the other? I saw her a couple of days ago on Ed. Taylor's ways, he checked. That was the one I thought of having Bee-lips hire. There's two more, he remembered now. One the State Road Department has up along the keys. The other's laid up in the Garrison Bight. How far are we now? He looked back to where the fort was well astern, the red-brick building of the old Postoffice starting to show up above the Navy yard buildings and the yellow hotel building now dominating the short skyline of the town. There was the cove at the Fort, and the lighthouse showed above the houses that strung out toward the big winter hotel. Four miles anyway, he thought. There they come, he thought. Two white fishing boats were rounding the breakwater and heading out toward him. They can't do ten, he thought. It's pitiful.

The Cubans were chattering in Spanish.

"How fast you going, Cappie?" the big one said, looking back from the stern.

"About twelve," Harry said.

"What can those boats do?"

"Maybe ten."

They were all watching them now, even the one who was supposed to keep him, Harry, covered. But what can I do? He thought. Nothing to do yet.

The two white boats got no larger.

"Look at that, Roberto," said the nice-speaking one.

"Where?"

"Look!"

A long way back, so far you could hardly see it, a little spout rose in the water.

"They're shooting at us," the pleasant-speaking one said. "It's silly."

"For Christ's sake," the big-faced one said. "At three miles."

"Four," thought Harry. "All of four."

Harry could see the tiny spouts rise on the calm surface but he could not hear the shots.

"Those Conchs are pitiful," he thought. "They're worse. They're comical."

"What government boat is there, Cappie?" asked the big-faced one looking away from the stern.

"Coast guard."

"What can she make?"

"Maybe twelve."

"Then we're O.K. now."

Harry did not answer.

"Aren't we O.K. then?"

Harry said nothing. He was keeping the rising, widening spire of Sand Key on his left and the stake on little Sand Key shoals showed almost abeam to starboard. In ten more minutes they would be past the reef.

"What's the matter with you? Can't you talk?"

"What did you ask me?"

"Is there anything can catch us now?"

"Coast guard plane," said Harry.

"We cut the telephone wire before we came in town," the pleasant-speaking one said.

"You didn't cut the wireless, did you?" Harry asked.

"You think the plane can get here?"

"You got a chance of her until dark," Harry said.

"What do you think, Cappie?" asked Roberto, the big-faced one.

Harry did not answer.

"Come on, what do you think?"

"What did you let that son of a bitch kill my mate for?" Harry said to the pleasant-speaking one who was standing beside him now looking at the compass course.

"Shut up," said Roberto. "Kill you, too."

"How much money you get?" Harry asked the pleasant-speaking one.

"We don't know. We haven't counted it yet. It isn't ours, anyway."

"I guess not," said Harry. He was past the light now and he put her on 225°, his regular course for Havana.

"I mean we do it not for ourselves. For a revolutionary organization."

"You kill my mate for that, too?"

"I am very sorry," said the boy. "I cannot tell you how badly I feel about that."

"Don't try," said Harry.

"You see," the boy said, speaking quietly, "this man Roberto is bad. He is a good revolutionary but a bad man. He kills so much in the time of Machado he gets to like it. He thinks it is funny to kill. He kills in a good cause, of course. The best cause." He looked back at Roberto who sat now in one of the fishing chairs in the stern, the Thompson gun across his lap, looking back at the white boats which were, Harry saw, much smaller now.

"What you got to drink?" Roberto called from the stern.

"Nothing," Harry said.

"I drink my own, then," Roberto said. One of the other Cubans lay on one of the seats built over the gas tanks. He looked seasick already. The other was obviously seasick too, but still sitting up.

Looking back, Harry saw a lead-colored boat, now

clear of the Fort, coming up on the two white boats.

"There's the coast-guard boat," he thought. "She's pitiful too."

"You think the seaplane will come?" the pleasant-spoken boy asked.

"Be dark in half an hour," Harry said. He settled on the steering seat. "What you figure on doing? Killing me?"

"I don't want to," the boy said. "I hate killing."

"What you doing?" Roberto, who sat now with a pint of whiskey in his hand, asked. "Making friends with the captain? What you want to do? Eat at the captain's table?"

"Take the wheel," Harry said to the boy. "See the course? Two twenty-five." He straightened up from the stool and went aft.

"Let me have a drink," Harry said to Roberto. "There's your coast-guard boat but she can't catch us."

He had abandoned anger, hatred and any dignity as luxuries, now, and had started to plan.

"Sure," said Roberto. "She can't catch us. Look at those seasick babies. What you say? You want a drink? You got any other last wishes, Cappie?"

"You're some kidder," Harry said. He took a long drink.

"Go easy!" Roberto protested. "That's all there is."

"I got some more," Harry told him. "I was just kidding you."

"Don't kid me," said Roberto suspiciously.

"Why should I try?"

"What you got?"

"Bacardi."

"Bring it out."

"Take it easy," Harry said. "Why do you get so tough?"
He stepped over Albert's body as he walked forward.

As he came to the wheel he looked at the compass. The boy was about twenty-five degrees off and the compass dial was swinging. He's no sailor, Harry thought. That gives me more time. Look at the wake.

The wake ran in two bubbling curves toward where the light, astern now, showed brown, conical and thinly latticed on the horizon. The boats were almost out of sight. He could just see a blur where the wireless masts of the town were. The engines were running smoothly. Harry put his head below and reached for one of the bottles of Bacardi. He went aft with it. At the stern he took a drink, then handed the bottle to Roberto. Standing; he looked down at Albert and he felt sick inside. The poor hungry bastard, he thought.

"What's the matter? He scare you?" the big-faced Cuban asked.

"What you say we put him over?" Harry said. "No sense to carry him."

"O.K.," said Roberto. "You got good sense."

"Take him under the arms," said Harry. "I'll take the legs." Roberto laid the Thompson gun down on the wide stern and leaning down lifted the body by the shoulders.

"You know the heaviest thing in the world is a dead man," he said. "You ever lift a dead man before, Cappie?"

"No," said Harry. "You ever lift a big dead woman?"

Roberto pulled the body up onto the stern. "You're a tough fellow," he said. "What do you say we have a drink?"

"Go ahead," said Harry.

"Listen, I'm sorry I killed him," Roberto said. "When I kill you I feel worse."

"Cut out talking that way," Harry said. "What do you want to talk that way for?"

"Come on," said Roberto. "Over he goes."

As they leaned over and slid the body up and over the

stern, Harry kicked the machine gun over the edge. It splashed at the same time Albert did, but while Albert turned over twice in the white, churned, bubbling back-suction of the propeller wash before sinking, the gun went straight down.

"That's better, eh?" Roberto said. "Make it shipshape." Then as he saw the gun was gone, "Where is it? What did you do with it?"

"With what?"

"The *ametralladora!*" going into Spanish in excitement.

"The what?"

"You know what."

"I didn't see it."

"You knocked it off the stern. Now I'll kill you, *now*."

"Take it easy," said Harry. "What the hell you going to kill me about?"

"Give me a gun," Roberto said to one of the seasick Cubans in Spanish. "Give me a gun quick!"

Harry stood there, never having felt so tall, never having felt so wide, feeling the sweat trickle from under his armpits, feeling it go down his flanks.

"You kill too much," he heard the seasick Cuban say in Spanish. "You kill the mate. Now you want to kill the captain. Who's going to get us across?"

"Leave him alone," said the other. "Kill him when we get over."

"He knocked the machine gun overboard," Roberto said.

"We got the money. What you want a machine gun for now? There's plenty of machine guns in Cuba."

"I tell you, you make a mistake if you don't kill him now, I tell you. Give me a gun."

"Oh, shut up. You're drunk. Every time you're drunk you want to kill somebody."

"Have a drink," said Harry looking out across the gray

swell of the gulf stream where the round red sun was just touching the water. "Watch that. When she goes all the way under it'll turn bright green."

"The hell with that," said the big-faced Cuban. "You think you got away with something."

"I'll get you another gun," said Harry. "They only cost forty-five dollars in Cuba. Take it easy. You're all right now. There ain't any coast-guard plane going to come now."

"I'm going to kill you," Roberto said, looking him over. "You did that on purpose. That's why you got me to lift on that."

"You don't want to kill me," Harry said. "Who's going to take you across?"

"I ought to kill you now."

"Take it easy," said Harry. "I'm going to look at the engines."

He opened the hatch, got down in, screwed down the grease cups on the two stuffing boxes, felt of the motors, and with his hand touched the butt of the Thompson gun. Not yet, he thought. No, better not yet. Christ, that was lucky. What the hell difference does it make to Albert when he's dead. Saves his old woman to bury him. That big-faced bastard. That big-faced murdering bastard. Christ, I'd like to take him now. But I better wait.

He stood up, climbed out and shut the hatch.

"How you doing?" he said to Roberto. He put his hand' on the fat shoulder. The big-faced Cuban looked at him and did not say anything.

"Did you see it turn green?" Harry asked.

"The hell with you," Roberto said. He was drunk but he was suspicious and, like an animal, he knew how wrong something had gone.

"Let me take her a while," Harry said to the boy at the wheel. "What's your name?"

"You can call me Emilio," said the boy.

"Go below and you'll find something to eat," Harry said. "There's bread and cornbeef. Make coffee if you want."

"I don't want any."

"I'll make some later," Harry said. He sat at the wheel, the binnacle light on now, holding her on the point easily in the light following sea, looking out at the night coming on the water. He had no running lights on.

It would be a pretty night to cross, he thought, a pretty night. Soon as the last of that afterglow is gone I've got to work her east. If I don't, we'll sight the glare of Havana in another hour. In two, anyway. Soon as he sees the glare it may occur to that son of a bitch to kill me. That was lucky getting rid of that gun. Damn, that was lucky. Wonder what that Marie's having for supper. I guess she's plenty worried. I guess she's too worried to eat. Wonder how much money those bastards have got. Funny they don't count it. If that ain't a hell of a way to raise money for a revolution. Cubans are a hell of a people.

That's a mean boy, that Roberto. I'll get him to-night. I get him no matter how the rest of it comes out. That won't help that poor damned Albert though. It made me feel bad to dump him like that. I don't know what made me think of it.

He lit a cigarette and smoked in the dark.

I'm doing all right, he thought. I'm doing better than I expected. The kid is a kind of nice kid. I wish I could get those other two on the same side. I wish there was some way to bunch them. Well, I'll have to do the best I can. Easier I can make them take it beforehand the better. Smoother everything goes the better.

"Do you want a sandwich?" the boy asked.

"Thanks," said Harry. "You give one to your partner?"

"He's drinking. He won't eat," the boy said.

"What about the others?"

"Seasick," the boy said.

"It's a nice night to cross," Harry said. He noticed the boy did not watch the compass so he kept letting her go off to the east.

"I'd enjoy it," the boy said. "If it wasn't for your mate."

"He was a good fellow," said Harry. "Did any one get hurt at the bank?"

"The lawyer. What was his name, Simmons."

"Get killed?"

"I think so."

So, thought Harry. Mr. Bee-lips. What the hell did he expect? How could he have thought he wouldn't get it? That comes from playing at being tough. That comes from being too smart too often. Mr. Bee-lips. Good-bye, Mr. Bee-lips.

"How he come to get killed?"

"I guess you can imagine," the boy said. "That's very different from your mate. I feel badly about that. You know he doesn't mean to do wrong. It's just what that phase of the revolution has done to him."

"I guess he's probably a good fellow," Harry said, and thought, Listen to what my mouth says. God damn it, my mouth will say anything. But I got to try to make a friend of this boy in case——

"What kind of revolution do you make now?" he asked.

"We are the only true revolutionary party," the boy said. "We want to do away with all the old politicians, with all the American imperialism that strangles us, with the tyranny of the army. We want to start clean and give every man a chance. We want to end the slavery of the *guajiros*, you know, the peasants, and divide the big sugar estates among the people that work them. But we are not Communists."

Harry looked up from the compass card at him.

"How you coming on?" he asked.

"We just raise money now for the fight," the boy said. "To do that we have to use means that later we would never use. Also we have to use people we would not employ later. But the end is worth the means. They had to do the same thing in Russia. Stalin was a sort of brigand for many years before the revolution."

He's a radical, Harry thought. That's what he is, a radical.

"I guess you've got a good program," he said, "if you're out to help the working man. I was out on strike plenty times in the old days when we had the cigar factories in Key West. I'd have been glad to do whatever I could if I'd known what kind of outfit you were."

"Lots of people would help us," the boy said. "But because of the state the movement is in at present we can't trust people. I regret the necessity for the present phase very much. I hate terrorism. I also feel very badly about the methods for raising the necessary money. But there is no choice. You do not know how bad things are in Cuba."

"I guess they're plenty bad," Harry said.

"You can't know how bad they are. There is an absolutely murderous tyranny that extends over every little village in the country. Three people cannot be together on the street. Cuba has no foreign enemies and doesn't need any army, but she has an army of twenty-five thousand now, and the army, from the corporals up, suck the blood from the nation. Every one, even the private soldiers, are out to make their fortunes. Now they have a military reserve with every kind of crook, bully and

informer of the old days of Machado in it, and they take
anything the army does not bother with. We have to get
rid of the army before anything can start. Before we
were ruled by clubs. Now we are ruled by rifles, pistols,
machine guns, and bayonets."

"It sounds bad," Harry said, steering, and letting her
go off to the eastward.

"You cannot realize how bad it is," the boy said. "I
love my poor country and I would do anything, anything
to free it from this tyranny we have now. I do things I
hate. But I would do things I hate a thousand times
more."

I want a drink, Harry was thinking. What the hell do
I care about his revolution. F—— his revolution. To help
the working man he robs a bank and kills a fellow works
with him and then kills that poor damned Albert that
never did any harm. That's a working man he kills. He
never thinks of that. With a family. It's the Cubans run
Cuba. They all double cross each other. They sell each
other out. They get what they deserve. The hell with
their revolutions. All I got to do is make a living for my
family and I can't do that. Then he tells me about his
revolution. The hell with his revolution.

"It must be bad, all right," he said to the boy. "Take
the wheel a minute, will you? I want to get a drink."

"Sure," said the boy. "How should I steer?"

"Two twenty-five," Harry said.

It was dark now and there was quite a swell this far
out in the Gulf Stream. He passed the two seasick Cubans
lying out on the seats and went aft to where Roberto sat
in the fishing chair. The water was racing past the boat
in the dark. Roberto sat with his feet in the other fishing
chair that was turned toward him.

"Let me have some of that," Harry said to him.

"Go to hell," said the big-faced man thickly. "This is mine."

"All right," said Harry, and went forward to get the other bottle. Below in the dark, with the bottle under the flap of his right arm, he pulled the cork that Freddy had drawn and re-inserted and took a drink.

Now's as good as any time, he said to himself. No sense waiting now. Little boy's spoke his piece. The big-faced bastard drunk. The other two seasick. It might as well be now.

He took another drink and the Bacardi warmed and helped him but he felt cold and hollow all around his stomach still. His whole insides were cold.

"Want a drink?" he asked the boy at the wheel.

"No, thanks," the boy said. "I don't drink." Harry could see him smile in the binnacle light. He was a nice-looking boy all right. Pleasant talking, too.

"I'll take one," he said. He swallowed a big one but it could not warm the dank cold part that had spread from his stomach to all over the inside of his chest now. He put the bottle down on the cockpit floor.

"Keep her on that course," he said to the boy. "I'm going to have a look at the motors."

He opened the hatch and stepped down. Then locked the hatch up with a long hook that set into a hole in the flooring. He stooped over the motors, with his one hand felt the water manifold, the cylinders, and put his hand on the stuffing boxes. He tightened the two grease cups a turn and a half each. Quit stalling, he said to himself. Come on, quit stalling. Where're your balls now? Under my chin, I guess, he thought.

He looked out of the hatch. He could almost touch the two seats over the gas tanks where the seasick men lay. The boy's back was toward him, sitting on the high stool,

outlined clearly by the binnacle light. Turning, he could
see Roberto sprawled in the chair in the stern, silhouetted
against the dark water.

Twenty-one to a clip is four bursts of five at the most,
he thought. I got to be light-fingered. All right. Come
on. Quit stalling, you gutless wonder. Christ, what I'd
give for another one. Well, there isn't any other one now.
He reached his left hand up, unhooked the length of
belting, put his hand around the trigger guard, pushed
the safety all the way over with his thumb and pulled
the gun out. Squatting in the engine pit he sighted carefully on the base of the back of the boy's head where it
outlined against the light from the binnacle.

The gun made a big flame in the dark and the shells
rattled against the lifted hatch and onto the engine. Before the slump of the boy's body fell from the stool he
had turned and shot into the figure on the left bunk, holding the jerking, flame-stabbing gun almost against the
man, so close he could smell it burn his coat; then swung
to put a burst into the other bunk where the man was
sitting up, tugging at his pistol. He crouched low now
and looked astern. The big-faced man was gone out of
the chair. He could see both chairs silhouetted. Behind
him the boy lay still. There wasn't any doubt about him.
On one bunk a man was flopping. On the other, he could
see with the corner of his eye, a man lay half over the
gunwale, fallen over on his face.

Harry was trying to locate the big-faced man in the
dark. The boat was going in a circle now and the cockpit
lightened a little. He held his breath and looked. That
must be him where it was a little darker on the floor in
the corner. He watched it and it moved a little. That
was him.

The man was crawling toward him. No, toward the
man who lay half overboard. He was after his gun.

Crouching low, Harry watched him move until he was absolutely sure. Then he gave him a burst. The gun lighted him on hands and knees, and, as the flame and the bot-bot-bot-bot stopped, he heard him flopping heavily.

"You son of a bitch," said Harry. "You big-faced murdering bastard."

All the cold was gone from around his heart now and he had the old hollow, singing feeling and he crouched low down and felt under the square, wood-crated gas tank for another clip to put in the gun. He got the clip, but his hand was cold-drying wet.

Hit the tank, he said to himself. I've got to cut the engines. I don't know where that tank cuts.

He pressed the curved lever, dropped the empty clip, shoved in the fresh one, and climbed up and out of the cockpit.

As he stood up, holding the Thompson gun in his left hand, looking around before shutting the hatch with the hook on his right arm, the Cuban who had lain on the port bunk and had been shot three times through the left shoulder, two shots going into the gas tank, sat up, took careful aim, and shot him in the belly.

Harry sat down in a backward lurch. He felt as though he had been struck in the abdomen with a club. His back was against one of the iron-pipe supports of the fishing chairs and while the Cuban shot at him again and splintered the fishing chair above his head, he reached down, found the Thompson gun, raised it carefully, holding the forward grip with the hook and rattled half of the fresh clip into the man who sat leaning forward, calmly shooting at him from the seat. The man was down on the seat in a heap and Harry felt around on the cockpit floor until he could find the big-faced man, who lay face down, felt for his head with the hook on his bad arm, hooked it around, then put the muzzle of the gun against the head and touched the trigger. Touching the head, the gun made a noise like hitting a pumpkin with a club. Harry put down the gun and lay on his side on the cockpit floor.

"I'm a son of a bitch," he said, his lips against the planking. I'm a gone son of a bitch now. I got to cut the engines or we'll all burn up, he thought. I got a chance still. I got a kind of a chance. Jesus Christ. One thing to spoil it. One thing to go wrong. God damn it. Oh, God *damn* that Cuban bastard. Who'd have thought I hadn't got him?

He got on his hands and knees and letting one side of the hatch over the engines slam down, crawled over it forward to where the steering stool was. He pulled up on it, surprised to find how well he could move, then suddenly feeling faint and weak as he stood erect, he leaned forward with his bad arm resting on the compass and cut the two switches. The engines were quiet and he could hear the water against her sides. There was no other sound. She swung into the trough of the little sea the North wind had raised and began to roll.

He hung against the wheel, then eased himself onto the steering stool, leaning against the chart table. He could feel the strength drain out of him in a steady faint nausea. He opened his shirt with his good hand and felt the hole with the base of the palm of his hand, then fingered it. There was very little bleeding. All inside, he thought. I better lie down and give it a chance to quiet.

The moon was up now and he could see what was in the cockpit.

Some mess, he thought, some hell of a mess.

Better get down before I fall down, he thought and he lowered himself down to the cockpit floor.

He lay on his side and then, as the boat rolled, the moonlight came in and he could see everything in the cockpit clearly.

It's crowded, he thought. That's what it is, it's crowded. Then, he thought, I wonder what she'll do. I wonder what Marie will do? Maybe they'll pay her the rewards. God damn that Cuban. She'll get along, I guess. She's a smart woman. I guess we would all have gotten along. I guess it was nuts all right. I guess I bit off too much more than I could chew. I shouldn't have tried it. I had it all right up to the end. Nobody'll know how it happened. I wish I could do something about Marie. Plenty money on this boat. I don't even know how much. Anybody be O. K. with that money. I wonder if the coast guard will pinch it. Some of it, I guess. I wish I could let the old woman know what happened. I wonder what she'll do? I don't know. I guess I should have got a job in a filling station or something. I should have quit trying to go in boats. There's no honest money going in boats any more. If the bitch wouldn't only roll. If she'd only quit rolling. I can feel all that slopping back and forth inside. Me. Mr. Bee-lips and Albert. Everybody that had to do with it. These bastards too. It must be an unlucky business. Some unlucky business. I guess what a man like me ought to do is run something like a filling station. Hell, I couldn't run no filling station. Marie, she'll run something. She's too old to peddle her hips now. I wish this bitch wouldn't roll. I'll just have to take it easy. I got to take it as easy as I can. They say if you don't drink water and lay still. They say especially if you don't drink water.

He looked at what the moonlight showed in the cockpit.

Well, I don't have to clean her up, he thought. Take it easy. That's what I got to do. Take it easy. I've got to take it as easy as I can. I've got sort of a chance. If you lay still and don't drink any water.

He lay on his back and tried to breathe steadily. The launch rolled in the Gulf Stream swell and Harry Morgan lay on his back in the cockpit. At first he tried to brace himself against the roll with his good hand. Then he lay quietly and took it.

FOR WHOM THE BELL TOLLS

EL SORDO ON THE HILLTOP

EDITOR'S PREFACE

For Whom the Bell Tolls begins with Harry Morgan's dying words as they might have been translated into magnificent seventeenth-century prose. "No man alone," Harry had mumbled. "No man," the author quotes from John Donne, "is an island, entire of itself; every man is a piece of the continent, a part of the main; if a clod be washed away by the sea, Europe is the less, as well as if a promontory were, as well as if a manor of thy friend's or thine own were; any man's death diminishes me, because I am involved in mankind."

Robert Jordan is involved in mankind. He is the first of Hemingway's heroes with a social purpose, "a feeling of consecration to a duty toward all the oppressed of the world." The feeling has been weakened during the course of the Spanish Civil War, but the sense of duty remains.

Jordan realizes that there are lies and injustice and self-seeking on his side as well as the other; but he sees no hope except in the victory of his side, and he will go on fighting for it to the end. And now, having abandoned all hope for the oppressed for himself, he finds that he can live "as full a life in seventy hours as in seventy years." He escapes from the fear of death and solitude, and he finds that love is possible for him in a sense that it was not possible for Hemingway's other heroes. His almost willing death is the end of a story, a legend that really began with the retreat from Caporetto.

This is the best of Hemingway's novels, but it is also the longest and most closely interwoven and the hardest from which to select one passage that will reflect the quality of the whole. Some of the finest scenes would give a false emphasis if printed by themselves—like the massacre in Pablo's village, which is balanced in the novel by the story of Maria and the Fascists—while the last chapter, which is also the best, depends for much of its force on what has gone before. But El Sordo's fight on the hilltop is a fine passage that can stand alone.

For Whom the Bell Tolls was published in the fall of 1940. It was a Book-of-the-Month Club choice, it was filmed with painstaking accuracy (though the political meaning was omitted and everything was prettified by Technicolor); and it has had a sale in all editions of more than 800,000 copies.

EL SORDO ON THE HILLTOP

E L SORDO was making his fight on a hilltop. He
did not like this hill and when he saw it he thought
it had the shape of a chancre. But he had had no choice
except this hill and he had picked it as far away as he
could see it and galloped for it, the automatic rifle heavy
on his back, the horse laboring, barrel heaving between
his thighs, the sack of grenades swinging against one
side, the sack of automatic rifle pans banging against
the other, and Joaquín and Ignacio halting and firing,
halting and firing to give him time to get the gun in
place.

There had still been snow then, the snow that had
ruined them, and when his horse was hit so that he
wheezed in a slow, jerking, climbing stagger up the last
part of the crest, splattering the snow with a bright, puls-
ing jet, Sordo had hauled him along by the bridle, the
reins over his shoulder as he climbed. He climbed as hard
as he could with the bullets spatting on the rocks, with
the two sacks heavy on his shoulders, and then, holding
the horse by the mane, had shot him quickly, expertly,
and tenderly just where he had needed him, so that the
horse pitched, head forward down to plug a gap between two rocks. He had gotten the gun to firing over
the horse's back and he fired two pans, the gun clattering,
the empty shells pitching into the snow, the smell of
burnt hair from the burnt hide where the hot muzzle
rested, him firing at what came up to the hill, forcing
them to scatter for cover, while all the time there was a
chill in his back from not knowing what was behind
him. Once the last of the five men had reached the hill-

top the chill went out of his back and he had saved the pans he had left until he would need them.

There were two more horses dead along the slope and three more were dead here on the hilltop. He had only succeeded in stealing three horses last night and one had bolted when they tried to mount him bareback in the corral at the camp when the first shooting had started.

Of the five men who had reached the hilltop three were wounded. Sordo was wounded in the calf of his leg and in two places in his left arm. He was very thirsty, his wounds had stiffened, and one of the wounds in his left arm was very painful. He also had a bad headache and as he lay waiting for the planes to come he thought of a joke in Spanish. It was, *"Hay que tomar la muerte como si fuera aspirina,"* which means, "You will have to take death as an aspirin." But he did not make the joke aloud. He grinned somewhere inside the pain in his head and inside the nausea that came whenever he moved his arm and looked around at what there was left of his band.

The five men were spread out like the points of a five-pointed star. They had dug with their knees and hands and made mounds in front of their heads and shoulders with the dirt and piles of stones. Using this cover, they were linking the individual mounds up with stones and dirt. Joaquín, who was eighteen years old, had a steel helmet that he dug with and he passed dirt in it.

He had gotten this helmet at the blowing up of the train. It had a bullet hole through it and every one had always joked at him for keeping it. But he had hammered the jagged edges of the bullet hole smooth and driven a wooden plug into it and then cut the plug off and smoothed it even with the metal inside the helmet.

When the shooting started he had clapped this helmet

on his head so hard it banged his head as though he had
been hit with a casserole and, in the last lung-aching,
leg-dead, mouth-dry, bullet-spatting, bullet-cracking,
bullet-singing run up the final slope of the hill after his
horse was killed, the helmet had seemed to weigh a great
amount and to ring his bursting forehead with an iron
band. But he had kept it. Now he dug with it in a steady,
almost machinelike desperation. He had not yet been
hit.

"It serves for something finally," Sordo said to him in
his deep, throaty voice.

"*Resistir y fortificar es vencer*," Joaquín said, his mouth
stiff with the dryness of fear which surpassed the normal
thirst of battle. It was one of the slogans of the Communist party and it meant, "Hold out and fortify, and
you will win."

Sordo looked away and down the slope at where a
cavalryman was sniping from behind a boulder. He was
very fond of this boy and he was in no mood for slogans.

"What did you say?"

One of the men turned from the building that he
was doing. This man was lying flat on his face, reach-
ing carefully up with his hands to put a rock in place
while keeping his chin flat against the ground.

Joaquín repeated the slogan in his dried-up boy's voice
without checking his digging for a moment.

"What was the last word?" the man with his chin on
the ground asked.

"*Vencer*," the boy said. "Win."

"*Mierda*," the man with his chin on the ground said.

"There is another that applies to here," Joaquín said,
bringing them out as though they were talismans,
"Pasionaria says it is better to die on your feet than to
live on your knees."

"*Mierda* again," the man said and another man said,

over his shoulder, "We're on our bellies, not our knees."

"Thou. Communist. Do you know your Pasionaria has a son thy age in Russia since the start of the movement?"

"It's a lie," Joaquín said.

"*Qué va,* it's a lie." the other said. "The dynamiter with the rare name told me. He was of thy party, too. Why should he lie?"

"It's a lie," Joaquín said. "She would not do such a thing as keep a son hidden in Russia out of the war."

"I wish I were in Russia," another of Sordo's men said. "Will not thy Pasionaria send me now from here to Russia, Communist?"

"If thou believest so much in thy Pasionaria, get her to get us off this hill," one of the men who had a bandaged thigh said.

"The fascists will do that," the man with his chin in the dirt said.

"Do not speak thus," Joaquín said to him.

"Wipe the pap of your mother's breasts off thy lips and give me a hatful of that dirt," the man with his chin on the ground said. "No one of us will see the sun go down this night."

El Sordo was thinking: It is shaped like a chancre. Or the breast of a young girl with no nipple. Or the top cone of a volcano. You have never seen a volcano, he thought. Nor will you ever see one. And this hill is like a chancre. Let the volcanos alone. It's late now for the volcanos.

He looked very carefully around the withers of the dead horse and there was a quick hammering of firing from behind a boulder well down the slope and he heard the bullets from the submachine gun thud into the horse. He crawled along behind the horse and looked out of the angle between the horse's hindquarters and the rock. There were three bodies on the slope just below him where they had fallen when the fascists had rushed the crest under cover of the automatic rifle and submachine gunfire and he and the others had broken down the attack by throwing and rolling down hand grenades. There were other bodies that he could not see on the other sides of the hill crest. There was no dead ground by which attackers could approach the summit and Sordo knew that as long as his ammunition and grenades held out and he had as many as four men they could not get him out of there unless they brought up a trench mortar. He did not know whether they had sent to La Granja for a trench mortar. Perhaps they had not, because surely, soon, the planes would come. It had been four hours since the observation plane had flown over them.

This hill is truly like a chancre, Sordo thought, and we are the very pus of it. But we killed many when they made that stupidness. How could they think that they would take us thus? They have such modern armament that they lose all their sense with overconfidence. He had killed the young officer who had led the assault with a grenade that had gone bouncing and rolling down the slope as they came up it, running, bent half over. In the yellow flash and gray roar of smoke he had seen the officer dive forward to where he lay now like a heavy, broken bundle of old clothing marking the farthest point that the assault had reached. Sordo looked at this body and then, down the hill, at the others.

They are brave but stupid people, he thought. But they have sense enough now not to attack us again until the planes come. Unless, of course, they have a mortar coming. It would be easy with a mortar. The mortar was the normal thing and he knew that they would die as soon as a mortar came up, but when he thought of the planes coming up he felt as naked on that hilltop as though all of his clothing and even his skin had been removed. There is no nakeder thing than I feel, he thought. A flayed rabbit is as well covered as a bear in comparison. But why should they bring planes? They could get us out of here with a trench mortar easily. They are proud of their planes, though, and they will probably bring them. Just as they were so proud of their automatic weapons that they made that stupidness. But undoubtedly they must have sent for a mortar, too.

One of the men fired. Then jerked the bolt and fired again, quickly.

"Save thy cartridges," Sordo said.

"One of the sons of the great whore tried to reach that boulder," the man pointed.

"Did you hit him?" Sordo asked, turning his head with difficulty.

"Nay," the man said. "The fornicator ducked back."

"Who is a whore of whores is Pilar," the man with his chin in the dirt said. "That whore knows we are dying here."

"She could do no good," Sordo said. The man had spoken on the side of his good ear and he had heard him without turning his head. "What could she do?"

"Take these sluts from the rear."

"*Qué va*," Sordo said. "They are spread around a hillside. How would she come on them? There are a hundred and fifty of them. Maybe more now."

"But if we hold out until dark," Joaquín said.

"And if Christmas comes on Easter," the man with his chin on the ground said.

"And if thy aunt had *cojones* she would be thy uncle," another said to him. "Send for thy Pasionaria. She alone can help us."

"I do not believe that about the son," Joaquín said. "Or

if he is there he is training to be an aviator or something of that sort."

"He is hidden there for safety," the man told him.

"He is studying dialectics. Thy Pasionaria has been there. So have Lister and Modesto and others. The one with the rare name told me."

"That they should go to study and return to aid us," Joaquín said.

"That they should aid us now," another man said. "That all the cruts of Russian sucking swindlers should aid us now." He fired and said, "*Me cago en tal;* I missed him again."

"Save thy cartridges and do not talk so much or thou wilt be very thirsty," Sordo said. "There is no water on this hill."

"Take this," the man said and rolling on his side he pulled a wine-skin that he wore slung from his shoulder over his head and handed it to Sordo. "Wash thy mouth out, old one. Thou must have much thirst with thy wounds."

"Let all take it," Sordo said.

"Then I will have some first," the owner said and squirted a long stream into his mouth before he handed the leather bottle around.

"Sordo, when thinkest thou the planes will come?" the man with his chin in the dirt asked.

"Any time," said Sordo. "They should have come before."

"Do you think these sons of the great whore will attack again?"

"Only if the planes do not come."

He did not think there was any need to speak about the mortar. They would know it soon enough when the mortar came.

"God knows they've enough planes with what we saw yesterday."

"Too many," Sordo said.

His head hurt very much and his arm was stiffening so that the pain of moving it was almost unbearable. He looked up at the bright, high, blue early summer sky as he raised the leather wine bottle with his good arm. He was fifty-two years old and he was sure this was the last time he would see that sky.

He was not at all afraid of dying but he was angry at being trapped on this hill which was only utilizable as a place to die. If we could have gotten clear, he thought. If we could have made them come up the long valley or if we could have broken loose across the road it would have been all right. But this chancre of a hill. We must use it as well as we can and we have used it very well so far.

If he had known how many men in history have had to use a hill to die on it would not have cheered him any for, in the moment he was passing through, men are not impressed by what has happened to other men in similar circumstances any more than a widow of one day is helped by the knowledge that other loved husbands have died. Whether one has fear of it or not, one's death is difficult to accept. Sordo had accepted it but there was no sweetness in its acceptance even at fifty-two, with three wounds and him surrounded on a hill.

He joked about it to himself but he looked at the sky and at the far mountains and he swallowed the wine and he did not want it. If one must die, he thought, and clearly one must, I can die. But I hate it.

Dying was nothing and he had no picture of it nor fear of it in his mind. But living was a field of grain blowing in the wind on the side of a hill. Living was a hawk in the sky. Living was an earthen jar of water in the dust of the threshing with the grain flailed out and the chaff blowing. Living was a horse between your legs and a carbine under one leg and a hill and a valley and a stream with trees along it and the far side of the valley and the hills beyond.

Sordo passed the wine bottle back and nodded his head in thanks. He leaned forward and patted the dead horse on the shoulder where the muzzle of the automatic rifle had burned the hide. He could still smell the burnt hair. He thought how he had held the horse there, trembling, with the fire around them, whispering and cracking, over and around them like a curtain, and had carefully shot him just at the intersection of the cross-lines between the two eyes and the ears. Then as the horse pitched down he had dropped down behind his warm, wet back to get the gun to going as they came up the hill.

"Eras mucho caballo," he said, meaning, "Thou wert plenty of horse."

El Sordo lay now on his good side and looked up at the sky. He was lying on a heap of empty cartridge hulls but his head was protected by the rock and his body lay in the lee of the horse. His wounds had stiffened badly and he had much pain and he felt too tired to move.

"What passes with thee, old one?" the man next to him asked.

"Nothing. I am taking a little rest."

"Sleep," the other said. *"They* will wake us when they come."

Just then some one shouted from down the slope.

"Listen, bandits!" the voice came from behind the rocks where the closest automatic rifle was placed. "Surrender now before the planes blow you to pieces."

"What is it he says?" Sordo asked.

Joaquín told him. Sordo rolled to one side and pulled himself up so that he was crouched behind the gun again.

"Maybe the planes aren't coming," he said. "Don't answer them and do not fire. Maybe we can get them to attack again."

"If we should insult them a little?" the man who had spoken to Joaquín about La Pasionaria's son in Russia asked.

"No," Sordo said. "Give me thy big pistol. Who has a big pistol?"

"Here."

"Give it to me." Crouched on his knees he took the big 9 mm. Star and fired one shot into the ground beside the dead horse, waited, then fired again four times at irregular intervals. Then he waited while he counted sixty and then fired a final shot directly into the body of the dead horse. He grinned and handed back the pistol.

"Reload it," he whispered, "and that every one should keep his mouth shut and no one shoot."

"*Bandidos!*" the voice shouted from behind the rocks.

No one spoke on the hill.

"*Bandidos!* Surrender now before we blow thee to little pieces."

"They're biting," Sordo whispered happily.

As he watched, a man showed his head over the top of the rocks. There was no shot from the hilltop and the head went down again. El Sordo waited, watching, but nothing more happened. He turned his head and looked at the others who were all watching down their sectors of the slope. As he looked at them the others shook their heads.

"Let no one move," he whispered.

"Sons of the great whore," the voice came now from behind the rocks again.

"Red swine. Mother rapers. Eaters of the milk of thy fathers."

Sordo grinned. He could just hear the bellowed insults

y turning his good ear. This is better than the aspirin, e thought. How many will we get? Can they be that oolish?

The voice had stopped again and for three minutes hey heard nothing and saw no movement. Then the niper behind the boulder a hundred yards down the lope exposed himself and fired. The bullet hit a rock nd ricocheted with a sharp whine. Then Sordo saw a nan, bent double, run from the shelter of the rocks where he automatic rifle was across the open ground to the big oulder behind which the sniper was hidden. He almost ove behind the boulder.

Sordo looked around. They signalled to him that there vas no movement on the other slopes. El Sordo grinned appily and shook his head. This is ten times better than he aspirin, he thought, and he waited, as happy as only hunter can be happy.

Below on the slope the man who had run from the pile f stones to the shelter of the boulder was speaking to he sniper.

"Do you believe it?"

"I don't know," the sniper said.

"It would be logical," the man, who was the officer in ommand, said. "They are surrounded. They have noth-ıg to expect but to die."

The sniper said nothing.

"What do you think?" the officer asked.

"Nothing," the sniper said.

"Have you seen any movement since the shots?"

"None at all."

The officer looked at his wrist watch. It was ten min-tes to three o'clock.

"The planes should have come an hour ago," he said. ust then another officer flopped in behind the boulder. he sniper moved over to make room for him.

"Thou, Paco," the first officer said. "How does it seem to thee?"

The second officer was breathing heavily from his sprint up and across the hillside from the automatic rifle position.

"For me it is a trick," he said.

"But if it is not? What a ridicule we make waiting here and laying siege to dead men."

"We have done something worse than ridiculous already," the second officer said. "Look at that slope."

He looked up the slope to where the dead were scattered close to the top. From where he looked the line of the hilltop showed the scattered rocks, the belly, projecting legs, shod hooves jutting out, of Sordo's horse and the fresh dirt thrown up by the digging.

"What about the mortars?" asked the second officer.

"They should be here in an hour. If not before."

"Then wait for them. There has been enough stupidity already."

"*Bandidos!*" the first officer shouted suddenly, getting to his feet and putting his head well up above the boulder so that the crest of the hill looked much closer as he stood upright. "Red swine! Cowards!"

The second officer looked at the sniper and shook his head. The sniper looked away but his lips tightened.

The first officer stood there, his head all clear of the rock and with his hand on his pistol butt. He cursed and vilified the hilltop. Nothing happened. Then he stepped clear of the boulder and stood there looking up the hill.

"Fire, cowards, if you are alive," he shouted. "Fire on one who has no fear of any Red that ever came out of the belly of the great whore."

This last was quite a long sentence to shout and the officer's face was red and congested as he finished.

The second officer, who was a thin sunburned man

with quiet eyes, a thin, long-lipped mouth and a stubble of beard over his hollow cheeks, shook his head again. It was this officer who was shouting who had ordered the first assault. The young lieutenant who was dead up the slope had been the best friend of this other lieutenant who was named Paco Berrendo and who was listening to the shouting of the captain, who was obviously in a state of exaltation.

"Those are the swine who shot my sister and my mother," the captain said. He had a red face and a blond, British-looking moustache and there was something wrong about his eyes. They were a light blue and the lashes were light, too. As you looked at them they seemed to focus slowly. Then "Reds," he shouted. "Cowards!" and commenced cursing again.

He stood absolutely clear now and, sighting carefully, fired his pistol at the only target that the hilltop presented: the dead horse that had belonged to Sordo. The bullet threw up a puff of dirt fifteen yards below the horse. The captain fired again. The bullet hit a rock and sung off.

The captain stood there looking at the hilltop. The Lieutenant Berrendo was looking at the body of the other lieutenant just below the summit. The sniper was looking at the ground under his eyes. Then he looked up at the captain.

"There is no one alive up there," the captain said. "Thou," he said to the sniper, "go up there and see."

The sniper looked down. He said nothing.

"Don't you hear me?" the captain shouted at him.

"Yes, my captain," the sniper said, not looking at him.

"Then get up and go." The captain still had his pistol out. "Do you hear me?"

"Yes, my captain."

"Why don't you go, then?"

"I don't want to, my captain."

"You don't *want* to?" The captain pushed the pistol against the small of the man's back. "You don't *want* to?"

"I am afraid, my captain," the soldier said with dignity.

Lieutenant Berrendo, watching the captain's face and his odd eyes, thought he was going to shoot the man then.

"Captain Mora," he said.

"Lieutenant Berrendo?"

"It is possible the soldier is right."

"That he is right to say he is afraid? That he is right to say he does not *want* to obey an order?"

"No. That he is right that it is a trick."

"They are all dead," the captain said. "Don't you hear me say they are all dead?"

"You mean our comrades on the slope?" Berrendo asked him. "I agree with you."

"Paco," the captain said, "don't be a fool. Do you think you are the only one who cared for Julián? I tell you the Reds are dead. Look!"

He stood up, then put both hands on top of the boulder and pulled himself up, kneeing-up awkwardly, then getting on his feet.

"Shoot," he shouted, standing on the gray granite boulder and waved both his arms. "Shoot me! Kill me!"

On the hilltop El Sordo lay behind the dead horse and grinned.

What a people, he thought. He laughed, trying to hold it in because the shaking hurt his arm.

"Reds," came the shout from below. "Red canaille Shoot me! Kill me!"

Sordo, his chest shaking, barely peeped past the horse' crupper and saw the captain on top of the boulder waving his arms. Another officer stood by the boulder. The snipe was standing at the other side. Sordo kept his eye where it was and shook his head happily.

"Shoot me," he said softly to himself. "Kill me!" Then his shoulders shook again. The laughing hurt his arm and each time he laughed his head felt as though it would burst. But the laughter shook him again like a spasm.

Captain Mora got down from the boulder.

"Now do you believe me, Paco?" he questioned Lieutenant Berrendo.

"No," said Lieutenant Berrendo.

"*Cojones!*" the captain said. "Here there is nothing but idiots and cowards."

The sniper had gotten carefully behind the boulder again and Lieutenant Berrendo was squatting beside him.

The captain, standing in the open beside the boulder, commenced to shout filth at the hilltop. There is no language so filthy as Spanish. There are words for all the vile words in English and there are other words and expressions that are used only in countries where blasphemy keeps pace with the austerity of religion. Lieutenant Berrendo was a very devout Catholic. So was the sniper. They were Carlists from Navarra and while both of them cursed and blasphemed when they were angry they regarded it as a sin which they regularly confessed.

As they crouched now behind the boulder watching the captain and listening to what he was shouting, they both disassociated themselves from him and what he was saying. They did not want to have that sort of talk on their consciences on a day in which they might die. Talking thus will not bring luck, the sniper thought. Speaking thus of the *Virgen* is bad luck. This one speaks worse than the Reds.

Julián is dead, Lieutenant Berrendo was thinking. Dead there on the slope on such a day as this is. And this foul mouth stands there bringing more ill fortune with his blasphemies.

Now the captain stopped shouting and turned to Lieutenant Berrendo. His eyes looked stranger than ever.

"Paco," he said, happily, "you and I will go up there."

"Not me."

"What?" The captain had his pistol out again.

I hate these pistol brandishers, Berrendo was thinking. They cannot give an order without jerking a gun out. They probably pull out their pistols when they go to the toilet and order the move they will make.

"I will go if you order me to. But under protest," Lieutenant Berrendo told the captain.

"Then I will go alone," the captain said. "The smell of cowardice is too strong here."

Holding his pistol in his right hand, he strode steadily up the slope. Berrendo and the sniper watched him. He was making no attempt to take any cover and he was looking straight ahead of him at the rocks, the dead horse, and the fresh-dug dirt of the hilltop.

El Sordo lay behind the horse at the corner of the rock, watching the captain come striding up the hill.

Only one, he thought. We get only one. But from his manner of speaking he is *caza mayor*. Look at him walking. Look what an animal. Look at him stride forward. This one is for me. This one I take with me on the trip. This one coming now makes the same voyage I do. Come on, Comrade Voyager. Come striding. Come right along. Come along to meet it. Come on. Keep on walking. Don't slow up. Come right along. Come as thou art coming. Don't stop and look at those. That's right. Don't even look down. Keep on coming with your eyes forward. Look, he has a moustache. What do you think of that? He runs to a moustache, the Comrade Voyager. He is a captain. Look at his sleeves. I said he was *caza mayor*. He has the face of an *Inglés*. Look. With a red face and blond hair and blue eyes. With no cap on and his mous